Victor Erofeyev, who has been hailed as 'the heir to the long-lost Russian avant-garde', is the author of the highly acclaimed novel *Russian Beauty*. It has been translated into twenty-six languages and is a bestseller around the world. His collection of short stories, *Life with an Idiot*, is currently being translated into English.

Victor Erofeyev was born in 1947. He lived in Paris for three years as a child, where his father was a high-ranking Soviet diplomat. A literary critic and dissident writer, he contributed to the 1979 collection *Metropol*, which led to his being banned from Soviet print until the Gorbachev era. He lectures at various American universities and writes regularly for *The Times Literary Supplement* and other papers. He has also written an introduction to *The Little Demon* by Fyodor Sologub for Penguin Twentieth-Century Classics. He is married with a son and lives predominantly in Moscow.

Andrew Reynolds is Research Fellow in Russian at Queens' College, Cambridge. Born in Swansea in 1964, he was educated at Dynevor Comprehensive School and Merton College, Oxford. His translation of *Russian Beauty* was highly praised in both Britain and the USA. The author of a number of articles and translations, he is at present working on a critical study of the poetry Osip Mandelstam wrote in exile in Voronezh. He is married with a daughter.

THE PENGUIN BOOK OF

New Russian Writing

Russia's *Fleurs du Mal*

Compiled with an Introduction
by Victor Erofeyev

Edited by Victor Erofeyev and
Andrew Reynolds

PENGUIN BOOKS

PENGUIN BOOKS

Published by the Penguin Group
Penguin Books Ltd, 27 Wrights Lane, London w8 5tz, England
Penguin Books USA Inc., 375 Hudson Street, New York, New York 10014, USA
Penguin Books Australia Ltd, Ringwood, Victoria, Australia .
Penguin Books Canada Ltd, 10 Alcorn Avenue, Toronto, Ontario, Canada m4v 3b2
Penguin Books (NZ) Ltd, 182–190 Wairau Road, Auckland 10, New Zealand

Penguin Books Ltd, Registered Offices: Harmondsworth, Middlesex, England

First published 1995
10 9 8 7 6 5 4 3 2 1

Typeset by Datix International Limited, Bungay, Suffolk
Printed in England by Clays Ltd, St Ives plc
Set in 10/13 pt Monophoto Garamond

Contents

Acknowledgements

'*Tifozny kvarantin*' ('Typhoid Quarantine') copyright © Varlam Shalamov 1978

'*Lyudochka*' ('Lyudochka') copyright © Viktor Astafiev 1988

'*Zolotoi shnurok*' ('The Golden Lace') copyright © Andrei Sinyavsky 1987

'*S koshelochkoi*' ('Bag-in-hand') copyright © Fridrikh Gorenshtein 1982

'*Tetrad' individualista*' ('An Individualist's Notebook') copyright © Yury Mamleev 1986

'*Vasily Rozanov glazami ekstsentrika*' ('Through the Eyes of an Eccentric') copyright © Venedikt Erofeev 1982

'*Lyubov' tigra*' ('The Fool and the Tiger') copyright © Valery Popov 1991

'*Kompromiss pyaty*' ('The Fifth Compromise') copyright © Sergei Dovlatov 1981

'*Trevozhnaya kukolka*' ('The Anxious Chrysalis') copyright © Sasha Sokolov 1986

'*Dukhovka*' ('The Oven') copyright © Evgeny Kharitonov 1995

'*Tsentral'no-ermolaevskaya voina*' ('The Central-Ermolaevo War') copyright © Vyacheslav Pietsukh 1988

'*The Night* Souper' copyright © Edward Limonov 1995

'*Kak s''eli petukha*' ('How They Ate the Cock') copyright © Evgeny Popov 1981

'*Poet i Muza*' ('The Poet and the Muse') copyright © Tatyana Tolstaya 1986

'*Opisanie predmetov*' ('Description of Objects') copyright © Dmitry Prigov 1979

'*Shestikryly serafim*' ('The Six-winged Seraph') copyright © Lev Rubinshtein 1984

'*Istoriya Maiora Simin'kova*' ('The Story of Major Siminkov') copyright © Anatoly Gavrilov 1990

'*Zasedanie zavkoma*' ('Next Item on the Agenda') from *Der Obelisk. Erzahlungen* copyright © 1992 by Haffmans Verlag AG Zurich

'*Solzhenitsyn, ili Golos iz podpol'ya*' ('Solzhenitsyn, or a Voice from the Underground') copyright © Igor Yarkevich 1991

'*Zhen'kin tezaurus*' ('Zhenka's *A to Z*') copyright © Victor Erofeyev 1993

The publishers are grateful to the following for permission to reprint the following:

Alfred A. Knopf for permission to reprint 'The Fifth Compromise' by Sergei Dovlatov

Virago Press and Aitken, Stone & Wylie Ltd for permission to reprint 'The Poet and the Muse' by Tatyana Tolstaya, published in the collection *Sleepwalker in a Fog*

W. J. van Oorschot, Amsterdam, Holland, for permission to use 'Through the Eyes of an Eccentric' by Venedikt Erofeev

Ardis Publishers, Ann Arbor, Michigan, USA for permission to use 'The Anxious Chrysalis' by Sasha Sokolov

Haffmans Verlag AG, Zurich, Switzerland, for permission to use 'Next Item on the Agenda' by Vladimir Sorokin

In all other cases, permission to use the stories has been granted by the individual authors or their Estates

Note on Transliteration
The transliteration conventions of *Oxford Slavonic Papers* (BS2979, 1958) have been followed, omitting diacritics. Exceptions have been made in order to facilitate pronunciation: the use of *yo* for the Russian ë, and the use of i for the soft sign (except at the end of words and between two consonants, where no indication of the soft sign has been given). The transliteration of the titles of stories and of Russian quotations (in Acknowledgements and Notes), however, conforms fully to the *OSP* system.

In certain cases well-established English spellings have been preferred (e.g. Alexander, Khrushchev, Herzen). Some apparent inconsistencies in the rendition of the authors' names are the result of using the authors' preferred, or the more common, English version (e.g. Victor Erofeyev).

Introduction

Russia's Fleurs du Mal

VICTOR EROFEYEV

In the last quarter of the twentieth century, evil has been the ruling power in literary Russia. With Baudelaire in mind, and in true anthology spirit, one may say that contemporary Russian literature has gathered a whole bouquet of *fleurs du mal*. The individual authors included here are by no means mere elements in my ikebana: each is significant in his or her own right. Nevertheless, from texts which are dissimilar and often in conflict, a curious archetext emerges. It does not simply give an impression of what is happening now in Russian literature. Let that be a job for learned Slavists. More significant is the fact that the texts taken as a whole form a NOVEL about the wanderings of the Russian soul. In that the Russian soul has been going round and round in circles of late and is still not out of the whirlwind, its experience is relevant far beyond the realm of 'Slavic' interests, and the tale of its progress thus turns into an exciting and audacious plot.

Once upon a time Stalinist writers dreamed of creating a unitary text of Soviet literature. My collection parodies their dream. If the collective reason of Soviet literature was teleocentric, in the new literature the flowers of evil shoot up all over the place, like weeds.

Bazarov, the hero of Turgenev's famous novel *Fathers and Children*, was a nihilist who affronted public morality, yet his key phrase was an expression of hope: 'Man is good, conditions are bad.' I would choose these words as the epigraph for classic Russian literature. The presiding spirit of the most significant part of this literature was the salvation of man and mankind. This is an impossible task, and Russian literature failed to cope with it so *brilliantly* that it guaranteed itself world-wide success.

The conditions of life in Russia have always been lamentable and abnormal. The desperate struggle of writers against these conditions obscured to a large extent the wider question of the essence of human nature. There was never any strength left for a more profound philosophical anthropology. As a result, despite all the richness of Russian literature, despite its unique psychological portraits, stylistic diversity and religious questing, the whole of its *Weltanschauung* was reducible to a simple creed: to *a philosophy of hope*, to the expression of an optimistic faith in the possibility of changes whose aim was to provide man with a worthy existence.

Konstantin Leontiev, the perceptive, unjustly neglected philosopher of the second half of the nineteenth century, was therefore right to speak of Dostoevsky's *rosy* Christianity, and of Tolstoy's too; the latter almost completely lacked any metaphysical essence and was very firmly oriented towards humanistic doctrines reminiscent of the French Enlightenment. The classics of Russian literature splendidly taught how one could remain *human* in unbearable and extreme conditions, without betraying either oneself or others; even today this sermon continues to have a universal educational significance. Nabokov's observation that Dostoevsky is a writer for adolescents, a writer forming young minds, is also applicable in part to many other Russian authors. But if for the West the experience of Russian literature became part of its general literary knowledge, and an injection of the Russian virus was unquestionably beneficial, Russian cultural life received such an overdose of literary preaching that, ultimately, it started to suffer from something similar to moral hypertonia, or the disease of *hypermoralism*.

It is true that at the beginning of the twentieth century a serious break with tradition took place in Russian culture. The rift was reflected in philosophy (for example, in the collection *Landmarks*, essays which described the national stereotypes of *progressive* consciousness), in the visual arts of the Russian avant-garde, and also in the literature of the 'Silver Age'. The 'Silver Age', which lasted for about twenty years and was rich in famous names and stylistic schools, seemed to the traditionalist mentality to be little more than decadence, but in fact its significance lay above all in its rejection of the preceding anthropology. Perhaps the most scandalous work of the period was Fyodor Sologub's short novel *The Little Demon*. Its postulate was that evil is not to be blamed on society, since evil has free rein in the human soul. The main character, the grammar-school teacher Peredonov, is cruel *for no reason*, sadistically sensual and irredeemable. *A philosophy of hope* is superfluous here.

However, Russian literature did not wish to part with its optimistic illusions. It followed in the footsteps of the Russian Populist belletrist Vladimir Korolenko, whose famous phrase stated that 'Man is created for happiness like a bird is for flight', and of Gorky with his proclamation 'Man – that sounds proud!' Both utterances became part of the foundation of Socialist Realism.

By mixing *humanism* (which was viewed not just as the philosophy of the Renaissance but also, more importantly, as a 'proto-Communist' doctrine) with a more straightforward love of man (that is, the 'voluntary' love of man for man), Soviet ideologues were able to represent anyone who had any doubts about humanism as an enemy of mankind. Such a deception engendered in Soviet culture what Andrei Platonov called an *orgy of humanism*. Subsequently these *orgies* turned into a literature of lies and ignominy graced by piles of gibberish and graphomania that are *unsurpassed* examples of kitsch.

On the other hand, from its very beginning non-conformist literature, from Zamyatin's novel *We*, through Bulgakov's satirical short stories and his novel *The Master and Margarita*, Pasternak's novel *Doctor Zhivago* and so on, right up to the entire corpus of Solzhenitsyn's work, has borne witness to a worthy resistance to tyranny and spoken out about desecrated human values.

Soviet and anti-Soviet literature strove to outdo each other in a humanistic tug-of-war. In the meantime, it was precisely under Soviet power that man, the very subject of humanism, showed the full measure of his capabilities. By showing what a nasty piece of work is a man, by performing miracles of baseness, treachery, time-serving, meanness, sadism, dissoluteness and degeneration, he proved that he was capable of anything and everything.

The Stalinist *Commedia*, which was played out on the gigantic stage of Eurasia, was in this sense instructive, and after the curtain went down an unbiased spectator could not have been blamed for drawing the most pessimistic conclusions concerning the nature of man. However, when the drama's most brilliant act reached its climax in 1953 with the death of its author and director, those spectators who were still alive hurried to put all the blame on 'Stalin's cult of personality', thereby providing evidence of, among other things, man's inability to analyse facts properly.

The clash of official state humanism and liberal humanism produced the philosophy of Khrushchev's 'Thaw', which was based on a 'return' to *genuine* humanistic norms. 'The warmth of goodness' became the dominant theme of a whole generation of poets and prose writers of the sixties (Evgeny Evtushenko, Bulat Okudzhava, Vasily Aksyonov, Fazil Iskander, Andrei Bitov, Vladimir Voinovich, Georgy Vladimov and others), who later came to be known as the 'men of the sixties'.

From their point of view, any criticism of humanism was an impermissible and unaffordable luxury, a luxury hindering their struggle with a hypocritical regime and their desire to bring that regime closer to the utopian model 'with a human face'.

At the end of the eighties the history of Soviet literature broke off in mid-sentence. It met with a violent death, one whose immediate cause had little to do with literature. Soviet literature was a hothouse flower of the socialist state system. As soon as the heating was turned off in the hothouse, the flower first faded, then withered away. The corresponding flower of the literature of resistance also grew sick; they were linked by a single root system.

The result was total confusion in the household of Russian letters. Writers were left without a literature.

But there were some exceptions. Even during the hothouse years a literature had begun to take form – critics would later call it an *alternative literature* – outside the sermonizing mainstream. Politically this *alternative literature* was 'vague', which made both the opposing ideological camps distrust it. Obviously it was not imbued with the Soviet ethos, but it was more a-Soviet than anti-Soviet. It was rather cool towards dissident literature, because it felt that the only differences between dissident and conformist writing were ideological, inasmuch as both evidently shared the same aesthetic criteria.

To the mind of the Russian *intelligentsia*, the *alternative literature* has learnt from a strange mixture of teachers: Gogol and the Marquis de Sade, Decadents from the beginning of the twentieth century and the Surrealists, mystics and The Beatles, Andrei Platonov and the previously unknown Leonid Dobychin, Borges, Nabokov and Pound. It adores the 'transsense' of the *Oberuity* and Hollywood blockbusters, pop-art and guitar poetry, Stalinist skyscrapers and Western post-modernism.

The loss of a common cause, a universally acknowledged truth, releases the energy that is indispensable for a free journey. Born in the dialectical game of losses and gains, the new Russian literature flutters out of its mine cage. The intensity with which it experiences freedom, it would seem, underpins its very existence.

The journey starts in Hell. There are two points of departure: Solzhenitsyn and Shalamov. Solzhenitsyn found it possible to sing a hymn of praise to the Russian soul even in the Gulag (*One Day in the Life of Ivan Denisovich*). Shalamov (*Kolyma Tales*) showed the limit beyond which any soul disintegrates. This was something new, or, at any rate, was read as such. Shalamov showed that suffering does not ennoble people (Dostoevsky's line), but makes them indifferent, so that even the difference between victims and executioners is erased: they are ready to change places.

The stories of VARLAM SHALAMOV, who spent seventeen years in prisons and labour camps, are written not by an Orpheus who has descended into the underworld, but by a Pluto who has clambered up from Hell and has recognized that hope is both an illusion and a heavy burden. For the *alternative literature*, this change of heart and mind, this 'Change of Landmarks', is crucial.

Just like the hero in his story 'Typhoid Quarantine', Shalamov was 'a representative of the dead. And his knowledge, the knowledge of a dead man, could not be of use to those who were still alive.'

A dead man sees everything through a dead man's eyes, which is the precondition for a dead prose of *defamiliarization*, alien to the fervently emotional Russian literature: 'Did he think about his family at that time? No. About freedom? No. Did he recite poetry from memory? No. Did he recall the past? No. He lived by a blunted, indifferent malice alone.'

Shalamov's Gulag came to be more a metaphor of existence than a depiction of political reality. For a while such an attitude towards man remained marginal. During Khrushchev's 'Thaw' the traditional quarrel between Westernizers and Slavophiles was resumed. The age-old problem of the split within Russian culture found expression in the confrontation of literary groupings. But, in spite of their differences, each party thought about the common good.

The literature of the twentieth-century *fin de siècle* has exhausted all the collectivist possibilities. It breaks into pieces, abandons shared values for marginal values, the canonical for the apocryphal. A new era began in the mid-seventies, an era of previously unheard of doubts not merely in the *new* Soviet man, but in *man* in general. The new Russian literature has called absolutely everything into question: love, children, faith, the Church, culture, beauty, nobility of character, motherhood, and even the wisdom of the common people, thereby destroying those Populist illusions in which the intelligentsia had kept believing through all the years of Soviet power. More recently it has called the 'Boring West' into question as well. This scepticism has increased with the passage of time. It is a joint reaction to the wild Russian reality and the excessive moralism of Russian culture.

The long-standing wall in classical literature which divided the agents of life and death (positive and negative characters) has come tumbling down, though in the best works the wall was more easily breached than the Berlin wall ever was. Anyone can unexpectedly and for no reason become the repository of a destructive principle: movement in the opposite direction is far trickier. Any emotion not touched by evil is called into doubt. Evil is wooed, advances made to it, and many leading writers either can't tear their eyes away from evil, bewitched by its power and *artistry*, or else they become its hostages. Some of them find in Socialist Realism elements possessing a crude charm, and are able to see genuine ontological models in its architectural forms. Beauty yields to expressive pictures of ugliness, beautiful forms give way to deformity. A mocking, shocking, *épatant* aesthetics is developed. There is heightened interest in 'dirty' words, in obscene language as a detonator of a text. The new literature fluctuates between 'black' despair and a totally cynical indifference.

In a literature which once bore the perfume of wild flowers and hay there is now a new smell – a stench. Everything stinks: death, sex, old-age, bad food, everyday life. The themes of violence, sadistic aggression, broken lives come to the fore. The number of murders, rapes, perversions, abortions, tortures, the number of scenes depicting various forms of humiliation (the army, prison, young thugs) and sexual deviation, grows apace. Faith in reason is repudiated and the role of chance misfortunes, of chance in general, increases. Writers are less and less interested in the professional lives of their heroes, who are left as a rule without a coherent biography. Many heroes are either mad or mentally inadequate. Psychological prose gives way to psychopathological prose. It is no longer the Gulag, but Russia herself, falling apart at the seams, that serves as a metaphor for life.

That Russia is a prison, one big labour camp, the continuation by other means of the Gulag and its merciless rules, is made abundantly clear in the prose of VIKTOR ASTAFIEV. The degree to which writers are involved with evil varies considerably. Some attempt to localize evil, to see external factors as the cause of the degradation, to blame it on the Bolsheviks, on the Jews. Astafiev chokes with anger: as one of the leading writers of *village prose*, he passionately hates urban culture, seduced and corrupted as it has been by the West, and symbolized by the *lubricious* dances described in sinister terms in 'Lyudochka'. However, Astafiev has provided evil with such *freedom of self-expression* that this evil cannot be blamed on the influence of Western culture alone, so that there seems little chance of defeating evil. In Astafiev's prose the patriarchal world of the countryside has been almost totally destroyed, and there is little hope that it can still be a source of salvation. Even that sacred image of Russian literature, the image of the mother who lives in the countryside and whose vocation it is to be the guardian of the basic values of life, is portrayed by Astafiev without sympathy. Obedience to an unhappy fate is the dominant theme: the presiding atmosphere is one of almost Eastern fatalism. Violent death seems as natural here as in war or in the deadliest districts of New York. The heroine's suicide is built into the story's very structure. Yet village literature cannot but offer a positive hero, an avenger from the people, a hero whose duty it is to take the law into his own hands and punish the disgusting hooligan who has driven the heroine to suicide. The scene of summary justice – a rather dubious victory for good – gives the author complete satisfaction. St George has killed the dragon. Behind the narrative one can glimpse the sensitive soul of the author himself, but the malicious notes of angry impotence which resound in Astafiev's work bear witness, on the whole, to the defeat of moralistic propaganda.

Such propaganda is still completely at home in the work of writers who are bound up with the overall humanistic spirit of the Khrushchev 'Thaw'. Yet in the work of FRIDRIKH GORENSHTEIN, the 'black sheep' of the 'men of the sixties', there is no longer any real hope that a positive hero can be found. The narrator himself is forced to become that hero, a narrator who has great difficulty in overcoming the repulsion he feels when confronted by life, and who functions as the *doppelgänger* of an avenging Antichrist. Such is the viewpoint from which he describes one day in the life of the old woman, Avdotiya. In this instance the use in the Russian text of the affectionate diminutive, *Avdotyushka*, is no more than sarcasm, a sarcasm precluding pity. The blame is laid in equal measure at the doors of the subject and object represented. The Socialist world is neither better nor worse than the heroine: they deserve each other. Russian literature's standard figure, the *little man*, who has to be protected and justified at all costs, turns into a foul, mercenary old crone, crawling through life like an insect in search of food to fill her craw.

Elsewhere Gorenshtein investigates the relation between evil and the national character. In his novel *The Psalm* Gorenshtein asserts that 'Humanists taught that there are no bad peoples. Moses' biblical teaching, however, if you think about it, said that there were no good peoples at all,' but he also stresses that each people is bad in its own way, since each possesses its own peculiar set of bad qualities.

Writers like Gorenshtein, Lyudmila Petrushevskaya and a host of others who are situated at the junction of two literary generations, find themselves split between a 'men of the sixties'' conviction that vices are socially motivated (their texts have a passionate social involvement and enthusiastically expose the evils of society), and the hopelessness of the *alternative literature*. In tandem with the new literature they start to suspect human nature itself, thereby joining the ranks of *helpless* observers who are astonished by the many 'roads' open to evil: envy, senility, the absence of human communication, national conflicts.

The degradation of the world no longer knows any 'humanitarian' limits, and the world is *dehumanized* in ways which mirror Ortega y Gasset's analyses. Writing and writers themselves are shown to be infected with a strain of this disease, a disease that is dangerous for everybody else, and this severely damages belief in the creative capabilities of man. But such doubts do not extend to the personality of the narrator, who mocks everyone else but considers himself or herself immune to such mockery.

YURY MAMLEEV is a different case altogether. His narrator begins with a self-definition borrowed from Dostoevsky's underground man: 'All right, so I'm a nasty piece of work.' Yury Mamleev's main heroine is death. In his works death is an all-devouring obsession, a feeling of rapture that one has discovered a taboo subject (the problem of death did not exist for Marxism), a black hole into which all thoughts are sucked. Death becomes the only real link between being and consciousness. Mamleev's writings provide no answer to the question as to what gives birth to this link: whether it is the unhappy Soviet (Russian) being, leading one to thoughts about a state of ontological misfortune, or whether it is the unhappy individual consciousness, so possessed by death that it is willing to live with the most unfavourable forms of being. Most probably, it is not the question but the result that matters: death destroys any humanitarian ideas. All that remains is the wild, terrified *squeal* of Mamleev's characters (the verb *to squeal* is Mamleev's principal verb), who wish to escape from their *idée fixe* about inevitable death, who try to save themselves from this obsessive thought in dirty beer cellars, in sects, in sex, in hallucinations, in murders – but nothing helps. Only stupidity can help. However, the very diversity of 'pathological' horrors, which are depicted in a conservative style close to the realistic prose of the nineteenth century, Dostoevsky's prose in particular, runs the risk of becoming thematically monotonous and self-parodic.

SASHA SOKOLOV would like to make all the horrors dissolve in the most 'imperishable' of narrations. To make them disappear is the task of the lyric hero, the author's double. In 'The Anxious Chrysalis' the certainty that the right choice has been made is tangible. In social terms, this means being one of the *superfluous men*, mocked by 'the stupid, crude, wingless laboratory assistants in scarlet Russian-style shirts'. Apart from the Redshirts, butterflies, moths and other gaudy and affected mummers put in an appearance at the masked ball of life, where thoughts about freedom and happiness find expression. Costumes are needed to cloak the banality of the ideas, but the metaphors and the complex syntax are the things that really matter. The integument is all-important. In the person of Sasha Sokolov, contemporary literature investigates the possibilities offered by aestheticism as a form of resistance.

A new haven is mapped out where the Russian soul, exhausted by evil, is prepared to take shelter: the Nabokovian alternative of *perfect* style, which blocks out reality more and more, to the limit, until it turns into a manifesto declaring that the only subject one can believe in is the authorial *I*, with or without the costume of the anxious chrysalis.

However, more often than not '*I* know what is to be done' gives way to 'there's nothing you can do'. The works of Sergei Dovlatov and Valery Popov, two writers who started out in Leningrad, and whose fates were very different, are exemplary in this respect. Dovlatov died an *émigré* in New York, while Popov became an influential literary figure in his home town – though Russian literature is one, of course, it doesn't divide into émigré and metropolitan literatures, even if this fact has only been sufficiently appreciated since Gorbachev came to power in 1985. In the writings of Dovlatov and Popov the idea that there is nothing to be done is suffused by the mitigating light of an almost Chekhovian humour. The war against evil has long since ended with evil's final triumph, but one has to go on living somehow.

The narrator of VALERY POPOV's story, a decent, typical *intelligent*, comes into contact with evil, the inevitable but morally always damaging contact of the occupied with the occupier. What is more, he starts feeling envious. He too would like to be able to break promises and laws as easily as his 'evil' heroes do, he's keen to become *a lord of life*, but he lacks the courage and boldness, and his upbringing and decency get in the way and do not permit him to transgress. Such a longing has not yet become second nature to the heroes of Popov's works, but one can see the beginnings of the process. It is a case not so much of social opportunism as of literary-metaphysical opportunism, an opportunism which entails an unfettered love of recounting interesting stories (a variation on the theme of *art for art's sake*), the neutralization of moral pathos and, as a consequence, the cancellation of *salvation*.

The theme of opportunism is developed by SERGEI DOVLATOV, who takes the final step in turning the depicted reality into a theatre of the absurd and who weakens once and for all, indeed, until it fades away altogether, the moralizing role of the narrator by foregrounding the theme of compromise, most obviously in the chapter names and the very title of his book *The Compromise*. Life under Communist power possessed a priceless comic quality. Sergei Dovlatov is not capable of changing that life, but he is capable of describing it, and the very act of describing reality becomes a transcending of reality, the transformation of the vile into a pure object of style. The more absurd, the merrier.

In contradistinction to both Sasha Sokolov's *light*, lyric double and Mamleev's *dark*, turbid narrator, Dovlatov's narrator is neither better nor worse than other people. He is just like everyone else. He knows that in a country in whose very name – USSR – each letter stands for a lie everything is built on deception, but he also contributes to the deception himself. He splits in two like a schizophrenic, living as a journalist who writes about a 'man doomed to be happy', about members of the Secret Police and the great construction projects of Communism, and as a private individual dissatisfied with the regime, a womanizer, a resourceful drunkard. One can get a real high from the internal and external inconsistencies. The result is, instead of *salvation*, a saving *cynicism*. It is this which has turned Dovlatov into a key figure for the new literature and made him a very popular author among the general reading public. Cynicism brings relief, softens the psychological difficulties involved in making the transition from totalitarian force to market forces, and the reader receives a much-awaited indulgence: he is no longer called upon to perform heroic deeds.

EDWARD LIMONOV is a virtuoso in the art of cynicism. His hero confesses: 'I am different. I know fear, as everyone does, but always feel an urge to break taboos.' Abnormalities or sudden candidness are what interest him, something which goes beyond the *norm*, the norm being the common enemy of the *alternative literature*. The strongest man triumphs, and has a good time while he is about it. The old idea of the superman is cleverly repackaged in the form of a little sentimentalist who loves beer, women and sausage (though not necessarily in that order). Limonov's hero is totally incapable of anything and at the same time is capable of *anything*. It depends on the position of the stars and the disposition of his nerves. His is the mentality of a typical hooligan, one extremely adept at taunting the imagination, especially in Russia. One can walk away calmly after being rebuffed by a singer in a bar, or one can stick a knife in her. Everything can change in a single second. Yesterday an avant-gardist, today an ultra-nationalist. Unpredictability is the essence of cynicism. The unstable balance between provincial complexes and megalomania is upset in the nineties by the politicization of the hero. Now convinced of the boring emptiness of Western life, he chooses the profaned Communist idea in order to throw down a challenge, as a means of going against the current. Life imitating art is a very Russian phenomenon; literary heroes have always spawned a host of followers, remoulding readers in their own image. The Limonov hero has fathered the author himself. A game with real evil has begun, in which real blood is being shed. And it is against such bloodshed that the following writers, who all share a type of *holy foolishness*, wish to cast a spell.

Venedikt Erofeev, Vyacheslav Pietsukh and Evgeny Popov, each in his own 'foolish' way, obscure their own views of the world. In Soviet times this obfuscation served as a means of political self-defence, but in essence it represented a rejection of rationalistic answers to the accursed questions of existence, a polemically brilliant powerlessness when faced with the problem of explaining the world.

VENEDIKT EROFEEV provided Russian prose with the special biological rhythm of an alcoholic confession. The result was authentically Russian. An alcoholic – a tender, shy, tremulous and boorish soul – proved to be more sober than the sober world. Venedikt stumbled his way towards a very serious and profound theme for Russian culture: that of a superficial, 'not being serious', devil-may-care attitude to life, an attitude which has its roots in the religious past of holy fools in Christ and wandering minstrels. He also provided a national solution: a 'natural' cycle of binges and hang-overs which became a rejection of the ideological calendars forced upon the people, a sort of narcotic trip bringing the good news about the incompatibility of the Soviet way and the Russian soul.

'Vasily Rozanov through the Eyes of an Eccentric' (the original Russian title) makes it possible to understand the yearning of post-Stalinist culture for literary and religious exemplars. The author represented the momentous meeting of Russian independent culture of the sixties and seventies with the 'Silver Age' as the only 'hope' for a contemporary intellectual who was planning to do away with himself, disillusioned as he was with the truisms of rationalism. The unforeseen but long-awaited contact with Vasily Rozanov's dizzying paradoxes put everything in its place. In showing itself to be an underground, *bashful moralism*, holy foolishness gave Erofeev's semi-hero, semi-author (such centaurs are widespread in the *alternative literature*) the strength to go on living and to curse the powers that be, helped him gain confidence in the rightness of his particular blend of self-abasement and national pride, and, above all, to feel his ties with the 'constellations'.

However dirty, unprepossessing and unhappy the Russian man may be, he is still convinced that he has within him something special, something which other peoples will always lack. 'The Russian soul encompasses everything,' asserts VYACHESLAV PIET-SUKH, with more than a hint of holy foolishness. Pietsukh is a conciliatory type of writer, and for him a bad peace is better than a good war. Good-natured and unwilling to go into naturalistic detail, his narrator prefers to carnivalize evil, to conceal violence by using the poetic manner of a folk tale. He plays with the evergreen stereotypes of Russia's past and the national tendency toward mythological thinking. His is an attempt to spellbind evil in some miraculous way, to talk about it in a jokey manner, to substitute good for evil on the sly, to beat swords into ploughshares. Yet when one looks more closely at 'The Central–Ermolaevo War', the feud between two villages, one can't help being struck by the overall stupidity, the scenes of torture and the various absurdities, and the finale turns into an involuntary parody of a happy ending precisely because of its charming fairy-tale quality.

The holy foolish writings of EVGENY POPOV are more mournful, although outwardly they too wear a bright motley and are indeed full of buffoonery. Popov too strives for a peaceful outcome, but this native of Siberia does not succeed in reaching an accord. Genetically close to village prose, Popov has departed from it by changing in effect just a few letters: in his short stories the village hicks turn into pricks, the eccentric holy fools into tools. The obscene puns acquired a metaphysical dimension. Popov tries to shed light on how the events being described are unfolding, but he gets confused, he prevaricates, and plays the fool himself, someone not capable of coping with the flow of life, in which stories surface about 'how some children were captured, hung up in the woods, cut open with knives, and their blood drained off into laboratory retorts.' Why? 'So that their blood could be handed in at the blood transfusion centre in exchange for vast sums of money.'

Giving up hope of any final knowledge of the world, Popov leaves indistinct, unfinished passages which present one with the opportunity either to think things through to the end in his stead and thus to increase the scope of the subject, to thicken the plot, or to reproach him for a cowardly agnosticism. Sometimes this obfuscation fails to achieve the desired effect, when it finds itself in the realm of common knowledge (in such cases the narrator is put in a weak position in relation to his reader), but sometimes the obscurities coincide with metaphysical riddles.

Like other writers with a tendency toward holy foolishness, Popov shows marvellously, though often completely unintentionally, the non-Europeanness of the Russian character, its inconsistency, the indeterminacy of its views and deeds, features which are connected with the complexity of the axiological structure of the Russian world.

The Western reader can breathe a sigh of relief: thank goodness he doesn't live in Russia, where human life is so cheap and where there is so much barbarity. But in fact the problem isn't Russia. The true significance of the new Russian literature does not lie in its exposure of the country, but in its demonstration of the fact that beneath the thin veneer of civilization man is nothing more than an uncontrollable animal. It is just that the Russian example is at times more striking than most.

Some of the advantages of Russia's 'culture lag' can be appreciated from the work of EVGENY KHARITONOV. He was the founder of modern Russian gay culture in the seventies, when homosexuality was a crime not just in theory but in practice, with the result that practising homosexuals were actively persecuted and imprisoned. The fact that Kharitonov was the first to discover homosexuality as a literary subject, plus the *forbidden* nature of the theme itself, led the writer to a plastic, *passive* style, thanks to which he became one of the best writers of his generation. A *new way of writing* about lóve emerged (not since the time of Turgenev has Russian literature known such a pure love): passionate, persecuted, bashful, gasping for breath, pre-thrombotic in its inner tension. And that is how the writer died: from a heart attack on a Moscow street, dying before he could achieve fame. Today the growing gay press in Russia glorifies Kharitonov, he is already a classic, his name is becoming a shibboleth.

A development contemporaneous with, and parallel to, Kharitonov's prose is the emergence of women's writing, a prose which is candid but which on the whole keeps its distance from feminist ideology, an ideology towards which TATYANA TOLSTAYA, for one, does not conceal her hostility. In Tolstaya's stories the powerful, masculine energy of traditional forms of writing contrasts derisively with the descriptions of unhappy, meaningless lives. Tolstaya is ready to embrace and reassure her unlucky heroes, but she fully realizes that to help them, let alone save them, is not just difficult, but almost impossible. Other people are the victors: the cunning, the evil, the distrustful. The predators win, but this does not mean that the predators are right; it's simply that there is neither justice nor logic in life, just some sort of pulsation and some passing dreams, it's a real pity, and there's nothing you can do; but although no one is totally good, there *are* some who are totally bad, there are some who are better and some who are worse, and one has to show all this in order to be able to distinguish the one from the other. Why? The question hangs in the air, especially as the form of writing encourages the author to indulge her refined tastes, her desire to fill up the space on the page with the juiciest, most eye-catching, most expressive words.

The vitality of the writing in Tolstaya's stories is, incidentally, somewhat suspect: it reminds one of the fresh look of well-made artificial trees set out in American interiors. Perhaps this is not the case, but the contemporary cultural context implacably transforms living greenery into an artful imitation.

The creation of a positive hero, an officer in a rocket battalion with ambitious plans for his future, in 'The Story of Major Siminkov', might seem at first to be a task more suited to a Socialist Realist writer. However, ANATOLY GAVRILOV's neutral narrative, conceived as not merely an echo but as a stylistic reworking of Pushkin's short story, 'The Shot', stands in opposition to both the former semi-official literature of the propagandistic genre (which pretended to be free and independent), and to the literature of denunciation and exposure which aims to horrify the reader with its tales of the vileness and violence of army existence. Accepting the army's own rule book, its arbitrariness and conventions, as facts of life, Gavrilov traces the human passion for self-affirmation. That the hero does not get on in the world results not from an error but from the whims of chance, from a totally farcical event, bringing to naught all creative efforts, and hurling the hero headlong to bottomless perdition. No one is to blame, and it is precisely this which causes the syndrome of horror and awe which paralyses any desire to make an active contribution to anything, and which leads the writer to the national creed of the advantages of the *contemplative* life, to the awareness that in Hell it is better simply *to observe*.

Stylistic imitation is a sign that the word is in bad shape, a symptom of an exhausted literature. The *alternative literature* has to deal with a dead word. One can adorn it lovingly, but it is difficult to bring it back to life. The Russian word, which on many occasions during the Soviet period, fell prey to ideals and raptures, promises and slogans, entered the seventies as a mere ghost of a word.

ANDREI SINYAVSKY's desire is to make an inspection and inventory of the word, to go back to basics. It might seem that Sinyavsky is close to Ionesco as he arranges in 'The Golden Lace' a parade of dead, schoolroom words, capable of expressing above all the absurdity of life. In actual fact, in Sinyavsky's case this return to the primer is meant to revive the word, to re-establish with the help of simple syntactical constructions its lines of communication with the noise of life. 'Do you intend to return to Russia?' 'No, I don't.' These are already the words of a confession taking form, but the attempted reanimation fails, and the author himself realizes that prose has come to a 'dead end'.

A dead language can't be treated. The condition which the literary critic in Sinyavsky recognizes and analyses is presented by Moscow *conceptualism* as the last word in art. The final years of the Communist regime saw the development in the radical wing of the avant-garde (Prigov, Rubinshtein, Sorokin) a subculture of Moscow conceptualism, a subculture with its own laws, public, semiotics, its own rituals of underground private exhibitions and performances, discussions, scandalous happenings, and its own network of personal relationships, all of which went to form a part of my generation's life that cannot be recalled without nostalgia.

Moscow conceptualism – hermetic, uncompromising, ironic and arrogant – combines a complete alienation from the word with, hidden behind the text, complete despair. Having begun with parodies of Socialist Realist painting and having transformed the aesthetics of Socialist Realism into a form of social drama, conceptualism was perceived initially as a protest, and was indeed close to artistic dissidentism by virtue of its didactic aims. However, the scope of its activity grew wider, and it turned into an independent elemental force not specifically connected with any political challenge. Moreover, the aesthetics of Socialist Realism gradually began to be perceived as some sort of national constant, something defining, something existentially repulsive yet significant. Because the conceptualists are always playing on their images, one has to treat their declarations with some caution, as some kind of never-ending literary game; yet their claim that they are making a final analysis of culture is utterly serious.

The fact that the word-as-whore is capable of guaranteeing satisfaction to any consciousness, from the totalitarian to the liberal, warns the conceptualists to be on their guard. The word is sent under conceptualist escort to carry out forced labour of a strictly masochistic nature: it is told to engage in self-destruction and self-flagellation. No general pardon is on the horizon. Usually the West finds such a brutal attitude to the word hard to take, since for the West the byword for distrust of the socialized word is Orwell's 'Newspeak'. Although conceptualism denies that its own word is relevant to life and makes much of its own intertextuality, its word is seen as expressing a distrustful attitude toward life and life's wearisome iteration, in which all moves have been exhausted, and this directly links conceptualism with the *literature of evil*.

Asserting himself as an author who creates independent characters, who works with ready-made constructions and who is capable of reproducing any type of writing, DMITRY PRIGOV takes to the poetic absurd a mass of ideological clichés and concepts, in particular those of a specifically Soviet nature, by playing around with political, national and moral taboos. One of contemporary poetry's brightest stars, Prigov uses his texts to mark out the dead zones of Russian–Soviet culture, inducing in his audience a liberating laughter and in this way facilitating the regeneration of meaning. The rapid dating of certain of his texts is a natural consequence of the ever-changing state of political affairs.

LEV RUBINSHTEIN has created an independent version of fragmentary writing based on counterpoint. The fragments consist of single-sentence, often ridiculous utterances containing various semantic and emotional content and a varying degree of authorial remoteness, ranging from zero-information content to attempts at autobiography, equalized at the level of the text to a unit of utterance. The humour arises because the fragment, laid bare and torn from its stereotypical context, is still so recognizable, though it loses a lot in translation. The existential coefficient of such a text is high enough, but is also extremely sad.

Although as a matter of principle VLADIMIR SOROKIN refuses to be called a writer, he accepts his status as the leading monster of the New Russian Literature. He puts his texts together from the leftovers of Socialist Realism, only to make them explode by means of unexpected leaps in the narrative, obscene language, and an extreme thickening of the textual brew, a text-concentrate whose main ingredients are sexual pathology and extreme violence, including cannibalism and necrophilia. Beneath the surface of the text lexical chaos and delirium are laid bare. The dead word phosphoresces thanks to verbal conjuring, shamanism, and a mystical glossolalia which vaguely hints at the existence of other worlds. Sorokin's texts are like meat from which all the blood has flowed away and which is writhing with worms. This dish, prepared by a disillusioned *romantic* meting out revenge on the world for its ontological ugliness, makes the reader feel sick and induces in him a state of aesthetic shock. But just as in the case of Mamleev, who to a certain extent may be considered Sorokin's teacher, the limited menu, the overreliance on the technique, gradually weakens the initial impression.

The totalitarian ambitions of conceptualism always seemed to me to be somewhat exaggerated. Having written my first essays on de Sade and Lev Shestov as long ago as the beginning of the seventies and having paid my dues to the literature of evil, I am nevertheless probably closer to what may be called a 'flickering aesthetic', a type of 'negative capability' which I view as an attempt to escape the postmodern canon, and which combines suggestive, seditious invention with an alluring laying bare of the devices of any discourse. Clearly it is this aesthetic which is responsible for creating, as the composer Alfred Schnittke wrote in a review of a collection of my short stories, 'that uncanny effect of coming into contact with something long familiar but completely imaginary, that shock from meeting both heaven and hell simultaneously, a shock taking place inside every one of us, that absolute mysteriousness of something that seems at first to be hackneyed and banal. You're not sure what takes your breath away more: indignation at the blasphemous themes and characters, or the release of tension in an atmosphere of unspoken but tangible, martyr-like holiness.'

Though the younger generation of writers tend to be over-persistent in their imitation of the model texts of the literature of evil, there is in their works a lessening of the tension that results from the actual experiencing of evil. A secondary style arises, *chernukha*, 'black stuff', a 'slanderous' and sensationalist 'dirty art' in which the horrors of life and pathological behaviour are treated as more of an amusement, a literary device, a tried and tested way of playing with extremes of feeling. Interest in the former political confrontations wanes more and more. The heroes of the resistance and the former Communist leaders fuse and are apprehended in the same way as comic book characters. IGOR YARKEVICH in his belated juvenilia sees all yesterday's battles as nothing more than a Vanity Fair. His alternative: Solzhenitsyn *or* me, a poor wanker, is resolved on the level not so much of slapstick as on that of the desacralization of the role of the contemporary writer, who is no longer so pained by the degradation of the language as the conceptualists, because in the final analysis it has not led to the death of literature.

The Russian literature of the end of the twentieth century has acquired a profound knowledge of evil. My generation became evil's mouthpiece, made evil a part of ourselves, provided evil with vast opportunities for self-expression. It was an unconscious decision; things just turned out that way. But it had to be like that. This literature is powerful precisely because there was no preconceived plan to voyage into the heart of darkness. Clear dividing lines have been erased. Life crosses over into death, good luck becomes bad, laughter turns to tears. Men and women have become all mixed up;

it is no longer possible to distinguish their 'minimal' differences. Writers are drawn to marginal sexual practices, perversions, sacrilege. Although the moralizing tendency in criticism has argued that *Satanism* has taken over Russian literature, that the new writers are of the Devil's party, what has actually happened in historical terms is that the pendulum has swung away from lifeless humanism. The hypermoralistic list has been corrected. A bright page of evil has been entered into the annals of Russian literature. As a result, the Russian classic novel will never again be a textbook on how to live or a source of ultimate truth. The correctives which have been added are too shocking, too blood-curdling. To give voice to the force of evil, a generation of powerful writers has entered Russian literature.

Evil has expressed itself. As the twentieth century draws to a close, the literature of evil has done its work. The ontological market of evil spoils one for choice. Evil's cup runneth o'er with black liquid.

What next?

Translated by Andrew Reynolds

VARLAM SHALAMOV

Typhoid Quarantine

The man in the white gown held out his rosy, washed hand, and Andreev put his sweaty, stiff military shirt into the outstretched fingers. The man jerked back his hand and shook it.

'I don't have any underwear,' Andreev said indifferently.

The orderly then took Andreev's shirt in both hands, turned the sleeves inside out with an agile, practised movement, and took one look . . .

'He's full of them, Lydia Ivanovna,' he said and bellowed at Andreev: 'How could you let yourself get so lousy?'

But the doctor, Lydia Ivanovna, interrupted him.

'It's not their fault,' she said quietly in a tone of reproach, stressing the word 'their', and took a stethoscope from the table.

Andreev remembered this red-haired woman for the rest of his life, thanked her a thousand times, and thought about her with warmth and tenderness. Why? Because she had stressed the word *'their'* in this, the only sentence that Andreev had ever heard from her. He thanked her for a kind word said at the right time. Did she ever learn of his thanks?

The examination was brief and did not require a stethoscope. Lydia Ivanovna breathed on a violet rubber stamp and pressed it to a printed form, leaning on it heavily with both hands. She wrote a few words on it, and Andreev was taken away.

The guard, who had been waiting in the entrance hall, did not take Andreev back to prison but to one of the warehouses in the centre of the settlement. The area around the warehouse had a barbed-wire fence with the prescribed ten strands and a gate, next to which stood a sentry wearing a leather coat and holding a rifle. They entered the yard and approached the warehouse. A bright light shone through the crack in the door. The door was made for trucks, not people, and the guard opened it with great difficulty. The smell of dirty bodies, sour human sweat, and old clothing struck Andreev's nostrils. A muffled hum of human voices filled the vast box. The walls were entirely covered with four-tiered bunks cut from whole larch trees. The bunks were built solidly, to last forever – like Caesar's bridges. More than a thousand people lay on the shelves of the huge warehouse. This was only one of twenty enormous warehouses packed with living goods. There was a typhoid quarantine in port, and there hadn't been any 'outgoing shipments' for more than a month.

There had been a breakdown in the camp's blood circulation system, whose erythrocytes were living people. Trucks stood idle, and the mines lengthened the prisoners' workday. In the town itself the bakery was not able to keep up with orders. Every prisoner had to receive a pound of bread per day, and bread was even being baked in private apartments. The authorities were growing ever more bitter over the fact that the town was slowly filling up with convict 'slag' that had been thrown out by the mines in the taiga.

There were more than a thousand human beings in the warehouse to which Andreev had been brought and which bore the then-fashionable title of 'section'. This multitude was not immediately noticeable. On the upper bunks people lay naked in the heat; the prisoners on and beneath the lower bunks wore padded coats, pea jackets and hats. No one will ever explain why a convict almost never sleeps on his side. Most of the men lay on their backs, and their bodies seemed like growths or bumps in the wood, like bent boards in the enormous shelves.

Sometimes people clustered in small groups either around story-tellers – 'novelists' – or around incidents, and given such a concentration of people, incidents occurred nearly every minute. The men were being kept in the transit camp and had not been sent to work for more than a month. They were sent out only to the bathhouse to disinfect their clothing. Every day the camps lost twenty thousand workdays, one hundred and sixty thousand hours, perhaps even three hundred and twenty thousand hours; workdays vary. Or twenty thousand days of life were saved. Twenty thousand days of life. Statistics is a wily science, and figures can be read in different ways.

Everyone was in his place when food was handed out, distributed to ten prisoners at a time. There were so many people that no sooner had breakfast been distributed than it was time for lunch. As soon as lunch had been served, it was time for supper. Only bread and 'tea' (warm boiled water) and half a herring were distributed to each man in the morning. No more bread was issued for the rest of the day. Lunch consisted of soup, and only kasha was served for supper. Nevertheless, there was not sufficient time to serve even this quantity.

The assignment man showed Andreev his place and pointed to the second bunk. A grumble of protest came from the top bunk, but the assignment man cursed back at the grumblers. Andreev gripped the edge of the shelf with both hands and unsuccessfully attempted to bring up his right leg. The assignment man's strong arm tossed him upward, and Andreev plunked down among the naked bodies. No one paid him any attention. The 'registration' and settlement procedure had been carried out.

Andreev slept. He awoke only when food was distributed, after which he would carefully and precisely lick his hands and fall asleep again. His sleep was not sound, however, since the lice refused to leave him in peace.

No one questioned him, even though there were many people here from the taiga, and the rest were destined to end up there. They all knew this, and for that very reason they wanted to know as little as possible about their inevitable fate. They were right, Andreev reasoned. They should not know everything that he had seen. Nothing could be avoided or foreseen. What use were extra fears? These were living people, and Andreev was a representative of the dead. And his knowledge, the knowledge of a dead man, could not be of use to those who were still alive.

Bathhouse time came two days later. Bathing and clothing disinfection were nothing but an annoyance, and all the prisoners prepared themselves reluctantly. Andreev, however, wanted to rid himself of lice. He had all the time in the world, and he examined the seams of his faded military shirt several times a day. But only the disinfection chamber held the promise of final victory. He went to the bathhouse willingly and, although they issued him no underwear and he had to pull his reddish military shirt over his naked body, he no longer felt the usual bites.

At the bathhouse, the usual portion of water was issued – one basin of hot water and one of cold – but Andreev managed to deceive the water man and get an extra basin. A tiny piece of soap was issued, but it was possible to gather discarded fragments from the floor and work up a good lather. This was his best bath in a year. So what if blood and pus seeped from the scurvy ulcers on his shins? So what if people in the bathhouse recoiled from him in horror? So what if they walked around him and his lousy clothing in disgust?

When clothing was returned from the disinfection chamber, the fur socks of Andreev's neighbour Ognev had shrunk so much that they looked like toys. Ognev burst into tears, for the socks were his salvation in the north. Andreev, however, stared at him without sympathy. He had seen too many men cry for too many reasons. Some pretended, others were mentally disturbed, and still others had lost hope and were desperately bitter. Some cried from the cold. Andreev had never seen anyone cry from hunger.

When they returned through the silent city, the aluminium-hued puddles had cooled, and the fresh air had a smell of spring. After the session in the bathhouse, Andreev slept soundly. Ognev, who had forgotten the incident in the bathhouse, said Andreev had 'had his fill of sleep'.

No one was permitted to leave, but there was one job in the 'section' for which a man could be allowed to cross through 'the wire'. True, this had nothing to do with leaving the camp settlement and crossing the 'outer wire' – a series of three fences, each with ten strands of barbed wire and a forbidden area beyond them circumscribed by another low fence. No one even dreamt of that. They could only contemplate the possibility of leaving the immediate yard. Beyond the barbed wire of the yard was a cafeteria, a kitchen, storehouses, a hospital – in a word, a very different life, one forbidden to Andreev. Only one person could pass through the fence – the sewage disposal man. And when he suddenly died (life is full of fortunate coincidences!), Ognev accomplished miracles of energy and intuition. For two days he ate no bread. Then he traded the bread for a pressed-fibre suitcase.

'I got it from Baron Mandel, Andreev!'

Baron Mandel! A descendant of Pushkin! Far below, Andreev could make out the long, narrow-shouldered figure of the Baron with his tiny bald skull, but he had never had an opportunity to make his acquaintance.

Since he had been in quarantine for only a few months, Ognev still had a wool jacket left over from the 'outside'. He presented the assignment man with the jacket and the suitcase and in exchange received the sewage disposal job. Two weeks later, Ognev was nearly strangled to death in the dark by criminals. They took three thousand roubles from him. The ability to leave and enter quarantine evidently provided a number of business opportunities.

Andreev scarcely saw Ognev during the heyday of his commercial career. Beaten and tormented, Ognev made a confession to Andreev one night as he returned to his old place:

'They cleaned me out today, but I'll beat them in the end. They think they know cards, but I'll get it all back!'

Ognev never helped Andreev with bread or money, nor was this the custom in such instances. In terms of camp ethics, he was acting quite normally.

One day Andreev realized with amazement that he had survived. It was extremely difficult to get up from his bunk, but he was able to do it. The main thing was that he didn't have to work and could simply lie prone. Even a pound of bread, three spoons of kasha and a bowl of watery soup were enough to resurrect a person so long as he didn't have to work.

It was at this precise moment that he realized he felt no fear and placed no value on his life. He also knew that he had passed through a great test and had survived. He knew he would be able to use his terrible experience in the mine for his own benefit. The opportunity for a convict to exercise choice, free will, did, in fact, exist – however minutely. Such an opportunity was a reality that could save his life, given the right circumstances. Andreev was prepared for the great battle when he would fight a beast with the cunning of a beast. He had been deceived, and he would deceive. He would not die. He would not permit that to happen.

He would fulfil the desires and commands his body had imparted to him at the gold mine. He had lost the battle at the mine, but it would not be the last he fought. He was the slag rejected from the mine. So he would be that slag. The violet stamp that Lydia Ivanovna had made on the piece of paper consisted of three letters: LPL, meaning Light Physical Labour. Andreev was well aware that such marks were totally ignored at the mines, but here at the Centre, he intended to get maximum mileage out of those letters.

Still, his chances were slight. He could say to the foreman: 'Here I am, Andreev, and I intend to lie prone here and not go anywhere. If I get sent to a mine, at the very first pass, just as soon as the truck brakes, I'll jump down, even if the guards shoot me. I don't care, I won't mine gold, no matter what.'

His chances were slight. But now he would be more intelligent and would trust more in his body. And his body would not deceive him. He had been deceived by his family, deceived by his country. Everything – love, energy, ability – had been crushed and trampled. Any justification the mind might seek was false, a lie, and Andreev knew this. Only the instinct of a beast, roused by the mine, could and did suggest a way out.

Precisely here, on these Cyclopian shelves, Andreev realized that he was worth something, that he could respect himself. He was still alive, and he had neither betrayed nor sold out anyone during the investigation or in the camp. He had succeeded in speaking the truth for the most part, and in suppressing his own fear. It was not that he feared nothing. No, but moral barriers had now been more clearly and precisely defined; everything, in fact, had become clear and precise. It was clear, for example, that Andreev was guilty of nothing. His former health was lost without a trace, broken forever. But was it forever? When Andreev had been first brought to this town, he thought he might live for another two or three weeks. To regain his former strength he would have needed complete rest for many months in resort conditions, with milk and chocolate. Since it was clear, however, that Andreev would never see any such resort, he would have to die. But that was not terrible; many of his comrades had died. Something stronger than death would not permit him to die. Love? Malice? No, a person lives by virtue of the same reasons as a tree, a stone, a dog. It was this that Andreev had grasped, had sensed with every fibre of his being precisely here at the city transit prison camp during the typhoid quarantine.

The scratch marks on Andreev's hands and arms healed faster than did his other wounds. Little by little, the turtle-shell armour into which his skin had been transformed disappeared. The bright, rosy tips of his frostbitten fingers began to darken; the microscopically thin skin, which had covered them after the frostbite blisters ruptured, thickened slightly. And, above all, he could bend the fingers of his left hand. In a year and a half at the mines, both of Andreev's hands had moulded themselves around the handles of a pick and shovel. He never expected to be able to straighten out his hands again. When he ate, he would grasp his spoon by pinching the handle with the tips of his fingers, and he even forgot that a spoon could be held in any other manner. His living hand was like a hook, an artificial limb. It fulfilled only the functions of an artificial hand. He could, if he wished, use it to cross himself when praying to God. But in his heart there was nothing but malice, and his spiritual wounds could not so easily be healed. They were never to heal.

At last, to his amazement, Andreev managed to straighten out his left hand one day in the bathhouse. Soon would come the turn of

7

the right hand – still bent claw-fashion. At night Andreev would quietly touch his right hand, and it seemed to him that it was on the verge of opening. He bit his fingernails in the neatest fashion and then proceeded to chew his dirty, thick, slightly moistened skin – a section at a time. This hygienic operation was one of Andreev's few amusements when he was not eating or sleeping.

The bloody cracks on the soles of his feet no longer hurt as much as they used to. The scurvy ulcers on his legs had not yet healed and required bandaging, but his wounds grew fewer and fewer in number, and were replaced by blue-black spots that looked like the brand of some slave-owner. Only his big toes would not heal; the frostbite had reached the bone marrow, and pus slowly seeped from them. Of course, there was less pus than there had been back at the mine, where the rubber galoshes that served as summer footwear were so full of pus and blood that his feet sloshed at every step – as if through a puddle.

Many years would pass before Andreev's toes were to heal. And for many years after healing, whenever it was cold or even slightly chilly at night, they would remind him of the northern mine. But Andreev thought of the future. He had learned at the mine not to plan his life further than a day in advance. He strove towards close goals, like any man who is only a short distance from death. Now he desired one thing alone – that the typhoid quarantine might last forever. This, however, could not be, and the day arrived when the quarantine was up.

That morning all the residents of the 'section' were driven out into the yard. The prisoners milled around silently, shivering for hours behind the wire fence. The assignment man stood on a barrel and shouted out the names in a hoarse, desperate voice. Those whose names were called left through the gate – never to return. Out on the highway trucks roared – roared so loudly that it was difficult to hear the assignment man.

'Don't let them call me, don't let them call me,' Andreev implored the fates in a childish invocation. No, he would not be lucky. If they didn't call for him today, they would call for him tomorrow. He would return to hunger, beatings, and death in the gold mines. His frostbitten fingers and toes began to ache, as did his ears and cheeks. Andreev shifted his weight more and more frequently from one foot to the other. He raised his shoulders and breathed into his clasped hands, but it was no easy thing to warm his numb hands and sick feet. It all was of no use. He was helpless in the struggle with the monstrous machine whose teeth were grinding up his entire body.

'Voronov! Voronov!' the assignment man called out. 'Voronov! The bastard has to be here . . .' In a rage the assignment man threw the thin yellow folder on to a barrel and put his foot down on the papers.

Suddenly Andreev understood. As lightning shows the way in a storm, so his road to salvation was revealed. In his excitement he immediately grew bold and moved forward towards the assignment man, who was calling out one name after the other. People disappeared from the yard, one after the other. But the crowd was still enormous. Now, now . . .

'Andreev!' the assignment man shouted.

Andreev remained silent and examined the assignment man's shaven jowls. When he had finished his examination, Andreev's gaze shifted to the remaining folders. There were only a few left. 'The last truck,' Andreev thought.

'Sychov! Answer – first name and patronymic!'

'Vladimir Ivanovich,' an elderly convict answered, according to the rules, and pushed the crowd aside.

'Crime? Sentence? Step out!'

A few more persons responded to the assignment officer's call. They left, and the assignment man left with them. The remaining prisoners were returned to the 'section'.

The coughing, stamping, and shouting quietened down and dissolved into the polyphonic speech of hundreds of men.

Andreev wanted to live. He had set himself two goals and was resolved to achieve them. He saw, with unusual clarity, that he had to lengthen his stay here as long as he could, if possible to the very last day. He had to control himself and not make any mistakes . . . Gold was death. No one in this transit prison knew that better than Andreev. No matter what the cost, he had to avoid the taiga and the gold mines. How could he, a slave deprived of all rights, manage this?

He had come to the conclusion that the taiga had been depopulated during the quarantine; cold, hunger, exhausting workdays, and sleeplessness must have deprived the taiga of people. That meant that trucks with prisoners would be sent to the mines from quarantine. (Official telegrams read: 'Send 200 trees.') Only when all the mines had been filled again would they begin sending people to other places – and not to dig gold in the taiga. Andreev did not care where he was sent. Just as long as it wasn't to mine gold.

Andreev did not say a word about this to anyone. He did not consult with Ognev or Parfentiev, his comrade from the mines, or with any of the thousand people who lay with him on those warehouse shelves. He knew that, if he were to tell them of his plan, any one of them would rush to tell the camp authorities – for praise, for a cigarette butt, for no reason at all . . . He knew what a heavy burden it was to keep a secret, but he could do it. Only if he told no one would he be free of fear. It was two, three, four times easier for him to slip alone through the teeth of this machine. The game was his alone; that was something he had learned at the mine.

Andreev 'did not respond' for many days. As soon as the quarantine was up, convicts were again used for work assignments, and the trick was not to be included in the large groups, since they were usually sent to do earth-moving with picks, axes and shovels. In smaller groups of two or three persons it was easier to earn an extra piece of bread or even some sugar; Andreev had not seen sugar for more than a year and a half. His strategy was simple and accurate. All these jobs were, of course, a violation of regulations in the transit prison, but there were many people who wanted to take advantage of free labour. People assigned to earth-moving details hoped to be able to beg for some tobacco or bread. And they succeeded – even from passers-by. Andreev would go to the vegetable storage areas, where he could eat his fill of beets and carrots and bring 'home' a few raw potatoes, which he would cook in the ashes of the stove and eat half-raw. Conditions demanded that all nutritional 'functions' be performed quickly; there were too many hungry people around.

Andreev's days were filled with activity and began to acquire a certain meaning. He had to stand in the cold every morning for two hours, listening to the scheduling officer call out names. And when the daily sacrifice had been made to Moloch, everyone would tramp back into the barracks, from where they would be taken to work.

Andreev worked at the bakery, carried garbage at the women's transit prison, and washed floors in the guards' quarters, where he would gather up the sticky, delicious meat leftovers from the officers' tables. When work was over, mountains of bread and large basins of starchy fruit pudding would be brought to the kitchen, and everyone would sit down, eat and stuff their pockets with bread.

Most of all Andreev preferred to be sent alone, but that happened rarely. His small-group strategy failed him only once. One day the assignment man, who remembered Andreev's face (but knew him as Muravyov), said to him:

'I found you a job you'll never forget – chopping wood for the camp director. There'll be two of you.'

Joyously the two men ran ahead of the guard, who was wearing a cavalry overcoat. The guard slipped, stumbled, jumped over the bottom of his coat with both hands. They soon reached a small house with a locked gate and barbed wire strung along the top of the fence. The camp director's orderly opened the gate, took them without a word to the woodshed, closed the door, and loosed an enormous German shepherd into the yard. The dog kept them locked up until they had cut and split all the wood in the shed. Later that evening they were taken back to camp. They were to be sent back to do the same job the next day, but Andreev hid under his bunk and did no work at all that day.

The next morning, before bread was distributed, a simple idea occurred to Andreev, and he immediately acted upon it. He took off his boots and put them on the edge of the shelf, soles outward, so that it looked as though he himself was lying on the bunk with his boots on. Then he lay down next to them, propping his head on his forearms.

The man distributing bread quickly counted off ten persons and gave Andreev an extra portion of bread. Nevertheless, this method was not reliable, and Andreev again began to seek work outside the barracks.

People kept accumulating in the transit camp. Rumour had it that no one was being sent to the taiga, but Andreev resolved to drag out his departure till the very end anyway. Soon thereafter he picked up a steady job – washing the floors in the camp SD, the Storage Depot.

The third and fourth level of the bunks had long since been emptied, as was the lower level.

Did he think about his family at that time? No. About freedom? No. Did he recite poetry from memory? No. Did he recall the past? No. He lived by a blunted, indifferent malice alone.

It was then that Andreev came upon Captain Schneider.

The professional criminals had occupied a place close to the stove. Their bunks were spread with dirty quilts and pillows of various sizes. A quilt is the inevitable companion of any successful thief, the only object that he carries with him from prison to prison. If a thief does not own a quilt, he will steal one or take it away from another prisoner. As for the pillow, it is not only a rest for his head, but it can be quickly converted into a table for endless card battles. Such a table can be given any form. But it is still a pillow. Card players will lose their trousers before they will part with their pillows.

The more prominent criminals, that is, those who were the most prominent at that moment, were sitting on the quilts and pillows. Higher up, on the third shelf, where it was dark, lay other pillows and quilts. It was there that the criminals maintained the young effeminate thieves and their various other companions. Almost all the thieves were homosexuals.

The hardened criminals were surrounded by a crowd of vassals and lackeys, for the criminals considered it fashionable to be interested in 'novels' narrated orally by prisoners of literary inclination. And even in these conditions there were court barbers with bottles of perfume and a throng of sycophants eager to perform any service in exchange for a piece of bread or a bowl of soup.

'Shut up! Senechka is talking. Be quiet! Senechka wants to sleep . . .'

It had been a familiar scene back at the mine.

Suddenly, among the crowd of beggars and the retinue of criminals, Andreev saw a familiar face and recognized the man's voice. There was no doubt about it – it was Captain Schneider, Andreev's cellmate in Butyrki Prison.

Captain Schneider was a German communist who had been active in the Comintern, spoke beautiful Russian, was an expert on Goethe and an educated Marxist theoretician. Andreev's memory had preserved conversations with Schneider, intense conversations that took place during the long prison nights. A naturally cheerful person, this former sea captain kept the entire cell in good spirits.

Andreev could not believe his eyes.

'Schneider!'

'What do you want?' the captain turned around. His dull blue eyes showed no recognition of Andreev.

'Schneider!'

'So what do you want? You'll wake up Senechka.'

But already the edge of the blanket had been lifted, and the light revealed a pale, unhealthy face.

'Ah, captain,' came Senechka's tenor voice with a languid tone. 'I can't fall asleep without you . . .'

'Right away, I'm coming,' Schneider said hurriedly.

He climbed up on the shelf, folded back the edge of the blanket, sat down, and put his hand under the blanket to scratch Senechka's heels.

Andreev walked slowly to his place. He had no desire to go on living. Even though this was a trivial event by comparison with that which he had seen and was still destined to witness, he never forgot Captain Schneider.

The number of people kept decreasing. The transit prison was being emptied. Andreev came face to face with the assignment man.

'What's your name?'

Andreev, however, had prepared himself for such an occurrence.

'Gurov,' he replied meekly.

'Wait!'

The assignment man leafed through the onion-sheet lists.

'No, it's not here.'

'Can I go?'

'Go ahead, you animal!' the scheduling officer roared.

They were taken out to work every day, but it was a case of free transit labour with no records kept. Best of all was to end up in a small group of one or two men, and that was precisely Andreev's goal.

It wasn't hard. You had only to linger in the back ranks when they lined everyone up before the gates. At first they would take large groups of three or four hundred to use for earthmoving projects in town that were not very advantageous to the camp administration. After that the groups got smaller and smaller. Finally Andreev's moment arrived: he got sent to the bakery together with a group of female convicts.

Once he was assigned to wash dishes and clean up the cafeteria for people who had served their sentences and who were about to be released. His partner was one of those 'goners' who were so emaciated they were known as 'wicks'. The man had just been released from prison, and it was difficult to determine his age. It was the first time this 'goner' had worked. He kept asking what they should do, would they be fed, was it all right to ask for something to eat before they began work.

The man said he was a professor of neuropathology, and Andreev recognized his name.

Andreev knew from experience that camp cooks (and not only camp cooks) did not like these 'Ivan Ivanoviches', as the intellectuals were contemptuously nicknamed. He advised the professor not to ask for anything in advance and gloomily thought that he himself would have to do most of the work, since the professor was too weak. This was only just, and there was no reason to be offended; Andreev himself had been a bad, weak 'partner' any number of times, and no one had ever said a word to him. Where were they all now? Where were Sheinin, Ryutin, Khvostov? They had all died, and he alone, Andreev, had been resurrected. Of course, his resurrection was yet to come, but he would return to life.

Andreev's suspicions were confirmed: the professor was a weak, albeit fussy partner.

When the work was finished, the cook sat them down and placed an enormous tub of thick fish soup and a large plate of kasha before them. The professor threw up his hands in delight, but Andreev had seen men at the mines eat twenty meals, each consisting of three dishes and bread. He cast a suspicious glance at the proffered refreshments.

'No bread?' Andreev asked gloomily.

'Of course there's bread – a little.' And the cook took two pieces of bread from a cupboard.

They quickly polished off the food. On such 'visits' the prudent Andreev always saved his bread in his pocket. The professor, on the contrary, gulped the soup, broke off pieces of bread, and chewed it while large drops of dirty sweat formed on his shaven grey head.

'Here's a rouble for each of you,' the cook said. 'I don't have any more bread today.'

This was magnificent payment. There was a commissary at the transit prison, where the civilians could buy bread. Andreev told the professor about this.

'Yes, you're right,' the professor said. 'But I saw that they also sold sweet *kvas* there. Or was it lemonade? I really want some lemonade, anything sweet.'

'It's up to you, professor, but if I were you, I'd buy bread.'

'Yes, I know, you're right,' the professor repeated, 'but I really want some sweet lemonade. Why don't you get some too?'

Andreev rejected that suggestion out of hand.

Ultimately Andreev managed to get himself assigned to washing floors alone at the bookkeeping office. Every evening he would meet the orderly, whose duties included keeping the office clean. These were two tiny rooms crowded with desks, each of which occupied more than four square yards. The work took only about ten minutes, and at first Andreev could not understand why the orderly 'hired' someone to do the job. The orderly had to carry water through the entire camp himself, and clean rags were always prepared in advance when Andreev came. The payment was generous – cheap tobacco, soup, kasha, bread and sugar. The orderly even promised to give Andreev a light jacket, but Andreev's stay came to an end before he managed to do that.

Evidently the orderly viewed washing floors as shameful so long as he could hire some 'hard worker' to do it for him – even if it required only five minutes a day. Andreev had observed this characteristic in Russian people at the mines. If the head of the camp gave an orderly a handful of tobacco to clean the barracks, the orderly would dump half the tobacco into his pouch, and with the other half would hire a 'political' to do the job for him. The latter, in turn, would again divide up the tobacco and hire someone from his barracks for two hand-rolled cigarettes. This man, who had just finished a twelve- or fourteen-hour shift, would wash the floor at night for these two cigarettes and consider himself lucky; he could trade the cigarettes for bread.

Currency questions represent the most complex area of camp economy. Standards of measurement are amazing. Tea, tobacco, and bread are the exchangeable, 'hard' currencies.

On occasion the orderly would pay Andreev with coupons redeemable in the kitchen. These were rubber-stamped pieces of cardboard that worked rather like tokens – ten dinners, five main courses, and so on. When the orderly gave Andreev a token worth twenty portions of kasha, the twenty portions did not cover the bottom of a tin basin.

Andreev watched the professional criminals shove bright yellow thirty-rouble notes through the window, folded to look like tokens. This tactic always produced results. A large bowl filled to the brim with kasha would inevitably emerge from the window in response to such a token.

There were fewer and fewer people left in the transit prison. Finally the day arrived when the last truck was dispatched from the yard, and only two or three dozen men remained in camp.

This time they were not dismissed to the barracks but were grouped in military formation and led through the entire camp.

'Whatever they intend to do, they can't be taking us to be shot,' an enormous one-eyed man next to Andreev said.

This was precisely what Andreev had been thinking: They couldn't be taking them to be shot. All the remaining prisoners were brought to the assignment man in the bookkeeping office.

'We're going to take your fingerprints,' the assignment man said as he came out on to the porch.

'Well, if it's come to that, you can have me without raising a finger,' the one-eyed man said cheerfully. 'My name is Filipovsky.'

'How about you?'

'Pavel Andreev.'

The assignment man found their files.

'We've been looking for you for a long time,' he said without a trace of anger.

Andreev knew that he had won his battle for life. It was simply impossible for the taiga not to have sated its hunger for people. Even if they were to be shipped off, it would be to some nearby, local site. It might even be in the town itself. That would be even better. Andreev had been classified only for 'light physical labour', but he knew how abruptly such a classification could be changed. It was not his classification that would save him, but the fact that the taiga's orders had already been filled. Only local sites, where life was easier, simpler, less hungry, were still waiting for their final deliveries. There were no gold mines in the area, and that meant there was hope for survival. This Andreev had learned during the two years he had spent at the mines and these three months in quarantine, spent under animal-like tension. Too much had been accomplished for his hopes not to be realized.

He had to wait only one night for an answer.

After breakfast, the assignment man rushed into the barracks with a list – a small list, Andreev immediately noted with satisfaction. Lists for the mines inevitably contained twenty-five men assigned to a truck, and there were always several of such sheets – not just one.

Andreev and Filipovsky were on the same list. There were other people as well – only a few, but more than just two or three.

Those whose names were on the list were taken to the familiar door of the bookkeeping department. There were three other men standing there: a grey-haired, sedate old man of imposing appearance wearing a good sheepskin coat and felt boots; a fidgety, dirty man dressed in a quilted jacket and quilted trousers with footcloths instead of socks protruding from the edges of his rubber galoshes. The third was wearing a fur jacket and a fur hat.

'That's the lot of them,' the assignment man said. 'Will they do?'

The man in the fur jacket crooked his finger at the old man.

'Who are you?'

'Yury Izgibin. Convicted under Article 58 of the criminal code. Sentence: twenty-five years,' the old man reported vigorously.

'No, no,' the fur jacket frowned. 'What's your trade? I can learn your case history without your help . . .'

'Stove builder, sir.'

'Anything else?'

'I'm a tinsmith as well.'

'Very good.'

'How about you?' The officer shifted his gaze to Filipovsky.

The one-eyed giant said that he had been a stoker on a steamboat based in Kamenets-Podolsk.

'And how about you?'

The dignified old man unexpectedly muttered a few words in German.

'What's that all about?' the fur jacket asked with an air of curiosity.

'That's our carpenter. His name is Frisorger, and he does good work. He sort of lost his bearings, but he'll be all right.'

'Why does he speak German?'

'He's from the German Autonomous Republic of Saratov.'

'Ah . . . And how about you?' This last question was directed at Andreev.

'He needs tradesmen and working people in general,' Andreev thought. 'I'll be a leather dresser.'

'Tanner, sir.'

'Good. How old are you?'

'Thirty-one.'

The officer shook his head. But since he was an experienced man and had seen people rise from the dead, he said nothing and shifted his gaze to the fifth man, who turned out to be a member of the Esperantist Society.

'You see, I'm an agronomist. I even lectured on agronomy. But I was arrested as an Esperantist.'

'What's that – spying?' the fur coat asked indifferently.

'Something like that,' the fidgety man responded.

'What do you say?' the assignment man asked.

'I'll take them,' the officer said. 'You can't find better ones anyway. They've all been picked over.'

All five were taken to a separate room in the barracks. But there were still two or three names left in the list. Andreev was sure of that. The scheduling officer arrived.

'Where are we going?'

'To a local site, where do you think?' the assignment man said. 'Here's your boss.'

'We'll send you off in an hour. You've had three months to "fatten up", friends. It's time to get on the road.'

They were all summoned in an hour – not to a truck, but to the storeroom. 'They probably want to change clothes,' Andreev thought. 'April is here, and it'll soon be spring.' They would issue summer clothing, and he would be able to turn in his hated winter mine clothing – just cast it aside and forget it. Instead of summer clothing, however, they were issued winter clothing. Could this be an error? No, 'winter clothing' was marked in red pencil on the list.

Not understanding anything, they donned quilted vests, pea-jackets, and old, patched felt boots. Jumping over the puddles, they returned to the barracks room, from which they had come to the storehouse.

Everyone was extremely nervous and silent. Only Frisorger kept muttering something in German.

'He's praying, damn him . . .' Filipovsky whispered to Andreev.

'Does anyone understand what's happening?' Andreev asked.

The grey-haired stove builder who looked like a professor was enumerating all the 'near sites': the port, a mine four kilometres from Magadan, one seventeen kilometres from Magadan, another twenty-three kilometres from the city, and still another forty-seven kilometres away . . . Then he started on road construction sites – places that were only slightly better than gold mines.

The assignment man came running.

'Come on out! March to the gate.'

Everyone left the building and went to the gates of the transit prison. Beyond the gates stood a large truck, the bed of which was covered with a green tarpaulin.

'Guards, assume command and take your prisoners.'

The guard did a head count. Andreev felt his legs and back grow cold . . .

'Get in the truck!'

The guard threw back the edge of the large tarpaulin; the truck was filled with people dressed in winter clothing.

'Get in!'

All five climbed in together. All were silent. The guard got in the cab, the motor roared up, and the truck moved down the road leading to the main 'highway'.

'They're taking us to the mine four kilometres from Magadan,' the stove builder said.

Posts marking kilometres floated past. All five put their heads together near a crack in the canvas. They could not believe their eyes . . .

'Seventeen . . .'

'Twenty-three . . .' Filipovsky said.

'A local mine, the bastards!' the stove builder hissed in a rage.

For a long time the truck wound down the twisted highway between the crags. The mountains resembled barge haulers with bent backs.

'Forty-seven,' the fidgety Esperantist squealed in despair.

The truck rushed on.

'Where are we going?' Andreev asked, gripping someone's shoulder.

'We'll spend the night at Atka, 208 kilometres from Magadan.'

'And after that?'

'I don't know . . . Give me a smoke.'

Puffing heavily, the truck climbed a pass in the Yablonovy Range.

Translated by John Glad

VIKTOR ASTAFIEV

Lyudochka

A SHORT STORY

A story told in passing, a story heard in passing, some fifteen years ago now . . .

I never laid eyes upon her, this girl, and now I never will. I don't even know her name, but I've somehow got it into my head that she was called Lyudmila, or, affectionately, Lyudochka.

> What's in a name? My name too soon will die
> When inscribed in your album, like the sad roar
> Of distant wave that broke on deserted shore,
> Like in wood's darkling heart a midnight cry.

And why do I remember precisely this? During these fifteen years so many events have taken place, so many people have been born and so many have died natural deaths, so many are in their graves, so many have perished at the hands of villains, drunk themselves to death, poisoned themselves, been burnt to death, disappeared without trace, drowned . . . So why then does this story, quietly and separately from everything else, live on in me and torment my soul? Could the answer lie in the tale's depressingly homely character, in its disarming simplicity?

Lyudochka was born in a small, dying village named Vychugan. Her mother and father both worked at the collective farm. Her father, from the strain of physically exhausting work begun, of necessity, at too early an age, and from the strain of long-standing, deep-rooted drunkenness, was pigeon-chested and feeble, restless and rather thick. Lyudochka's mother, worried that any child of hers ran the risk of being born an idiot, tried to conceive during one of the rare breaks in her husband's drinking-bouts, but for all that the little girl inherited in part her father's sickly condition and was born a weak, unhealthy, tearful child.

She grew like a wind-battered, frost-bitten blade of grass, she played little, was rarely seen smiling or singing, at school she always had pretty low marks, but she quietly and without any fuss always tried her best, and was never right at the bottom of the class.

Lyudochka's father had long since disappeared from their lives, and his leaving had scarcely been noticed. Without him mother and daughter lived freer, better, brighter lives. Her mother had occasional lovers, sometimes they would drink and sing at table, and stay the night, and one tractor driver from the local State Timber Enterprise, who ploughed up the garden for her and received a good meal for his efforts, stayed on there for the whole spring. He began to get the hang of running the farmstead, of country life, started to make things run more smoothly, seeking to improve and strengthen their way of life. He covered the seven kilometres to work on his motorcycle, and at first he used to take a gun with him and would often plop on the floor from his rucksack crumpled birds which looked as if they'd already moulted, or sometimes he would pull a hare out of his rucksack by its yellow paws, and would hang it on nails and neatly remove its skin. This skin, turned inside out, with a white fur trim and with red specks scattered across it like stars, would then hang for a long time over the stove, indeed for so long that cracks would start appearing, and at that point they would clip off the fur, spin it together with a flaxen thread and use it to knit soft, fluffy shawls.

The permanent guest couldn't be said to treat Lyudochka either well or badly, or indeed to relate to her at all. He didn't shout at her, insult her, or reproach her, but nevertheless she was still a bit afraid of him. The two of them lived in the same house, and that was all. When Lyudochka had reached her seventeenth year, had got through her ten classes at school, and grown into a young woman, her mother told her to go and find work in the town: there was no point in her staying in the village, and she and 'the guv'nor' – Lyudochka's mother doggedly refused to call the lodger 'husband' or 'father' – were planning to move to the timber enterprise. Mother promised to help Lyudochka until she got settled, with money, potatoes and whatever else God might provide: hopefully when they got old she would help them in turn.

Lyudochka arrived in town on the local train, and spent her first night there in the station building. The following morning she went into a hairdresser's, which was next to the station, and having spent a long time waiting for her turn, spent even longer getting herself suitably made up for town life: she had her hair curled, and a manicure. She also wanted to have her hair dyed, but the old hairdresser, whose own hair was dyed the colour of a bronze samovar, advised her against it: 'Your 'air is so-o-o soft, so-o-o fluffy, your little 'ead looks like a dandelion, and a perm and all them chemicals will only split your 'airs and make them fall out.' Lyudochka was quick to agree: in fact she didn't really want to dye her hair, she'd simply wanted to spend a bit longer in the hairdresser's, in a warm room where the air was thick with the aroma of eau-de-Cologne . . .

Though quiet and reserved in a country sort of way, Lyudochka none the less had her wits about her in the way country folk do, and she offered to sweep up the hair on the floor, prepared soapy shaving solutions for someone, passed someone else a towel and by evening had got to know the whole set-up there. She ambushed the old lady who was known by her patronymic, Gavrilovna, as she left work, the one who'd advised her against dyeing her hair, and asked if she could become one of her apprentices.

The old woman looked Lyudochka up and down very carefully, studied her few papers, gave her a gentle interrogation, and then went with her to the City Public Utilities department, where she completed all the paperwork necessary for Lyudochka to start work as a hairdresser's apprentice.

What is more, Gavrilovna also took the apprentice in, having first laid down certain straightforward house rules. Lyudochka was to help her with the domestic chores; had to be in by eleven o'clock; no boys in the house; not to drink wine or smoke; to obey her landlady in all things; and to respect her as she would her own mother. And in lieu of rent she was quite happy to accept a lorry-load of firewood from the timber enterprise.

'As long as you're an apprentice, you can live 'ere with me, but as soon as you've learnt your trade you'll 'ave to go to live in a 'ostel, and God willing, you'll make your own way in life.' Then, after an awkward pause, Gavrilovna added: 'If you get up the spout, you're out through that door. I never 'ad any children myself, I don't like the squealing brats, and what's more, like all old 'airdressers, I'm a martyr with me legs. In bad weather I scream all night with them.'

It should be noted that in doing this, Gavrilovna was making an exception to her rules. For some time now she had been uneasy about taking in lodgers as a whole, while she had refused to take any girls at all.

Once, a long time ago, under Khrushchev, two girl students from the Financial Technical College had lived with her. They wore trousers and warpaint. They were smokers. As far as smoking and the rest of it went Gavrilovna gave it to them in no uncertain terms. The young ladies scowled, but put up with the various living conditions: they smoked outside, came home on time, didn't play their music too loud. Then again they didn't sweep or wash the floor, didn't clear away the plates after them, didn't clean the bathroom. All that wouldn't have mattered. But they were always trying to re-educate Gavrilovna, kept on referring to the lives of the great and good, and forever insisting that she didn't live correctly.

But she could have lived with that and all. The trouble was that the little madams weren't very good at distinguishing what was theirs from what was someone else's, so they might scoff all the pies she'd just made, or dig all the sugar out of the sugar-basin; and they were never in a rush to pay the rent, and had to be reminded a dozen times about it. Yet even that would have been just about bearable. But they started to treat Gavrilovna's kitchen garden as their own: not in the sense, mind, that they weeded or watered it, no, they simply picked off everything that was ripe, making use of nature's gifts without so much as a by-your-leave. Once they ate, with a little pile of salt, the first three small cucumbers from the heavily manured row. Gavrilovna had, as always, tended and cared for those first cucumbers on her knees. She'd got the manure for the row in the winter, and she'd only just managed to lug it in her rucksack from the stables, where she'd given the lame Slyusarenko, the old scoundrel, some vodka for it. And she'd even talk to the cucumbers, saying: 'Well, then, grow, grow, get strong, my babies! And then we'll make some lovely soup from you!' as she'd sprinkle them with water warmed in a barrel by the sun.

'Why did you eat the cucumbers?' Gavrilovna challenged the girls.

'What's all the fuss about? We felt like it. What, are you too mean to let us have them? We'll buy you a real whopper at the market!'

'I don't need a real whopper! That's what you need. To keep yourselves amused. But I was hoping to use those cucumbers . . .'

'Yourself, yes? You're an egoist!'

'What am I?'

'An egoist!'

'And you're, you're — you're just whores!' Offended by the unfamiliar word, Gavrilovna brought the conversation to an abrupt end and booted the young ladies out of her house.

From that day on her only lodgers had been young men, most often students. Gavrilovna would whip them quickly into shape, teach them the basics of housework, how to wash the floors, do simple cooking and wash clothes. She even taught two of the most intelligent lads from the Polytechnical Institute to cook using a traditional Russian stove. Gavrilovna had invited Lyudochka to live with her because she recognized in her someone from the same country stock as herself, a kindred soul, a country girl who hadn't yet been ruined by the city. In addition, being on her own was beginning to get her down — if she were to be laid up in bed, who would be beside her to lend a helping hand? And as for the fact that she'd made strict rules from the word go, well, she really had no choice: give the youth of today half a chance, show the slightest signs of weakness, and they'll ride roughshod over you.

Lyudochka was an obedient girl, she listened to what she was told, but she made slow progress in her apprenticeship. She found it extremely difficult to pick up the hairdresser's art which had seemed so simple to her at first, and when the appointed period of study came to an end, she was unable to pass the exams to become a fully qualified cutter. In the hairdresser's she supplemented her income by working as a cleaner, remained on the staff and continued to practise. She would use the electric clipper to scalp the hair off lads who were on their military training programmes before the final call-up, she'd give schoolboys short haircuts, leaving a small tuft of hair above the now almost bald foreheads. She practised the more stylish haircuts 'at home', cutting the hair of the really mod and terrible youngsters from the Carsteng suburb, which was where Gavrilovna's house stood, in styles that made them look like Old Believers. She arranged the hair of flighty young disco queens in the fashion of the trendiest Western pop-stars, and didn't take any money from them for this.

Gavrilovna, who sensed a weakness in her lodger's character, dumped all the housework, indeed the whole running of the household, on to the girl. The old woman's legs were paining her more and more, the veins protruding on her calves were black knots. Lyudochka's eyes burned whenever she rubbed ointments into the warped legs of her landlady, who was seeing out her last year of work before her pension. The smell from these curious ointments was so overpowering, and Gavrilovna's cries so heart-rending, that the cockroaches fled into the neighbouring rooms, and the flies dropped dead, every last one.

'Well, look at what this work of ours does, look at the price we 'ave to pay for others' beauty!' pronounced Gavrilovna in the darkness when the pain had eased somewhat. 'Take a look at the delights awaiting you, 'cos even though you're muddle-'eaded, you'll still make some sort of 'airdresser sooner or later. What on earth drove you from the village?'

Lyudochka put up with everything. She put up with the mockery of those girlfriends who had completed their training successfully. She put up with her loneliness and lack of a proper home in this unfriendly city, and with Gavrilovna's testiness, though it must be said that Gavrilovna bore no malice towards her and didn't kick her out even after Lyudochka's stepfather had failed to deliver the promised load of firewood. Moreover, for her patience and efforts, for helping around the house and for easing her pain Gavrilovna promised to arrange a permanent residence permit for Lyudochka and even to put the house in her name, as long as she would continue to behave as modestly as she had so far, look after the house and the yard, graft in the garden, and look after her when she finally lost the use of her legs.

From her workplace by the station Lyudochka would take the tram to the end of the line. From there she would walk through the decaying and declining Carsteng park or, to put it in human language, the park of the *Carriage and Steam Engine Depot*, which had been planted and laid out in the thirties and ruined in the fifties. Someone had had the bright idea of digging up a trench and laying a pipeline the whole length of the park. The hole was dug, the pipe was laid, but, as is usually the case here with us in Russia, they forgot to cover it up again.

Black with crooked joints and for all the world looking like a grass snake trampled by cattle, the pipe lay in sweating clay, it hissed and sent forth steam, its hot slops gurgling boisterously. With the passage of time the pipe had been covered over by soapy mucus and mire, and a hot river formed above it, whirling round iridescent, poisonous rings of engine oil and various everyday objects. The trees above the trench were sick and wilted, and their bark had peeled away. Only the gnarled poplars, whose bark had also popped and burst, their horned dry branches trembling on their tops and their paw-like roots planted firm on the ground, still grew, littering everything with their down and in autumn strewing their brittle, blighted leaves all around. A little bridge made from four wooden blocks had been built over the trench. Every year the

Jacks-of-all trades from the depot had made some sort of handrails for it out of the low sides of old open wagons, so that the blind-drunk and the halt and other poor wobbly beggars wouldn't tumble into the hot water. The children and grandchildren of the depot's craftsmen had been equally assiduous in vandalizing annually these same handrails.

When the age of steam had passed and the depot building was taken over by new engines, diesel locomotives, the pipe became totally clogged up and ceased working, but nevertheless some sort of hot magma, a cocktail of dirt, engine oil and soapy water, kept flowing along the trench. No one bothered to provide handrails for the bridge any more. With the passing of the years all sorts of wild trees and wild weeds crept towards the trench and grew to their heart's content: elders, raspberry bushes, osier beds, thistles, wild currants which bore no berries. Spreading wormwood, sportive burdock and thorns grew everywhere. In one or two places the impenetrable undergrowth was broken by bird-cherries with their crooked trunks, two or three daphne willows and one stubborn birch tree black with mould stood there, while lopsided limes, which had retreated some twenty metres, flowered in mid-summer, modestly rustling their leaves. Replanted fir trees and pines tried to take root here, but before the fir trees could reach maturity the locals, the inhabitants of the Carsteng urban settlement, who always had an eye to the main chance, would cut them down for the New Year, and the pines were nibbled by goats and all sorts of mischievous cattle, and so many branches were broken off for no good reason by idlers who hung around and had nothing better to do, that all that was left of the trees were a few branches out of arm's reach and harm's way. The park, with its stubborn remains of the frame of its gates of steel, with its basketball and other posts set up here, there and everywhere, and with unwanted poplar saplings springing up all over the place and choking everything, looked as if a bomb had hit it or as if it had been overrun by some fearless enemy cavalry. There was a perpetual stench in the park air, because people used to throw puppies, kittens and dead piglets into the trench, all kinds of everything, everything that was superfluous to living requirements and which cluttered up the home and human existence. This was why the park was forever, but particularly in winter, black with crows and jackdaws, and the corvine cawing deafened the surrounding area and grated on the ear.

But man cannot exist without nature, just as the animals he keeps around him cannot live without nature either, and seeing as the closest one could get to nature around there was the Carsteng park, people were always pleased to know that there was somewhere where they could relax. Along the sides of the trench stood concrete benches which forced their way into the weeds, concrete because the children and grandchildren of the depot's glorious workers vandalized the wooden benches – and everything else made of wood for that matter – in demonstration of their power and their preparedness for more serious business later. All the thickets above and alongside the trench were covered with dog, cat, goat and some other animal fur. Bottles of various hues and forms protruded from the dirty trench and its foam in a continuously clinking mass: tubby bottles, flat bottles, short bottles, green bottles, white bottles, black bottles. Tyres, piles of paper and wrapping material rotted in the trench; foil glinted silver in the light of sun and moon; torn bits of cellophane quivered. Occasionally some surprises turned up in the river itself, into which the trench's evil-smelling effluent flowed playfully: a deflated Crocodile Gena, the children's favourite, who had given up his rubber ghost; a red rubber ring from the hospital; a forlorn condom, sadly shrivelled and stuck together; the remains of an ancient wooden bed; and many, many other goods.

As is always the case in any self-respecting town, both in the Carsteng park and in its vicinity, slogans, banners and portraits would be displayed on public holidays, hung from pipes welded and bent into shape for this express aim. To begin with everything was fine: you knew what to expect. The same old portraits, the same old slogans. And then it was All Change. What had been 'The Cause of Lenin and Stalin Lives and Triumphs!' became 'Leninism Lives and

Triumphs!' Where once there had been 'The Party is Our Guide!', now there was 'Glory to the Soviet People, the Victorious People!' The locals also proved themselves capable of independent ideological thinking: one local wit added, to the slogan 'Workers of the Soviet Union! Your Future is in Your Hands!', the words 'And in Your Feet!' The railway depot had always been noted for its extreme vigilance, class awareness and sense of civic duty. From then on, not one piece of graffiti appeared on the gantry – the lofty-sounding name given to this iron construction.

But when five portraits were removed from the very heart of the gantry at a stroke, to reveal in all its naked glory Lenin's slogan 'Our Party is the Intelligence, Honour and Conscience of Our Times!', even the railway workers were lost for words.

The local school, with its old and ideologically sound cadres, was also shaken up a bit. A young woman literature teacher from Leningrad, who had been allocated to the school after she'd graduated, shouted out during a meeting: 'Can one really expect any kind of moral stance from a town where since 1942, literally in the town centre, on the gates of the armaments factory in letters three metres high, shine out the words: "Our Target is Communism!"?'

Well, it's pretty clear that such a school-ma'am won't last long in the Carsteng suburbs: she'll soon be sent home, or perhaps be packed off to some other place.

It stood to reason that in such an 'urban-type settlement', in such splendid surroundings as the Carsteng park, there'd be some real scum, all locally bred. They got drunk there, played cards, had fist and knife fights, sometimes with fatal results, with the thugs from the town itself in particular, who also couldn't resist the attractions of this enchanted realm. They'd also grab girls there, and once the local yobs almost nailed that free-thinking Leningrad teacher – but she managed to outrun them, being the sporty type.

The commander-in-chief of the Carsteng gorillas was Artyomka-Suds, who had a foamy mane of white hair, a thin face and crooked, nimble legs. However much Lyudochka tried to do something with the locks on the wild head of Artyomka, who had been named by his railwayman father after the heroic Artyom from the film *We are from Kronstadt*, all her efforts were in vain. Artyom's curls, which from a distance did indeed resemble soap-suds, turned out on closer inspection to be like the sticky macaroni in the canteen at the railway station, boiled and then plopped in a slippery pile on to an empty plate to lie there untouched, stuck together in a glutinous mass. And, of course, Artyomka-Suds hadn't really come to Gavrilovna's home to tame his mop of hair. As soon as Lyudochka was otherwise engaged with scissors and comb, he started grabbing hold of different parts of her anatomy. At first Lyudochka jumped sharply away, trying to keep out of range of Artyom's fingers and bitten fingernails, and then she started to beat down the roaming hands. The client didn't give up however, and so Lyudochka hit the Carsteng chief with the trimmer, but so awkwardly that a red liquid appeared from Artyom's head of locks, as if from chicken feathers. It proved necessary to pour iodine from a flask on to the bold bonce of this randy young man. He started howling, as though his trousers were on fire, his chubby lips producing a hissing sound as he gasped for breath and from then on made no more thuggish demands. What is more, Suds ordered the whole Carsteng gang not to touch Lyudochka and not to let anyone else paw her either.

From that time on Lyudochka didn't fear anything or anyone in the settlement, and would walk from the tram stop to Gavrilovna's house through the Carsteng park at any time of the day and night and at any time of the year, answering the suggestive remarks, jokes and wolf-whistles of the riff-raff with a knowing smile that showed she was among friends, and with a slightly disapproving, but also all-forgiving shake of the head.

One day 'leader of the gang' Suds forced Lyudochka to go with him to the town's central park. There was an enclosure there, fenced off with a painted railing, a high enclosure with a strong surround and a wire gate. In one wall there was a niche where a crescent-shaped cutting had been made, a sort of entrance into a cave; in this niche, jerking, swaying, shaking, jumping up and down on benches, were youths whose hair hadn't been cut for ages and whose clothes were a mess. One individual, who looked remotely like a woman and who was almost naked, was screeching into a fat microphone held lewdly in the hand. At first Lyudochka thought that the said individual was screaming in a foreign language, but when she listened more closely she could just make out the words: 'Come to me. Luv. Or else . . .'

In the enclosure-cum-menagerie the people seemed to find it natural to behave like wild animals. Some young slut, who was all black and red from her make-up and who was being tightly embraced by a young lad in a T-shirt with something scrawled all over it, was yelling from the heart of the dance-floor: 'You cheeky sod! Pighead! Wot you doing? Be patient! Can't you wait until dark?' 'No he can't!' shouted someone, neither boy nor man, from the sidelines. 'Show the lads her tits, boy! Crack her cherry right here in front of us!'

On all sides the enclosed mob roared in mocking laughter. It howled, seethed, bubbled, and belched forth the stench of alcohol. The herd raged and raved, turning their dancing into a shameful, demonic display of flesh and madness. People dripping wet, people boiling with unbridled lust and unleashed passions, people mocking everything that was human, everything that had come before them and everything that would come after, were exhausting themselves as they hung on to one another behind the wire, choking themselves and partners alike in the heat, and throwing themselves at the wire, just like war heroes who blocked gun emplacements with their bodies, except that these were prisoners who only resembled human beings and who had nowhere to run to. The music helped the herd get even wilder, madder, more possessed, its beat finding a rhythmic echo in the herd's convulsions: a music of crashes, booms, screeches, thunderous drum rolls, groans, howls.

To begin with Lyudochka looked around like a hunted animal, and then went to skulk in a corner of the enclosure, her eyes searching all the time for Suds — she'd need his protection if they attacked her. But although Suds had been swallowed up by this seething mass of grey scum, the young militiaman walking around the dance floor with a bunch of keys and wearing a smart peaked cap reassured Lyudochka. The militiaman fiddled with his keys, jangling them to make it clear to everyone that there was a force here ready to resist any fits of passion. From time to time this force went into action. The militiaman would stop for a second, nod his peaked cap, and in rapid response to this nod four lads wearing the red armbands of volunteers would appear from the elder bushes. The militiaman, pointing imperiously at the enclosure, throws the lads the clanging keys. The lads then rush into the enclosure and start chasing after some creature – in the evening light you couldn't tell whether the creature was male or female – that starts flapping and flailing against the wire like some headless chicken. Trying to keep hold of the bars, of the hands stretched out in solidarity, this wretched sacrificial victim, this poor bare animal with blood oozing from flayed skin, yells from a red, daubed gash of a mouth: 'Bastards! Fascists! Narks! Queers!'

'They'll give you fascists and queers down in the pig-sty . . . Just you wait and see . . .' Such is the parting shot the herd, slightly calmer now, offers in triumph, or maybe in compassion, a sorrow tinged with perverse pleasure that someone else has copped it.

Lyudochka was scared to leave her corner of the railed-in pen, and she still hoped that Suds would slither out from the darkness, so that in his wake and that of his gang, even if following at a distance, she'd be able to make it home safely. But some scruffy lout in skin-tight trousers, or perhaps they were leggings or even tights, spotted her and dragged her from her corner. The lad was evidently still a schoolboy, but he knew his stuff when it came to sex. He held the girl tightly to his pigeon chest, and started pressing his hardness against her in time with the music. Lyudochka was no prim and proper little prude, no babe in the woods, no Mummy's sheltered little girl: after all she hailed from the countryside, she'd seen how the animal kingdom lived and knew a bit about people's country matters too. She gave the flash disco dancer a hard shove, but he was an old hand and didn't loosen his grip, and bared a crooked tooth. Indeed, for some reason this was the only tooth to be seen in his mouth. 'So what's with you? What's your problem? Let's be friends, eh, peach?'

Lyudochka nevertheless managed to escape her wooer's attentions somehow, and beat a hasty retreat from the enclosure. As soon as she reached home, still panting heavily and holding her head in her hands, she kept repeating:

'How horrible! How horrible!'

'Let that be a lesson to you to watch where you 'ang around!' was Gavrilovna's refrain when Lyudochka had, through force of habit, told her all about her recent adventures.

Tidying away the top Lyudochka had knitted and her skirt with small pleats, Gavrilovna gave Lyudochka a lecture, saying to the child that if she managed to qualify as a hairdresser and stuck with the job, then she'd find her a suitable working lad without the help of any of these old disco dances, for there were other people besides riff-raff in this world. Or a sensible widower perhaps: she had one of the latter in mind, and although he was both older than Lyudochka and had children, he was a reliable man, and age didn't matter, indeed there was a lot to be said for older men. A middle-aged man's years give him common sense, respectability, experience, while a woman's youth and comeliness are a comfort and joy to man. In former times the man had always been older than his bride, and was therefore thought of as the master. He would keep the house, livestock and all they owned in perfect order, keep a watchful eye on his wife, look after her and the children. And if a decent, well-established man did turn up, she could let them both live with her – who else could this lonely old soul leave the house to? And then in her declining years obviously they'd look after her: her legs had already given up on her as it was.

'And them dances, me treasure, are a mockery of the soul, that's what they are, tempting the flesh like that: men and women rubbing against each other, getting inflamed with passion, and what sort of a basis for living together can that be? In all me born days I've never been to none of these dances, that's why I 'aven't covered myself in any shame, me only dances have been waltzes around the customers' chairs in the hairdresser's salon.'

Lyudochka, as always, was completely and utterly in agreement with Gavrilovna, who not only was a clever person but who'd also experienced a lot in life. She reckoned that she'd been very lucky, after all it wasn't everyone's lot to have such a mentor, an older and wiser friend. Such good fortune certainly didn't happen to everyone: for example, it was said that all sorts of things went on in the hostel, it was Sodom and Gomorrah there, endless dissipation, and awful living conditions on top. Often the water was shut off, there were queues to use the gas stove and the room for washing clothes; lads would drop in and remove the fuses or smash the lights so that they could lie in wait for the young girls in the dark . . .

Lyudochka cooked, boiled, cleaned, scraped, whitewashed, painted, did the washing and ironing, and she didn't find it any trouble to keep the house spotlessly clean, indeed she enjoyed doing the work, and of course if, God willing, she were to get married, she would already know how to do everything, she'd be a fully independent housewife, able to do all these things without any help, and her husband would love and appreciate her for that.

True, Lyudochka didn't get enough sleep, she sometimes suffered from giddy spells and nose bleeds, but she would block her nose with cotton wool, and lie on her back, and everything would be OK, she wasn't the sort of cry-baby who runs to hospital at the first sign of trouble; and anyway her nose was small and neat, and the amount of blood that flowed from it was nothing to write home about.

It was about this time that the railway community saw the return of one of its natives, not from distant exile but from a place far closer to home, in fact from that very same timber felling enterprise where Lyudochka's stepfather worked, the return of someone who was known to everyone in the area and who went by the nickname of Botfly. There's nothing more to tell of him: his name says it all. His face did in fact resemble that of some dark insect buzzing around a meadow tormenting the life out of beast or man. The only way in which a real botfly differed from the creature born in the Carsteng settlement was that instead of feelers a dirty swelling of a moustache stuck out from under Botfly's nose. When he smiled, or rather when he snarled, it moved to reveal his rotten teeth, which seemed to be made of small lumps of concrete.

Vicious and all screwed up from an early age, Botfly started robbing at an early age too: in school he used to take the little ones' pocket money, biscuits and sweets, things like rubbers, ball-point pens and badges. He was particularly persistent in his attempts to get hold of chewing gum of any variety, but most of all he liked the type wrapped in silver foil. The soft-hearted teachers of the railway school managed to keep him there until the seventh year, but by then the fourteen-year-old Botfly was already carrying a knife, and had no need to steal anything from anyone: the local youngsters used to pay him tribute, as if he were a Khan, bringing him everything that was his wish and command. It was in the seventh year too that Botfly committed his first crime: in a fight at a tram-stop he stabbed one of the town thugs and was entered in militia files as a young man with 'behavioural problems'. In the same year he was convicted of the attempted rape of a postwoman and received his first sentence – three years. Suspended. But this brave warrior couldn't have given a toss about this suspended sentence, and went on living the life his heart desired. He started a new line of business, learning how to carry out with impunity pirate raids on dachas on the town's outskirts. If the dacha owners didn't leave him something to eat and drink and didn't leave the doors unlocked, he would smash their windows, vandalize their verandas, break the crockery, stamp all over their belongings, rip up the bed linen, urinate in the jars of flour and oats, and, if he felt like it, defecate smack in the middle of the dacha. He'd draw a Jolly Roger on the stove, and would hang on the door some public information poster he'd brought with him from town which carried the warning: 'Beware of fires!' He'd hide close by, waiting for the owners, who would then fall over themselves in their rush to leave out alcohol and tins of food, and even some fuel, some dry logs, as was the custom in hunters' cottages in days gone by, and they would leave a friendly note for him: 'Dear Guest! Eat, drink and be merry – but for God's sake, please don't burn our house down!'

Botfly lived all winter off the fat of these blessed lands full of booty, but he was caught in the end all the same, and the three suspended years became three years in prison.

Since then the hero of the Carsteng settlement had spent most of his time in corrective labour camps, occasionally returning to his native settlement as if for a well-earned break.

On such occasions the local thugs fell into line behind Botfly, picking up knowledge and know-how, bowing their heads respectfully before their Mr Big, this hardened gang-leader who was a fully qualified member of the criminal underworld. But despite the authority Botfly enjoyed among the local lowlifes, he liked to fleece his gang in various trivial ways, by playing cards, hunt-the-thimble and other games.

For the people of the Carsteng settlement, who were always in a state of alarm anyway, these were times when they lived in even greater fear.

On that fateful summer evening Botfly, who was between jobs, was sitting in the park on a concrete bench, his man of leisure's arms sprawled along its concrete block of a back. The sleeves of his rust-red shirt were rolled up to his elbows, his arms were sunburnt to his wrists and covered with tattoos. Bracelets and signet rings flashed in the light. A mass of figures flickered on the latest digital watches he wore on both wrists; in the triangle made by the wide-open neck of his shirt, against a dark spread-eagle tattoo, a cross glittered on a fine chain made of good quality imitation gold. His cornflower-blue jacket with shiny buttons and claret-coloured wedges at the waist, the garb of a jockey, doorman or some foreign customs official, was a 'recent acquisition' and kept slipping off his shoulders. His lads would rush behind the bench and drag the strange 'tail-coat' out of the tall weeds, and when they had picked off the burrs and bits of clay, they would respectfully drape the cape over their 'dear guest's' shoulders. These lads, their ring-leader Suds included, knew that under the chain, below the free-flying eagle which was tormenting a bare-breasted victim, was a message inspiring awe and fear: 'I believe in Jesus Christ, Lenin and Chief Security Officer Nalivaiko'.

Botfly reached lazily for the bottle of expensive cognac which was propped up against the back of the bench, took a couple of swigs and then passed it on to his obedient buddies.

'I could really do with a bit of fluff! A nice piece of ass, that's all I ask!' Botfly played around with words in which real longing could be heard, and ground his teeth from time to time in such a way that it seemed that those weren't rotten teeth sticking out beneath his moustache, but a mouthful of rocks, and that burning with the undying flame of passion, he was crushing these rocks – 'and smoke bellowed from the jaws!'

The lads, their eyes goggling at such a man of rare qualities, kept trying to set his mind at rest:

'We'll find you a piece of ass, don't worry! No need to fret! They'll soon start pouring from the disco, we'll grab you some nice chicks. As many as you can handle . . . Just leave a little wine for us, that's all . . .'

'Screw the wine! Screw the money! Screw life!' Botfly took another swig of the bottle, spat between his feet, grew sullen, and rolled his head along the rib of the concrete block. Was he in a bad way, a real bad way, he couldn't stand it any longer. And appreciating that such desperateness had been earned, paid for by a life of suffering, by unbearable deprivations in places with harsh rules and restrictions on each and every freedom, the lads hid their eyes in shame, sighed, and hoped and prayed in silence that the disco would finish soon.

'Aha, der's a nice gel come to play, perhaps it can yet be my birthday,' said Botfly in a mock Georgian accent, livening up.

'That's Lyudka. Don't touch her,' said Artyomka-Suds, staring at his feet.

'Why not, she got the clap, or is she a virgin?'

'Yeah, the clap. She's all poxy.'

'But we don't care, but we don't care, as the song goes . . . Poxy, ugly or whatever – as long as I get my end away, who cares?' Botfly leapt up from the bench and grabbed Lyudochka by the belt of her raincoat. 'Where're you off to in such a rush, darling? Wait a mo, no need to go, you're someone I'd like to get to know . . .'

Botfly grabbed a fistful of raincoat, crumpling it and through it Lyudochka's dress, dragged the girl towards him, and tried to sit her on his lap. Lyudochka struggled with ever-increasing urgency and determination.

'Greeeat that you're fighting back, darling! Your man likes a bit of rough stuff . . . It makes him wild . . . Keep still. Sit down, you tart!'

Lyudochka refused.

'What do you mean, tart? I'm Lyuda. Let me go!'

'Yeah, it's Lyuda all right. She's local. We know her.'

'Ah, Lyuda, Lyuda, Lyuda, I'm really in the mood-a . . .' sang Botfly, as if he hadn't heard his mates, and with a predatory grin bared the grey teeth beneath his moustache. 'I don't think you heard me right. Your man wants it! Wants it very badly! What did they teach you in school about obeying your elders?'

'Nothing . . . I mean . . . nothing . . .'

'Fancy that!' guffawed Botfly. 'All airs and graces! . . . Why you such a rude bitch? And who's asking you anyway, whore?' Botfly tipped Lyudochka over the bench and leapt after her, bellowing as he tried to catch her as she crawled away on all fours through the tall weeds. 'Waa-it a minute! Don't raaash, daarling! – No raaash!' – Botfly grabbed hold of Lyudochka's raincoat, pulled her towards him, rubbed her face in the dirt. 'Keep your clucking mouth shut, chick!' There was a crack as he tore open her dress. Lyudochka was trying all the time to yell out, but the only sound that passed her lips was: 'An-kay . . . an-kay . . . an-kay . . .' And suddenly a cry forced itself through, and what was in fact a stifled squeak seemed to her a scream that could be heard at the end of the earth.

'There's true love for you!' Artyomka-Suds shook his shaggy head. 'With a serenade . . .'

His pals, who were three in number, responded with a feverish chuckle.

'Can we go and watch?'

'Take a look. No skin off my nose,' Artyomka said with a shrug of the shoulders; it required a special effort on his part to resist the temptation to take a look for himself.

'Keep still, you swine!' came the words from the tall weeds. 'Where d'ya think ya off to? Where you going? Unless you want to get into some even hotter water! . . . Cool it now, damn you!' Botfly smashed his fist against something and cut his hand against the bits of glass which were everywhere in the long grass.

Lyudochka was still trying to call out. In the suffocating darkness, dirty fur fell from the mixture of this year's and last year's tall weeds into her open mouth, or so it seemed to her, and stopped her breathing; the nausea which had grown tight in her chest suddenly found release in a convulsion, and her throat, in the grip of this spasm, jolted into action.

Botfly went sprawling. He leapt out of the bushes, forced his way through the undergrowth, all the while flicking something off his best jacket and shirt, and snarled in a fury: 'The fucking bitch! She puked up all over my tails! It's covered in her crap!' Botfly stretched out his arms like a scarecrow, looked down and moaned. 'And my daks! My daks!' He tried to smooth out his trousers then, noticing red on his hands, set about sucking the blood from his fingers and spitting it out. A greedy swig of cognac was followed by an imperious nod of his head in Lyudochka's direction.

'Thanks, but we'll wait for our tarts. From the discos . . . we'll . . .' the boys babbled.

Botfly hurled himself at them, bloodying their shirts, twisting, crunching up the lads' rags along with the imitation gold chains, the mementoes of camp life he had so generously given them.

'No way, suckers! Scared of getting dirty, are we?' he whistled through the gaps in his teeth. 'I'm in the shit, and you all come up smelling of roses! It won't wash! Not a chance! Who put me on to that tart? Who the fuck does she think she's keeping herself for?'

Botfly shoved the boys over the bench, towards the tall weeds, then thrust his hand into the pocket where he kept, suspended on a loop, a graceful Finnish knife fashioned by the craftsmen of the locomotive depot, and warned them: 'Grab your cue, join the queue, and don't dare miss the pocket!'

Lyudochka was blindly feeling her way over the ground, groping the earth, groping herself, she crawled through the tall weeds, crashed into bushes, kept sneezing in between fits of vomiting, and all the time was looking for something, searching, searching, and trying to pull the ripped rags around her. Suddenly she gave a piercing howl as she spotted Big Chief Artyomka looming before her, and started beating and scratching him. To tell the truth, on seeing this crumpled, torn creature Artyomka-Suds lost his nerve and tried to throw her coat with its ripped sleeve on to her shoulders. But she wasn't going to give him the chance . . .

'Suds! Suds! Suds! . . .' Screaming his name, Lyudochka escaped from the undergrowth's dirty sticky paws, rushed like mad through the gnawed poplars, slipped and fell on the little bridge, all the time shouting 'Suds! Suds!'

When at last she had run all the way to the familiar surroundings of Gavrilovna's house, which was now like home to her, Lyudochka crashed into the gate, tearing it from its weak wooden hinge, fell over the fence, crawled along the pathway which had recently been washed by the rain, collapsed on to the step of the porch that she herself had recently scraped and scrubbed, buried her head in the door-mat, and blacked out.

The young girl came to on the old divan, on her own sheets, and straight away felt something cold and slippery beneath her. She felt under her – oil cloth. Gavrilovna was a thrifty landlady.

'You've come round? That's good. That's marvellous. Come on, drink some of this water with red whortleberry, it's a bit sour but it will wash the bitterness out of your soul . . . Come on, drink, drink some, and stop trembling, stop trembling,' droned Gavrilovna reassuringly, leaning over Lyudochka.

At first Lyudochka drank greedily, gulping it down, but the

drink seemed to come up against some kind of valve in her throat, a valve holding back bubbling nausea. And she pushed away the hand that was offering her the cup.

'A woman 'as to look after 'er 'eart, all the rest wears well . . . And a woman isn't born for violence, but for some quite different purpose . . . OK, so they've cracked your cheerie, that's no big deal. That's no great loss nowadays: men marry any old girl nowadays, no one cares less about such things nowadays . . . But as for those scoundrels and 'ooligans, I'd twist their 'air for them, yes I would! . . . And you're a fine one too, I must say! How many times did I tell you not to walk through the park alone at night, that it's a watering hole for 'ooligans and tarts and all sorts of filth. But, oh no, none of you listen to us oldies . . .'

'I want to go home to Mummy.'

'To Mummy? Of course you can, me precious. Go tomorrow morning, for a day, or two, as you wish. I'll tell them at work and I'll clear up for you in the salon, and you can clear off home . . . But look at the mess we've got here in your room! . . . I'll tidy this up too: I may be bow-legged, but I can still get about.'

In Lyudochka's native village, Vychugan, there were now only two houses which were still intact. In one of them the old lady Vychugan-ikha had stubbornly lived out her last days and stubbornly died; the other was occupied by Lyudochka's mother and stepfather. In the very distant past they used to sing in the village:

> Vychugan's the place where we all dwell.
> Working all day, at night singing so well.

But Lyudochka's stepfather now sang different words to the same tune:

> Vychugan's the place where we all dwell,
> We don't work, but can we drink, by hell!

The whole village had become choked by wild, unchecked natural growth, and the path to it was almost untrodden by human feet.

Virtually all the houses in the near-deserted village were marked with the wooden crosses of boarded-up windows. Everywhere one looked there were tottering starling houses, collapsed wood and wattle fences around farmyards, formerly tended but now neglected fruit trees were dying everywhere, while between the mute cottages poplars, bird-cherries and aspens, whose seeds had been brought there on the wind from the forest, grew like wildfire. In contrast, the old village birches were wilting. And the limes were wilting. And the blackcurrant bushes in the tall weeds were wilting, and the raspberries in the kitchen gardens had run wild and formed a dense crowd, though they had allowed the quick-witted, sharp-tongued nettles into their midst. The apple tree which stood where a field began seemed made of bone. That was where the Tyuganovs' cottage had once been, but the Tyuganovs had disappeared long ago, the cottage had gone to rack and ruin, and bits of it were removed for firewood. The saplings on their land had dried up too, the bushes nibbled by sheep and goats alike. The apple tree, left all alone, had been stripped of its bark and its leaves, a poor naked wretch. Just a single bough still kept its bark and flowered every spring, though where on earth it found the strength to flower no one knew.

During Lyudochka's last summer at school, every flower on the lonely bough became fertilized, and suddenly large red shiny apples appeared on the otherwise bare tree. 'Kids, don't eat these apples. They're a bad omen!' commanded the old woman Vychuganikha. 'Everything's a bad omen these days . . .' everyone answered her, nodding in agreement.

The apples kept on coming. They totally overpowered and smothered their very own leaves with their size and weight, cracked the bark, and sapped the tree of its last strength. And then one night the living bough of the apple tree broke, unable to bear the weight of its fruits any longer. Its bare, flat trunk remained behind the houses that appeared to have retreated to give the tree living space, and it now looked like a cross with a broken cross-beam in a country churchyard. A monument to a dying Russian village. Yet one more. 'And thus it shall be,' prophesied Vychuganikha, 'that one day soon a stake will be driven into the heart of Russia, and ne'er a soul will be left to hold her wake, tempted and destroyed as she will have been by evil spirits . . .'

It was terrifying listening to Vychuganikha. The peasant women, trembling, crossed themselves awkwardly: they'd forgotten whether it was from right to left or left to right. Vychuganikha humiliated them and showed them again how to make the sign of the cross. And after growing old alone, the women eagerly and submissively started believing in God again. After all, they had nowhere else to go, no one else to turn to, no one else to believe in.

'We are unworthy, no doubt,' they prattled, 'we swear and drink, without our men who were killed in the war and who perished in the prisons we've had to stop being women and become men . . .'

'We are all filthy creatures, not worthy to believe in Him. But try we must,' instructed the strict Vychuganikha.

The women set up their icon shelves and placed icons they collected from lofts and sheds on them, they lit icon-lights, using instead of icon-lamps tins which used to hold small fish, fish with the foreign-sounding name 'sprats'. They rolled candles made of wax and tallow on their naked, wizened thighs, took their embroidered towels, now threadbare, out of the trunks. Despite having been a member of the *Komsomol* in her youth, Lyudochka's mother had now become as superstitious as the old women. Once Lyudochka chuckled as her mother furtively crossed herself, and received a box on her ears for her pains.

Lyudochka left the village behind her and came out on to a green hill which was overrun with burnt-out tufts of coltsfoot and the still blossoming yellow suns of globeflowers, tall buttercups and dandelions. A tethered cow stood among the globeflowers, her hanging udder almost touching the tops of the wild flowers. This was Olena. Used as she had been to collective life, she now wandered around the empty neighbouring hamlets, bellowing there mournfully as she called her friends, and received no reply. This was why they had to tie her up, knocking in a stake at a new location every day. There was no cowherd, as there were no other cows. Olena, an old, kind cow, whose name Lyudochka had thought up once upon a time, ate badly when tethered, and her udder was all crumpled up. Olena recognized the person who had christened her, and moved towards her, but the rope kept her in check, and she mooed resentfully. Lyudochka threw her arms around Olena's neck, pressed her close and burst out crying. The cow licked away her salty tears with its large and now green tongue, and breathed loudly in sympathy.

The women of Vychugan had all died off, women who had been made widows by war and national victories on all fronts of the battle for socialism. In early spring the earthly span of the stronghold and bastion of the village of Vychugan had come to an end: the earthly span of Vychuganikha herself had ended. Her relatives had disappeared without trace, and there were no men in the village. Lyudochka's stepfather had called upon some friends from the timber enterprise to lend a hand, they had brought the old woman to the country churchyard on a sledge pulled by a tractor, but there was no money for the wake. Lyudochka's mother managed to scrape together some food for the table, they sat for a while, had a drink, had a chat – after all, as they said, Vychuganikha had to be the last of the Vychugans, the founders of the village, the forefathers of the hamlet.

Lyudochka's mother was washing clothes in the kitchen. On catching sight of her daughter she wiped each of her hands on her apron in turn, then, holding on to the small of her back, straightened up slowly, and finally placed her palms on her swollen stomach.

'O, Lord! Look who's come to see us! So that's who the cat was foretelling when it was licking its paws!' Leaning sideways against the ancient bench by the wall, her mother pulled her headscarf off her incredibly tousled hair and, gathering her thick hair with a comb unhurriedly, making the most of this unexpected moment of rest, continued: 'This very morn I noticed that the logs kept on falling out of the stove on to the hearth – a sure sign that we should expect guests. But what guests, I thought? Who's likely to visit us, I wondered? And now here you are! Why are you propping up the lintel like that? Come on in. It's your home too you know.'

While talking and moving her hands, her mother looked closely at Lyudochka, taking everything in with a swift but perceptive glance. Lyudochka's mother had had her full share of experiences, suffering and toil during her forty-five years, and immediately understood that some misfortune had befallen Lyudochka. She was pale, with scratches on her face and cuts on her legs, she'd become gaunt, her arms were hanging listlessly, and there was indifference in her eyes. From the way in which Lyuda hurriedly and firmly pressed her knees together when her mother looked at her stomach suspiciously, and from the way in which she immediately made a big effort to look more cheerful, it didn't need a lot of brains to guess which particular misfortune had befallen her. But through this sorrow, or rather not sorrow, but more an inevitability, all women must pass sooner or later. And each woman has to go through this misfortune alone, and has to cope with it herself, for if the birch bends with the first wind, it does not break. And just think how many more misfortunes like this, how many more battalions of sorrows, still lay ahead, oh-ho-ho! . . .

Insomuch as Lyudochka's mother had got used to meeting and coping with all her sorrows and disasters and with her life as a whole on her own, she'd also grown accustomed to thinking that inscribed on a woman's heart was the word: 'endure'. Therefore it wasn't from harshness of character, but from her well-established practice of being independent in all things, doing everything herself, that Lyudochka's mother didn't rush to meet her daughter half way, didn't make it easier for her, didn't try to lighten her burden. Lyudochka must learn to cope with her burden, with her lot on her own: let her be tested by misery and misfortune, let her be hardened through suffering. After all for her part she, like any Russian woman, had enough delights of her own to be going on with, especially now she was pregnant, and she had to take care and not exhaust herself for as long as God or fate decreed. During the years of cold and hunger she, with her drunkard of a husband, just about managed to have and raise a child, and now it was necessary to find somehow and somewhere the strength for a second one. Or failing that, to preserve what remaining strength she still had in her, or which was indeed no longer in her, but in her roots, from her ancestors.

'You got a day off work or what?'

'What? Yes, that's it.'

'That's good. It's as if I knew you were coming. I'd kept some eggs and smetana back for something like this . . . Our eggs aren't like those town eggs of yours, our egg yolks are like little suns . . . And the guv'nor has extracted some honey.' Mother shook her head and burst out laughing. 'He's getting used to the ways of the world. The bees have stopped stinging him. With a bit of luck he'll give you some honey. We'd prepared a churn ready to sell . . . You see we're going to move to the timber enterprise after all . . . As soon as I give birth . . .' She wiped her smile from her lips, puckered her swollen, cyanotic face, averted her gaze and gave a deep, guilty sigh: 'What a bright idea of mine to have a baby so well into my forties . . . they say it's hard to give birth at such an age. But what can you do? The guv'nor wants a child. He is building a house in the settlement . . . and we'll sell this one. But the guv'nor doesn't mind if we put the house in your name instead . . .'

As before, mother persisted in not calling her new husband 'husband' or 'spouse' or 'better half'. Perhaps she was embarrassed to do so in front of her daughter, but most likely it was because it was her custom to distrust any signs of order and stability in her life. She didn't want to believe fully in her good luck so that later, if things turned out badly after all, it wouldn't be so difficult to overcome, to use the language of the town, the separation, or in country speech, your man dumping you, and there wouldn't be so many tears.

'What would I need a house for? What would I do with it? I'm fine as I am . . .'

'If you're fine as you are, that's fine, there's an end to it. But we need the money. If only someone would give five hundred roubles for the slates and the glass. But no one will. Who needs this house? Who needs this God-forsaken village?' Suddenly tears began to pour down mother's face, and for a while she sat gazing out of the window, beyond the kitchen garden, in the direction of the river and beyond, into the darkening distance of the forest's uneven stubble and the shadow of a forgotten black haystack in the middle of a green desert, in which it seemed that a small wedge had not been scythed, but had been hacked out of pied, marbled flesh – clearly a forester from the central farm estate had mown it and made a small rick for his horse.

'Dear, dear me, what will become of us? Who can benefit from such ruin?' mother asked, addressing her question to the expanse before her and, having received no reply, dried her face with her damp, patched-up apron. 'So I'll finish washing the clothes then, and you go and milk Olena and bring in some firewood. After his shift the guv'nor slogs away on the new house, he'll be home late, he'll be starving after his labours.' Something bordering on affection crept into her voice. 'We'll make him some soup. Go and get some of last year's sauerkraut out of the cellar, and some gherkins. I don't go down to the cellar any more, but you climb down, under an overturned barrel, inside a cornbin, you'll find a cask of home-brewed beer that the guv'nor hid, there's not a lot left after last year's harvest, perhaps you'll both have a drink, you'll be tired . . .'

'Mum, I still haven't learnt how to drink or cut hair.'

'That's good. That's good,' mother began melodiously, her mind clearly elsewhere. 'How come you haven't learnt how to cut hair yet?' she said, suddenly realizing what Lyudochka had said. 'Oh well. You'll learn some day. Little strokes fell great oaks. As they say, what man has done man can do.' Mother carried on thinking her own thoughts, carrying on her own private conversation. 'And as far as learning to drink's concerned – it's a skill not worth having. All it brings is destruction and depravity. It ruined our exhausted village it did, did that bane.' And once more withdrawing into herself, as if she was already dreaming, she added: 'Still, it must have been God's will . . .'

'All of a sudden everyone's remembered God! Everyone's turning to him with great hopes, and with complaints to him, as if they're taking them to the village council . . .' began Lyudochka, but she sensed that her words, even the sounds were hanging in a vacuum, and then falling flat, settling on the walls like dust. Her mother wasn't listening and hadn't even heard her.

And when Lyudochka was milking the cow on the flowering, grassy mound, she kept looking and looking into the distances beyond the river, kept remembering, remembering. It seemed to her that her memory, her soul too perhaps, continued to live there, on the other side of the river, and that she could be heard there, but there was no one there to respond.

She had enough memories to keep her going the entire milking.

When Lyudochka had climbed back up to the kitchen gardens, she stopped and, still holding the milkpail, for some reason started thinking about her stepfather, about the difficulties he'd had in getting used to running the farmstead, and about how eagerly he'd tried. He was incapable of doing almost anything in house and garden alike, but then again he knew how to look after cars and his motorcycle, he could use a rifle and was handy with saw, axe and spade. For a long time he couldn't tell one type of vegetable growing in the garden from another, he was helpless and hopeless with the beehives, the bees made his life a misery and chased him away from their hives and around the meadow where he kept them. The cows and horses wouldn't let him near them. He was a real fool when it came to haymaking – he treated it not as work, but as a holiday, a time for fooling around, he wallowed in the hay, liked to sleep in the cabin, ran barefooted through the meadow, loved throwing his cap in the air and catching it again. Wearing men's longjohns, Lyudochka and her mother would stack the hay, working from above, while her stepfather would bring it to them on a pitchfork, picking up a mere handful of hay and often spilling it all before he reached them, and sometimes he'd bang a sheaf down on top of them and knock the women over. Once he knocked Lyudochka down with his pitchfork, she fell headlong and could have been maimed, and he just stood there pointing his finger at her, unable to say a word because he was laughing so much. That was the first time she'd ever seen him really laugh out loud, baring his yellow teeth. And as a reaction to the fright she'd had, she giggled along with him too.

On the bank of the river Lyudochka and her stepfather together set about stacking the last rick – mother had rushed off to sort things out in the house and prepare something to eat. When they had finished stacking the rick and had tied up its top as best they could using withies to stop the hay blowing away, her stepfather gestured in the direction of a bend in the river where much of the bank had been washed away and said: 'You go over there, and I'll comb out the rick.'

Lyudochka bathed in her childhood river, washing off the dust from the hay and the chaff with that feeling of profound, relaxing pleasure which only people who have worked well and to their heart's content in the heat of the sun in the hayfields can know, people who have stacked, without set-backs or problems with the weather, a mass of the finest hay. Fodder for the cows means faith in the future and a winter free from all cares.

As she hopped along the path across the meadow, shaking the water out of her ear, Lyudochka suddenly heard a roar from beyond the bend in the river like that of some wild animal, she heard howling, rumbling, slapping noises. She ran to the top of a knoll, and the following picture met her eyes: her stepfather, like a kid from nursery-school, was gurgling upon a sand-spit, kicking his knobbly pale legs through the water, slapping the water with arms black to the elbows, splashing about and catching the splashes in happy, wide-open jaws where metal teeth glinted.

This stockily built man with a weather-beaten head greying on all sides, with deep furrows on his face, tattooed all over, his long arms slapping his belly, suddenly skipped along the sand-spit, and a hoarse roar of joy burst from the burnt-out or rusty core of this person whom Lyudochka barely knew. It started to dawn on her that this person had had no childhood, that childhood had caught up with him or was catching up with him, that it had returned to him only now, and that every man is supposed to live this childhood at one time or another, to have his full share of playing, running, sinning, crying. And whosoever takes away some part of a man's life commits a crime against that man and against life itself, indeed, this thief of life is himself a violent criminal, trying to take that which does not belong to him.

Lyudochka was rather startled by these grown-up, clearly defined and straightforward thoughts, the like of which she'd never experienced before. But then she was nobody's fool, in her loneliness she could talk to herself with the best of them, but as soon as she was in other people's company, in society, she'd grow shy and become that stupid, pale little girl they'd taken her to be in school, scarcely able to move her lips and giving the dates of the reign of the Roman Emperor Augustus, which she'd learnt off by heart, in a whisper. For some reason she could never get the year when Christopher Columbus discovered America right. She'd read about America and seen a few things on television, and would have been happy telling you all about that, but it wasn't America that was needed, but the date – and there you had it, bottom marks, and a scolding to boot: 'When you've cleared your head of silly thoughts, you can learn it all again and get it right. I don't want pupils with poor grades in the reports!'

Lyudochka stepped back into the bushes, and walked alongside the course of the river back to the high road. Changing into a dry, comfortable dress at home, she laughed as she told her mother how her stepfather had been carrying on in the river.

'And where on earth was he supposed to learn all about bathing? All he's known since childhood is life in exile and in the camps, armed guards, guards watching even in the camp bathhouse. The life he's had . . .' Mother stopped sharply, her look became harsher and, as if she was trying to prove something to someone, continued: 'But he's a decent man, perhaps even a good man.'

From that time on, from the time she'd watched her stepfather bathing, Lyudochka stopped being afraid of him, but they didn't grow any closer as a result. Her stepfather wouldn't let anyone get close to him. And now, this minute, in the meadow on the outskirts of her deserted native village, Lyudochka was suddenly overcome by such a strong, melancholy longing, such an irresistible need for some living soul, that the thought came to her that perhaps she should run to the timber-felling station, run seven kilometres, find her stepfather, rest her head on his hard chest and cry her eyes out. He might stroke her hair, pity her, comfort her . . .

'I'm planning on taking the morning train back. If that's OK with you?'

Her mother turned quickly to her, tried in vain to work out exactly what was bothering her, some thoughts nagging at the back of her mind, stayed lost in thought for a moment and then sighed, having managed to suppress the anxiety inside her:

'Oh well, if you must, yes of course . . .'

'My, that was quick!' said Gavrilovna in astonishment. 'What, not enough room for you at your parents'?'

'They're getting ready to move.'

'They're moving? Well of course then. No point in getting under their feet, you're far better off here . . . What did they give you?'

'All this here.' Lyudochka kicked the sack standing on the floor and burst out crying when she recognized the cord which had been attached to it in place of a strap. This cord consisted of four strong strands: two brown, made of wool, which had turned black with the passage of time, and two silky-white. A long time ago the people of Vychugan had swapped something or other for the end of a cable from a tourist launch, untwined all the strands and were able to make enough cords to supply the whole village. Really strong cords. There it was, that tightly woven cord! Her mother used to tell of how she would tie this cord to Lyudochka's cradle, put her foot in a noose at the other end, and would peel the potatoes, or prepare the cowswill, or spin wool, or repair clothes, while at the same time rocking the baby's cradle. 'And you really loved howling, you did. I would rock you and rock you, sing to you and sing to you:

> Rock-a-bye baby, on the tree top,
> When the wind blows, the cradle will rock,
> When the bough breaks . . .

And still you'd be crying. I'd curse you and yell at you to shut up, damn you, and you'd be so frightened you'd just bawl even more . . .'

'Wot you crying for now?'

'I feel sorry for Mummy.'

'Mummy, eh? No one feels sorry for me though . . .' Gavrilovna fell silent for a while and then added in a changed voice: 'There's, er, something you should know, girl . . . Yes, uhm . . . You see, Artyomka, old soap suds, 'as been taken in for questioning . . . You scratched 'im real good . . . it's clear evidence. But 'e's been ordered to keep mum, on pain of death. And this is the main thing . . . some of Botfly's boys called, with a warning. Just one squeak out of you and they'll nail you to a post and burn my house down.'

Gavrilovna's house was filled with a long and heavy silence. Eventually Gavrilovna stirred herself, felt through space for Lyudochka's head, pressed her to her sagging bosom, under which, somewhere in the far, far distance, Gavrilovna's worn-out old heart danced and skipped along, swaying drunkenly and missing its beat.

'This hearth and home is my only comfort and joy. I've laid down my life for it, worked like a horse, looked after my little garden, not for myself but in order to earn some money, I've gone without food myself, and not once did I use my leave for a holiday. Other decent folks would be going either to seaside sanatoriums or dispensaries for the workers, whereas I'd be chucking my instruments into my old grip and be off to my old country stamping grounds to help them keep the lice away . . . I've suffered from enough scabs, itches and shingles to last me a lifetime, just to come by these few kopecks, to save up for this cottage. I'm ashamed to admit it, but it must be owned – I even used to water down the eau-de-Cologne . . . And I also did my share of cutting hair in prisons.

It's only recently, now that I'm about to retire, that I have been moved to the woman's salon, on to some lighter work . . .'

'Yes, I understand. I'll go and find a place in the hostel,' Lyudochka nodded her head, but didn't move away from the bosom that had warmed her and kept on listening to how this human heart was suffering, hurrying ever onward to some unknown destination.

'Just for a while. Just for a while, my dear. That bandit won't stay out of trouble for much longer . . . 'e'll soon get fed up, soon wear 'imself out walking the streets . . . 'E'll end up back inside, and then I'll 'ave you back . . .' Gavrilovna ran her hands through Lyudochka's hair and combed it for her, and started to sob in the twilight: 'Lord! Why is it that good people 'ave no peace and happiness? Why are their lives just one long line of worries and suffering? Will they ever find any relief . . .?'

As soon as Lyudochka had reached her teens and was old enough to make the journey on her own each day to and from the heart of the collective farm where the secondary school for children from seven to seventeen was situated, practically all the running of the household was shifted on to her shoulders. One spring, towards Easter probably, or before some major spring holiday at any rate, after she'd whitewashed the stove, washed the windows, scraped the wood and dusted everywhere, she was rinsing the floor matting by the edge of the still frozen river when she slipped and fell in a place where the ice had already thawed. The water there was not very deep, but it was cold. The sun was already getting warmer by then, so she didn't rush home, deciding instead to finish the work off first. And she caught a chill. She developed a high temperature, and the outcome was that she ended up in the regional hospital. As in any of our hospitals, let alone a regional one, there were no spare beds, and, as is common practice in our hospitals, and not only in the regional ones, Lyudochka was put to lie for the time being in the corridor, which, with all its cold winds and draughts, was not exactly the best place for someone suffering from pneumonia.

During that night, which turned out to be long, endless, she discovered at the end of the corridor, half-hidden behind a stove, a young man whose head was covered with stiff, dried bandages. He was dying. From the night nurse she found out his simple and for that very reason all the more terrible story.

Recruited from some region near the Volga, the lonely lad had caught a cold while working as a woodcutter, and a furuncle had appeared on his temple. At first he didn't even pay any attention to it, and continued to travel to his work in the forest. But his head ached more and more unbearably, and the lad went to see the timber enterprise's own medic.

The medic he saw was a doctor's assistant, a young lady with a perm full of ringlets that made her look like a lamb, with cheap gold in her ears and on her fingers, a young lady who had found it a great effort during two years' study at the regional medical institute to learn how to measure temperature and blood-pressure and give painful injections and enemas. Now wearing a stethoscope instead of the usual amulet around her slender neck, a starched white doctor's cap and white coat, pressing her fists down into the little pockets of her white coat, this prima donna of the medical world inquired without even a show of interest: 'Well, what do we have here?' and rather squeamishly pressed the swelling on the lad's temple. 'Perfectly normal. Just a boil. Why do people waste my time with such rubbish?' was the diagnosis.

Only two days later this very same student medic was obliged to accompany personally the young woodcutter, who had lost consciousness, to the regional hospital. And there, in a place not equipped for complicated operations, the doctors were forced to perform an emergency trepanation on the lad's skull, and saw that the lad was beyond help – the pus had worked its way through the cranium and had started its job of destruction. The young man's not very convoluted brain was strong, and it rotted away slowly. A man who only a few days before had been totally fit now had to meet, for no reason at all, an excruciating and implacable death.

He was already in his death agony when he was moved, at the

request of the other patients, out of the overflowing ward into the corridor, and placed behind the stove.

The lad's heart was working overtime with quickened, powerful shoves, his lungs expelled the overheated air with a whistle, his ruined throat and burnt tongue both gave out the same sound, 'psykh psykh psykh', as if behind the stove a rubber tyre was being inflated using a faulty pump.

Lyudochka got out of bed and waited for her giddiness to subside, then looked beyond the stove. Pressing her fists to her breast, she looked long and hard at this man in torment. Moved by an instinct of compassion, which has still not totally perished in humankind, she laid her hand on the young lad's face – his bandaged head frightened her. The lad gradually went quiet, the pump inside him stopped pumping air so feverishly, his glutinous eyelashes came unstuck as he opened his eyes which were swimming in liquid mucus, and, coming back from non-being, he made one last effort – he made out the weak light and someone standing there in this light. Realizing that he was still alive, still here in this world, the lad tried to say something, but the only sound that came from his lips was 'an-kay . . . an-kay . . . an-kay . . .'

With the female intuition passed down to her from time immemorial, Lyudochka guessed that he was trying to say thank you to her. In his short life this man must have been infinitely lonely and miserable, since no other reason could have brought him to the middle of nowhere, have driven him to those deadly timber-cutting areas. He must be one of those, thought Lyudochka, you hear being read about on the radio: those lads who hadn't loved their fill or worked their fill, or read the book of life to the end, or who hadn't had the chance to finish smoking one last cigarette, or something like that, before going off into battle, or in this case, before signing up for demanding, debilitating work. And although Lyudochka had always found school difficult, and her difficulties had included literature and the Russian language, and in particular trying to remember what participles and gerunds were, nevertheless she had always been filled with pity for those who were talked about in poems, that is, for 'those who had gone early into the bloody battle'.

But this man was dying not in war, he was dying out of battle, dying young, with beautiful black eyebrows, and perhaps he'd never even had the chance to love someone, perhaps he didn't even have any family . . .

Lyudochka picked up something distantly resembling a stool, something with bent aluminium supports instead of legs, sat down alongside the young woodcutter and held him by the hand. She had to wait a long time for the unstable, slippery seat under her to lose its chill. The lad gazed at her with inexpressible hope, his lips, cracked from his fever, quivered in an attempt to say something. Lyudochka thought that he was saying a prayer, and tried to help him, regretting for what was probably the first time in her life that she'd never made the effort to learn even one prayer properly, but had only picked up snatches of prayers from the old women in the village, who themselves didn't know a single prayer from beginning to end: 'God who is just! God of all glory . . . Forgive your slave his intended and unintended trespasses alike . . . put out his fever, send down from heaven your healing power . . .'

The lad moved his fingers weakly: he could hear her, but he almost certainly didn't understand the words, and it was the sound and the ancient rhythm that were getting through to him. And so she tried her best to remember some poems, or more accurately lines from poems, which she'd read by chance in some girls' albums, in school textbooks, but above all in the local paper *The Farmer's Beacon*: 'No leaves now whisper in the golden copse . . .'; 'Love is a storm at sea, love is an evil ocean, love is joy and misery . . .'; 'And for a long time shall I be held glorious by my people, as a builder of Communism's great construction projects . . .'; 'And also say my parting word to her, hand over the wedding ring . . .'; 'In order to live, to live, and on the bounteous fields of the collective farm, my happy labour freely give . . .'

Lyudochka recited all sorts of nonsense, stretching her rather limited memory just in order to distract the lad from his pain and from his fear and foreboding of his imminent death.

But eventually she exhausted her stock of poems and herself, she started to rock back and forth on the rickety, slippery stool. Lyudochka fell silent and, it would appear, dozed off.

She was awoken with a start by a weak moan which sounded like a puppy whining. Through the rough-hewn window at the other end of the corridor, dawn was breaking. Tears which made the lad's burning face look molten now became visible. Lyudochka squeezed his hand to let him know that it was right to cry, that tears ease the heart's suffering, and she thought: perhaps it really is good, perhaps this lad's never even cried once throughout his entire adult life. But the dying lad didn't answer her squeeze with one of his own, and Lyudochka's blood ran cold. He wasn't crying in order to make things easier, something else caused his tears, something eternal, something well-concealed. For it was only here and only now that he'd understood the value, or more exactly the meaning, of any compassion, including hers, as he lay dying on the hospital bunk behind a dirty stove whose paint had peeled away. He'd understood that yet one more in the long line of betrayals of the dying had come to pass.

Why is it that the people around someone who is departing this life show so much fussy kindness and false sympathy? Why it's simply because they, the living, will remain alive. They will still be here, and he will not be. But after all he loves life as well, he deserves to live. So why is it then that they remain, while he departs, growing more and more distant, leaving the living and all living things behind, or to be more accurate, why do they cowardly draw away from him? But no tears, no despair or other expressions of grief can shield them from the most penetrating gaze of all, the gaze of a dying man, in whom at this very moment, at the parting of the ways, in the dying of the light, everything has come into focus, all vision and all his sense of life, a life he still holds dear, still needs.

The living, the living are betraying him! And it's not his pain or his life which matters to them, they value their compassion, though they are equally keen for his sufferings to end as quickly as possible so that they can stop suffering too. When his last breath leaves him, they, the living, will tiptoe away, thinking of themselves and not of him, and will disappear taking with them a mixture of secret joy and triumph. For the time being at least, death has no dominion over them, has nothing to do with them, and perhaps later on too, due to pressure of work, death won't notice them, will forget about them once again or will prolong their days on account of their sensitivity, their humility and their loving compassion for their neighbours.

The lad with a final uncompromising, unreconciled effort freed his fingers from Lyudochka's grasp and turned away – he hadn't been expecting from her a mere cold comfort, he'd been expecting a sacrifice from her, a willingness to be with him to the end, to the bitter end, and perhaps even to die too. Then a miracle would have come to pass: the two of them together would have become stronger than death, they would have come back to life, and in this lad, already as good as dead, would have appeared a surge of such power that it would have swept away everything blocking the road to resurrection.

But no one, not one single person on this earth had proved capable of such an unprecedented act of bravery, such a desperate, selfless, heroic sacrifice for his sake, for the sake of this lad. For no, she was no Decembrist's wife, following an exiled loved one to the ends of the earth. And where are they anyway, today's Decembrists' wives? Standing in the queues for wine . . .

The lad's hand flopped down and hung at the side of the bed, his mouth, hotly open, remained like that, but he made no more sound; his eyes didn't close immediately, but slowly, as if unwillingly somehow, without his consent, they were covered bit by bit by his eyelashes, eyelashes robbing him of the raging light that burned within, a light which bore no resemblance at all to the misty oblivion of death.

Lyudochka, like some guilty thing surprised while committing some bad, secret act, stood there for a while, then straightened her dressing gown and crept back stealthily to her bunk, and put her head under her blanket. But she heard how the nurse discovered the dead lad behind the stove, how she said quietly: 'His sufferings are over, the poor child.' She heard how they took the dead man away on a stretcher, how they folded up and took away his mattress and bed . . .

Ever since that night a feeling of profound guilt before that young woodcutter, that dead woodcutter, had never left Lyudochka. And now, in her sorrow, in her loneliness, when everyone seemed to have abandoned her, she felt particularly sharply, physically even, the total isolation of the dying man, and now it was her turn to drink the cup of loneliness to the dregs, to know what it was to be totally abandoned, totally forsaken, to endure people's shows of sympathy. She felt the space around her getting smaller and smaller, just as it had done alongside that bed behind the peeling hospital stove.

Why had she lied, why had she deceived both the lad and herself, why? For if there really had been in her a readiness to stay with the dying man to the end, to suffer his torment in his stead, as in times gone by, then perhaps in actual fact she would have discovered inside her strengths she didn't even know she had. And even if there had been no miracle, even if the dying man hadn't taken up his bed and walked, been resurrected, all the same the consciousness of the fact that she was capable of self-sacrifice for the sake of her neighbour, capable of giving all of herself to him, to the last dying breath, would have made her above all strong, self-confident, and ready to resist evil forces.

But now, now she understood to the very quick of her soul, not abstractly but instinctively, what she'd once upon a time read about and indifferently learned by rote from school textbooks, how heroes chained up in solitary confinement cells managed to survive. Of course, they themselves were the creators of their own indomitable spirit, but this spirit was also the creation of others who were just as strong in spirit, who were capable of sharing their suffering . . .

Just take those very same Decembrist wives, those noblewomen, for example.

But to tell the truth, the thing is that the girls of the modern school didn't believe in the possibility of self-sacrifice, still less that such young aristocratic madams raised in luxury could have sacrificed themselves. And as for the women she knew, who weren't born with silver spoons in their mouths, why for a crust of bread, for a small tip, or on account of some insult they'd be prepared to scratch one another's eyes out, and would use such foul language when arguing with a man, be he the foreman or even the head of the collective farm, that your ears would . . .

Lyudochka suddenly thought about her stepfather. No doubt he was one of them, one of the strong. But how, what was the best way to try to get closer to him?

There had been a time when in the village club lads who were a bit drunk would push in their manly way the young village schoolgirls like Lyudochka, mere small fry, off the benches and on to the dirty floor, and sit there like kings, on their own; and they only lifted the girls back off the floor when the girls had developed bodies worth fondling and groping.

But what about those others, the town girls, on the disco floor?

Surely they too had been knocked off their feet, on to the dirty floor? So why then had she joined Gavrilovna in condemning them? In what ways was she better than them? In what ways were they worse than her? In times of misfortune and loneliness all people are alike . . . So you shouldn't go around . . .

There wasn't any room in the City Department of Municipal Services hostel yet, and Lyudochka continued to lodge with Gavrilovna. So that 'them scum' wouldn't notice, Lyudochka's landlady ordered Lyudochka to return home only after dark, and not to go through the park but to go the long way round. However, Lyudochka disobeyed her landlady and kept on walking through the park without looking around, as if in a dream. And here in the park the lads once again waylaid her, trying to scare her with the threat of Botfly, while all the time cunningly edging her towards the tall weeds behind the bench.

'What d'you think you're doing?'

'Why, nothing! How about some nice kebabs? C'mon babe, light our fire!'

'My, my! Aren't you keen! Got the hots eh?'

'And why not? It's all the same now, now that your cheerie's cracked, as Gavrilovna puts it. The cake's been cut – time for some more slices . . .!' The drunken Carsteng braves kept on pushing and pushing Lyudochka in the direction of the bushes. Botfly was not among their number. A real shame. Lyudochka had in her raincoat pocket one of Gavrilovna's old, discarded cut-throat razors. She'd decided to cut off Botfly's manhood at its very root! 'I sired you with this, I shall slay you with it too!' – she remembered someone's howler in a school essay.

Lyudochka would never have hit upon the idea of such a terrible vengeance herself, but she'd heard stories at work about how one desperate woman had taken the law into her own hands in this way. Indeed she'd heard about all sorts of weird and wonderful things in the station hairdresser's! Scissors and tongues were at it hammer and tongs there from morning till evening. Lyudochka had even been on the point of going to church secretly, till she heard at work that there'd been such a crush there when they'd been blessing the Easter cakes, such pandemonium, real Babel, and so she decided not to go after all. There were more than enough problems to be going on with as it was. As was her wont, she tried broaching the subject with Gavrilovna by means of a few faltering sentences, saying that she'd quite like to go with her to church; but Gavrilovna came down on her like a ton of bricks, and without mincing her words said that one had to prove that one was worthy enough to believe in God, and that it wasn't like being in a *Komsomol* construction brigade, that orgy when the lorries roll in from town. As she said, Lyudochka's sin ought to gather a bit of moss first, the memory of it should fade a bit first, and only then, perhaps, could the two of them, old blasphemers that they were, be allowed to approach His martyr's feet.

'It's a shame your great leader isn't here – he's such a fine figure of a man . . .! What a pity!' repeated Lyudochka aloud and then said even louder into the darkness. 'Now push off boys! You've done enough damage already! You've already ripped one dress and ruined my raincoat! I'll go and slip into some old clothes. I'm poor enough as it is, I have to slave away cleaning.'

'Go on then. But don't forget, love and betrayal are as incompatible as genius and villainy.'

'My, what a way you have with words! I bet you're top of your class!'

'I always get top marks in everything. As good as Botfly. You should try me sometime – I'm sure you'll be impressed with what I can do.'

'And you'll be impressed by what I can do too.'

Lyudochka went and changed into her old worn-out dress, one from the village which bore a mark where her *Komsomol* badge had been, and with little pockets below the waist. She untied the cord which had been attached, in place of a strap, to the sack she'd brought from the village, took off her shoes and laid them out neatly next to each other on the rug near the divan, was about to reach for a piece of paper, but then decided to look first for a ballpoint pen in the knick-knacks box, among the buttons, needles and other women's odds and ends. She eventually found one, but it hadn't been written with for a long time, and the ink had dried. Having made a few scratches on the paper, Lyudochka angrily threw the pen on the floor and, shouting out 'See you!' to Gavrilovna who was lording it in the kitchen, left the house. Next to the porch she pulled on her old galoshes, and stood for a while outside the gate, taking so long to shut it that it seemed as if she wasn't used to doing it. On the way to the park she read a new notice which had been nailed to a post about how workers of both sexes were being recruited for work in the timber industry. 'Perhaps I should go there, take the train?' flashed through her mind, but immediately this thought was cut across by a second: there, down in the woods, there were Botflys aplenty, each one more terrible than the last.

In the park she searched for the poplar she'd noted a good while ago, a poplar with a gnarled bough growing across the path. She threw the cord over it, then skilfully made a noose – after all she wasn't a country girl for nothing, and although she was a quiet one, she knew how to do lots of things. She could cook, wash clothes, wash dishes, milk cows, reap hay, chop wood, heat up the bath-house, and draw a rope tight and secure it to hang out the washing. It was true that she wasn't able to harness a horse – but then again no horses had been kept in her village for over ten years now. And she just couldn't, she was afraid to put her hands under the chickens to feel the eggs, still less could she chop off cockerels' heads, and she hadn't learnt, although she'd tried, how to drink or swear.

Oh well, if she'd lived longer in this brave new world, no doubt she'd have soon experienced those delights too.

Lyudochka climbed up on to the ossified remains of a bough that jutted out from the trunk of the poplar like a tusk, tested this sliver gingerly, with the sensitive sole of her foot, steadied herself, pulled the noose towards her, put her head through it and said in a whisper: 'Kind God, Merciful God . . . but then, I'm not worthy . . .' And she switched to those who were closer to her: 'Gavrilovna! Mama! Stepfather! I never even asked what your name was. Good people, forgive me! And you, Lord, forgive me, even though I am unworthy, I don't even know whether you exist or not . . . If you exist, forgive me, in any case I lost my *Komsomol* badge long long ago. No one even bothered to ask about that badge. No one asked about anything – no one cares about me . . .'

She was, like all withdrawn people, stubbornly determined at heart and capable of drastic actions. When she was a girl she was always the first to jump in the river to test the water. And here too, with the noose around her neck, just as she had in her childhood, before she took the first plunge, she covered her face with the palms of her hands and, arching her feet, threw herself as if from a high, steep bank into the still, deep, oblivious water. Into the boundless, bottomless pool.

Lyudochka had never taken any interest in what happens to

people who hang themselves and didn't know that their tongues stick out horribly and that they invariably urinate. She had just about enough time to feel how everything had become painful and hot deep inside her, she guessed where the pain was, and tried to grab hold of the noose in order to free herself, snatched at the cord with frenzied fingers, but only succeeded in scratching her neck, and was also just able to sense a warm trickle which dried up almost as soon as it started to flow. Her heart began to expand, to swell up, there was no longer any room for it in her ever-tightening breast, the space available there was getting smaller and smaller. It seemed as if her heart was bound to break her ribs and tear open her chest: the pressure in it was so great, its blows, its strokes so powerful. But her heart soon got tired, it grew weak, started to contract, grow quiet, grow smaller, and when it had shrunk to the size of a walnut, it started to slow down, down, and then disappeared without a sound and without a trace, borne away somewhere into the emptiness.

And then all the pain and all the sufferings left Lyudochka, flying away from her body, and stopped for ever. And her soul? But who needs it, that simplest of souls, which had taken refuge in the simplest, most ordinary of bodies?

'Where the hell's that lying bitch got to? Is she prick-teasing us or what? I'll give her . . .'

One of the lads, who were now tired of languishing in the Carsteng park, got up from his seat, creaked his way over the rickety, derelict bridge and resolutely made his way along the edge of the park towards the line of poplars dimly lit up by distant street lamps and distant lights in people's windows.

'Let's get the fuck out of here! Scarper! She's . . .' The scout hurtled in leaps and bounds away from the poplars, away from the light.

An hour later, or two perhaps, sitting in the grubby station restaurant, the reccy man recounted with a nervous chuckle how he'd seen Lyudochka, her whole body still trembling, swinging back and forth at the end of a rope, doing the twist in such a way

that first her arse and then her front faced you, with a real whopper
of a tongue sticking out, and something dripping from her naked
legs.

'Well, who would have thought it!' groaned his pals. 'What a
dirty trick . . . What a bastard! If she was still alive, I'd show her
how to go hang . . .! From my pole . . .!'

'It's a real turn up for the books! A real choker! Silly fool's gone
and hung herself! What for?'

'We have to warn Botfly. Don't forget his threats . . .'

'Yeah, you're dead right. He's a real animal, and he's got his
claws out. One final toast, chaps! A final toast! Let's drink, brothers,
for the soul of this brave girl to re-ssst in pee-ece.'

'Let's hope it won't be our last! So one more for the road! For
the ditch! One for the bitch! Now let's go before we're nicked . . .'

'The silly idiot! And when life is so happy and glorious in our
mar-vel-less young countre-ee . . .'

It was decided not to bury Lyudochka in her native village, for as
soon as the last home there became empty the village itself, that
former haven for people, would be wiped from the face of the earth –
the collective farm would turn everything into one huge ploughed
field, and plough over the cemetery too. After all, there seems no
point in having that cemetery there casting its shadows amidst the
wide open space of the collective farm, or being on living folks' minds
all the time, a reproach and a reminder, making them depressed.

In the standardized, anonymous town cemetery, amidst standard-
issue gravestones and crosses, Lyudochka's mother was trying to
keep the mound of her stomach covered with the ends of a light-
brown shawl. She kept her belly warm with the palm of her hands
too – it was raining, and she was taking care to stay warm and dry.
But she kept on forgetting herself, and would lift the shawl to her
mouth and start chewing on the woollen material, and through this
thick damp lump would come, like the cry of a beast at night or the
boom of the skulking, hollow-sounding bittern from the dense
Vychugan swamp: 'Lyu-u-u-dochka . . .'

The women from the station hairdressers' looked around in terror, and, quietly pleased that the funeral hadn't dragged on too long, hurried off to the wake.

When the funeral was over Gavrilovna, unable to stand any longer, wobbly on her pins which did indeed seem to be about to go from under her, collapsed on to the old leather couch where Lyudochka had slept, and shrieked: 'Ly-u-u-dochka!' She moistened and soiled a picture of her lodger, which had been blown up from a school photograph. Bright as a button in a school uniform without any creases, Lyudochka had come out very well on the photo, really life-like, why, wasn't there even a smile there? Gavrilovna somehow managed to see a concealed, shy smile in this photo.

'I cared for 'er like she was my own daughter,' she announced, blowing her nose on an old kitchen towel. 'We went 'alf on everything, on every little bit of food. I was hoping to get 'er a 'usband, and was planning to put the 'ouse in her name . . . Oh my grey-winged little dove . . . oh my darling little swallow, my little birdie! What 'ave you gone and done? Why did you do this to yourself?'

Lyudochka's mother was no longer crying out loud, evidently feeling self-conscious in someone else's home, surrounded by people she didn't know. Only tears, restless tears, which filled to the brim that soul of the Russian woman, that soul whose depths no one has ever measured, the soul whose worth and depth are unknown, fell of their own accord all down her face, they appeared on all the recent and not so recent wrinkles, making even her neck and her ears wet, ears that she'd had pierced ready for earrings back in her youth, but that had never ever known the weight of earrings. Nevertheless her tears didn't prevent her from looking after the women's work there, from seeing that the guests had plenty to eat and drink, insomuch as Gavrilovna had packed up completely and wasn't able to cope with such mundane matters. Her closed eyes looked like black circles as she lay in her room, arms folded across her stomach, with nothing more to say, no more tears to shed, and not looking like one of the living.

When mother's tears fell and made a sound against the plates with meat and potatoes or against the bowl containing the *kutya*, she would say: 'I'm so sorry!' and would quickly dab the table with a crumpled grey rag. 'Pour yourselves some more drink, have some more food. Eat and drink to Lyudochka's memory – for God's sake, remember her,' she kept saying.

Lyudochka's stepfather, who was wearing a new black jacket and a white shirt and who was the only man there, downed one glass of vodka, then a second and growled: 'I'm going for a smoke.' He threw on his nylon jacket with a knitted collar, a jacket which had had holes splashed all over it, the burn marks from electric welding, went out on to the porch, lit up, spat, looked around, looked at the street and the smoking chimney of the Carsteng boiler-house, and set off in the direction of the park.

It was there that he found a jolly company swarming round that brave young man – Botfly. The company had recently gained new members, closed ranks and grown stronger. The militia were keeping an eye on them though and were slowly putting together evidence of criminal activity, so that they would be able to arrest and imprison, without any fuss and at a stroke, the whole rebellious band.

The lads, worn out by the effort of finding things to keep them idle, were still attacking the passers-by just as before, and sprawled on the bench, just as before, was a creature, neither man nor boy, wearing a crimson shirt, with bracelets, watches and rings on his fingers and a crucifix round his neck. Their leader. Lyudochka's stepfather, wearing his jacket with the knitted collar, looking like someone who'd had a chest-full of grapeshot, stopped dead before the indestructible concrete bench, pressing down through the soles of his Czech boots as if to leave a clear imprint in the mud.

'What can I do you for, mush?'

'I've come to take a look at you.'

'Well, you've seen me, now fuck off! I don't yet charge for private viewings.'

'So it is you then who's the big boss, Botfly?'

'Perhaps it is. You taking the piss?'

'Well well. A poet too! You like your little jokes, don't you?' Lyudochka's stepfather suddenly shot out his hand, ripped the crucifix from Botfly's neck and hurled it into the undergrowth. 'At least leave that unsullied, you sack of shit! Keep your filthy paws off God at least, leave him for decent people.'

'You . . . you . . . sucker! . . . Why I'll . . . I'll cut your dick down to size! Arab-style!'

Botfly shoved his hand into his pocket. The whole Carsteng gang froze, waiting with fear and lust for the breathtaking, bloody business to unfold.

'Aha, so you like fooling around with knives too?!' said Lyudochka's stepfather, his mouth twisted. As quick as lightning he grabbed Botfly's wrist before Botfly could do anything, held his hand inside the pocket in a tight grip, and then with a loud crack ripped out the knife together with the surrounding cloth. Botfly's superb Finnish knife with a mother-of-pearl handle made from the keys of an accordion that he'd pirated landed with a plop in the muddy trench.

Immediately, without giving Botfly any time to come to his senses, Lyudochka's stepfather seized with his huge hand the collar of his tailcoat together with the crimson shirt and dragged the ladies' man, now fighting for his breath, through the rampant, impenetrable weeds. Botfly tried to free himself, tried to kick the man, but only managed to kick off his boot instead and scatter his valuables all over the bushes. Lyudochka's stepfather lifted up the swordsman and, like Stenka Razin throwing the Persian princess into the Volga, tossed him into the polluted waters of the drainage trench. Botfly's naked belly flashed into view for a second, revealing red stripes left by a blade – on several occasions he'd tried to fake madness in the camps by slashing his stomach. The lads who rushed to pick up their boss's boot and search for his watches and rings in the tall weeds were amazed by how the buttons on the English tailcoat had cannoned off in all directions. They didn't come off with bits of material, didn't break across the holes, like the ones made here. These tin, or perhaps nickel or maybe even silver buttons from overseas had shot away from the tailcoat, leaving behind on the coat-breast little silver hooks. Flashing like bullets, the buttons had flown in all directions, and one had even shot right on to the other side of the trench, flushing a bird out of the burdocks.

The greenish-black thickets, which were covered in snot-like down and muck, resounded with such a howl that if at that very moment the long silent, rust-choked hooter of the locomotive depot had started to wail, it wouldn't have been audible above this terrible cry.

The crows took wing, the stray dogs from the Carsteng park went wild, and an old one-eyed goat broke loose from its tether.

Lyudochka's stepfather wiped his hands on his trousers and started to walk away.

The Carsteng gang of thieves, Botfly's minders, blocked this man's way. He fixed his steely gaze upon them. Under this gaze the Carsteng lads felt like the small scummy plants growing next to the trench which, if they didn't part and give way, this chap would simply trample underfoot! The lads felt that this was a real Mister Big, a lord of life, a professional, not some amateur. This criminal boss had never dirtied the knees of his trousers, it was a long time since this one had been on his knees before anyone, even before the most terrible camp guard. He walked on half-bent legs, with a slightly springy, almost playful animal-like gait, ready to pounce, ready to act. With his chest puffed up and his shoulders pushed back, it was as if he had tensed his whole being in readiness to meet any threat. This was a two-legged creature formed by a merciless time, all stains had been removed from the bright whites of his eyes, and from their depths the sharpest crystals, his pupils, protruded. The sparks flashing from their facets were a metallic fire from the dark depths, wreathing not in consciousness, but beyond it, they came from that place in which a fury inherited from cavemen, a fury passed through the dark, thick woods of the ages, was bubbling away, an all-destroying, all-conquering, merciless fury.

A low, terrifying growl came from deep inside his belly, from under the swollen Neanderthal mounds of his forehead, from under the crushed eyebrows, while from his eyes there kept on flashing and flashing the undying sparks and the undying flame that had made those same eyes molten and empty, made them eyes that saw nothing and no one.

These nasty, petty little criminals were just playing at what it would be like to enjoy total freedom to do anything, scratching from the tree of life a sticky gum, a little piece of the action, enjoying a learning period in familiar surroundings before entering for real the world of crime, or even perhaps before eventually deciding, having got the madness out of their systems and having finished mucking around in a belated childhood, to give up as a bad job all this risky business, and return to the boring, everyday world of their fathers and grandfathers, to daily toil and cheerless reproduction. And now they'd understood in a single second, they'd understood with the pathetic convolutions of their tiny minds, that existence alongside such operators as this terrifying creature was the harshest, not the coolest of lives, and that it would be better therefore to leave such a life well alone. Though when, of course, all the barriers between that world and this world are removed, and that day's coming nearer all the time, when there really will be nowhere to turn, well, then indeed it will be 'All Hail to the Conquering Hero!' then, indeed, it will be necessary to be under the wings of just such a boss . . .

The lads set about their more pressing business with relief: three or four of them dragged the almost cooked Botfly, who was squeaking barely audibly, out of the trench. Another one dashed off in the direction of the tram stop to call an ambulance, someone else rushed to some old wooden barracks in which two or three windows were still intact and where those spurned by society, creatures who'd turned to drink and old folk abandoned by their children, tended to hang out. That was where he hoped to track down the victim's mother, to delight the ruined old woman with yet one more account of another of her own dear son's escapades, a son who had, it seemed, spent his last night under the roof of the barrack he knew so well. His glorious, stormy path from children's corrective labour colony to strict-regime prison camp had come to an end in a muddy death. The oppressed, robbed, slashed, stabbed, beaten inhabitants of the railway community, who'd lived in constant fear of such attacks, would now be able to breathe a sigh of relief and would be able to live in relative peace and quiet until the coming of the next Botfly, no doubt also spawned and raised by their good selves.

When he had reached the edge of the park, Lyudochka's stepfather stumbled suddenly, and thanks to his ingrained habit of always being on his guard, of being able to see everything and hear everything, spotted on a bough which overhung the path a fragment of a pied cord which, for some reason, the militiamen hadn't removed. Some force from his past, some evil force which he himself didn't fully understand lifted him up high, he grabbed hold of the bough, which creaked and broke away from the trunk, leaving behind an iodine-coloured spot the shape and size of a horse's eye. Lyudochka's stepfather held the branch in his hands for a while, sniffed it for some reason, and then said quietly, for his own benefit:

'So why then didn't you break when we needed you to?' And with a sudden madness, his rage and anger not yet cooled, he snapped the bough into little pieces. After chucking the broken pieces away, he stood for a while, observing from under his sullen brows how an ambulance limped and crawled across the corrupted, mangled, hummocky park, till at last it reached the trench to offer its first aid. He lit a cigarette. Some people were trying to roll a stained and creased ball into the white ambulance, and a foul liquid flowed over its whiteness. Lyudochka's stepfather spat out the butt of his cigarette and was about to walk away, but he stopped immediately and turned back, undid the coloured cord which had been drawn tight, took it from the broken poplar branch, stuffed it into the side pocket of his jacket, touched his chest and, without looking back, hurried off to Gavrilovna's home, where the wake was already drawing to a close.

There was still plenty left on the table. The town women hadn't been able to polish off all the drink, there were too few of them for that. Lyudochka's stepfather drank a glass of vodka, listened carefully to his own thoughts, and had another glass. He stood over the table for a while, looking at his wife who'd come over all timid and at the women who were keeping a cautious silence and who had already started self-consciously busying themselves, washing and sorting out the plates and cutlery borrowed from various neighbours. He tore his eyes away from the bottle with regret – everyone could see it required a real effort on his part – and, signalling to his wife it was time to leave, hurriedly set off for the evening train.

His wife rushed after him, following at a respectful distance, but she couldn't keep up with him – her man's steps were too long and too angry as he stamped loudly over the asphalt. But suddenly he stopped and waited for her, took her bag and the suitcase with Lyudochka's belongings, helped the heavy woman up on to the first iron step on the ladder into the carriage, found her somewhere to sit, threw the bundle on to the rack above them, used his heel to push the suitcase under their seat, and all this without saying a single word. Then, resting the side of his head against the window, he made out that he was now calmer, or perhaps he really was, and fell asleep. After all he got well and truly tired at work, building the house, and looking after the farmstead. And she wasn't exactly much help to him in her present state, was she?

Lyudochka's mother had always sensed in 'the guv'nor' that something hidden deep inside him, that terrible, monstrous force, which he had never, thank God, let loose in her presence and, perhaps, never would. Recovering slightly from the awe and terror which had gripped her for some reason, she thought about herself and in silence fashioned something like a prayer: 'Lord, help me give birth to a healthy baby this time at least and keep her from harm. The child won't be a hindrance or a burden to us, even though we are old I admit, our child will be as a son and a daughter, a grandson and a granddaughter to us all at once, it will give us strength, keep our lives on an even keel ... And for my dear daughter, my little drop of scarlet blood, this innocent victim of life, forgive me, Lord, if you can . . . I never did evil to anyone, and I didn't mean to harm her so . . . Forgive me, forgive me, forgive me . . .'

Lyudochka's mother didn't even realize that she was whispering out loud, or that she'd been doing so for some time, enunciating the words with trembling, dancing movements of the lips, or that her whole face was once again soaked in tears, but 'the guv'nor' didn't appear to hear her, and he didn't even go out into the corridor for a smoke. And she uncertainly rested her head upon his shoulder, leaning against him gently, and it seemed to her, or perhaps it really was so, that he lowered his shoulder slightly so that it would be more comfortable and more convenient for her, and even seemed to press her to his side, as if he were keeping her warm.

The local militia turned out not to have the resources or the evidence to break Artyomka-Suds and make him squeal after all. Having received yet another strict reprimand, he was allowed to go home. In fulfilment of the authorities' command to come to his senses fast, but above all because he'd been scared out of his wits, Artyomka-Suds enrolled in a communications tech: not the sort where the polytechnic lads work with the latest, highly sophisticated apparatus, computers and technology, but in an affiliated institute, where they teach them how to climb poles, screw in attachments and make the wires taut. And it was the shock of it all that made Artyomka-Suds get married very soon afterwards, and in heroic shock-worker style, quicker than anyone in the settlement, only four months after their wedding, a curly-headed child was born, happy and smiling. At the christening Artyomka-Suds's father, a pensioner who'd been honoured for his fine work record, said laughing that this baby was a real flathead, because he'd been dragged into this world by forceps, and therefore he wouldn't even be as brainy as his father and that if he ever had to climb up a pole he wouldn't know which end to start from.

A few months later the fourth page of the local paper featured a short item about the moral health of the town. It stated that for the three-month period under review three murders had been committed in the town, one hundred and five burglaries, fifteen assaults whose aim had been to strip people of their clothing, and one attempted bank robbery, thwarted by the vigilance of the militia. No major robberies or crimes with particularly serious consequences had been noted, there had been only eight rapes, thirty-two cars stolen and eleven raids on dachas. Of course, it was still early to talk about there being complete peace and security and a completely healthy moral climate in the town, but thanks to crime prevention initiatives and the increased attention paid by the local powers to the ways in which the moral health of society could be improved through sporting activity, and in particular thanks to the opening of a swimming pool within the grounds of the locomotive depot, where hot water had been going to waste for so long, the crime figures, when compared to the figures from the same period in the previous year, showed a decrease in the level of criminal activity of 1.7 per cent.

Lyudochka and Botfly didn't figure in this account. The head of the regional section of the Directorate of Internal Affairs had only two years to go to his pension, and he had no desire to undermine such encouraging statistics with dubious cases where foul play hadn't been proved. So Lyudochka and Botfly, who had not left behind them any suicide notes, possessions, valuables or witnesses, were marked down in the Directorate of Internal Affairs' registration book as suicides, who, for no good reason and while being of unsound mind, or in simple terms, without thinking what they were doing, the stupid fools, had taken their own lives.

Translated by Andrew Reynolds

ABRAM TERTS (ANDREI SINYAVSKY)

The Golden Lace

Like a number of other people I sense that Russian prose writing is in need of renewal. People are bored with the old prose, the writers at least, if not the readers. It bores Russian literature itself. Socialist Realism is finished. How much longer can we go on writing prose which is no more than an endless complaints book about the Central Committee of the Communist Party of the Soviet Union, illustrated with quotations from Chingiz Aitmatov's *The Place of the Skull*, Valentin Rasputin's *The Fire* or Viktor Astafiev's *A Sad Detective Story*? These illustrations may well help life in Russia to return to a semblance of normality, but they really have no relevance to the future development of Russian letters, if only because Alexander Solzhenitsyn's short story 'Matryona's Home' got there first, in 1963. It blazed the trail a quarter of a century before all this earnest latter-day Village Prose. To think that a quarter of a century has passed and we are no further on! After the achievement of 'Matryona's Home' it is quite profitless to go on playing the same thing over and over again in Russian, Kazakh or Kirghiz prose versions.

I don't see tackling ever more controversial political themes as the way forward either, or translating social energies into sexual energies. In short, it is beginning to look as if we have come up against a brick wall.

The Russian Futurists undoubtedly felt much the same way at the beginning of the century, but their sense of impasse came at a time when Russian poetry had soared to new heights with Symbolism, primarily, and Acmeism. This meant they were positioned a great deal better than we are. In Russia Futurism exploded in this context of a great rise in the fortunes of poetry and it led Russian letters to new levels of attainment. That is not our present situation. Our explosion will have to take place in a desert.

We may take some comfort from the fact that immediately before beginning their advance the Futurists were unaware of having any positive mission to perform. Reading their 1912 manifesto, *A Slap in the Face of Public Taste*, we are struck today by the vehemence of its negation, coupled with a positive programme which is decidedly weak and vague. On the positive side, we find little more than the assertion that they are 'standing on the ice floe of the word "we" in a sea of catcalls and outrage', or that 'What we hymn is the mystery of the potent infinitesimal.' This is gibberish, yet from it emerged Velemir Khlebnikov, Vladimir Mayakovsky and Boris Pasternak, to say nothing of its other results. We lack any comparable force of repulsion.

I fully recognize that I am drawing these damning parallels between Russian Futurist poetry and our contemporary new prose, with its ambition of scaling an equally formidable barrier (which so far it has been unable to achieve). Taking a historical perspective, it is only fair to say that ours is a more daunting barrier to scale. There are two reasons for this. The first is that we are dealing with prose, which develops more slowly than poetry. The second, and more important reason, is that our springboard was and still is not symbolism but, in the main, the far more primitive phase of Socialist Realism. The first general reaction against Socialist Realism was, and to this day remains, simply Realism, retreat to an artistic movement which has been known since the nineteenth century. Russian Village Prose is at best a harking back to Gleb Uspensky. Now Uspensky was a distinguished and honourable writer, but it is difficult to see how anyone can leap from his way of writing into a new Russian prose. For all that, we are aware of an insistent voice telling us that jump we must. The development of a new style cannot be accompanied by a wholly despairing intonation.

I offer here a prose piece as an example of an equally dead-end but interesting condition which has been called here in France 'death of the subject, death of the object'. It is something currently taxing and tormenting Abram Terts, and seems to me to be in some measure the form for the new Russian prose. The text is called *The Golden Lace*.

'Do you have my fine shoe?' 'Yes, I do.' 'Do you have my golden candlestick?' 'No, I do not.' 'Do you have my new kerchief?' 'No, I do not.' 'What sugar do you have?' 'I have your good sugar.' 'What boot do you have?' 'I have my own leather boot.' 'Do you have my goose?' 'No, I have my own.' 'Do you have my old knife?' 'I have a splendid knife.' 'What lantern do you have?' 'I have your old lantern.' 'Have you a new table?' 'I have an old table.' 'Have you a great house?' 'I have a great and splendid house.' 'Have you the small polecat?' 'Yes, I do.' 'Do you have a golden knife?' 'I have a golden knife.' 'Do you have a silver candlestick?' 'I have a pewter candlestick.'

'Is it you who have my golden lace?' 'It is.' 'What sugar do you have?' 'I have bad sugar.' 'Are you tired?' 'Yes, I am tired.' 'Are you too warm?' 'No, I am cold.' 'Have you any cheese?' 'No, I do not have anything.' 'Have you good coffee?' 'I do not have good coffee: I have good tea.' 'What tea do you have?' 'I have your tea.' 'What do you have that is bad?' 'I have a bad shoe.' 'Are you thirsty?' 'I am tired.' 'What do you have that is fine?' 'I have a fine cloth cloak.' 'What boot do you have?' 'I have an old leather boot.' 'Do you have the silver lace?' 'I do not.' 'Do you have anything?' 'I do not have anything.' 'Do you have anything good?' 'I do not have anything good.' 'What do you have that is bad?' 'I have the bad horse of my kind friend.' 'Have you any bread?' 'I do not have any bread.' 'What cheese do you have?' 'I do not have any cheese, I have some bread.' 'What eagle does your brother have?' 'He has my neighbour's great eagle.'

'What lace do you have?' 'I have the golden lace.' 'Do you have the blacksmith's iron hammer?' 'I do not.' 'Do you have anything good?' 'I do not have anything good.'

'Do you like tobacco?' 'No, I do not.' 'What, then, do you like?' 'I like tea and coffee.' 'Which do you like, the ram or the calf?' 'I like neither the ram nor the calf: I like coffee and tea.'

But on the other side: 'What do I have?' 'You have a great eagle.' 'Do you like this pie?' 'No, I do not like pie, but I like that pâté.' 'Is it a red kerchief that I have or a yellow one?' 'You have neither a red nor a yellow handkerchief, but you have my golden lace.'

'Is it my eagle the hunter has or his own?' 'He has neither yours nor his own; he does not have an eagle, he has a polecat.' 'Where have you put my little knives?' 'I do not have them; I am looking for them.' 'Are you looking for donkeys?' 'I am looking for donkeys and bulls.'

'What does this officer have?' 'What does which officer have?' 'The officer whom the colonel does not like.' 'He has the boot-maker's leather boots.'

'How many horses do you have?' 'I have five horses.' 'Do you want my knife?' 'No, I do not want it.' 'Where do you see three great elephants?' 'I see them at our rich neighbour's. He has three great houses.' 'Does the house have a cupola?' 'No!' 'Does the soldier have a shako?' 'Yes!' 'What friends does the Turk have, these or those?' 'He has neither these nor those. He has no friends.'

'Have you seen the waistcoats of my young brother?' 'No, I have not seen them.' 'How many woodcock have you seen in the forest?' 'I saw ten woodcock there and three wild boar.' 'About which wild boar are you talking?' 'I am talking about the three great wild boar.'

'What drinking glasses do you have?' 'I have splendid new drinking glasses.' 'Do you want this splendid candlestick?' 'No, I do not want it.' 'Can you give me your horse?' 'I cannot: it is at my brother's.' 'Do you see the great horns of this billygoat?' 'I see three billygoats and ten bulls with splendid horns.'

Meanwhile, however: 'What does the poor blacksmith have?' 'He has iron tongs.' 'Do these people have doves or geese?' 'They have neither doves nor geese: they have three small nightingales and twenty-two sparrows.' 'How many socks do you have?' 'I have forty-eight.' 'Where are my shoes?' 'Here!'

'What is it you see?' 'It is the sea that I see.'

'Is it an iron or a pewter pot that he has?' 'He has a good pewter pot.' 'Do you see nightingales there in the park?' 'I see nightingales and sparrows.' 'How many wings does a nightingale have?' 'It has two.'

'What's the time?' 'Half six.'

'What is this shoemaker going to fetch?' 'He is going to fetch the student's shoes.' 'Is there a cat or a mouse in your father's house?' 'There are neither cats nor mice in our house.' 'Can tigers eat deer?' 'They can.'

'Do you want some pepper to sprinkle on your gammon?' 'No, thank you, I do not like pepper.' 'Can your brother-writers write?' 'They could but they do not want to.' 'Why do they not want to?' 'Because they are too lazy.'

'What woman does this youth see?' 'He sees a young and beautiful woman in a black dress.' 'Where does he see her?' 'He sees her in church.' 'Do you see a great horse?' 'Yes, I do.' 'Where is the coachman going with my father's horse?' 'He is going to a new stable.' 'Are you going to church.' 'Yes, I am going there with my sisters.'

'Why do you need salt?' 'I want to salt my meat.'

'How many sisters has the kind son of our carpenter?' 'He does not have a single sister, but he has five brothers.' 'Does this murderer have brothers?' 'No, he does not have any brothers, but he does have two sisters.' 'Where are the mothers of these charitable maids?' 'They are in church.' 'Do herring have much roe?' 'They have little roe.' 'What fish have much roe?' 'Sturgeon do.'

'Do you see this fine funeral?' 'Yes, I do.' 'Whom do you see there in chains?' 'I see the murderers of our good neighbour, the skilful blacksmith, in chains.'

'What gloves do these gentlemen have?' 'These gentlemen have very good leather gloves.' 'Do you see this famous versifier?' 'Yes, I see him every day.'

However: 'What do I see there in the street?' 'You see a pretty woman with very pretty little children there.' 'Does the bootmaker bring you your boots?' 'My bootmaker does not bring me my boots, but my tailor brings me new clothes.'

'What cards do you have?' 'I have clubs.' 'I thought that you had hearts.' 'No, I have clubs, spades and diamonds.' 'Is that a lap-dog I see there?' 'No, it is not a dog but a pig.' 'What does your son play?' 'He plays the violin.' 'But why are you buying an umbrella instead of a cane?'

'Who is cooking the beef?' 'The chef is cooking it.' 'Are you a Frenchman?' 'I am afraid I am a Russian.' 'Who is the gentleman who has such a very high forehead?' 'He is an Englishman.' 'Do you wish to sell me your hat?' 'No, I do not wish to sell you it because I have need of it myself.' 'May I take off my boots prior to taking off my gloves?'

'Do you not write too much?' 'No, I write too little.' 'Who is that madwoman there in the market?' 'It is the wife of that madman whom you often see at a concert.' 'Does the shepherd have many billygoats?' 'The shepherd has few billygoats.' 'Does this woman have good wares?' 'Yes, she has exceedingly good wares.' 'What does she have?' 'She has good silver knives, forks, steel penknives, scissors, spectacles, and other metal and glass wares.'

'What is more precious than beauty?' 'Virtue.' 'Could you perhaps lend me a few francs?' 'I have often lent you money, but you have never repaid any of my loans.'

'How much time did you spend at your doctor's?' 'I spent two and a half hours with him.' 'What were you doing there for such a long time?' 'We were playing cards.' 'What is the tailor doing now?' 'He is mending the clothes which I sent him.' 'Why does this young soldier drink so much?' 'Probably because he is thirsty.'

'What have you had stolen?' 'I have had a fine watch stolen, and a golden lace which I bought in Paris.' 'Do you have white gloves?' 'No, I have yellow gloves.' 'Have you seen the book which I have written?' 'Yes, your publisher sent it to me.' 'Have you read it?' 'I have not read it, but have glanced through it briefly.' 'Why do you not write as you should?' 'I cannot write better.' 'Go on, shoot! It is your turn now.' 'I am afraid I shot just now.'

'Do you intend to return to Russia?' 'No, I do not.'

'What do you like to do?' 'I like to read and, especially, to write.' 'Do you read very much?' 'We men of letters do not have time to read very much.' 'Do you want to buy this castle?' 'I would like to buy it, but I have no money.' 'About whom are you talking?' 'I am talking about the person whose house burned down yesterday.' 'Why is this child crying?' 'Because it was given scissors to cut its nails, but has cut its fingers.' 'Carve me a slice of beef!' 'With the greatest of pleasure.'

'Has your brother used the horse which he bought yet?' 'Yes, he has used it.' 'Have you told your brother to leave the train?' 'No, I did not venture to tell him to do so.' 'Why did you not venture to tell him to do so?' 'Because I did not want to waken him.' 'Will you soon be bringing me my dinner?' 'It would be better for me not to dine at all rather than dine so late.' 'Which fork do you have?' 'I have the fork which my brother gave me.'

'Have you seen the brave captain's golden sword?' 'I have not seen his golden sword, but I have seen his silver helmet.' 'Why does this young man affect such an arrogant appearance?' 'He considers himself a great artist, he who plays the piano only with extreme mediocrity.'

'Will your brother buy this horse?' 'He will not buy it, because he has not the means with which to buy it.' 'How long have you been wearing this large hat?' 'I have been wearing it since I returned from Germany.'

'But who has golden laces?' 'Nobody has.'

'Who is knocking at the door?' 'It is I! Please be so kind as to open the door for me.' 'What do you want?' 'I have come to request that you return the money I lent you.' 'If you would be so kind as to come tomorrow I shall return it to you.'

Why has this drunkard, who all his life has drunk only wine, asked on his deathbed for a large glass of water? 'When you are dying,' he said, 'it behoves a man to make peace with his enemies.'

Translated by Arch Tait

Bag-in-hand

Avdotiya woke up in the early hours and immediately remembered about her little bag.

'Oh my, my . . .' Avdotiya began wailing. 'Oh, oh, carrying that can of milk yesterday, the handle broke, it's all worn out . . . I have to get it stitched up before the shops open.'

She glanced at her little old alarm clock. Once upon a time that alarm clock used to get Avdotiya up out of bed together with the others . . . Who? What does it matter? What personal history has Avdotiya got nowadays?

Soviet citizens remember all the detailed ramifications of their personal history, thanks to the innumerable forms they have to fill in so very often. But it was a long time since Avdotiya had filled in any forms, and of all the various state institutions, her interest was reserved for the grocery stores. For Avdotiya was a typical grocery-store granny, a social type unrecognized by socialist statistical science, but actively involved in the consumption of the product of socialist society.

Before the weary working population comes pouring out of its workshops, factories and institutions in the evening; before, worn to a frazzle by rush-hour travel on public transport, it squeezes itself into the hot, cramped, suffocating shops, Avdotiya has time to dart round them all, like a little mouse . . . She'll pick up a few Bulgarian eggs in one place, a little bit of Polish ham in another, a Dutch chicken in yet another, a bit of Finnish butter somewhere else. The topography of the food-hunt, so to speak. She never even thinks any more about the taste of a good Russian apple from Vladimir, or a sweet dark-red cherry, and she gathers berries outside Moscow to eke out her pension, not for eating. Off she'll go, bag in hand, into the woods that are still left alive, getting there ahead of the alcoholics, who follow Michurin in expecting no favours from nature and collect the raspberries to make booze. They'll strip the woods so bare there'll be nothing left for a bird to peck or a squirrel to gnaw. First they fleece their little brothers in the forest, then they perch themselves on the shoulders of their brothers and sisters among the working people.

Our Avdotiya will sell a little bagful of raspberries from the Moscow woods, and she'll buy a kilogram of bananas from Peru. She'll sell a few bilberries and buy some Moroccan oranges. It's a fine life under socialism. The western fighters for peace are quite right. It's just a pity their visual propaganda doesn't make use of our Avdotiya's weighing scales and Avdotiya's added value.

Avdotiya the grocery-store granny was an old hand at shop-plundering, she was experienced, and her weapon was her little bag. Old Avdotiya loved her little bag, and as she made ready for her working day, she would croon to it:

'Ah, my little provider, my own little Daisy-Cow!'

Her plan of action was all drawn up in advance. First to 'our shop' – that's the one next door to her house. After that to the bread shop. After that to the big department store. After that to the milk shop. After that to the shop run by the Tatars. After that to the vegetable stall. After that to the bread shop opposite the stall. After that to the shop beside the post office . . .

It was never calm in the big shop. When you plunged in there, the waves grabbed you and bore you away . . . From the grocery section to the delicatessen, from the delicatessen to the meat section . . . And always elbows on every side, elbows and shoulders, more elbows . . . The good thing was they couldn't really 'nudge' you here – there was nowhere to fall. But an elbow to 'the mug' – nothing could be simpler.

Now they've wheeled out a trolley piled high with flat tins of herring. This kind of situation is manna from heaven to Avdotiya . . . No queue or order of any kind, just straightforward pillage. Free-for-all grabbing. It's not the cunning of the fox Avdotiya requires here, but the cunning of the mouse. It's just like a circus act: hup, one, two – and the trolley's empty. Some folks have grabbed nothing but empty air, and they're furious. At the head of the pack are the strong, skilled housewives, with three or four tins. A few little old women are up there with them. Our Avdotiya has three tins in her little bag . . .

If the grocery-store grannies ever combine forces, then they're truly formidable. Once seven old women, including our Avdotiya, stormed a counter in chain formation. The leader, Matveevna – she's in hospital with a fracture just at present – was holding herself up with a crutch. They swept all before them and secured their Polish ham.

Of course, you always have to assess the situation in advance, it's pointless getting involved in that kind of tangle over there in the meat section . . . Something's just been wheeled out, but just what isn't clear. It's something between a scrum and a scrimmage. A few people smiling stiffly – they're the ones who try to make a joke of their brutality: but most of the faces are seriously vicious. This is work . . .

Oh, you get away from there, Avdotiya! You've grabbed your herring, now get out. Herring may not be meat broth, it tickles as it slips through your guts, and it hurts when it makes you belch . . . But it's what you fancy, and you can't always be following doctor's orders, you have to please yourself sometimes. A bit of potato will kill the salt, and some sweet tea will settle everything down. Now you've grabbed your fatty herrings, get away, Avdotiya, while you're still in one piece. Get away, Avdotiya . . .

But it was a bad day, nothing going right. Avdotiya grasped the situation too late. There was no space left to turn round, not even room to draw breath . . . And there was a new smell – home-grown coarse tobacco and tar – tar from new roads in the satellite towns . . .

They've arrived ... There are the tourist buses outside the supermarket. Every bus a requisitioning detachment's mobile head-quarters to which the plundered purchases are carried back. The entire bus weighed down with bundles, sacks and string bags. The troops move off in various directions – men and women with fine strong arms. The scouts are nimble boys and girls.

A freckle-faced girl comes running up:

'Uncle Parshin, Aunty Vasilchuk said to tell you they're selling vegetable fat.'

'What kind of fat's that, lop-ears?'

'Yellow,' says freckle-face, nodding gleefully. 'I pushed in and I saw them selling it ... And a man in there bashed Aunty Vasilchuk with his shoulder ...'

But Uncle Parshin wasn't listening any longer.

'Vanyukhin! Sakhnenko! Get the churn!'

Off ran the combat detachment with a forty-litre milk churn ... Oh, there's so many of them, oh, I can't stand it ... And now they've shoved in another milk churn ...

'Oh! He ... Help! Help me!'

The satellite town folk work smartly, transporting sausage, cheese and grain through the air. It's harvest time. If you don't reap, you don't eat. And if you don't eat, when you pick up the Party newspaper, you get irritated. And ideological wavering in the satellites would be bad news. Who are the satellite towns, anyway? Only the best fighters in Russia ... 'Just as long as we're fed, we'll give anyone a thrashing ... Just whistle for us, Central Committee, just give us the word – "Comrades, stand to!" But we can't do nothing if there's nothing to eat, Comrade Central Committee. The satellite towns are your support, Father Central Committee, and there you go feeding that rotten whore, Moscow. And even round Moscow you can't always find any vodka to top up your tank.'

Our Avdotiya made her escape. And she saved her little bag too ... Avdotiya's lived a long time on this earth, she knows a thing or two. It's not the truth she seeks, just groceries. But this day's not going to go according to plan. She called into a delicatessen. Quiet, calm, the air's clean and the counters are neat and empty. Could at least have put something on them, for appearance's sake. Even if it was only a bone for a dog. The salesgirl sits there with her cheek propped up in her hand. People come in, swear and spit. But our Avdotiya went in and stood there, taking a pause for breath, then asked:

'Have you got any nice fresh fillet steak, love? Or some nice tender sirloin?'

'I think you're in the wrong place, granny,' the salesgirl answered. 'It's not a delicatessen you need, it's a doctor ... Can't you see what's on the counter?'

Our Avdotiya didn't take offence.

'Thanks for the advice,' she said.

Off she goes to another delicatessen, and when she goes in — there's something there! She snatched a pair of kidneys from right under the nose of some dim-wit. The kidneys were lying on a dish in damp isolation, like anatomical specimens, and the dim-wit was perusing them and sniffing them. Taking off his glasses and putting them back on again, Avdotiya dashed across to the cash-desk and paid for the kidneys.

'That's not right,' cried the intellectual. 'I was first.'

'You were sniffing them, but granny here paid,' answered the sales assistant.

'Have you got any more?'

'There aren't any more ... Why don't you buy some of the special, we don't have it very often.'

The intellectual took a look — he couldn't make out what it was. He read the label: 'Egg with Caviare'. He took a closer look — yes, it was a hard-boiled egg, not fresh, cut in two halves. And the sulphurous yoke was dotted with black sparrow droppings.

'Where's the caviare?'

'That's as much as there's supposed to be. Thirty grams. What d'you expect for that price?'

The price is one for which, in the days of Khrushchevian voluntarism, on the eve of the historical Plenum of October 1964, which set a fundamentally new direction for the development of agriculture, you could have bought two hundred grams of good caviare in any ordinary delicatessen. Swift is Russia's flight, as though the dogs were barking at her heels . . . But where are we going in such a hurry? Why not sit down and catch our breath, think things over and wipe the sweat from our brow? Just you try suggesting it. The political commentators will laugh you to scorn.

So this is the life of Avdotiya, the little old grocery-store granny without any personal history. She's adapted to it. If a political commentator peers out from her little television, he'll see her regaling herself on kidneys. The commentator's face twists and warps, and his voice roars distortedly, because her television's been out of order for ages. But what can she do about it? They've forbidden the consumption of caviare and freshly smoked sausage, but at least they still let you chew on kidneys. And there's other food that hasn't been totally requisitioned yet. Russia's abundance is unlimited. In one place they queue for Indian tea, in another they queue for Bulgarian eggs, in yet another they queue for Romanian tomatoes. Just stand there for a while and you get them.

Our Avdotiya went into the milk shop. That calm and pacific food product, milk – the non-alcoholic drink. Children drink it, and people on strict diets. Sometimes the queues in here are calm too. But not today, when they're selling prepacked Finnish butter . . .

Avdotiya goes in and listens: the queue's buzzing like a circular saw that hits a stone when it's running at full speed . . . The queue's face is hyper-tense, white with red blotches. A real blood-and-milk complexion . . . Avdotiya pushes in backwards, following her backside into the Tatar's shop, where the manager is a Tatar and his wife sells fruit juice . . .

The Tatars are under siege by plundering hordes from the Ukrainian steppes . . . Makhno's anarchists . . . All in the same uniform – neck-scarves and double-breasted fur-trimmed plush jackets. Beefy scarlet hands, crimson faces and garlic breath . . . But then, just recently even Russians – especially militiamen for some reason – have garlic breath . . . Maybe it's the sausage, maybe they try to camouflage the rotten ingredients with garlic . . .

The anarchists shout at each other:

'Teklia, ver's Tern?'

'Gonfa shampayn viz Gorpyna.'

While the satellites plunder the basic products, Makhno's warriors plunder the luxury goods. They bring their sacks of pumpkin seeds or early pears to the market, stuff the sacks full of money, and then fill the sacks up with expensive delicacies.

There's Gorpyna helping Teklia hoist a sack full of champagne on to his shoulders. There's Tern clutching rucksacks bulging with bars and boxes of chocolates in both hands. It brings back memories of the old partisan gun-carts with their axles greased with tar, loaded high with plundered landlords' property. But this is a different kind of pillage. Inspired not by Bakunin, but by Marx. Goods-money-goods . . .

The Soviet shop is an object-lesson in the history and economy of the state – and in politics and morals and social relations . . .

'How much they giving?'

'Still won't be enough for everyone . . .'

'Two kilos each . . .'

'You in the queue?'

'Nah, I'm standing here for the good of my health.'

'What?'

'Sod off . . .'

You can add a few more words in your own language if you like. Everyone gets the message. But a foreigner in Russia is a privileged individual. He can sod off to the foreign currency shop, Beriozka, or the Central Market. The Central Market abounds in high-quality food-stuffs and foreign cars. Our country is quite capable of producing sun-soaked tomatoes and cool-scented cucumbers, dessert pears with sweet oily flesh and aromatic peaches so lovely they serve to decorate a festive table as well as any flowers. Our country is quite capable of spreading its counters with the delicate yellowish-white carcasses of geese, ducks, chickens and turkeys. Mounds of fresh meat. Lumps of unsalted, mouth-watering bacon fat, spicy fish, rich whitish-creamy cottage cheese, thick soured cream . . . Here at the Central Market, it's still NEP, here there is no continuous advance towards Communism, no overfulfilment of the plan, no grandiose space flights, no struggle for peace . . .

The Central Market is a nice place . . .

But where's our Avdotiya got to? We've completely lost sight of her . . . There she is, in an itinerant queue – there are some like that. A shop-porter in a blue overall is dragging along a trolley, and on the trolley there are foreign cardboard boxes. No one knows what's in the boxes, but a queue forms anyway and runs after the trolley. New people keep on joining. Avdotiya's somewhere in the first third of this long-distance queue . . . She should get some . . .

Her grey hair is soaking wet and itchy under her headscarf, her heart is in her mouth, her stomach is squashing her bladder, and there's a rasping ache from her liver somewhere in the small of her back. But she mustn't fall behind. Fall behind and you lose your place in the queue. The shop-porter is hung over, and he wants to clear his head with a breath of fresh air, so he drags the trolley along without stopping. Someone in the queue, worn out, says:

'Can't you stop for a bit, we're tired, start selling the stuff . . .'

The woman from the retail organization, following behind the trolley with her fat backside and short dirty overall, tells them:

'You make any fuss, and I won't sell anything.'

The queue rounded on the timid rebel and put him in his place.

'If you don't like it, go home and cool off . . . What a fine gentleman – can't even stand a walk in the fresh air! They know better than us where they're supposed to sell the stuff. Maybe they have orders from the boss.'

Our Avdotiya runs on after the others. The drunken porter deliberately swings to and fro. Over towards the tram-stop, then back towards the bus-stop . . . And the woman with the fat backside is laughing . . . She's been drinking too . . . They're just taunting everybody, the monsters . . .

In the present state structure they share direct power over the people with local militia inspectors, house managers and other folk in state service ... Once Avdotiya turned up in tears at the Mosenergo electricity supply office, where she'd been directed by some kind people. The girls working there, still young and unspoiled, asked her.

'Why're you crying, granny?'

'I haven't got the paper to pay the electricity. They say they'll cut off the electricity. What'll I do without electricity? I can't cook or wash in the dark.' She held out her old payment book, all used up – a kind neighbour had been filling it out for her.

'Ah, your payment book's finished. Here, have a new one.'

They gave her a brand new one, and didn't take a kopeck. How our Avdotiya thanked them, what good health she wished them. And how many times she must have been mocked and taunted in various offices to feel such fear of public servants! But these girls were better than servants, they were real providers!

Avdotiya runs on, although she already has black spots in front of her eyes. The porter turns this way, the porter turns that way. And whichever way he turns, the queue follows him, like a tail. On one steep turn the engineer Fishelevich dropped out of the queue with a clanking of yoghurt bottles and a crunching of bones. Couldn't stand the pace. But the rest stick with it, even though their strength's almost gone. Then luckily the porter tried to be too clever, turned too sharply, and the cardboard boxes tumbled off right in the middle of the pavement ... A few burst, and egg white and yolk came running out.

The queue was delighted – they were going to get eggs. They felt better already. Something they needed, and they didn't have to run after it any more. The queue stood there, breathing heavily, resting while the porter and the woman with the fat backside conferred in obscene language. Volunteers were even found to carry the boxes from the middle of the pavement over to the wall of the building. Selling began ...

The Russian heart and the Russified heart are easily appeased ...

Difficulties and injuries are quickly forgotten – too quickly forgotten.

Following the catastrophe, the porter and the woman with the fat backside have decided in consultation that at the workers' request they will allow each customer ten whole eggs and ten cracked ones . . . And instead of calling them 'table eggs', they will dub them 'dietary eggs' and increase the price shown on the label. But at the same time they will give out polythene bags free of charge. Good. Our Avdotiya took her ten whole eggs in one polythene bag and her ten cracked ones in another, paid the new price, put everything in her little bag and went away happy.

She called into the bakery and bought some bread half a black loaf and a long white one. No queuing for bread in Moscow yet. If there's ever a queue for bread, it will mean the beginning of a new stage of advanced socialism. In pursuit of the struggle against cosmopolitanism they'll ban the consumption of American, Canadian, Argentinian and other grain. For the time being, however, this question remains in the province of peaceful coexistence. International flour bakes good bread. A bit of meat to go with it would be good, too. Since she didn't get any nice young chicken, a little bit of meat would do nicely . . . And there's the meat shop, right there in front of our Avdotiya. The meat shop's buzzing, the meat shop's humming. And that means they're selling. Our Avdotiya goes inside.

The queue's far from small, but it's not unruly. Meat queues are usually some of the most violent. Maybe it's the smell that transports people back to the times of our ancestors, when the leaders of various caves fought each other for a prime cut of mammoth sirloin? A human being can turn wild as easy as drinking a glass of beer . . .

Those are the kind of thoughts that come to you in a Moscow meat queue, as your nostrils are assailed by the smell of tormented flesh. Our Avdotiya began sniffing, too, our toothless predator. She spotted something . . . that little piece lying over there . . . not too big, not too small . . . Ah, if she could just get that one . . . Our Avdotiya would pamper it like a child, wash it first in cold, cold water, then in lukewarm water, clean out all the little bits of tough tissue and tendons, cut out the marrow-bone to make a bit of soup. And she'd use the soft meat for a nice matching set of cutlets, like twins. She could try begging the queue for that piece in the name of Christ the Lord. The queue didn't look vicious.

Just as she thought that, she took a closer look – and she froze . . . Standing there in the queue is Kudryashova, Avdotiya's old enemy . . . Kudryashova is a hardened bread-winner, the backbone of a large family of voracious children, and our Avdotiya has often beaten her to the goods . . . Kudryashova has sloping shoulders and hands like meat-hooks. Kudryashova can carry two bags for long distances which our Avdotiya wouldn't even be able to lift – as long as the load consists of foodstuffs. And Kudryashova is a fine child-bearer. Her eldest is already in the army, and her youngest is still crawling. Kudryashova is a strong woman, well adapted to queues. She can take on the average male at fisticuffs on equal terms. But when it comes to grabbing – and, as we know, that's sometimes what's required in the retail sector – then our Avdotiya is quicker and smarter than Kudryashova, just as a sparrow is quicker than a crow. One day she might snatch a head of cabbage out of Kudryashova's grasp, another day a ready-wrapped piece of Tambov ham.

'You just wait, you witch,' Kudryashova threatens and abuses her, 'you just wait till I nudge you.'

'And I'll call a policeman,' answers our Avdotiya. 'You and your silly nudging!' But really she's afraid. 'Oh, she's going to nudge me, she is.'

Now seems like the right time to explain what this word 'nudge' means. It comes from an old Slavonic form, the meaning of which is still preserved in a modern Ukrainian word. In modern Russian, it translates as 'to shove', but it's not quite that. A different intonation can change the meaning of a word, so that in usage, if not in grammar, there are actually two words. To shove means to push or to shift someone away from yourself. Sometimes someone who's shoved you will say sorry, beg your pardon. But if they 'nudge' you, there won't be any apology. Because when they nudge someone they try to make sure he gets smashed good and proper.

'Oh,' quailed our little Avdotiya. 'Oh, she's going to nudge me.'

But the queue is calm, not bellicose at all, and Kudryashova is calm. She glowers at Avdotiya out of the corner of her eye, but she doesn't say anything. Why could that be? The reason lies, not in the meat, but in the butcher.

An unusual kind of butcher has appeared at this particular retail outlet. An intellectual butcher, more like a coarse-boned professional surgeon from the common people, with a white cap set on his greying head, firmly moulded, well-fed features and spectacles. The butcher is jolly and cynical, like a surgeon, not gloomy and filthy, like a butcher. He regards the queue as a target for cheerful mockery, not a partner in neurotic altercation. He is superior to the queue. He grabs up the pieces of meat in hands that are huge, but clean, and sets them on the meat tray on the display counter. In response to the queue's murmuring and demands for quick service, he offers a word-perfect rendition of *Eugene Onegin* . . .

'Come on,' grumbles a woman with a tired-looking face, obviously not standing in her first queue of the day, 'get on with it . . . You're here to serve the customers.'

'Chapter two,' the butcher replies:

> The village where our Eugene pined
> Was in itself a charming spot:
> There friends of pleasures less refined
> Might thank the heavens for their lot . . .

A strange picture. One that summons up strange ideas. And leads to unexpected conclusions. The first conclusion is that Pushkin should be read to the meat queue by a butcher and no one else. This, in fact, is the main conclusion, and worth pondering for a while in the stuffy atmosphere of the shop. The butcher may jangle Pushkin's lyre with a cynical and vulgar hand, but he rouses kindly feelings. The crowd is silent – following the final stage direction in *Boris Godunov*. It stands there calm and quiet. Not really listening to

Pushkin, but hearing him. Just let some prominent Pushkin special-
ist or famous actor try reciting Pushkin to a meat queue – they'd be
lucky if jeers were the only response. Vicious hatred would be more
likely. No, culture must be brought to the people by the authorities.
What kind of culture is that, then, and what kind of Pushkin? We
can answer that by approaching the question from a different angle.
By answering a question with a question. Have you ever watched
the sunrise? Not over luxurious tropical greenery which knows all
about the sun, which lives for the sun and anticipates its appearance
with academic certitude. And not over a calm, grassy forest meadow,
which is itself a particle of sunlight, which believes in the sun and
experiences its rising as the most intimate of feelings. We had in
mind sunrise over the lifeless rocky cliffs of the north. What good,
you might ask, is life to the dead? What would the cold rocks want
with the sun? The rocks lie there calmly, ponderously, monoto-
nously in the depths of night, remote under their covering of ice
and snow; the rocks greet the grey light of the brief day with
indifference, their breasts insensitive to the keen blasts of the wind.
But still the sun rises over them. A feeble imitation of the torrid,
fructifying sun or gently caressing sun that we know, a sun which
would strike fear and anguish into the subtropical foliage or the
forest glade. And suddenly the cliffs change. The rocks become
pink, moss and lichen appear, and a rather unprepossessing insect
crawls out of a cleft to join in the brief holiday. Perhaps it is not
even aware of where the light has come from, or why the wind has
died down, or why its indifference to the cold has been replaced by
a new feeling, or rather, sensation, of warmth and calm. But if the
southern sun, or even the mild temperate sun, were to rise over the
northern cliffs, it would mean disaster. The cold rocks would crack,
the lichen would dry out, and the unprepossessing insect would
shrivel up and die. The cold north needs a cold sun.

. . . The butcher picks up the piece of meat in his huge white hands.
A really fine, juicy piece. And a bone like sugar loaf. Our Avdotiya
just can't believe her eyes. What happiness!

'Happy holiday!' She says that to flatter the butcher, so he won't change his mind.

'Thank you very much,' replies the butcher, 'which holiday's that? State holiday or Church holiday?'

The murmuring fades away. The people are in a good mood, even though the queue is cramped. And when people are relaxed, awareness follows.

'It's tough enough for us,' someone says, 'but what about the old folks on their own?'

Avdotiya reaches out for the meat. The butcher doesn't give it to her. Avdotiya begins to get really worried. But she needn't.

'Allow me to put it in your bag for you,' says the butcher.

With the meat already in the bag, Avdotiya, happy, turned to go, but the butcher called after her:

'Thank you for your custom.'

'God grant you good health,' answers our Avdotiya.

Avdotiya has gone outside and she walks along with a smile on her face. She goes round the corner, takes the piece of meat out of her bag, jogs it up and down like a child, kisses it. Some nice young chicken might be better, but Avdotiya doesn't have any chicken, she didn't get any, and this meat is all her own. Our Avdotiya's day started badly, but it's turned out well. While she's in luck, she might as well make the best of it. Avdotiya decides to visit a shop a long way away, one she rarely goes to. 'Never mind, there's a little bench on the way, I'll sit down for a bit and then go on. Maybe I'll pick something up . . .'

Our Avdotiya sets off. She walks, rests, walks on again. Then suddenly she sees a fool coming towards her. She knows his face to look at, but not his name.

This fool was no longer young. His head got badly sunburned, so he always wore a cap. This sharp-nosed fool travelled around on public transport and cut silhouettes of people out of paper. They caught a good likeness, but they cost money. At one time, the fool used to work as an artist in a tannery. Then one day, instead of the slogan 'We shall fulfil the five-year plan in four years', he wrote

'We shall fulfil the five-year plan in six years'. What could he have been thinking of? But then, the fool's own brother, a colonel and a hero – medals, four-room flat, honoured veteran of the Great Patriotic War – suddenly announced one day in public that, 'Today, by order of the Supreme Commander-in-Chief, comrade Stalin, snow fell in the city.' And at that time, not only was comrade Stalin no longer in this world, he wasn't even in the mausoleum. How could he have ordered the snow? They thought it was a poor joke from the colonel, but they looked closer and saw he was quite sincere, and there was an unhealthy gleam in his eyes. In short – bad genes. Maybe that was it, and the fool was just a fool. But they do say that in a spot well away from his own district, where he wasn't known so well, the colonel's younger brother approached the very jaws of a raging, bloodthirsty, hours-long queue standing in the baking sun beside a kiosk where they were selling early strawberries, and said: 'In the name of the Supreme Soviet of the USSR I request you to serve me three kilograms of strawberries.' And he held up his right hand, palm forwards. There was nothing in his hand, but the people obeyed him, and he got his three kilograms of strawberries . . . There's a fine fool for you . . .

The fool sees our Avdotiya and says:

'Granny, they're selling Soviet sausage in store number 15 . . . And there's no one in there.'

A man walking beside him overhears and says:

'What a load of nonsense . . . All our sausage is Soviet, we don't have any Jewish sausage here.'

'Fine tasty sausage,' answers the fool, 'smells real good. Haven't seen any like it for ages.'

'He's not right in the head,' Avdotiya whispered to the man, tapping her own headscarf.

'Ah.' The anti-Semite understood and went on his way.

Store number 15 was the one Avdotiya was going to. The shop is as long and narrow as a hose-pipe and too filthy for words. The sales assistants are all dirty, crumpled and unkempt, standing behind the counter looking like they're just out of bed and they had vodka instead of coffee for breakfast. The cashier is drunk too, and so is the customer she's facing. They babble at each other, but they can't come to any understanding. She speaks in Ryazan dialect, and he speaks in Yaroslavl dialect. All the shop-porters have tattoos on their bony arms and their sunken, alcohol-corroded chests . . . One has Stalin tucked away in his bosom, peeking out from behind a dirty vest as if it were a curtain, another has a grinning eagle, and a third has a maritime chest – a sailor with the inscription 'Port Arthur'.

Avdotiya knew all about this shop, and she rarely came here. But here she is today. Avdotiya goes in, looking round her, sees the picture described above, and feels like backing out. But then she glanced into the far corner, with the 'Delicatessen' sign. She glanced, and she couldn't believe her eyes. The fool had been telling the truth. Lying there on the counter was beautiful sausage, such as Avdotiya hadn't even thought of in an age. Firm as dark-red marble, with a white patterning of firm pork fat, but you could see at a glance it would taste juicy.

A miracle, that's what it was. How had several cases of Party-standard smoked delicatessen sausage turned up here, as though they'd come straight out of the stocks in the Kremlin? And why hadn't the shop staff plundered it all themselves? They must have been really drunk to put it on sale. And the label hanging there said 'Soviet Sausage'. The fool hadn't been lying. This was prime meat – pork and beef – and it smelt of Madeira . . . The closer Avdotiya came, the stronger the smell was. If you sliced it fine and put it on bread, you could dine on it in fine style, breakfast and supper, for a long time.

There was once a time when Avdotiya didn't take her supper alone. When there was a steaming samovar of pure gold, and Filippov's breadrolls. He was handsome. And Avdotiya had a long tawny braid. It was 1925 – no, 1923. Half a pound of sausage in a crackling paper bag. The sausage had a different name then, but it was the same one . . . When he brought it he'd say: 'Try this, Avdotiya Titovna. It's made with Madeira.' And he used to bring a little piece of smoked sturgeon . . . 'Try a bit,' he used to say.

'Right then, old girl,' the drunken, unkempt salesgirl behind the counter says to Avdotiya, 'you buying any sausage? Be another ten years before you can get sausage like that.'

But Avdotiya doesn't answer. There's a lump in her throat. 'Which one d'you want?' asks the salesgirl. 'How about this one?' And she lifts up a fine firm stick of smoked sausage. But Avdotiya can't see, her eyes are full of tears.

'What you cryin' for?' asks the salesgirl. 'Son-in-law thrown you out, has he?'

'I haven't got a son-in-law,' Avdotiya scarcely manages to answer, and she sobs and sobs.

'Must've 'ad something stolen,' suggested the porter with the maritime chest. 'You 'ad something stolen, old girl?'

'Yes, stolen,' Avdotiya answers through her tears.

'Was it you, Mikita?' The question is aimed at the one with Stalin peeping out from behind the curtain of his vest . . .

'Never even laid eyes on 'er,' answers Mikita. 'Only thing you could steal from an old crow like that is 'er piles.'

'Stolen,' says Avdotiya, and the tears keep on pouring down . . . It's a long time since she's cried like that.

'If you've 'ad something stolen, go to the militia, don't stop the shop working,' says the salesgirl, and puts the stick of sausage on the scales to weigh it for the anti-Semite. He must have changed his mind and decided to believe the fool. More and more people keep turning up. The fool has done a good job spreading the word about the Soviet sausage.

Indeed, Soviet sausage really deserves a special mention of its own. Together with orange queues, sausage queues form the main axis of the trade war between the state and the people.

We haven't stood in any genuine sausage or orange queues, because our Avdotiya avoids them. Avdotiya's cunning, so are the satelliters. And Makhno's Ukrainians are rarely seen in these queues, which are found more often in the outlying areas of the city, where they might suddenly start selling goods in short supply. So who does stand and fight in these queues? The railway stations. And who are the railway stations? They are the USSR itself. But the USSR only queues for oranges very unwillingly. Instead of apples and pears, the USSR grows an abundance of 'Kalashnikov' automatic rifles. And the Third World grows oranges. A natural exchange, beyond the bounds of Marx's *Capital*. The orange is an alien, unfamiliar fruit. Bitter and sour, it sets the USSR belching. The orange isn't a really serious fruit – it doesn't go with vodka. It's only good for the kids to suck on. But sausage is a different matter altogether . . .

The sausage shops of Moscow are filled with the spirit of the railway stations, with their stuffy atmosphere. You have the feeling that any moment your head will be set spinning by a barked announcement: 'Attention, boarding is beginning for train number . . .'

And then the trains will set out directly from the sausage shops for the Urals, Tashkent, Novosibirsk, Kishinev . . . The railway station people are not violent. The satellite towns are cunning, but the stations are patient. Cunning is elastic, but patience is strong as iron . . . Iron knows how to wait. And iron has its own reasons. It knows how far which products can be transported. After all, education has made great strides in the USSR, and the queues have a high percentage of educated people – there are engineers standing there, physicists and chemists. Standing there and calculating . . . Meat and butter will travel as far as Gorky. But meat goes bad before it reaches Kazan, while boiled sausage survives. You can carry smoked foods, tea and tinned foods out beyond the Urals. And those oranges to amuse the kids. But nothing's better than genuine smoked sausage. So the iron stands and waits patiently. The USSR queues up for smoked sausage. 'Ah, my lovely, wouldn't you be just fine with a bit of bread and butter, like in the good old days.'

Avdotiya came to her senses.

'I'm first,' she yells. 'I was first in the queue.'

Useless. They brushed her aside. Avdotiya got angry. She got really angry. 'People nowadays are no better than scavengers, people nowadays are just rotten swindlers.' Our Avdotiya got really carried away in her resentment. Her scarf slipped off her head. She bruised her fist on someone. She bruised her elbow on someone else. Avdotiya even heaved and strained and tried to 'nudge' someone. But then she got nudged herself. Some man nudged her with his backside, without even bothering to turn around. And his backside was a progressive, Young-Communist-League, reinforced-concrete backside.

Avdotiya came to in hospital. She came to and her first thought was for her little bag.

'Where's my bag?'

'What bag?' asks the nurse. 'You'd do better to worry about whether your bones will knit. Old bones are brittle.'

But Avdotiya mourns and can't be comforted.

'There was some meat in it, and three tins of herrings, and bread, and two lots of eggs . . . but most of all I want the bag back . . .'

The engineer Fishelevich was a patient in the same hospital. Hospital is like jail – people get to know each other quickly.

'Yury Semyonovich.'

'Avdotiya Titovna.'

'What's wrong with you, Avdotiya Titovna?'

'I got nudged.'

'What kind of illness is that?' Fishelevich asked ironically. 'Now I, for instance, have a fracture of the right arm.'

Avdotiya took a close look.

'That's right,' she said, 'they shoved you out of the queue on the right. I remember that. But don't you be upset. Going without eggs isn't nearly as bad as going without sausage.'

One of the other patients there was an Honoured Teacher with a fracture of the pelvis. She tried to make them both feel ashamed:

'How can the two of you tell stories like that?'

'What stories?' asks Avdotiya. 'It's all God's truth. Bulgarian eggs and Soviet sausage.'

'And now you've decided to tell anti-Soviet jokes about the Warsaw Pact!' The teacher is indignant and rebukes them even more firmly, especially Fishelevich. She shames him with the official line on the Jewish question, and vows to carry out her civic duty.

'Wait, please,' says Fishelevich, scared, and he takes out from his locker a thick book in a brown binding. He has been reading this book a lot, and everyone thought he was reading a novel.

'Here,' says Fishelevich. 'It says that "Soviet" sausage is rightfully regarded as one of the finest of smoked delicatessen sausages. Its meat filling, prepared from top-quality lean pork and beef, is mixed with finely diced pork fat, which forms an attractive pattern when it is sliced. The taste and aroma of "Soviet" sausage are enhanced with cognac or Madeira and spices. It is recommended that the sausage be cut thinly, in almost transparent slices.'

After that Fishelevich often read aloud from the book. The patients learned a lot of things they didn't know before. About cervelat and layered sausage, and about fish soup made with sterlet, which is best served with cabbage pie – a piece of the boiled fish may be served in the dish with the soup.

'Are you fond of fish, Avdotiya Titovna?'

'Yes, I am.'

This reading matter gave the teacher a fever, and she stopped coming out of her ward. But Avdotiya just listened and lapped it up. 'Ah, if I could just get all that in my little bag!' Her little bag was her provider and her closest friend. She dreamed about it at night several times. How could she take another bag with her on her round of the queues? Avdotiya grieved and mourned.

Then one day the nurse said:

'Rodionova, there's a package for you.'

Rodionova is our Avdotiya's surname. Avdotiya looked, and saw her little bag . . . She looked again – it really was her little bag, she wasn't dreaming . . . No meat, of course, and no eggs, and only one of the three tins of herring. But someone had put in a bottle of yoghurt, a bag of honey-cakes and about a kilogram of apples . . .

How little old Avdotiya stroked and cuddled her little Daisy-Cow . . . And then she suddenly thought – who could have brought the package? Avdotiya had no one at all. She reached into the bag and there was a note in the bottom in clumsy handwriting: 'Eat and drink, granny, get well soon.' And a signature – 'Terenty'. What Terenty?

Terenty was, in fact, the shop-porter with the maritime tattoos, the one with 'Port Arthur' on his chest.

Which just goes to show that even in the very darkest of souls, the spark of God's light has not been totally extinguished. In this lies our only hope.

Translated by Andrew Bromfield

An Individualist's Notebook

This old, battered notebook was found beside a rubbish-tip by one Ivan Ilyich Puzankov, a nightwatchman. He would've used it to wrap fish in, but in his drunken state he began to read it. By the time he'd read a few pages, he was gasping, convinced the DTs were upon him. Actually, what alarmed him most was the fact that he wouldn't be able to drink any more vodka, though he was still 200 grams short of his regular litre. However, fiercely adjudging that us proletarians had never yet been beaten, Ivan Ilyich crawled off regardless to the nearest beer-bar. There he sold this improbable notebook for a half-pint of beer and some sprats to a shifty-eyed, sick-looking intellectual, who preserved it in spider-webs and incomprehensibility.

The Individualist's Notebook

All right, so I'm a nasty piece of work. Yes, and I'm all the nastier for writing about this so lovingly; I'm cursing myself – useless bugger, demented halfwit, you want a good thump – but I'm in love just the same! And how! In seventh heaven.

Still, it's a bit off, loving yourself that way . . . Especially after all that's happened . . . oh, yes, that was quite something! Actually it all started from the fact that it wasn't myself I loved, but her. That's truly amazing – loving another human being. Deep down in your benighted soul, unburdened by gravity and the terrors of egoism, to feel so light, just so light, and somehow ennobled. Yes, I'd confer that on anyone in love – a title of nobility.

She was an extremely high-class girl; infernal to a degree, poetical and given to sleepwalking. I loved her passionately, but in a sad sort of way. I would hug her to myself, gaze into those soft eyes of hers with a kind of piercing madman's stare, and she would cry. She cried because the expression in my eyes was decidedly not of this world. And anything that wasn't of this world would call forth streams of tears. She didn't cry like other people, either, but in some unearthly fashion; it wasn't tears she wept, but thoughts; she would start thinking, she'd drift off somewhere, and tears would flow at the mere touch of her despairing thoughts.

She was a very nervous person. Which of course was just what I needed. At nights I would kiss her lonely, cold feet, and whisper nightmares to her. I would stroke her translucent skin, in its softness also not of this world, pierce her flesh . . . and murmur, murmur . . . of my terrors, of my profound despair at living among people, of death. I spent the entire honeymoon telling her about death. I spoke metaphysically, with little yawning abysses, with awesome, sinister pauses, when everything would come to a stand-still; and prostrating myself before her beautiful, naked, inaccessibly mystical feet, I would howl in a shrill voice, begging her to save me from my fears, from life, from death . . . Poor little creature, how could she endure all this!

All the pus, all the paranoid ulcers of my miserable soul I spilled out before her eyes, in ecstasy, squealing, riven with anguish. And this I called true love. Yes, that's how we loved one another, whole days on end wandering our locked rooms, alone with our nightmare, and the dark, taciturn sky, watching us through the windows.

Zina was quite often silent, becoming ever more wrapped up in herself. For my part, I would whimper, and look at her, and construct entire worlds. She was frightened of my worlds, and appeared to weep for them. Actually, in her own way she was quite abnormally schizoid, and could take the simplest, most trivial phrase and play around with it, construct a whole 'world', then go off into it and hide. But she'd have had to fly some to keep up with me, oh yes, sir! Anyway, that's how we looked at one another, lonely, dishevelled, each from our own worlds, singing our secret stories. We lived on our nerves, on our nerves, yes, the whole time!

You think we didn't sign up at the Registry Office, go through the formalities, get our names down ...? I'm supposed to be a mystic, so there was none of that? Oh, there was, there was, all of it. The Registry Office, the idiotic wedding, with the idiotic relatives and the potato salad, and even 'Let's have a kiss, then!' ... Actually, the way I felt, it was as if somebody else'd got married off, not me ... That lot had nothing to do with me ... And my bride seemed to me like a fairy-tale creature, descended from her celestial abode, while all around us were nothing but swines and mongrels ... That's why the impression I'm left with of our wedding is of one long grunt. I took an instant dislike to her parents, hated them with a fierce animosity, for the very reason that through Zina, these creatures had had the audacity to become my equals.

I must say that if there's one thing I can't stand it's ordinary people, who make up 90 per cent of the world. I'm ready to bet that any murderer, pervert or alcoholic is better and more noble than your average man ... At least there might be some repentance and fear in a criminal's miserable soul, and a drop of sweat on his brow, from some sort of feeling, but your ordinary person doesn't even have that much – he's a speaking machine, anti-spiritual, pathologically stupid, and regarded as possessing sound good sense. But in comparison with him, any cretin with so much as a smidgen of originality is a veritable philosopher. Just take a look at the eyes of your average man, see what's there: a cycle of ideas, fixed forever, locked up in their own bestial stupidity, and a total absence of the higher emotions. As far as your average man is concerned, first place in the hierarchy of values is occupied by the thing, the material object, the money, but not the idea, not the feeling, and never a nasty whiff of repentance ...

And why is that? It's because the ordinary person is too stupid to apprehend the spiritual and in order to bolster himself, he's forced to cling to externals, and set a higher value on material evidence of whatever kind, or worse still – to some sort of intellectual folly, assuming our ordinary person should suddenly latch on to an idea.

Her family conformed exactly to that familiar plan. Even in terms of his personality, her brother was pathological with it. An extremely uptight, niggardly young man, he denied himself all pleasure except hoarding money. I remember one evening, after he'd munched his way through a crust of black bread and an onion, he delved into his suitcase and drew out a huge wad of notes, and began stroking them ecstatically, drooling, pressing them to his heart and mumbling, 'This is the only thing that makes me feel like an intellectual.'

He needed money not in order to spend it, but to feel like a human being, to give him self-esteem, and he placed money above everything else in life. He actually had an attack of nerves once, seriously, when he heard somewhere that Churchill used to read Shakespeare.

'How can a great man be bothered with rubbish like that?' he declared, blenching. Yes, that came as a real blow to him, psychologically.

He had absolutely no faith in poetry, or painting, or religion, all of which he considered mere fancy. He was sincerely convinced that people not only don't believe in God, but never have done, and that the sort of person who might believe in God, in idealism, in poetry, simply didn't exist, and anything that had been written in books about such a person was mere propaganda.

'How can you prefer the invisible to the visible?' he would say.

His parents, well-off engineers, were just as stupid, but not quite so pathological.

In the beginning, when I was still at the courtship stage with Zina, I was very quiet and withdrawn, so that they took me for just an excessively shy and tongue-tied young man, but in general pleasant enough. Anyway, they made no objection to the marriage. However, two days after the wedding, I showed my true colours. We were staying at her place to begin with, so everything was out in the open. My guiding principle was to go my own way, but not to object verbally; on the contrary, to agree with everybody and appear, at least superficially, to be going *their* way. That was essential: physically, I couldn't bring myself to talk with them, let alone argue. I felt crushed and humiliated as it was, on a par with some sort of idiotic, useless, material substance, sitting with them at the same table, compelled to listen to them. My nerves were in a terrible state.

'Sasha (that's what they call me) – Sasha says he's really house-proud, and he's going to help us look after the dacha,' Zina's mother shouted to the whole kitchen.

But every Saturday I ducked out of socializing with them, preferring to go off into my own world. I mean, my own little worlds I practically worshipped, feasted my eyes on them, and they were as close and as dear to me as my own body . . . And I stewed in their juice, as if in my own blood, and didn't like people touching them . . .

However, her parents soon saw through me. I remember lonely evenings drinking tea, when the whole family was assembled. The dead lamp with its dark-blue shade had a certain wisdom and individuality, compared with these commonplace persons seated around the table, who were in no way worse than anyone else.

While I said nothing to them about anything, I could feel an inexpressible delicacy and tenderness in my heart. My thoughts were sentimental, otherworldly, and able, it would seem, to raise the dead.

'Sasha, why don't you go down to the dacha, why don't you buy cutlets, why don't you learn some poems?' Zina's mother asks me, tentatively.

'I'll definitely do all that on Saturday,' I reply, calmly and imperturbably.

But inside I'm beginning to feel sick because they're looking at me as at another human being, their equal.

'Why can't they sense my singularity?' I'm thinking, 'Can I be ordinary!? Actually, when I answer them, I become ordinary. It's terrible.'

'But it's the same every time, you always promise to do everything on Saturday,' says Zina's mother, impassively. 'That's four months gone by already, and you haven't done a thing.'

Her eyes are watering with malice. Zina's father looks as if he's dreaming he's at an official reception. I say nothing. They're struck by my otherworldliness. They can't define it in words, they're lost in conjecture, but they *can* sense a vague something. And they find that so scary that Zina's brother drops a slice of bread on the floor.

'Maybe you think you're cleverer than us?' her mother asks me, coldly.

Again I respond with some nonsense or other, which makes the whole situation even more sepulchral.

'Maybe you'd like to speak to him?' they ask my Zina.

Defensive tears, however, well up in her eyes . . .

Yes, there were quite a few jolly evenings of that sort.

Poor Zina – she loved her parents unthinkingly – had to flap around between me and them. I found it difficult to control her during the day (they kept confusing her with their common sense), but at nights, and whenever we were left alone *tête-à-tête*, I was her lord and master. At that point my worlds went into action. In the end, in order to shut myself off from her parents, I decided to answer all their questions with my own made-up words, so that they could understand nothing, and were horrified. 'With a ring of other-speech, I shall auto-partition myself from external cretins.' I would tee-hee then in my mind.

So now if they tried to elicit from me whether I loved Zina, I would answer, 'Yip-yap-yoof-woof.' And if, for instance, they were to ask me why I didn't think much of some fashionable actor, I would say, 'Ribble-fribble-cribble.' And if they got all angry and neurotic, reflecting on my assertion that the moon was hollow, I would respond monosyllabically, 'Moo.' To each question, I would have a different reaction.

The funniest thing was that they thought I was just acting the goat. Anyway, that couldn't go on, and I started whining to Zina at nights, that we should move out to my place. She knew perfectly well what I was up to, and reckoned I was still treating her parents fairly decently. She couldn't stand the idea of moving into my filthy, solitary rooms, crammed with prehistoric furniture, like something out of touch with this life. But she knew she would find tenderness there. Tenderness, which fogs the mind, and which can perhaps even be transformed into torment, into torture; tenderness, which hung poised over our unfathomable fear . . . We moved into my flat . . .

And I was absolutely fine there, at peace, out of touch . . . And I opened up before my darling wife genuinely, truthfully, the whole way . . . 'Isolation, separation,' I used to squeal in her earhole at nights. But she started having nightmares, and I loved to watch her having them. My nose for such things was quite extraordinary; the minute a nightmare presented itself to her in her sleep, I would ease myself awake, jump up on the bed, without waking her, light a little candle (stored for the purpose in my bedside table) and sit calmly and pleasurably gazing at her face. Her face was extremely expressive; white and tender, quivering slightly, as if there were snakes crawling underneath the skin. She was obviously frightened . . . Later, when it was all over, I would waken Zina and begin whispering transitions, mysterious dreams to her, inflaming in her a pathological pity for myself, and then violently take her.

In the agony, the drama of the sexual act, I sought a release and a refuge from those Higher Powers, which created us against our will. During all those minutes, my thoughts and words, directed at Zina, were the creations of the Spirit in its most mysterious, and stark-naked intimacy.

'Complication, copulation,' I now squealed in her ear. In the mounting squal of the sexual act I could force her to see the entire life of man, fragile and doomed, like sperm itself, vile, decaying, in its rising, its clinging passionately to delicious pleasure, and its fall into nothingness. I made her imagine that the sweat of voluptuousness was the sweat of death, and that the exhausted end of the sexual act was also the symbolic end of our human life, a life just as ill-begotten and as doomed to speedy extinction, as an eruption of semen.

Finally, she would get into such a state that she would kiss the residual splashes of my sperm, tenderly, achingly, murmuring that they were the tears of a broken life. 'I'll drink deep, deep,' she would moan ecstatically.

And all these little acts I made her carry out in profound secrecy, by candle-light, under the blanket, like something deeply vile, yet intensely intimate and personal.

And when we weren't shuddering in physical tremor, but lying serenely contented, in spiritual vein, do you imagine that we were any less wrecked?! Absolutely not. It was just how we saw it. After all, our condition was one of peace, a state of the mind, as if we had no bodies.

Indeed, we had no bodies, but we did have eyes . . . And naturally, she cried a lot. She used to rush around my solitary, schizophrenic rooms, where every stain frightened her, and seemed like an entire world. Moreover, I used to starve her. Hunger, of course, tends to enhance the body's otherworldliness and fragility; it calls forth torrents of whimsical sublimations, wonderful desires. I mean, no thinking person will ever admit to being hungry; instead they think, I'm missing something, something obscure and mysterious. That's how I was able to awaken her higher faculties. Spirituality, spirituality – I wanted as much spirituality as possible.

My other method consisted of arousing her fear of death; for my own part, I have a pathological dread of death, to the point of convulsions, and I reckon that the Creator still owes me an answer, on bended knees, as to why I'm so festeringly mortal, and like unto die – albeit theoretically – at any minute.

Well, sir, at that point we had various trifling illnesses, she and I, so that we had abundant grounds for our fears, sure enough.

Murmuring sweet nothings to her in the troubled half-light of our room, I would kiss her exquisitely swelling left breast, with its affecting little mole – a place on herself which she too loved, and couldn't look at in the mirror without weeping – and I would say, 'This will die,' clinging with my lips to her blissful throat, I would whisper, 'This too will die,' and achingly, mystically gazing into her eyes, into those pure, unfathomable eyes of hers, I would pronounce, 'And even that which lies behind these lovely eyes, will also die . . .' And she would understand that her soul would perish, her poor, gentle, lost soul, like a little boat on some remote forest pond. Through this constant emphasis on the reality, and at the same time the horror, the absurdity of death, as the ultimate end of the 'I', in tandem with the calculated arousal of unrestrained love for this doomed 'I' of mine – I brought her to a bizarre state of being, like that of a dream, in which someone is holding your hand, but you can't wake up, and never will wake up. Just before the end, her mind on death, as if whipped up by fear, she would start throwing plates, moaning, trying to climb the walls, especially when in my solitude, worn out by the horror of death, seeking an answer to nothing, I hid myself in that dark, cobwebby corner and tearfully kissed my own hands and feet.

Poor little thing, she kept on forgiving me. Out of kindness, I have already said, out of affection. I mean, you must realize that over all the gloom, the pathological terror, the hotchpotch of ideas, lay an unearthly, sickly cast of tenderness. Such tenderness, as unites two people in the death cell. The tenderness in the glance of a man being led through the streets to the guillotine, and who sees amidst the crowd Her – the one who might have been his Only One, and who does not know, and never will know it. And finally that tenderness with which a mother gives her own child poison, in order to save his soul from mortal sin, and to grant him the Kingdom of Heaven.

That's how our days passed, but of course not everyone measures out their life in days – for me, this was one long spiritual outburst, an endless wind, rushing into the Unknown.

Did she understand me? What was in her eyes, enfeebled by the touch of madness? For me, she was what I thought of her, but what did she think of me?

Yet with every drop of my sweat, with every suppurating wound of my neurotic soul, my soiled idealism, I loved and pitied her, seeing in her the living tiny scrap of my 'I', tugged this way and that, arrayed in female garb.

As I stroked the sovereign white skin of her thigh (all the while quietly running to seed), it was as if I was caressing my own heart. I so enjoyed seeing myself outside of me, and at the same time wanted to devour that little blob of my 'I', to absorb it into myself.

However – and here begins the final act of the drama of our relationship – the more I wanted to absorb her, to make her my own, the more I found myself bumping into something hard and impenetrable, as far as I was concerned, some little alien kernel of the spirit. It was something inimical, resilient, some kind of 'not I', from which I was repulsed, and retreated into myself.

Gradually, at first only on certain days, as if I was coming to my senses out of the creative vortex of love, I began to look on her with horror, through other eyes. In her peculiar inclination to domestic comfort, and her yearning for security, I suddenly caught a glimpse of materialism. Not that I myself rejected that, but it began to dawn on me that she attached more than minimal significance to externals. It also became clear that there was a very great deal I could not express to her, and that many, many of my secret wild fantasies sounded much more cosmic in the pristine Solitude of my own soul.

Zina subtly detected my cooling-off, and at first felt a sense of relief: I was no longer tormenting her. She became childishly joyful, like a butterfly, fluttering out of the gloom. And she attached herself even more strongly to me, in gratitude for the peace. There was something strange and wildly unreal in the fact that amid the sepulchral atmosphere of our rooms, the dereliction of our cupboards and armchairs, stored with the tears of my dreams and falls, her animated, idiot voice kept on delightedly twittering, as if she had just been rescued from the abyss within herself and in her beloved.

Yes, at first it was as if my silence – the terrible spectre of the end of love – had resurrected her ... Poor little creature ... She so longed for basic human happiness, and animal warmth ... Why then had she fallen in love with me?

More and more the chief token of our relationship came to be our undimmed scrutiny of one another, over a pot-bellied teacup, and despite the fact that in an environment like ours, the cheery, cosy little teapot looked ever so slightly tinged with madness, Zina was content even with that. Alas, her moment of happiness did not long endure. She began to realize, horror-stricken, that along with the departure of the nightmares and visions, I had also left her – I, whom she loved so much – and that the price of a healthy mind was the end of love. She then became dreadfully, hysterically distressed. I can remember lonely days, inexplicably torn out of the encircling world, when the two of us would be sitting in our apartment in the pure afternoon light, which now divided us more than the most profound darkness; she would rush around the room, wailing: 'Sasha, Sasha, where are you?' And from the lonely sanctuary of my armchair, sitting by her side at the window, I would answer: 'I've gone to my own world.'

And tears of pain, as if they had been wrenched out of her, would burst into her eyes, while I kept coldly and eerily silent: within the forbidden charmed circle of my Solitude, my little world became even more profoundly secret, and dear to me, even sweeter than when I had first discovered it.

With every passing day I withdrew farther and farther from her, and from the surface of life; it could be compared to an invisible flight, a journey into unknown depths; in the beginning, the faint and smoky lineaments of reality were still visible; later, as the motion accelerated, they were glimpsed more and more intermittently, until finally they merged into one far-off, indistinct and hazy outline . . . Where is the world, where is Zina?! She began to strike me as quite commonplace, simple, easily grasped; I caught myself thinking I could see no difference between her, and that tree looking in at us through the window.

Along with the loss of spiritual interest in her, I also lost interest in her flesh; her body began to frighten me: it was – as I recall – very close, and dear to me, and at the same time was becoming remote. At nights, in the confused little world of our apartment, when my night vigils were in full swing, continued out of sheer inertia, tapping my fingers on her naked, transparently white back, I would often find myself wondering if it wasn't the wall I was tapping. Her body was leaving me, going off into the shadowy far reaches of a world not mine.

I tried physically to stimulate myself, yelling: 'Mysteriousness, mysteriousness, let's have more mysteriousness,' and I would place her body, prior to taking it, in various crazy, absurd positions; mystery – yes, that's what was still lacking.

Zina realized it was no longer possible to establish spiritual contact with me, and lapsed into a kind of weak-minded decisiveness; occasionally in a despairing mock-frenzy of kissing, she would suddenly begin biting me, with an insane urgency, as if she wanted to bite through my outer casing, and peer into my soul. Biting, while her eyes cloud over with rapid, fleeing tears. Yes, she understands everything.

Either that, or she would suddenly begin muttering poetry to herself, all jumbled up with her own crazy thoughts, and start to hallucinate, even, as if the entire abyss lay open before her enfeebled eyes.

In this way, pathetically doomed and alone, wholly focused on herself, on her own torments, she would again arouse me, in a disturbing, delicious surge; it seemed as if the spirituality in her had reawakened, and I plunged joyfully into her gentle, evanescent shoulder.

But these were mere hysterical outbursts, scarcely hinting at the full horror of the truth.

I was already aware that I looked on her as upon an object, a teacup, which one can smash, without any movement of the heart.

There was a blank, chilling void in my soul.

In the end I grew intolerably rude to her; communications between us were brutally and crudely severed; I did nothing but yell at her, and only just refrained from beating her; she was quite numb from suffering, and simply went with the flow. Without making either a clean break, or any attempt at rapprochement with her, I became even more obdurate in my selfishness, and did absolutely nothing for her.

But the more roughly I used her, the more tenderly I used myself . . . and that tenderness reached such a pitch that I strove to detach myself wholly from my surroundings, feeling an inexpressible self-pity.

Often, convulsively secluded in my own room, I would sit by the heavy drawn curtains, and with my eyes half-closed, write stories. But in my hand – my snow-white, slender fingers – there was no pen; these wonderful, mysterious, half-created works were composed for myself, in the dumbstruck, the forbidden temple of my soul, half-dreaming, no attempt to pin down my thoughts for a rough draft, since I could understand myself from the merest hint. I loathed all paper, readers, pens, letters, my friends and my enemies both – and on that account I made no notes, preserving everything in the solitary coils of my pure 'I' . . . I savoured voluptuously the very fact that no one, apart from myself, could hear my stories.

Meanwhile, these fragmented, schizophrenic scenes played on. My beloved Zina kept whining, crying because it meant she was a fool, if I didn't want to talk to her. Her parents slammed the doors, and sent for the militia. Meanwhile I kept building my worlds. A soft light played over our rooms, various people's stupid ugly mugs came and went, and my poor little heart composed unheard-of feelings. I felt so much better, so inexplicably, strangely better. And my world grew apace, as they left me in peace.

Zina quite often left me to go back home, but on the other hand, much to my surprise, a strange new visitor started calling on me at nights. I called him Yury Arkadievich. And He would come so quietly, so enigmatically.

I would be lying at nights, under my sweaty, thought-drenched blanket, feeling only the sweetness of existence – the oneness of my body. Then at precisely two a.m., there would be footsteps in the hall – so soft, and mystical, like the movement of a pendulum. And in my wretched soul – in response – a desperate, aching feeling, as if my beloved comes to me from afar . . . I was terribly afraid I would scare Him off. He was so quiet, and not of this world. He would dust off the chair, place a cushion on it for comfort, and sit down. I would say nothing. And there would be such a blinding light in my brain, that it was as if neither England, nor the moon, nor Zina existed, and only Yury Arkadievich and I existed. A total absence of any kind of external reality. Nothing but the reality within, the genuine reality. As in the world beyond.

Yury Arkadievich would be silent at first, metaphysically silent and aloof. His face was remote and distant, like that of an Eastern sage, and He would gaze silently at his hands – so soft and gentle, so white – in mystical contemplation, lightly stroking them, in perfect bliss, in a manner inaccessible to mortals. Undoubtedly, He was very much in love with himself. Then we would sit and talk. He would do most of the talking, while I listened, awestruck.

'Your work's no good, my dear Sasha, no good at all,' He would reproach me. 'Not enough maniacal frenzy. Not cut off enough. No, my dear sir, you're still only *en route* towards God.'

'Which God, Yury Arkadievich?' I timidly enquired.

'Your inner God. The solipsistic one. The one that lurks in our "I", and in no other place. Because there is nothing, except that superior "I".' Yury Arkadievich would smile blissfully. 'And we must discover that God, my dear Sasha, and gradually become Him.'

'And you must urge me on, Yury Arkadievich,' I listened agog. 'Drive me towards that God, please.'

'A little more "I", more "I-ness",' He would sternly answer me. 'You have yet to discover your immortal essence, you are neither the Creator, nor the master of your own world, you simply take refuge in it . . . That's why it's so flawed and unstable. It's still not a world, but only a beginning, a mere drop . . . And you must spit in humanity's ugly mug, yes. Spit in all seriousness, conscientiously.'

And then Yury Arkadievich would be gone. He totally overwhelmed me with his own emanation and solipsism. I could feel they had already crossed all boundaries.

And indeed I well understood that there was much, in both quantity and quality, I had still not achieved, and that Yury Arkadievich was right to urge me on to new horizons. I was still weak, and very young, nervous, and too dependent on external circumstances.

Occasionally, by way of distraction from the solipsistically blinding truth of Yury Arkadievich, I would pose myself a really stupid question: 'Who is He?' Not in essence, of course – I knew that perfectly well – but to outward appearance? Did He exist on the 'hallucination-delirium' plane, or the so-called 'real' one? If on the 'hallucination-delirium', well, then, I would do Him honour, and when He appeared again, fall down and bow at his feet, sir, yes. Because that would mean He had come from the world beyond.

However, He might've been on the 'real' plane, just as in a drug-induced euphoric state I quite often forget everything, talk to passers-by on the street, and sometimes make them a present of my keys. Then I remember nothing about it. So even He could turn out to be one of them.

Anyway, one day I saw Yury Arkadievich in a shop, queuing up for galoshes. He was standing there quietly and patiently, like everybody else, as if He was hiding. And He was showing the solipsistic radiance around his head to no one, the crafty devil.

But that too could have been a 'hallucination'. And in the long run I concluded that the 'hallucination-delirium' plane, and the so-called 'real' one were effectively the same, and it was foolish to try and distinguish them.

Zina has walked out on me for good, I think. Yury Arkadievich scared her stiff. During one of his visits, she spent the night in an adjoining room, heard everything, and screamed wildly a couple of times.

I was left with a certain sadness myself, after a visitation by Yury Arkadievich: I felt downcast, because I was still only *en route* to my internal God, that I was still a weak, snivelling wretch, with too much faith in the reality of my surroundings; I felt that the genuine, solid growth still lay ahead of me, but for the present there were only buds.

Yury Arkadievich could also see this perfectly well, and not wishing to hurry the pace of events, began visiting me less and less often.

Meanwhile life tormented me as before; already I could scarcely appear on the street; I only rarely went out into the kitchen, or the hall; I felt painfully humiliated that I was forced to speak to people, to be with them in the underground, even to stand near them. The very sight of the city, the buses, traffic lights, humiliated me. 'The whole world must dance to my tune, and have no existence in its own right,' I would wail hysterically to myself, caressing my soul.

'Why doesn't anyone notice how great I am?' I howled bitterly into my pillow on one occasion. Yury Arkadievich – I remember it well – appeared on the instant.

'You're praying for recognition from the world, young man,' He said angrily, 'Well, how can you beg recognition from something which itself needs *your* recognition? It's not you that needs to beg the world, but the world that must beg you, for its right to exist.'

In my mind I already understood Him, but these magnificent ideas had yet to reach my skin, tender and cut to pieces as it was by the people who encircled me.

And I would run around collecting things, building castles in the air, making threats, but it was hard for me all the same.

However, I soon found consolation. I can't imagine why I hadn't thought of it before. I have in mind a grave matter, apropos the dear departed. I shall begin with the fact that death entered my soul along with my mother's first kiss – a cruel death, moreover, 'atheistic', a precipice overhanging nothingness.

In my childish dreams and terrors, in the distorted outlines of objects in the darkness – I could already see that unimaginable, all-negating nothingness.

In my sweat-soaked, trembling little body, and pathetic, pulsating little veins – in my own consciousness of myself – I could feel that nothingness spilling out over the whole world, from the vanishing stars, to the squashed flies, that cold, inexorable nothingness, lying in wait, biding its time.

And it seemed that if after death, supposing once in a million years, for only a minute, even, we might look out again on some kind of world, and feel our 'I' – then by that act we annihilate this unbounded horror, a chill eternity of utter negation. After all, I will never again exist, never.

Later on there were many theories, books, dissertations, triumphantly and for all time purporting to free us from that blank nightmare, but – never forget! . . . that first intimation of death was allowed entry into our soul, along with our mother's first kiss, along with the first light of day, from childhood on. And because of that it lived in the depths of my soul, lurking within me like some terrible monster.

However, that's only one side of the question. After all, death may have been atheistic, but it was a mystery none the less. And they couldn't kill a mystery. And that's why, ever since childhood, I've kept alive a prayerful reverence and trepidation in my heart, before the frozen features of the dead.

I needed no fairy tales, no songs of any kind, as long as I could gaze upon the departed dead.

And that profound horror of nothingness left me, moved somewhere off-centre, and by contrast, the consciousness of extinction aroused in me only a sense of mystery. That was made easier, obviously, insofar as I couldn't see myself dead, but only other people, while that horror of nothingness sprang up always in darkness, in solitude.

And now this side of death has taken a serious grip of me, even unto my very bowels.

Life was so bleak, with its utter hopelessness and materialism, its bestial stupidity and clarity, that Death – uniquely seen and felt by everyone, the Great Mystery, but a mystery that smacks you in the teeth – appeared as a genuine oasis amid a torrent of decrees, of porridge, televisions and impenetrable 'logic'.

There was something profoundly intimate and mystical about the observation of death, which I could make my own, belonging only to me . . . In a word, a great many complexes were woven into one at this point: the estranged, and the voluptuous, the wild and the repressed.

Autumn was already drawing on. I picked out for myself a grimy, mud-spattered cemetery on the outskirts of Moscow. Nearby, touching the heart with its own mystical ordinariness, stood a sort of half-canteen, half-beer-bar. I used to arrive there while it was still morning – always the same old stuff: would the deceased be there now? To make certain, before dropping into the pub, I would phone the cemetery boss. The boss, a sour-faced, half-drunk old geezer, invariably recognized my voice and answered me at tedious great length, about who was being buried, what age they were, what they had died of, and where they had found a spot for the grave. He was convinced that my interest in all this was some sort of official business, beyond the reach of his dull wits. Because of that he was really quite frightened of me.

When I got a favourable answer, I would first of all lose myself in a filthy, darkening corner of the canteen, by a low-level window, out of which I could see the ramshackle gates of the graveyard, just about ready to fall apart. I would order up a glass of beer, and two or three sprats. Then I would close my eyes, and go off into a trance.

My worlds stealthily entered me, along with the sharp-tasting drops of alcohol, their warm, spontaneous thoughts, and the soft, distant footfalls of the approaching funeral party. The first phase of my spiritual voyage of discovery passed entirely in that beer-bar, in grimy warmth, in expectation, waiting amid the flies, the stolidly chewing faces, and the cats, half-crazed with repletion.

My entire being quivered, and I foreknew the knock of the approaching corpse; an incomprehensible, doomed feeling of joy, wholly self-contained, entered my soul. I began stupidly tee-heeing, yes, I'm here alive, and he's dead.

That thought had an extraordinary effect on me, raising my self-esteem, the intimacy and blessedness of my life to unbearable heights. I would ever so gently stroke my knees, luxuriating in the fact of my existence, and everything around me: the ceiling, the cats, the chairs, the fat women, all seemed dead and motionless, encircling with their mindless, hostile wall, the delicious, solitary tremor of my 'I' and my flesh.

At the peak of ecstasy, I was so immersed in the purity of this thought, that I felt quite feeble-minded, and this was extremely pleasant.

I was giggling, pouring beer over myself, pulling the cats' tails.

Then the next phase began. Deeply affected, staggering a little from my thoughts, I went out to meet the funeral procession. My earlier joy had evaporated, and I now gave myself up completely to a transport of otherworldly mystery. Bobbing up and down slightly, I tottered along behind the coffin, and I kept thinking that they were burying some part of me: half of my leg, a precious drop of my soul, or simply a finger.

Thus I felt as if the coffin's inimitably mysterious path to the grave was my own bitter-sweet journey somewhere within that space between our world, and the world beyond the grave, when our spirit is leaving us, but hasn't yet gone. The soul still can't cut loose from the dreams, the weeping and wailing, and the visions of this world, which now takes on, at the moment of separation, some kind of other, unreal sense; and I would look with a fresh eye at the tall trees lining the cemetery paths, in which the sound of the wind was now transformed for me into the parting songs, never before heard, of this earthly world, revealing its hidden face only at the point of death; but from far off, a dark mysterious rhythm was already entering this same soul – the rhythm of the abyss beyond the grave.

This phase came to an end at the graveside itself. And when the corpse was placed alongside the pit, the first thing I did was to try and look into his face. Now and again, as a counterpoise to the grand and the dramatic in my make-up, the forces of idiotic hilarity spill out and take over. I would have a sudden urge to spit in the deceased's face, and occasionally an absurd feeling of anticipation would grow, that the deceased would suddenly awake, and spring up; I'd close my eyes tight, and open them: what if he made a run for it?

However, the basic content of this phase was death itself, and contemplating the face of the dead man.

I was intoxicated with the coldly rigid features of the corpse; and it seemed to me that if I were to stare into that face, stare long and hard to the point of madness, then I would strip away that frozen, nightmarish death-mask, and beyond it glimpse the riddle of life, the riddle of my own self. My heart missed a beat, surrounding nature assumed a subtle, fantastically morbid aspect; every little bush became either an imp, or a Faust. Even the fat, ridiculous relatives at the graveside seemed significant. I was being borne beyond imagining to the Altar of the Great Mystery, and in the turns and twists of the road that led there, I came to love my doomed self, with even more heart-rending intensity. And after the burial, wandering the silent alleyways of the cemetery, I would prostrate myself, shrilly praying for pity, before the green trees, the dogs and the sturdy beggars who happened to cross my path.

We take pity on people because there's something they lack: money, intelligence or a woman. But I was howling about another kind of pity: a warm, crazy, sexually deranged pity for one's own pristine, doomed 'I', for one's trembling, perishable existence, so precious, and so casually abandoned before this incomprehensible world – that was the kind of fierce, pathological pity I asked for; but the trees in their solitude made no answer, the dogs barked and ran away, and the beggars crossed themselves and cleared off . . . And I realized that that kind of pity, I could get only from myself, and that out of that pity, something truly great must arise . . .

So that's how I live now, in empty solitude. I go to my beloved cemetery almost every other day. I eat right here, beside the mystery. Everyone knows me now. The relatives of the deceased, the next in line, are forewarned about me. Some of them are extremely friendly, and will stand me a vodka after the burial; others give me a wide berth; still others think I'm some kind of government agent, and refuse to go on with the funeral.

I've had fits of ecstasy several times, when I've been in some sort of witless stupor, or in delirium, beyond the frontiers of my worlds, and climbed up, elbowing them all out of the way, to kiss the departed dead. One old geezer hurled his galoshes at me at one point . . .

A couple of times my beloved Zina has come running up to me in my cemetery beer-bar. She just looks at me, looks at me wide-eyed, then sighs and hurries away . . . I've nothing to say to her any more . . .

However, Yury Arkadievich – thanks be to God! – has begun to visit me again, albeit in the mornings now.

The last time He winked at me, and fixing me with His eye that way, said: 'Well, Sasha, wouldn't you say your youth's at an end? Isn't it time you were setting off on that decisive, mystical journey?'

. . . At which point, the individualist's notebook breaks off.

Translated by Stephen Mulrine

VENEDIKT EROFEEV

Through the Eyes of an Eccentric

1. I left home, taking three pistols with me – one I stuffed into my shirt, the second I stuffed into my shirt also, and the third, well, I can't remember where.

And stepping out into the alley, I said: 'Call this a life? It's a heaving of the waters, it's the wreck of the soul.' As I understand it, the Divine Commandment, 'Thou shalt not kill', extends even to oneself. ('Thou shalt not kill thyself, no matter how nasty it gets'), but today's nastiness, and today full stop, lie beyond the scope of the Commandments. 'For it is better for me to die than to live,' said the prophet Jonah. And that goes for me too.

It was raining everywhere, a fine drizzle, or maybe it wasn't raining anywhere, I couldn't have cared less. I set off in the direction of Gagarin Square, screwing up my eyes now and again and cowering, as an index of my grief. My heart was swollen with bitterness, my whole being was filled with anguish; I felt an ache to the left side of my heart, and another to the right. My loved ones had all abandoned me.

Whose fault that is, whether theirs or mine, will be sorted out on the Day of Judgement, when He shall come, etc., etc. They simply got fed up laughing at my Saturdays, and crying at my Mondays. The two or three lone ideas, which barely managed to keep me warm, have also vanished, dissolved into thin air. And to crown all, the very last creature that might have detained me a while on this earth, has run out on me. She was on her way out, and I caught up with her on the stairs. 'Don't leave me, my white-bellied darling!' I told her – then I cried for a half-hour, and caught up with her again: 'Stay, my bosom of bliss!' She turned round, spat on my shoes, and left me forever.

I might have drowned myself in my own tears, but I had no luck there. I tried to do away with myself for six whole months, I threw myself in front of trains, but the trains all kept pulling up, just short of my loins. And at home I knocked in a hook overhead, to make a gibbet, and traipsed around the city for a fortnight, with a sprig of orange-blossom in my buttonhole, looking for rope, only I couldn't find any. I even went the length of walking on to firing ranges, during large-scale manoeuvres, and standing by the main target, while all the Warsaw Pact countries let rip at me, and the shells flew harmlessly past. Whosoever got me those three pistols – a four-fold blessing upon thee!

I hadn't reached the square yet, and I was gasping for breath, so I sank down into a flowerbed, mute and misshapen. My heart was still swollen, my tears ran down fore and aft, I was so comical and pathetic that they had to give all the old women that looked at me smelling-salts and chloroform.

'First of all, wipe the sweat from your brow.' Whoever died sweaty? Nobody ever died sweaty. You're a godforsaken wretch, but try and recall something refreshing, something really reviving . . . like, for instance, as Ernest Renan said: 'There is a moral sense in the consciousness of every man, and for that reason there is nothing to fear in being godforsaken.' Exquisitely put. But that won't revive me – where is it in me, this moral sense? I haven't got one.

Even the fiery Hafiz (the fiery halfwit Hafiz, I can't abide him), the fiery Hafiz said: 'In each man's eyes shines his own star.' Well, I haven't got a star, not even in one eye.

And Alexei Maresiev said: 'Each of us must carry his own commissar in his heart.' But I don't have my own commissar there either. No, call this a life? This isn't a life, it's a shitty outfall, a maelstrom of slops, heart-wreck. This world is plunged in darkness and rejected by God.

Without getting up from the ground, I drew out my pistols, two from my armpits, the third from I don't remember where, fired off all three at once into all my temples, and keeled over on the flowerbed, my mind pierced clean through.

2. 'Call this a life?' I said, rising up from the ground. 'It's a puff of wind, it's a swirling mist, it's a gob of spit round your neck, that's what it is. You missed, you clown. Yes, you loathsome disease, you missed out of all three pistols, and now you haven't a single bullet left in any of them.'

I started to foam at the mouth, or maybe it wasn't just foam. 'Hey, take it easy! You've still got one remedy, the ultimate remedy, that Italian speciality – poisons and potions.' Yes, there's always Pavlik the chemist, he lives right on Gagarin Square, old stay-at-home bookworm Pavlik, that goggle-eyed wimp. Stop moaning, you're forever moaning! I don't remember who said it, either Averintsev, or Aristotle: *'Omnia animalia post coitum oppressi sunt,'* i.e., 'Every creature gets depressed after intercourse.' Yes, well, I'm depressed the whole time, before as well as after.

And that best of all *Komsomols*, Nikolai Ostrovsky, said: 'I can no longer see out of one eye, and with the other, I can see only the lineaments of my beloved.' But I can't see out of either eye, and my beloved's taken her lineaments off elsewhere.

And Schopenhauer said: 'In this world of appearances . . .' (Oh, the hell with it, I can't go on, I'm having spasms.) I jerked my shoulders a couple of times and set off again for Gagarin Square. I chucked all three pistols in amongst the Persian cyclamens and the wallflowers, and God knows what else.

Pavlik's bound to be at home, mixing up his chemicals and poisons, concocting a remedy for blenorrhoea – that's what I thought, as I knocked at his door:

'Open up, Pavlik.'

He opened up, without giving me so much as a twitch of his cheek or a flicker of his eyebrows; he had eyebrows enough to have raised at least part of them at me, but he didn't bother.

'Can't you see I'm busy?' he said, 'I'm mixing up chemicals and poisons, concocting a remedy for blenorrhoea.'

'Don't worry, I'm not stopping. Just give me something, Pavlik, some sort of hemlock, or strychnine or whatever, give it me or it'll be the worse for you, when I die of a broken heart, right here on your pouffe!' I clambered on to his pouffe, pleading with him: 'Have you any potassium cyanide? Acetone? Arsenic? Glauber's salts? Bring them all here and I'll mix them up and drink the lot, all your essences, all your potassiums and ureas, fish them all out!'

'No, I won't,' he said.

'Well, that's just wonderful. Terrific. Anyway, Pavlik, who needs your prussic acid, or whatever you call this stuff? What do I want with your lousy chemicals – I, who have mixed and drunk all the toxins of existence? What are they to me, who have tasted the poison of Venus? I'll just stay and break my heart right here on your pouffe. You keep on curing blenorrhoea.'

Incidentally, as Professor Botkin said: 'You need at least a couple of gonococci to catch blenorrhoea.' But as for me, idiot that I am, I haven't a single gonococcus.

And Miklukho-Maklai said, 'If I hadn't done anything before I was thirty, I'd have done nothing after it.' So what about me? What have I done before thirty, to have any hopes of doing anything after?

And Schopenhauer said, 'In this world of appearances . . .' (Oh no, I can't go on, I'm going into spasm again.)

Pavlik the pharmacist raised all his eyebrows at me, and stood goggle-eyed, same as he used to when he was a kid. He carried on where I left off:

'But Vasily Rozanov said: "Each of us has his own Passion Week in life." This is yours.'

'Yes, this is mine all right. Yes, sure, Pavlik, I'm having my Passion Week now, and it's got seven Good Fridays in it! That's fantastic! So who exactly is this Rozanov?'

Pavlik said nothing, just kept on mixing his poisons and chemicals, deep in some sort of private reverie.

'So what's this secret of yours?' I asked him, but he didn't answer that either, just kept on brooding over it. I flew into a rage and leapt up off the pouffe.

3. A half-hour later, saying goodbye to him at the door, I was stuffing three volumes of Vasily Rozanov under my arm and knocking a paper stopper into a flask of hemlock.

'He's a dyed-in-the-wool reactionary, of course?'

'And how!'

'Nobody more shameless?'

'Not one.'

'Nobody deeper dyed, more loathsome?'

'No, not a soul.'

'Delightful. Backward-looking?'

'Right into the bone, as our girls say.'

'And he ruined his life for some crackpot religious notions?'

'He did. God rest him.'

'What a sweetheart. Of course, he knocked around with the Black Hundreds, pogroms and all that?'

'Up to a point, yes.'

'Magical man! How did he manage to work up the spleen? Where did he get the nerve, and the free time? And not a single original thought his whole life?'

'Nothing but fantasies. And those almost exclusively of a malignant strain.'

'And during his life, and after it – he achieved no fame?'

'None whatsoever. Only ill-fame.'

'Yes, yes, I've heard of him. ("Hang on, Pavlik, I'm going in a minute.") I heard about him in my callow youth from our teacher Sofiya Solomonovna Gordo, about that bunch of renegades, that vile conspiracy: Nikolai Grech, Nikolai Berdyaev, Mikhail Katkov, Konstantin Pobedonostsev – "*He spread his owl wings*" – Lev Shestov, Dmitry Merezhkovsky, Faddei Bulgarin – "*The trouble isn't that you're a Pole*" – Konstantin Leontiev, Aleksei Suvorin, Viktor Burenin – "*The dog runs along the Nevsky*" – Sergei Bulgakov, and a whole heap of other bandits. Yes, Pavlik, I've heard of the dark, baleful light shed by that constellation 'of obscurantists, from my teacher Sofiya Solomonovna Gordo. I'm up to speed on that gang.'

'Sofiya Solomonovna Gordo is a fine woman, and I'm not going to argue about the "gang". That's common enough, and doesn't grate on the ear — don't drop the hemlock bottle — but the word "constellation" does grate, it's both meaningless and inaccurate, and as Johannes Kepler said: "Every sort of constellation is nothing more or less than a chance company of stars, having nothing in common either in their structure, their significance, their dimensions, or their accessibility."

'Well, all right, let's say I know that too, having heard about it from our class teacher Bela Borisovna Savner, a woman with the most amazing . . . ("Okay, Pavlik, I'm going!") So anyway, according to you, this civil servant Vasily Rozanov went one better than all the rest, outdid them in sheer bloody murder?'

'Absolutely all of them.'

'Topped the lot?'

'Topped the lot.'

'A real man-eater. So how did he die then? How did this bloodsucker die? One word, that's all, then I'll go.'

'He made a good death. Turned to the true faith about an hour and a half before the end. He had time to make confession and receive the Eucharist. You ask too many questions. Now, goodnight, you parasite.'

'Goodnight.'

I bowed, thanked him for the hemlock and the books, twitched three more times and cleared off.

4. So — have a drop of the hemlock first, then read? Or read first, then swig the hemlock? No, a read first, and a swig later. I opened it up at random and started from the middle (that's what people always do, when they've a bit of classy reading in their mitts).

And this is what was in the middle:

'A book ought to be expensive, and that's the first evidence of love towards it – the willingness to buy it. A book shouldn't be lent out. A book out on loan is like a cheap tart. It's lost something of its soul, and its purity. Reading-rooms and public libraries are places of resort, corrupting the people, like brothels.'

I mean, really, what a creep. But get this, after a few more pages, when he's no longer talking about corrupting books, but about prostitutes proper:

'One can allow a kind of purified prostitution for "merry widows", that is to say, for that class of women who are not suited to monogamy, who are incapable of comprehending the true, superior virtue of monogamy.'

That was followed by a farrago of nonsense about the compatibility of Christian principles with the 'sins of the flesh', and about how Christianity, if it seriously wants to compete with Judaism, ought to become at least partly phallic. My head began to fill up with something unpleasant, and I got up and drilled a hole in each of the four walls, to let the air in.

Then I slumped down on the settee and continued reading:

'My God, my Eternal Father, why hast Thou given me so much sorrow?' 'My soul is weary. Worn out with a terrible weariness. My morning is without light. My night is without sleep.' This is an obscurantist – and suddenly his soul is weary? 'Is there any pity in this world? Beauty, yes, meaning, yes. But pity?' 'Do the stars have pity? A mother pities, and thus she will be higher than the stars.' 'People are rude, horribly rude, and that's the sole reason, or the main reason, why there's so much pain in life, so much hurt.' 'Oh, how can my weak nerves endure such a gigantic portion of vexation!'

(No, with this 'murderer' there was quite a lot to talk about; in fact it was ages since I'd come across any creature with whom you could have so much to 'talk about'.)

'It is sorrow alone that reveals to us the great and the sacred.' 'Pain, all-embracing, causeless, and almost unremitting. It seems to me I was born in pain. My condition is at times so grave, that if it were any worse, I couldn't go on living – my constitution wouldn't stand it.' 'I don't want truth, I want peace.' 'Oh, the sad trials I have undergone! Why did I want to know everything?'

'I can only either laugh or cry. Do I actually, seriously reflect? Never.' 'Sorrow is my constant companion.' 'Laughter can't kill anybody, laughter can only crush you.' 'Patience can overcome any kind of laughter.' 'In general, laughing is an undignified activity, a base category of the human soul. Laughter comes from Caliban, not Ariel.'

'He wept. And He reveals Himself to tears alone. He who never weeps, will never see Christ.' 'Christ is the tears of humanity.' 'Lord God Eternal, stay by my side, never leave me.'

(Well, there you are! Maresiev and Kepler, Aristotle and Botkin all missed the point, but he hits' the nail on the head. 'Collegiate counsellor Vasily Rozanov, creating his works.' Yes, Schopenhauer and Sofiya Gordo, Hafiz and Miklukho-Maklai, were full of dismal rubbish, and the soul protested, but here it doesn't. And it won't protest now, no matter what it has to deal with, paradox or platitude.)

'Russian bravado and Russian idleness, coming together to overturn the world – that's revolution.' 'It has two dimensions – length and breadth, but not the third – depth.' 'Revolution is when a man is transformed into a pig, breaks dishes, fouls the nest, sets fire to the house.' 'Arrogance and malice – those are the ingredients of any revolution.'

And on the Decembrists, my beloved Decembrists:

'And they keep on writing the history of that farce. And memoirs, and all sorts of peacock feathers. Even Nekrasov, with his "Russian Women".'

And on Nikolai Chernyshevsky (yes, that suffering martyr, who was called upon 'to remind the rulers of this world of Christ'):

'Don't you realize that civilization isn't these pathetic little Buckles and Darwins, these piddling Spencers in their twenty volumes, it isn't your Chernyshevsky, all that riff-raff of the Russian Enlightenment, with their bast sandals and footcloths, that we ought to have kicked up the backside long ago?' 'And don't you realize that we should have boxed this wretched Spencer's ears, we should have punched Chernyshevsky's ugly mug, same as we'd do to a stable-boy stinking out the drawing-room? That we shouldn't have had any kind of truck with them? That we should simply have led them out by the hand, the way one removes from the table those gentlemen who, instead of sitting down to eat, begin making a stink.' (Stink? How can a martyr do that?)

And on Count Tolstoy:

'In particular I dislike Tolstoy and Solovyov. I don't like their ideas, I don't like their lives, I don't like their very souls. The meanest dog, crushed by a tram, stirs more movement in my heart than all their "philosophy and journalism". This "crushed dog" maybe explains a few things. They (Tolstoy and Solovyov) had not a shred of humility in them; on the contrary, they delighted in crushing other people.'

And on Maxim Gorky (at least I *think* it was Maxim Gorky):

'He keeps trying to catch something somewhere, in some sort of murky water, some sort of self-respecting fish. But mostly it escapes, his bait's lousy, his hook's blunt. But he doesn't get downhearted. And he casts his hook again.'

And on the 'founder of political waffle in Russia', Alexander Herzen:

'Throughout his whole life – not one natural or elevated thought – his mind set on grubbing up a little money, or lecturing people on how they should live. When he was a high school student he used to deliver the same sermons to his mother in his letters. And the movements of his heart are lacking in any kind of passion, slow and sluggish. Like a reptile crawling along.'

Anyway, I fell asleep on that crawling reptile at dawn, hugging my reactionary. To begin with it was the spiritual side of my being that fell asleep, and thereafter my fleshly side fell asleep also.

5. And when my spiritual side awoke, my fleshly side was still asleep. But my renegade woke up before any of them, and if I hadn't already got to know him, I'd have thought he was behaving very strangely:

To begin with, having splashed his face with water, he launched into 'God Save the Tsar', in a vile, tuneless voice, but putting more heart and naturalness into it than all the subjects of the Russian Empire, counting from the time of the ill-starred Khodynka Field. Then he showered all the children in the world with kisses and set off on foot to church. Standing in the midst of the worshippers, he looked now like some foreign asset-stripper, now like 'a demon, fearfully snatching at the cross', now like Abadonna, newly crawled out of his bottomless pit, now again like something with a deal of commitment, but it was hard to say what exactly that commitment was to, and what it was costing this Abadonna.

(Meanwhile I was still lying on the settee, crossing and uncrossing my legs, and observing.)

Emerging on to the porch, he gave alms to two beggars, but for some reason or other, after looking them over, he gave nothing to the rest. He thanked Kleinmikhel for something, boxed Zhelyabov's ears in passing, shed a tear or two and told the local constable that there was nothing more sacred in the world than the function of the police.

Then he hesitated a moment. Going round the back of a file of Socialists and People's Willers, he pinched Vera Figner's buttocks, that 'manly lady' (she didn't bat an eyelid), and abstractedly gave all the rest a cuff on the head. ('Oh, you rascal!' I said, in a transport of delight.)

But he meanwhile, having cuffed his last head, scowled and came towards me in the little hut, with a pile of old coins in his pocket. While he was taking them out, turning them over in his hands and blowing on each coin, I raised myself up from the settee and asked in a whisper:

'Is that really interesting – blowing on every single coin?'

And without a word he said to me:

'Yes, it's damnably interesting – have a go yourself. But why are you still dead to the world at this hour? Are you feeling sick – or have you been out whoring all night?'

'Yes, I have, and with three of them, no less. I was given them yesterday to read, because yesterday I felt lousy. "A book lent out . . ." and so forth. Anyway, I feel slightly better today. But I tell you, I was so bad yesterday that when the deputies in the city Soviet looked at me they heaped ashes on their heads, rent their garments and girt their loins round with sackcloth. And unto the old women that beheld me were given smelling-salts . . .'

I couldn't contain myself, and I ran through the whole of my previous day from memory, from the pistols to the crawling reptile. And at that point he was just exactly what I needed, my numismatist-friend: he couldn't contain himself either. He pronounced a number of commonplaces on the blasphemy of self-slaughter, then something about souls 'tissued out of filth, yearning and sorrow', and those 'shrinking violets who transform their broken hearts into a comic opera', about Shernval and Greenberg, about Amvrosy of Optina, about the mysterious emotions of the Jew, the sexual enigmas of Gogol, and God only knows what else.

This most subtle-minded mischief-maker, hypochondriac, misanthrope, downright boor, entirely formed of raw nerve-ends, began lampooning just about everything we're accustomed to revere, and singing hymns of praise to all those things we despise – all the while demonstrating lofty and systematic reasoning, and a total lack of system in exposition, with a bitter intensity, a gentleness distilled from black bile, and a 'metaphysical cynicism'.

Not knowing how further to express my delight (I couldn't shout, 'Oh, you rascal!' again), I crossed over to the chair, and invited him to flop down on my settee. And in three thousand words I told him what he couldn't know: about the Dnieper Dam and Ribbentrop, Belsen and *Belomor*, about the murder of the Tsar's children at Ekaterinburg, about the Traditionalists and the Renovationists (at this point he began to press me for more detail, but I didn't know any more), about Pavlik Morozov, and his kulak murderer Danilka.

All that oppressed him to the point that his countenance darkened and he went into a slump. It wasn't until some time later that he started to speak again: about the perverted ways of man, about his own sins against mankind, though not against God and His Church, about the sweat of Gethsemane and Original Sin.

So I told him about Original Sin likewise, and about posthumous rehabilitation, about Peking and the Kizlyar pastures, about the Taimyr labour camps and Nuremberg, about the absence of all guarantees and all meaning.

'When the Israelites journeyed to the south, to the Ishmaelites, they exchanged all that they possessed for balm. But what shall we exchange for balm, if we go south to the Ishmaelites? An oath, a guarantee, a pledge, a deposit – what can we offer instead of all that? What can we swear by, who can we vouch for, where can we find even one pledge? I mean, even old man Laban, who had lost faith in everything, swore by his daughters, because he didn't know what else to swear by. But in the whole of Russia, has any one of us so much as even one daughter? And if we have, will we be able to swear by those daughters . . .?'

My companion, who loved daughters, blew his nose and said: 'How true.'

6. And at that point I spewed out a barrage of gloomy and ridiculous sentiments: 'Everything's changed here, there isn't a word or a breath left of what used to be "everything". All the clowns, the mystics, the hucksters, the conjurors, the neurotics, the astrologers – they all shipped out somehow, even before your demise. Either that or they died off afterwards, hanged themselves back home in Russia. And a good thing too, no doubt. The people left behind were sensible, simple, decent hardworking folk. There's no shit, not a whiff of it, nothing left but diamonds and emeralds. I'm the only thing that stinks. Well, and maybe a few other renegades, they stink too.

'Our lives are short and stupid, theirs are long and smart. We're no sooner born, than we're already snuffing it. Meanwhile they, the scum of the earth, are long in years and will abide forever. Somehow it's the Jew that's eternal. It's Koshchei that's immortal. Not a single one of their ideas is short-lived, they need to mature, while we dwindle. It wasn't for parasites like us that Prometheus stole fire from Olympus, it was for them, for the scum . . .'

'Oh, give over,' said Rozanov to me at this point. 'Stop talking rubbish . . .'

'If I shut up and stop talking rubbish,' I said, 'the very stones'll cry out. And they'll start talking rubbish. Yes, indeed.'

I blew my nose and continued:

'They're in a state of total ignorance. "The monstrous ignorance of Oedipus", only it's exactly the reverse. Oedipus knifed his father and married his mother through ignorance, he didn't know it was his mother and father, and he wouldn't have done it if he'd known. But with them, no, it's something else again. They marry their mothers and kill their fathers, completely oblivious to the fact that it's disgusting.

'And you really ought to know what sort of hard cases they are, all these modern Russians. Nobody in Russia is ticklish, I'm the only person in the whole of Russia that laughs out loud when I'm tickled. I've tried myself to tickle three girls and upwards of a dozen blokes – not one could muster so much as a grimace, or a laugh. I tapped them all with the butt of my hand under the knee – no reflex whatsoever. True enough, their pupils react to light, but only feebly. None of them has a single stone in their kidneys, no trembling in their limbs, no lassitude at their hearts, no protein in their urine. Out of all the people of my generation, I was the only one they wouldn't take into the Red Army, and that was just because I had heartburn, and two boils on my back . . .'

('Ho-ho!' laughed my companion. 'Excellent!')

'And that's what torments me, this contrast between them and me. "Congenital idiots weep," said Darwin, "but cretins never shed a tear." That means that they're cretins, and I'm a congenital idiot. On second thoughts, no, we're as distinct as the tears of an idiot from the smile of a cretin, as diarrhoea from constipation, as my mild idiocy from their utter cunt-brained stupidity (a thousand pardons!). They've deprived me of my last breath, in and out both, terrors have assailed my soul on all sides, I expect nothing from them – no, I tell a lie, I expect fantastic atrocities and unspeakable swinishness from them, that'll come soon enough, it'll begin in the East or else the West, but it'll come all right. And when it starts, I'll bale out, instantly, without a second's thought, I've been down that road, I've got my poison handy, God's benison. I'll take off, so as not to see the madness of the sons of men . . .'

I uttered all this choking with tears. And when I'd finished, I leaned back in my chair, blinking and trembling all over. My companion watched me for a minute, then said:

7. 'Don't torture yourself, my friend, why torment yourself? Stop shaking, you creature of impulse! Every day you commit thirty sins you know about, and a hundred and thirty you don't, so you'd better worry about them first. Why should you lament the sins of the world and load them on to yourself? Deal with your own sins first. Among the general "madness of the sons of men", there's a place for your own (how did you so delightfully express it?) – "cunt-brained stupidity". "The world's eternally in a state of panic, and that's how it lives." And even the contrary: "We often find ourselves being untruthful, in order not to cause one another unnecessary pain." He, however, is constantly truthful. It'll be a blessed thing, if you betake yourself to His grace. In essence, you're just setting out on the path towards reverence for the Cross. So – you think you've lived a long time, my friend? Well, it's actually been no time at all, negligible. And what's more, since the Crucifixion, just sixty such intervals have elapsed. It all happened quite recently. "So lay aside your bombast", it's all only just beginning.

'Let them go ahead and say that a house of prayer, converted to a den of thieves, can't be made a house of prayer again. "Yet the gentle path will outlast the way of iron. The rails will be torn up. The machines will be broken. But the fact that man weeps at the mere threat of eternal separation – that will never end, never run out." "We must rid ourselves of the iron, it is a snare and a delusion, and put our faith in gentleness." "The true iron is tears, sighs and yearning. And our only nobility is that truth, which can never be destroyed."'

He said a good deal more, but no longer as well or with such warmth. And unsteadily, like the morning mist, he rose up from the settee, and like the morning mist, began to shimmer, then spoke a few more fine words – about sighing, about the feeding-trough and the swine – and vanished, like the morning mist.

Yes, that was well said: 'It's all only just beginning!' No, I'm not talking about that, not about myself – for me it all began long ago, and not with this Vasily Rozanov either, he simply inspired hope in me. In me it began ten years earlier – everything that had been poured into me since adolescence kept splashing about inside me, like slops, overflowing my belly and my soul, seeking a way out, and the one course of action remaining to me was that most tried and trusted of methods: to spew it all up using two fingers. One of these two fingers turned out to be the New Testament, the other, Russian poetry, that is, all the Russian poetry from Gavrila Derzhavin to Marina Tsvetaeva (Marina, who wrote 'Tragedy' with a capital T).

Things got easier for me. But for a long time afterwards I was pale and listless. The higher functions of my brain had been extinguished, owing to only one tiny part of it being actively stimulated – the vomiting reflex of the medulla oblongata. I needed something more fortifying, and it was this numismatist that gave me strength – on that very day, when I was pale and enfeebled beyond all measure.

He performed the same function as the Bosnian student who planted a bullet in the Archduke Franz-Ferdinand. Before him there had been an accumulation of causes, but that's how they would have remained, an accumulation of causes. Strictly speaking, nothing began with him, he just brought it all to a head, but without him, the Archduke's assassin, strictly speaking, none of it would have happened.

If he were to ask me now:

'Do you feel your vile spirit getting a little more godly?'

I'd answer: 'Yes, I do.'

I'd answer differently from how I would have answered the day before yesterday. Hitherto I spoke in a stupid, pathetic voice, a voice in which there was nothing but tinkling and bleating, the bleating of a lost sheep, alternating with the tinkle of a dropped drachma. But now I'd learned a thing or two about missionary work on the new model, and I was prepared to take it up, even if nobody asked me. To be 'clumsily' beneficent, and to anathematize 'mere trivia'.

Indeed, it was well said: 'O man, why do you not follow the path of gentleness?' That reminds me of the question a certain British gentleman asked a cannibal chief in Kalimantan: 'Sir, why do you eat your wives?' Well there's no better missionary to my knowledge than Vasily Rozanov, lolling around there on my settee.

Yes, what was it he said, on his way out? About sighing, and swine?

'A sigh is richer than a kingdom, richer than Rothschild. The entire history of the world, its origin and eternal life, are but a sigh. We are holy, while they are respectable. God will come to a sigh. He will come to us. But tell me this, please, will God really come to a respectable person? We have sighs. They have none.'

'And then I realized where the feeding-trough and the swine were . . .'

8. '. . . And where the crown of thorns was, and the nails, and the torments.'

And if I have to, I'll defend all this, to the best of my ability.

But if they start telling me that Rozanov was a bit of a coward in his everyday life, I'll first of all say that that's rubbish, that we only know a few facts, not what lies behind them. And even if that is actually the case, we can dodge round it by some sort of sneaky quibble, like for example saying that cowardice is actually a good thing, cowardice is a positive virtue. It's based on a profound understanding of the world, and consequently, wariness of it. On the other hand, bravery of any kind is an essentially negative virtue, since it consists of a lack of cowardice. And anyone who would argue the contrary is a halfwit.

If they try and tell me that he behaved badly in little things, that he was occasionally prone to reactionary ideas, and that as for his supposedly unshakeable principles, well, by his own admission he 'changed his convictions as often as his gloves', demonstrating his belief that every betrayal is followed by rebirth – if that's what they say, then I'll answer them after their own fashion: that all these are the declarations of a man who complained about his 'obsession with trivial details', and yet whose vision (perhaps the only man in Russia) was never once obscured by trivial detail.

Yes, not once, in his entire life, did this man ever pretend to be virtuous, while everyone else did. And for a fiery virtue, one can excuse a feeble vice. Of course, in order to avoid the condemnation of the purists, the actual vice needs to be devoid of any sort of extremity. To escape the reproaches of various brain-fuckers like Hamlet, for instance, Gertrude, before she got herself remarried, should have waited a little longer, at least until her *shoes were old*. The Redeemer was knowledgeable about everything, except sin. And not even we can be adept in every sin – so as to know their value, and be repulsed by them all. We can be involved in a minor deception, be mixed up in some pettifogging injustice – so what? – it's like a vaccination against smallpox – it saves us from the *gigantic lie* (every halfwit knows what I'm talking about).

And if I'm told by women that he looked frightful, that his nose was pudgy, and he had little shifty eyes and foul breath, and all that sort of thing, I'll answer them, the bitches, in this fashion: 'Well, so what if he had shifty eyes? That's the only sign by which you can identify an honest man: his eyes are never still. That signifies the man has a conscience, and is incapable of really major-league rottenness. With criminals on the grand scale, the eyes never waver, whereas with the better part of my acquaintance they're always on the move. Napoleon's eyes never wavered. But Rozanov said if he ever ran into Napoleon he would bite off his head. Now, how can a man have bad breath, who could even contemplate biting off Napoleon's bonce?

He was neither antisocial nor aggressive, so anyone who knows this life's no joke (and he knew that better than most), shouldn't talk nonsense – people like that are happy and kind, and that's why he was the happiest and kindest of men. Only frivolous people are antisocial or aggressive.

And if (shame on them!) they start talking about Rozanov's notorious 'erotic indispositions' – well, there's scarcely any point in denying it. But with a monastery standing squarely in his heart, from his early youth to his death, why shouldn't he indulge himself with the odd heathenish high jinks, if indeed, as might be imagined, that's all they were, fun and games? Why shouldn't we permit the odd excursion into sexual pathology to a man in whose heart the Holy Virgin remained immutable? It didn't cause the slightest harm, either to Rozanov or to the Holy Virgin.

We ought to erect a monument to him, no matter what people said about him. We ought to erect three monuments to him, one in his home town, one in St Petersburg and one in Moscow. And if anyone's going to remind me that the deceased himself used to insist: 'There's only one fitting memorial for a man – an earthen grave and a wooden cross – and only a dog deserves a monument', then I'll tell them, idiots that they are, that if monuments actually serve any purpose, then it's solely to remind us about somebody who, for reasons which either do or don't depend on ourselves, has undeservedly slipped from our memory. There's absolutely no point in erecting a monument to Anton Chekhov in Yalta – every dog there knows him without one. But as for Anton Denikin in Voronezh – there ought to be one – every dog there's forgotten him, and every dog ought to remember him.

9. In a word, this is it: that vile, poisonous fanatic, that venomous old bugger, saved my – no, he didn't give me a panacea for my moral infirmities – but he saved my breath and my honour (no more, no less, breath of life and honour). All thirty-six of his works, from the fattest volumes to the slimmest, penetrated to my heart, and stuck there, like the three dozen arrows in the belly of Saint Sebastian.

Anyway I set off from home that same night, flinging on something like a cape, with the books tucked under my arm. At that hour, nobody flings on capes and goes out to their pharmacist-mate's toting chauvinists under their arm. But that's what I did, my path illuminated by nothing, save a few wan constellations. The signs of the Zodiac passed in review, and I sighed, sighed so deeply that I almost dislocated everything I had. And when I had sighed, I said:

'The hell with Miklukho-Maklai, whatever rubbish he said. Before thirty, after thirty, what's the odds? I mean, really, take the Emperor Nero – what had he done at my age? He'd done absolutely nothing. True enough, he'd managed to chop off his brother Britannicus' head. But the main work lay ahead of him: he still hadn't raped a single one of his nieces, he hadn't set fire to Rome from all four corners, and he still hadn't suffocated his mother with a satin cushion. And it's the same with me – the best is yet to come!

'Ho-ho, so what if we are, all in all, dog-shit, and they're diamonds, what the hell! I know what kind of diamonds they are. And what kind of nasty tricks they'll play, even nastier than they've played already, I know that too! Burn out their throats and hearts, oh my Creator, they won't even notice, they won't even realize that Thou hast singed their throats and hearts, yes, go right ahead!'

Well, there you have it! And I've got the ideal thing for them, I've just remembered: an ancient formula for cursing somebody out: 'May you be cursed in your house and in your bed, in your sleep and on your road, in your speech and in your silence. And may all your senses be cursed: sight, hearing, smell, taste and your entire body from the top of your head to the soles of your feet!' ('A first-rate formula!')

And may you be cursed at your coming in, and your going out, in the woods and on the mountains, in victory or defeat, in bed and under it, with pants and without! If your days are wretched, woe betide you! If your days are happy, woe betide you! (If they're happy, a fourfold woe!) In your literacy, and your illiteracy, in all your sciences and literatures, may you be accursed!

On your couch of love, and in your councils, on your toilet-seats and at your music-stands, after death and before conception – may you be accursed. So be it. Amen.

Anyway, if you agree to these conditions, we'll look after you like precious objects, and you'll cherish us, if you're prepared to melt in the rays of my kindness, the way that trollop Snow Maiden melted in the rays of Yarilo – if you agree, I'll lift all the curses from you. I'd be less anxious about what's going to become of my country, if you were to agree. But can you be persuaded, you bastards? Not a hope.

All right then, the curse stays in place.

You may be emeralds, what the hell, and we're the opposite. You'll pass on, that's obvious, but we'll abide. Emeralds sink right to the bottom, but shit floats and so will we, hollow maybe, stinking maybe, but floating just the same.

Right now I'm like those numskull knights who came back from Peter the Hermit, crammed full of all sorts of junk, with their brains cleaned out, and their faces fixed in the direction of the Holy Sepulchre. The signs of the Zodiac passed in review. The constellations turned in their courses and twinkled. And I asked them: 'Hey, constellations, surely now you feel more kindly disposed towards me?' And the constellations answered, 'Yes, now we do.'

Translated by Stephen Mulrine

The Fool and the Tiger

I

Hurrying out of the lift, key in hand, I stopped dead. The front door of my flat had disappeared. Or, to be more precise, it had been well and truly smashed in and was hanging limp, up against the bathroom door. I rushed forward, as if to an unconscious man. I lifted the door and it collapsed in my arms – like a woman – having been softened up by that almighty blow.

'Well . . . looks like they've done the flat,' I thought, 'but at least they haven't done me in.'

The floor in the hall was sprinkled with whitewash that had come in with the door, thrown from the wall by the force of the blow. Leaving a trail of white footprints, I went into the study and opened the creaking drawer of my desk. My wallet was there, on top and half open, with the sides folded back; it was like a wounded bird lying with its wings spread out. With trembling fingers I unfastened it. The money was there, thank God.

I lowered myself slowly onto a chair and wiped my forehead with the back of my hand. I looked back at the smashed door, but now with a wry smile on my face. After all, my uninvited guests would have to have been pretty strange burglars not to have worked out where the money was.

In less of a hurry now I went into the kitchen. I was right. The little panel door below the sink had been viciously torn out. Rusty pipes and valves were sticking out of the half-darkness. Tiny bits of cloth were scattered about down there as well. It was clear what had happened. The damned valve had burst again. Water had poured out and the plumbers, who loathe water more than anything else, gave vent to their rage in their own way. They came to stop the water and, while they were at it, smashed up my flat. I turned on the tap. A worn-out thread of water gurgled out of it and that was all; it dried up. The position was clear; it was familiar; and it was typical. You can't do anything about it when something like that happens. There's no one to go to and you can't prove anything. Of course, you can always exchange a few punches with somebody, if you like, but I wasn't in the mood.

I sighed, picked up the rubbish and took it to the refuse-chute on the landing. There was nothing in my way now that the door had been removed. Then I went to the phone, as it was still in one piece, and called a friend of mine who can get things done.

'I see . . . you want Phil on this one,' he said.

'Phil? . . . Yeah, I think I remember . . .'

'You know . . . years ago . . . used to hang around with the wee'yun.'

'But they, at least I thought they . . . years ago . . . didn't they both get nicked?'

'That's right – and he carried the can for the wee'yun as well – the wee'yun already had a little boy by then.'

'Well, um . . .'

'Anyway, he's doing well now – he's a deputy for construction at some big enterprise. Yeah, and he remembers you perfectly. He was asking about you the other day – we were having a bevy. He'll sort the thing out for you, the whole thing.'

It was tempting, of course; he'd sort out 'the whole thing' – but at what price?

'Do you . . . know anyone else?' I wondered.

'I could get you anyone you wanted,' he said with a laugh. 'Musicians, police, grave-diggers even . . . but on this occasion you need Phil.'

I gave in: 'OK . . . tell me where I can find him.'

*

II

In the outer office a gorgeous blonde with a fancy hairdo was sitting behind a typewriter. She was the sort you might see in the outer office of any organization. Actually, these days I wasn't surprised when I met that kind working as a teacher or in institutions that administer the arts. Nowadays it isn't the name of the organization that really makes the difference: what matters are the opportunities it can provide – the actual type of work is of secondary importance.

'Excuse me, I wonder if I might ask . . .' I began.

'Certainly not,' she snapped back almost before I'd opened my mouth.

'But . . . perhaps, on second thoughts, you would be so good . . .' I insisted.

'I'll give you, "be so good", where you don't want it!' was the rude and rather curious expression she came out with, before jumping up and noisily removing the paper from the typewriter. Then, swaying her hips, she went to the door of the inner office. I slipped in behind her and we entered a large, somewhat bare room.

The man behind the desk had a pale retreating forehead that extended as far as a small tuft of grey hair at the back of his head. He was leaning far forward. Suddenly a smile appeared on his protruding face, revealing a crescent of metal teeth.

'Well then, you old brute, at last you've thought to come and see me!' he said. His tone was affectionate, his voice hoarse.

I didn't remember him at all. So much had changed in all those years. He, on the other hand, seemed to remember everything. They say that people who have been inside have very good memories: as time passes each detail of the life they led before they went in is more clearly and tenderly remembered. As it turned out, in this particular case, I was one of those fond details.

'Well, hello . . .' I greeted him, somewhat lamely.

'You remember the benders we used to have at Bob's?' His smile broadened further. 'Yes, I see . . . you're not the man you used to be . . . but a jazz musician will always recognize one of his own.'

'Well!' I exclaimed.

I honestly couldn't remember him, but no one could forget the 'benders' at Bob's. That was a great time, thirty years ago now, when we all played jazz together and called each other by foreign names like Nick, Fred and Bob. It didn't last. It all disappeared, other people became the lords of life . . . that can't be helped. In any case, now all we had in common were memories.

'You know, of course,' he said in confidential tones, 'Val is back in prison, Jaga has gone abroad . . .'

I felt I must have memories in common with both the imprisoned Val and the *émigré*, Jaga, but in actual fact I didn't remember either of them.

'And, as for you, I've been following your work for a long time,' said Phil, looking me straight in the eye, apparently moved – he must have been thinking of my literary efforts.

'Oh, well . . . it's all rubbish,' and with that, embarrassed and confused, I dismissed the subject.

I kept hesitating, not knowing whether or not to ask him how he was. I felt too awkward. After all, his life had been so hard he might find the question offensive. He might even take it as a hint that I wanted to get down to business.

So we just stood there staring at each other. It was probably eye-strain that produced the tears that followed.

'Philipp Klementich, I wonder if you could spare a moment to look at these papers?' asked the secretary, in a jealous tone.

'Shut up! Can't you see I've got a friend here?' he said dismissively.

Clearly he was upset and would rather we had been alone. I think he was put out mainly by the fact that she did not belong to our generation – or our sex. She, for her part, decided quite simply that if I was a friend, then there was no need to stand on ceremony.

Looking at her watch, she said: 'Look, Phil, have you gone mad? We should have been at Zoika's half an hour ago and now we've got no place to go!'

'. . . Justht go, vill you,' he said coldly, not without hostility, waving her away.

'Murder would be too good for you!' she spat out at him, before turning and making for the door.

This display of feelings embarrassed me somewhat, not least because I, apparently, had been the cause of it.

'You could go to my place,' I muttered, to my own surprise.

She turned round and stood motionless in the doorway, looking towards the window.

Phil, as if he hadn't heard my last remark, continued to look at me with that now frozen smile. This dumb scene lasted for quite a while. Then suddenly Phil got up and slowly went to the hook in the corner. He put on a checked flat cap, which seemed to squeeze his huge bird-like head more firmly on to his shoulders. He put on a long black raincoat. Then he set off and we, uncertain and confused, watched him. Thus was my invitation accepted. Evidently Phil felt that no further explanation was called for.

III

Outside, I pointed to the wine shop and asked: 'Shall we get something?'

'Well, what about a little *brandwijn*?' he said absent-mindedly.

I thought for a moment: '*Brandwijn*' must mean 'brandy'. A bit strong to start with, perhaps, but at least it would get things going.

For some reason he was absolutely delighted by my broken front door. 'Now then, Irina Evgenievna,' he said patronizingly, 'this is how real people live! Not like the cheapskates you get nowadays, putting doors on their flats.'

She shrugged her shoulders in contempt. 'Hell,' I said to myself, 'she's hardly going to like me after this and, when it comes down to it, quite a lot can depend on a woman.'

Phil went into my empty, slightly run-down flat (I've been meaning to sort it out for ages). He shook his head: whether it was in amazement or delight I don't know.

'There you are!' he said, returning to the lecture he was giving little Irina. 'None of your fancy furniture, carpets or any of that rubbish. What counts is what you've got up here!' he said, slapping himself on that pale retreating forehead of his.

'Actually, I don't like this flat much,' I said, slightly embarrassed by the good impression I was making. 'It's nothing special. The door, after all – it was only today, I think, or perhaps yesterday, that it was smashed in . . .'

'You got that?' he challenged Irina in the same strict tone. 'He doesn't even know how many days he's been without a front door.' Apparently I reminded Phil of a far-off and much-loved golden age of disinterested friendship. While with every passing moment Irina took me for more of a fool, my reputation with Phil was rising – at least as someone to pass the time of day with.

He was about to open the bathroom door, but I held him back: 'Hang on . . . you know, the . . . um . . . sink's broken!'

The thing was that on my birthday one of my friends had given me a small bottle of English eau-de-Cologne and that outrageous symbol of imperialism had slipped out of my hands and fallen into the sink. In terror I had closed my eyes and covered my ears. There was a crash. 'Well,' I concluded, 'that's the end of my little present.' When I finally opened my eyes I could hardly believe what I saw. The bottle of eau-de-Cologne was still in one piece; it was the sink that had been smashed to pieces.

I told this to Phil. He looked at me with a condescending smile and said: 'OK, I'll tell you what; by all means put that story in one of your novels, but I wasn't born yesterday – I'm an engineer, you know.'

It was a long time since I had first noticed that people who lead the most fantastic lives have a way of insisting that works of art conform to strict rules, that they provide instruction and so on. Phil was a case in point.

'Here we are, then,' I said and dragged my 'coffee table' into the middle of the room – it was, in fact, an old transistor radio that didn't work. I put out glasses.

'Ah, you've got a good set-up here,' said Phil, laughing, 'it's like a Mongolian yurt in here.'

'Oh yeah? Really?' said Irina, who for some unknown reason had taken offence – as if she had spent her whole life in a Mongolian yurt and knew what it was like.

'You go in,' continued Phil, ignoring her, 'there are shelves on the walls of the yurt and on each shelf there's one of our old Record wireless sets. When the batteries run out a Mongol goes off to the nearest settlement and brings back a new one.'

He certainly liked the sound of his own voice.

'Really?' said Irina.

'The kitchen's that way,' Phil commanded her.

She flapped off in that direction.

'When were you . . . .in Mongolia?' I asked casually, as we were on the subject. I thought I'd try to establish some of the landmarks in the extraordinary landscape of Phil's life.

'Well, you know,' he answered calmly. 'I did my porridge. Then I worked in Siberia – I'm in the building trade, you know – then I worked in Mongolia; by then I was already a foreman.'

'Yeah . . . not bad,' I said enthusiastically. 'How old are you, then?' I studied the protruding face, which might have been covered in flour it was so pale.

'How old do you think?' he asked, drawing himself up, half jokingly, half in pride, striking a Napoleonic pose in profile. In this ludicrously self-important position he froze, like a marble bust.

'Well . . . cheers!' We solemnly emptied our glasses.

'The first time I heard about you was when Polinka – you remember Polinka? – told me you were a great bloke,' he remembered.

Polinka! How could I forget Polinka – my first, my most desperate love!

'What do you know about her, anyway?' I exclaimed jealously.

'It's a sekwet!' His fingers played in the air. 'We were in the first year together at University.'

'You and Polinka?' I exclaimed.

Then I suddenly saw him lean over towards my transistor-table and, with a grunt, pull the cardboard back off it.

'Don't!' I exclaimed with a passion quite out of proportion to the circumstances. 'Don't!' I pushed the radio away from him. 'It hasn't worked for ages – leave the damn thing alone!'

'Don't worry . . . take it easy!' said Phil severely, using what was obviously his favourite expression. Pushing me firmly to one side, he stuck his little white hand inside the radio and one by one turned the valves in their sockets. Then he plugged it in and turned it on. Mellow, rhythmic jazz burst forth, making me jump and shaking the window panes and the walls as well.

'Fantastic! How did you do it?'

'. . . It's a sekwet!' he chuckled.

The only thing that troubled me was that, as at his office, he was ignoring the lady. He was obviously retaliating for some offence she had given him. 'But,' I thought, 'enough is enough.' Then, as if on cue, she appeared from the kitchen, with a haughty look and carrying a tray. Coldly she arranged the cups and poured the tea.

'Look,' I exclaimed, 'the steam is dancing to the music!' but they continued to insist on their estrangement. 'Come on,' I pleaded, putting an arm round each of them (brandy was splashing about in the glass I was holding). 'Don't row, I beg you. Everything's fine, for God's sake!' I began to push their heads together and with difficulty succeeded.

IV

I woke up, for some reason, on the sofa in the study. I was fully dressed. Both halves of the large double window in that room had been thrown wide open; high up in the sky was the fluffy white wake left by a pair of unseen planes flying parallel to one another.

Then, suddenly, a door banged shut. Obviously, there was someone in my flat. I became aware of a cold draught drying the bitter sweat as it appeared on my forehead. Suddenly brisk, resonant footsteps were coming towards me. My heart missed a beat. I tried to raise myself, but felt so sick and weak that I fell back again.

I wondered who was walking around my flat and at once

remembered, horrified, that I didn't even have a front door. I strained my ears, trying to work out how many of them there were. There seemed to be just one. The footsteps reverberated into the kitchen, which sound was followed by the hoarse gurgle of the tap. Funny thief! He'd obviously decided to treat himself to a cup of tea. I chuckled and immediately my head was gripped by a sharp pain. Then suddenly the steps were heading determinedly in my direction. My heart stood still.

The door of the study began to creak its way open. Heroically I rose to meet the dangerous intruder. A dirty silvery moon boot shoved its way through what was still a narrow gap. This was followed by a knee, in old, yellowed jeans, then by a tray with cups on it and, finally, with the shining metal of his smile and eyes sparkling, by a face I knew. I groaned and collapsed back on to the sofa.

'Well, you disreputable old brute!' he said affectionately, his voice as hoarse as ever. 'Still with us, are you? What about some tea!'

'Tea?' I murmured. 'Why not coffee? In the . . . there was some tinned white coffee.'

'That'll be right! Not a drop left, mate,' he said, baring his teeth. 'You certainly went for it last night, with the bottle and the rest. It's a wonder the walls are still standing.'

'. . . Me?'

'Well, who else, then – eh, me was it? . . . You were giving away money left and right, to all sorts of girls.'

What? 'To girls?' I collapsed again.

'Don't you remember?' he laughed. 'Well, take it easy! . . . No harm done; I drank a hell of a lot in my own time – drank like a fish. I threw up all over Siberia before I learned how to drink. You can't get on at all in the building trade unless you know how to drink.'

The kettle whistled and he turned and went off to the kitchen. With a pounding heart I rushed to the desk and opened the drawer. My wallet was there, on top; it had been opened and was empty. I felt weak again. The steps were now on their way back, so I quickly shut the drawer.

'Well, you old brute,' said Phil, returning with the tea, 'are you planning to get up, then?'

Holding on to the wall, I sat up.

'Tell me,' I said, taking a miserable little sip of tea and summoning my courage, 'you didn't by any chance take my money out of the drawer, did you?'

For a while he looked at me in silence.

'Yes, I did!' he said severely. 'If I hadn't, the way you were going last night there wouldn't have been any left.'

'Yeah, well, you see . . . I saved it up to have some decorating done,' I said pointing at the dilapidated walls.

'OK, I'll do your decorating for you,' he said gloomily. 'It's something I can do – when I can't do something, I say so. We'll do it all in one go. I'd very much like to fix this place up for you like somebody's flat I saw in Moscow recently.'

'And how much . . . would it cost?' I asked – I could at least try to find out, in this crafty way, how much of my money was already in the possession of my severe friend.

'For God's sake, calm down, you lunatic!' he shouted. 'Don't worry, I won't rip you off. There are plenty of other ways of making money – using one's friends . . . well, that really would be the limit!' he said contemptuously.

Sweat was running down my face. As it happened, I *had* allowed myself to consider the vile possibility of someone ripping off one of his friends.

I was feeling quite anxious: for some reason he was trying very hard to inspire me with the idea of our long lost friendship and an inseparable group of people, all held together – after all these years – by the most sacred of ties. He must have a reason for carrying on in this way – unless he was just doing it for kicks.

'. . . Oh . . . and there's the sink, too, of course, the sink!' I exclaimed.

'. . . You're like some kind of Japanese – ticking like a meter!' said Phil scornfully.

Undoubtedly, I should have been ashamed of myself. Here was a man interested in friendship, while all I cared about was the sanitary ware. It was utterly disgraceful!

'Tell me, though . . . did I behave very badly yesterday?' I asked, moving from a most excruciating subject to a slightly less excruciating one.

'What do you mean, "badly",' said Phil severely. 'You behaved just as you wanted to. This is *your* place, isn't it – not your mother-in-law's!'

'Absolutely!' I exclaimed, abruptly rising to my feet.

At this point a door swung to. Irina, looking like a queen and wearing my dressing gown, had emerged from the bathroom. With an opulent shake of her head she threw her wet hair over her shoulder and sat down with us.

'The trouble with Phil,' she said turning to me, trustingly now, as if to an old friend, 'is that he hasn't got any friends. He despises everyone. Now, thank God, at least he's got one . . .'

I looked at her, terrified, as if to ask, 'Who do you mean?'

'What do you mean, "who"?' she said aloud and with a tender smile. '*You*, silly!'

'Irina Evgenievna,' Phil broke in with his hoarse voice, 'you should have been at work long ago!'

'You raving alcoholic!' she said, offended, and sprang to her feet. Immediately she dressed and went to the door or, to be more precise, to the place where it once was. 'You'll be sorry for this!' she said vindictively.

'Take it easy,' said Phil with a flick of his wrist.

Irina rushed off. I had spent all that money on the brandy and poisoned myself to no purpose: here we were, no further on than we'd been at the beginning!

Phil didn't so much as glance after Irina. He remained completely motionless. Then he got up and shuffled slowly to the phone. He dialled.

'Good morning,' he said curtly and then listened for some time to a penetrating voice that could be heard a long way from the receiver. 'What dithguthting things you do thay,' he said in a fastidious tone and, holding the phone with two fingers, put it down. Having by this time completely forgotten about me, he grimly wound his scarf about his neck.

'Are you going to the office?' I inquired.

He took a long gloomy look at me.

'Let's go, then, as long as you won't be shocked,' he laughed and shrugged his shoulders.

Surely there was no possibility of my being shocked?!

V

We set off for his office on foot. Like two commanders coming up to the front line, with every step we ran into more evidence of recent action: houses destroyed, camp-fires, overturned wagons. Some people ran up to us and shouted something. Phil was unmoved by this or anything else, but carried on walking, slowly, his Napoleonic profile lowered and inscrutable.

Crossing a ditch by a bridge of planks we came into one of those small courtyards, hemmed in on every side by very high walls, that are known (mainly in St Petersburg) as 'well-courts'. It was damp. The surrounding buildings were derelict – without window panes, doors or roofs. From somewhere far off came the sound of blows ringing down on something. We went through into a second courtyard, which stank – as places do that have no roof – like an open sewer. There, next to a small two-storey building, I saw something that I found really quite disturbing. An unshaven man in a beret and earth-coloured overalls was breaking white porcelain basins with a huge sledgehammer. He would put the basin upside down on the ground and with a resounding blow smash it into little pieces. Beside him was a large heap of broken bits. The man swinging the hammer chucked the newly broken fragments on to this heap, brought up another brand new basin, still covered in packaging. He took a small crow-bar and wrenched off the little planks of wood that secured the basin, put it in position and savagely brought the sledgehammer down on it. This exercise, though totally inexplicable from my point of view, didn't surprise Phil in the least. On the contrary, he carried on as if nothing out of the ordinary was going on. He nodded in a cool, official way to the man with the hammer and, springing across the planks to the other side of the ditch, went into the building.

'We've got a little kindergarten going here,' he felt it necessary to explain.

The other man followed us, scraping his hammer along the ground after him. Inside was a dull black telephone, sitting on a sort of structure that looked like a rickety counter from which meals might have been distributed at one time. Phil squeezed the receiver between his ear and shoulder and, nodding in my direction, said to the other: 'You're off to his place tomorrow.' He began to dial. The man with the hammer made no reply and Phil, most characteristically, didn't mention my address. Perhaps he thought I was so popular that no address was required.

'We want to stick pictures on the walls,' said the man with the hammer, pointing to the bare walls.

'Might as well use bank notes,' said Phil laughing, still dialling.

The other man plodded back to his work and soon we could once more hear the sound of his fierce blows with the hammer. Phil dialled again. Suddenly I felt I realized why we had been wandering around all over the place like this. It was simply that Phil had no wish to turn up at work, because he knew what was waiting for him – a whole pile of problems he was thoroughly fed up with, coiled up like so many snakes, not to mention a few new worries carefully prepared by dear old Irina.

Slamming the phone down Phil went out in the courtyard. I followed, like a good second. Phil was looking more and more gloomy; evidently, certain thoughts were putting him under ever greater strain. A man in a safety helmet rushed up to him and croaked in a strange triumphant tone: 'A thousand frames were delivered and they're all crooked!'

'Take it easy!' was Phil's hoarse reply.

The messenger went off, obviously delighted. It is an astonishing thing, of course, this particular characteristic of ours – doubtless found nowhere else – that we are thrilled by disaster on a grand scale. We take an extraordinary perverse delight in our own misfortunes; our attitude is: 'we couldn't care less how bad things are, we're having a good time!' It isn't hard to imagine two of our citizens thus: '. . . So, you lost five hundred million – that's nothing. Look, an industrial complex was built where we live and the upshot of that project – nine hundred million down the drain!' The speaker is gripped by a fit of grim ecstasy, while the other is literally twitching with impatience, desperate to come out with information on losses on a much larger scale! That state of mind certainly makes it hard for us to live up to the Soviet ideal of the 'creative' citizen!

VI

We arrived at work.

'Philipp Klementich is out! . . . I have no idea!' said Irina abruptly, her voice full of triumph. The nature of her jubilation was not hard to grasp. Here she was, with her important boss away; she had no idea where he was, though it probably had nothing to do with work.

When we walked in she was opening the post. She ripped open a large envelope with some kind of official seal, quickly read the contents and pronounced a satisfied, vindictive 'mm'. Then she noticed us. Phil looked at her in silence, stone-faced, as she lifted her head higher and higher, growing in independence and haughtiness all the while as if to say: 'God, why do I waste my energy on this?'

We turned and walked down the corridor. It was like running the gauntlet. For some reason the walls were lined with women, all of them with children. From the filthy looks they gave us it was clear they regarded Phil and me as much hated enemies.

'That's one of his cronies,' came an ominous whisper from behind. 'That's where all the money goes, into their pockets – public money it is, too.'

I gave an involuntary shudder, rather taken aback by my, shall we say, too rapid and assured rise into the sphere of Phil's closest friends. The man himself continued to walk in silence, giving nothing away. Irina was following discreetly, holding the letter she had just opened. Sitting outside the door of Phil's office, with his hands folded on an imitation leather portfolio, was a policeman – judging from the thickness of his glasses, he was from the Fraud Squad. Phil greeted him, but extremely coldly. He did not invite him into the office.

A mountain of a woman with a moustache shouted out: 'The kindergarten was supposed to be ready in April and he hasn't done a damn thing yet – spends all his time boozing with his friends, that's all.' On this particular occasion her remarks were specially for our benefit, but it was obviously not the first time she had expressed herself.

Walking into Phil's office and shutting the heavily padded door behind us, we cut ourselves off from the not inconsiderable commotion and noise of the demonstrators outside. Phil slowly shuffled over to his desk and sat down, looking pretty gloomy. Irina, triumphant, almost danced up to the desk and plonked the letter down on the table in front of the boss. Evidently its contents were guaranteed to humiliate my friend – and in no uncertain terms! Yes, it seemed that he had gone a bit too far and that his all-conquering outrageous nerve, which had brought him so much success, had finally given rise to a revolt of the worst possible kind – a revolt of women. When the welfare of their young is at stake, as in the case of a kindergarten, tigresses discover hidden reserves of courage.

The door squeaked open, revealing a group of people, most of whom were, once again, women, although they were led by an aggressive little old man.

'You called the commission, I believe?' the old man said to Irina.

She glanced rather warily at Phil, but none the less proclaimed with great pride: 'Yes, it was I who called!'

Phil, summoning his most dazzling metallic smile, got up from behind his desk and went to meet the commission at the door as if he was about to embrace them, there on the threshold, like long awaited guests. When he had come up to them he grabbed the handle of the door and slammed it viciously in their faces. Interestingly enough, the commission troubled him no further – they must have set off at once for a higher authority.

'Thank you, Irina Evgenievna,' said Phil, chuckling, 'I'll pay you back!'

Poor old Irina, left without any support, flinched slightly, but said with increased haughtiness: 'Philipp Klementich, I should like to know when you will have the materials needed for the kindergarten?'

'. . . Today,' said Phil in a straightforward, unruffled manner.

'You've been saying "today" for the last six months!'

'I said today and I mean today,' said Phil if anything more impassively than before.

He slowly fastened his raincoat, which he had never taken off, and confidently made for the door. Rather less confidently I set off after him. Obviously there would come a time when he would actually get round to the work he was supposed to do for me.

There were no women left in the corridor: doubtless they had rushed off after the commission in its search for people with more clout. Only the policeman remained, sitting in the same place.

'Goodbye,' said Phil to him.

Without looking back, Phil (with me following) walked straight out of the building. A dark blue pick-up van was parked outside. Out of the back window appeared the familiar head and shoulders of the man who had swung the hammer.

'Do you need me, Philipp Klementich?'

'No one needs you, mate,' joked Phil gloomily. The other bared his teeth. Phil bent down and climbed into the van. Then I got in. I knew I probably wouldn't get anything out of this trip, but it was the only chance I had.

'Where to, Philipp Klementich?' asked the chauffeur, looking back over his shoulder.

'To the warehouse,' said Phil quietly but significantly.

'Ah!' came the surprised and delighted response of the chauffeur, who immediately got into gear and accelerated away. Clearly this trip was something of a pleasant surprise. I had a vague feeling that this business had something to do with me, but what exactly I had no idea.

'Philipp Klementich,' said the man with the hammer politely, turning to the boss, 'the Japanese called and said he'll pick up the breakage tomorrow, but he wants a hell of a lot – eighty tonnes!'

'Well, you'd better get on with it, then,' shouted Phil fiercely.

With that it appeared to me that I had worked out what was going on – a clever game it was too. Some Japanese – typically enough – was buying up all sorts of breakage and scrap from the building trade over here. Phil and his team were doing everything they could to supply him with this kind of material. The only thing that worried me was that Phil, with his indomitable obstinacy might turn everything he touched into scrap from the building trade.

That was more or less how things were turning out. On both sides of the road everything we passed lay in ruins: houses that had been destroyed, various rusty constructions that appeared to have been yanked up and were out of position – it was, in short, the sort of wasteland that Japanese lovers of scrap must dream about.

Suddenly a beautiful house flashed by. It stood alone; perhaps it had been a villa at some time, but now it had no window-panes or roof and there was a big sign at the front that read: 'Danger'. I wondered what the 'danger' might be or what the sign was there for. Who might have turned what had once been a place of comfort and repose into a place of danger? I wondered if the area had been declared dangerous to keep people away, so that certain goings-on might not be discovered.

'Oh . . . I hope . . . this business with the Japanese . . . it's all being done by the book, isn't it?' I asked, emerging from my reverie.

'The boss doesn't like doing things by the book!' said the hammerer with a loud resonant laugh.

'You'll be walking home in a minute if you're not careful, mate.' Phil interrupted harshly.

We rolled into an empty enclosed courtyard. Under a rusty awning a short flight of steps took us to a door covered in shiny tin. Phil delivered a message in Morse code via the doorbell. The door opened heavily from the inside and we walked into a basement. There were all sorts of weird and wonderful things in there: colourful gas stoves, obviously not made in the Soviet Union, brilliant white sanitary ware shining in the dark and wallpaper wrapped in bright cellophane on shelves that had been knocked up clumsily. It occurred to me that the door by which we had entered was probably the only way into the place. We were met by a big fat woman in overalls.

'You get thinner every day!' said Phil in a friendly hoarse tone. They laughed for a moment before disappearing into a little office, where they shuffled a few papers around. Then they came out and Phil shouted:

'Load up!'

Interestingly he didn't help with the loading himself, but stood by teasing the proprietress in a friendly sort of way – although, of course, that kind of thing may be just as important; who knows, it may be more important than anything else.

We loaded eight sinks, four lavatories, six rolls of linoleum, twenty rolls of wallpaper and ten tubes of glue that was more or less impossible to find in the shops. Although there were plenty of things that I needed among what was loaded, I was not favoured with the slightest hint that might have raised my hopes. Moreover (and this alarmed me quite considerably), as we were saying goodbye the proprietress came up to me and said gratefully:

'Thank you. Now, at long last, the children will get their kindergarten.'

I was amazed. What did I have to do with it and what was she thanking me for? In any case I hoped all these things had not been bought legally by his enterprise – but I couldn't be sure. Then, suddenly, it occurred to me that they may have been bought by his enterprise all right, but with my cash – the material might have been bought with my money! I gave Phil a very dirty look, but he was giving nothing away; he just sat there.

Was it possible that on top of all the other stupid things I'd done in my life I had now become a sponsor – somehow I did not like the word.

The sinks were moving around in the body of the van and knocking against my legs. I moved my legs – on principle. However much I liked children, I wasn't going to have my legs broken for them.

From one unexpected direction or another we suddenly arrived in a familiar courtyard and stopped by the building that – I was supposed to believe – would so soon be filled with the echoing voices of children. Getting out of the van I noticed that the ambush prepared earlier had been transferred. There they all were: the women, wretched with suffering, and their children, the members of the commission with the old man at their head and the seemingly motionless officer from the fraud squad, who had none the less got there before us – rather like the tortoise in the fable.

Phil, silent and unperturbed, got out of the pick-up van. Then we started hauling the goodies out, springing over the ditch by the plank-bridges and carrying them inside, like so many Volga dockers.

With each fresh trip we made the roar of the crowd changed, becoming gradually ever less malicious and contemptuous and more and more delighted. The first person to come up to me (as I stood, exhausted and breathing heavily) was the man from the fraud squad.

'Thank you very much. You're a real friend!' he said, squeezing my hand. Then he got into his grasshopper-green Moskvich car and sped off, greatly relieved.

I was thoroughly confused. I didn't know whose friend I was and certainly couldn't see how I could be the children's.

By this time the women were surging around me.

'Well, thank you very much . . . at least there's one good person about!'

Perhaps I am a good person, but I couldn't work out how they could possibly have guessed.

'Fedya, give the dear man a sweet!'

Fedya hesitated a little. Then he stuck his hand into his mouth and pulled out a half-finished fruit drop, which he offered to me. Touched by Fedya's generosity I took the sweet and put it in my pocket. The joyous clamour of the women with the old man at their head passed out of the courtyard into the street and was gone. Clearly something wonderful and unexpected had happened to them, something they had been tired of waiting for and had stopped believing could happen.

Phil was walking around the unloaded material in a business-like fashion, going from one item to another and making notes in a little book.

'What's going on . . . why does everyone keep on thanking me?' I asked him.

'This stuff's rubbish! We'll fix you up with the very best Finnish stuff,' he said, avoiding a straight answer and waving contemptuously at the equipment we had brought from the warehouse.

'But it wasn't, by any chance . . . bought by means of a transfer, was it?' I was curious to know, although by now I was understanding ever more clearly the terrible fate that had befallen me.

'Look, mate: a transfer wouldn't buy you a coffin to bury yourself in!' laughed Phil, now acknowledging his victory. 'The thing was that a construction account was needed for this kindergarten business, but my bosses went and opened a repair account. I had to sort that out with them and you know the rest – I was being hassled.' Looking a little guilty he took me by the sleeve.

'Yeah, but surely . . . you could have bought these things . . . with the hard currency . . . you get from the Japanese?'

'I can't hold on to the hard currency!' said Phil in his hoarse way. 'These boys – my bosses, that is – fancy a bit of hard currency every now and again!'

'But why . . . give it to them?'

Phil, by now confident of a complete moral victory, smiled broadly.

'Why give it to them? Because I need them and they don't sign any papers at all without baksheesh.'

'Can't anything in this world be done in an honest way any more?'

'In an honest way, eh?' Phil bared his teeth. Apparently my naïve questions had finally driven him mad. 'You like doing things in an honest way, do you? Take it, then! It was all bought with your money!' and, breathing deeply, he suddenly began to throw things into a dirty puddle at my feet: brand new wallpaper, sinks, lavatories, one of which broke. 'Take it,' he said, 'the children can wait.'

'OK, OK, I don't mind; you can have it,' I sighed.

'Valery, you're a superstar, mate!' he said joyfully, making faces like a child. '. . . Yeah, well, stop twitching like a lunatic, will you,' he said, returning to his severe, friendly tone. 'We'll fix you up with the very best Finnish stuff, yeah, and we'll get it all done in one go!'

VII

Yes, they do a remarkable job in working me out as someone to rip off, and somehow they manage to do it 'all in one go'. Above all the thing is done, the calculations are made, instantaneously and, as it were, effortlessly – sometimes even from a great distance. I remember how last spring a film director called me all the way from Tashkent and, with compliments and assurances, invited me to come out on, as he put it, 'a delicate mission'. Having heard so much about eastern hospitality and, above all, being broke at the time, I immediately went out. It turned out that the mission was indeed a very delicate one: I was to write the script of a film that had already been shot. That is to say, they had spent three years, shooting a three-hour film, without a script. The idea had been to make it up as they went along, but they made up so many things that in the end they themselves did not know what kind of film they had produced. On top of this, they had obviously been living it up over the three years. Although it was in no way necessary to the movie, it was being filmed on the Black Sea. It included appearances by a hell of a lot of beautiful girls who had absolutely nothing to do with the subject, which, incidentally, was non-existent. By now the director had spent several millions but did not have a connected piece of work to show the Arts Council. He was headed for big trouble and only I could save him. He was absolutely right there. There was just one town in the whole of this immense country where such a fool could be found: St Petersburg. In horror I studied the material they gave me. Someone or other – there was no way of knowing who – went into some luxurious rooms; then he went out again; some couples were dancing. What made it worse was that there was no way of filming some more or throwing something out; I had to make do with what there was, only able to change the order of the episodes and having to think up the words for a finished piece of mime. I don't mind admitting I was excited by the great challenge the task posed for my imagination. For two months I sat in a pretty dreadful hotel room, was insulted by the maids and, by the way, did not run into any eastern hospitality at all. In the end I managed to turn the original mosaic into a picture that was pretty well put together. I was feeling pleased and proud. The day I left the appreciative director informed me that, unfortunately, the bank was closed that day. Alas, he could not pay me the money he had promised. 'Well, perhaps I should stay, then?' I muttered, already feeling doomed and understanding everything. 'There's no need for that,' he cried indignantly. 'Get on the plane and the money will be waiting for you when you arrive. I'll send it by telegraph.' Naturally, I am still waiting for it. But, to give credit where credit is due, at least the man from Tashkent did not take any money from me, which is more than can be said for Phil. In any case, the moral is that things have a remarkable way of repeating themselves: your character determines your fate. And if the world is divided into two halves, consisting of those who deceive and those who are duped, come what may I would always prefer to be among the latter.

VIII

'My deaw thir,' came the sound of Phil's voice rousing me from my thoughts. 'All verk and no play mak'th Jack a dull boy!' he said, beckoning me from the pick-up van.

'No, I'd better be going.' Somehow I'd had quite enough of playing around already.

'Come on, let's have some fun. We'll go see old Irina. I want to give her a good talking to – it's time I sorted her out!'

'Don't!' I said, rushing to get into the van.

'To the office!' commanded Phil, slamming the door behind me.

As ever the car shook when we went round corners. Something told me to beware that having a good time with Phil might turn out to be even more of a strain than working with him. He quietly hummed a jaunty little jazz number as we went along, occasionally winking to me in a friendly way. He was utterly convinced that he had purchased my eternal gratitude (and, what's more, characteristically enough, with my own money!).

We arrived at the office and started getting out of the van. At that very moment a whole crowd of people were going off to have lunch together.

'It seems her ladyship is nowhere to be seen!' the hammerer told Phil.

'Obviously she's fasting!' said Phil chuckling.

I thought about leaving, but it seemed to me that when I was around Phil was more restrained than he might have been otherwise – especially with Irina.

That was when she appeared: she was walking with her nose in the air, ignoring us. She had someone in tow, young, swarthy and in high-heeled boots. Phil was standing very still, looking at the ground.

Instinctively I hoped, against all logic, that he hadn't seen her. But the way he was standing, dead still, indicated that unquestionably he had. Steeling herself, she resolved to sail past without saying anything, but at the last moment she cracked and walked straight up to Phil and addressed him in an exaggeratedly professional manner:

'Philipp Klementich, do you by any chance need me at the moment?'

He neither moved nor said anything. Everyone could feel the

tension. Phil's silence and motionlessness were more frightening than any shouting or rowing would have been. Those who were passing stopped talking, stood still and watched in amazement.

'Ruslan, darling, hang on, will you? I'll be back in a minute,' she said affectionately to her companion, rather demonstrably touching his shoulder.

Darling Ruslan took a few paces and, without turning round, stood and waited.

'Well?' Irina hissed.

'To your post, please,' said Phil, unperturbed and pointing the way.

Irina swore, pretty openly, turned and went into Phil's office. Phil, inscrutable as ever, shuffled along in his moon boots, slowly walked over to the desk and sat down behind it. Irina was being deliberately provocative as she went up to him with a pen and notepad. Phil said nothing, ignoring her completely.

'Perhaps I might go and have some lunch after all?' she asked, not being able to stand it any longer.

'Any trouble from you and you'll be on your way!' said Phil in a barely audible whisper.

'What have I done, then?' she said, immediately giving in.

'Listen ... if it wasn't for ... this soppy young lad,' and he nodded at me, 'I'd tell you *what*!'

'Well,' I thought to myself, 'that "soppy young lad" has certainly been pretty useful.'

The door opened and there was darling Ruslan, looking a little dishevelled.

'Off you go, darling. Philipp Klementich and I have some very important matters to attend to,' said Irina capriciously.

'Oh!' shouted Phil joyfully, half rising from his chair. 'Here's someone to run and get us some vodka! Give us a tenner, will you,' he said aside to me.

I couldn't see why on earth I should pay for this whim of his, but I couldn't bear the sight of Ruslan standing there like a lamp-post – so I handed over my last tenner.

'You're a good sport, Philipp Klementich!' said Ruslan, suddenly breaking into a smile and he stomped off at top speed.

'What a jerk!' said Phil contemptuously when he had gone.

'As for you, you're a swine, but I like you,' said Irina, coquettishly tapping Phil's nose with her pencil.

Soon Ruslan was back with the vodka. Breathless but delighted he handed it over to the boss, who ripped the tin lid off with his teeth, spat it out and filled the glasses.

'Not for me,' I said, but he paid no attention.

'Philipp Klementich,' said Ruslan, delicately sipping his vodka, 'there's something I'd like to ask about work.'

'You'd have been better off asking at work, then,' said Phil chuckling.

'Do you mind?'

'Well, what is it?'

'We're painting some holiday flats at the moment with some new stuff . . .'

'Yes, I know. Isn't that remarkable!'

'The thing is, a lot of the people who come for their holidays get swellings and throw up because of the paint . . . one of them was even taken off in an ambulance . . .'

'That's their business. Anything else?'

'. . . Shall we carry on painting?'

'Does it make *you* feel sick?'

'Not really . . . I've kind of got used to it . . .'

'Get on with it, then!'

That's Phil. It was a situation in which the average person would feel pangs of conscience, become nervous, hem and haw. Not Phil. He immediately disposed of the whole issue, cutting it away, as it were, at one blow. 'Get on with it, then!' And all the questions that would have driven other people out of their minds were answered without hesitation, 'all in one go'. That was Phil all over. It's for that very reason he manages to hold on to a top job, however many complaints are made against him, precisely because he gets things done – everything and always – even things that ought not to be done.

The hammerer appeared.

'Philipp Klementich . . .' His eye caught mine and he wavered. 'Shall I do it . . . for the Japanese?' He looked from Phil to me and back again.

'Get on with it!' Phil barked hoarsely.

The hammerer went out.

Soon we could hear the sound of blows ringing out from the courtyard. My fortune was being smashed to pieces. Phil sat there, poker-faced, gloomy.

Well, that was it – apparently I wasn't needed any more. It seemed to me that I had come full circle. It was ending as it had begun: with the breaking of basins. Along the way I had managed to calm and soothe Phil, mothers and their little children and a fraud squad officer. Now I was about to bring more joy into the life of the insatiable Japanese. The fact that I had been upset myself was immaterial!

'Give me some of yours, will you!' said Phil, nodding at Irina's glass.

'You are awful!' she replied, playfully splashing the rest of her vodka into his glass.

I couldn't stand being there any longer. They didn't want me for anything any more, not even as a 'soppy young lad' – there was more than enough soppiness to go round as it was!

'Ciao!' I said, making for the door.

Phil didn't even look at me. He may have been indifferent to my leaving. But if he had been, it is more likely that he'd have nodded after me in an absent-minded way and maybe even come out with some insignificant phrase. No, his complete silence and the fact that he did not move a muscle could only be interpreted as his response to an outrageous insult and a great tragedy. He had opened his heart to me (even if it wasn't the purest heart in the world), he had brought me into his holiest of holies, he had revealed his professional methods (even if they weren't ideal) – and I had spat on all this from a great height and left. There was nothing I could possibly do to redeem myself. Dear old Irina was most perceptive in grasping the boss's state of mind.

'Of course, when it's not his affairs that are being discussed he doesn't want to know!' she shouted after me.

That was wonderful: 'When it's not his affairs that are being discussed.' In actual fact it was precisely my basins that were at that very moment being pulverized – noisily and within earshot – to please the Japanese. Another extraordinary thing was that, although Phil was giving them to the Japanese, if I had taken one I'd have been depriving the children. But, enough of that! Though I was willing, just, to help the mothers and children, there was no way that I was going to help raise the already high level of Japanese industry!

I opened the door.

'He'll be back!' I was vexed to hear Phil remark casually to Irina as I left.

'. . . Be back, will I? We'll see about that,' I thought to myself.

IX

Outside I was dazzled by the bright sunlight. The driver of the pick-up van tooted his horn at me and I walked over to him.

'Get in. I'll give you a lift.'

'I haven't got any money,' I said throwing up my hands in grief. I'd had enough of Phil's henchmen too.

'Go on, get in!' said the driver heatedly. I could see that for some reason he really wanted me to, so I got in. We set off.

'And what if the boss needs you?'

'Oh! He's not going anywhere. He'll probably get himself plastered, but you can be sure he'll be there, at the helm! The evening's another story; he'll want me then.'

'Where will you take him – in the evening, I mean?'

'To restaurants and bars, where else? First we'll pick all the boys up, then we'll go to a bar. But I'm fed up with it all: I unscrewed the table in the back of the van,' he nodded back towards the empty space between the seats. 'They won't be drinking in this van any more. I said the fastenings wouldn't hold; there's no way they'll know. And I took the thing out. It was either that or sitting waiting for them to come out of the bar and then having them get in here and unpack a whole lot of food and drink on the table back there. I never get home before two – my wife's not talking to me any more, you know. The worst thing, though, is that they never give me anything. They might at least offer – "try a bit of this" sort of thing. You know, I might like to give my daughter some salmon or caviare . . . but no – never! They make pigs of themselves, drink a hell of a lot, throw things around and then: "Take me here," "Take me there." I have to drag them all home after everything else. That's it, anyway – this bar's closed!' Once more he nodded back over his shoulder.

'Who are they . . . the ones he drinks with?' I was curious to know.

'Who are they? That's easy enough – big shots. They're the sorts that are desperate for someone like Phil. If it came to it, they could have him go to jail for them, then after a bit they could get him out again. They're from the executive committee, maybe even higher up than that. I've seen them close up and know them for what they are: nothing but scum. They get arse-holed, then they try to get some birds.' He spat. 'And those basins you paid for, old Grinya's already knocked hell out of them. They'll go to the Japanese – there's some rare element that can be got out of them. And our people, Phil's lot – they couldn't give a damn. Anyway, they're not drinking in my van any more – no way!'

We turned a corner.

'And my wife has to drag our daughter all the way across town to a kindergarten near her factory; and a three-year-old has to be woken up at half five! There's no kindergarten where we live – there hasn't been one for ten years . . . If you gave them half a chance they'd wreck everything.'

'They've had rather more than half a chance already,' I thought.

'And . . . at our hostel there still aren't any basins on the second and third floors.'

'I don't have a basin either!' I remembered.

'You don't have one either?' and he turned to look at me.

X

The decorating the lads did for me in my flat set me back exactly half as much as had been taken from me by my very dear friend, Phil, who apparently had no intention of returning a kopeck.

Although I didn't see anything of him now, strangely enough my understanding of him was deepening. Every time the driver, Nikolai, came to see me about the work being done on my flat he grumbled loudly about having to drive drunk men home in the early hours of the morning. All of them – and Phil was particularly insistent on this – demanded to be taken home without fail, however drunk they might be. Their homes, apparently, were their sanctuaries. Incidentally, *à propos* of this, it would appear that the time Phil spent the night at my place he must have been making a rare exception. I was deeply touched by this knowledge. According to my new friend, Nikolai, Phil's home was exemplary: the flat was extremely well decorated, he had three sons, all very sporty, and a gorgeous wife. In other words, his home kept him going: that's where he found spiritual repose. On the other hand, somehow I find it difficult to believe you can split your life into two separate portions sharply divided by a line running down the middle.

Now he had disappeared, as if mortally offended that I had dropped him, neglected his spiritual life (if one can call what happened in his office 'spiritual life'). At the same time, as if goaded by the offence, he could hold on to the money he owed me – which was very convenient, of course. The main thing, though, was unquestionably the insult he had suffered in the depths of his heart. He told himself that as soon as I had understood that my mercenary interests would not be satisfied I had immediately left, spitting on every tie that bound us together. That's more or less how he explained it to himself. It was, of course, a decidedly lop-sided version of what had happened and in order to believe it himself –

that the root of the problem was my desecration of our friendship rather than his theft of my money – he had to keep himself in a permanent state of aggressive hysteria, claiming that everyone he dealt with was a bastard or a swine – and to him of all people, 'him with his open heart, while they' and all the rest of it. Living like that couldn't be easy – I sympathized with him.

It is only in a state of heightened tension, by bringing all one's feelings to white heat, that it is possible to pull the sort of tricks he had done with me and at the same time feel justified and even insulted. It's not easy. And all that just to end up knocking back some vodka with a few tough guys in a dirty pick-up van and for the umpteenth time boozing oneself into a state of righteousness.

Day in and day out achieving the impossible, and in the process flouting all moral constraints, may give him an excuse for thinking of himself as an extraordinary man, but in the final analysis it doesn't get him anywhere. Perhaps, the day we first saw each other again, after all those years, he really was moved by some pure, delicate feelings – and then he immediately went and smashed them to smithereens, like one of the basins. I wondered if, at the end of the day, his gains would outweigh his losses.

Things were especially hard for him now. Before he had at least the consolation of blaming me: 'Everyone knows,' he'd say to himself, 'what these idealistic types are like.' But now that option (like the table in the van) was no longer open to him.

One would expect that, leading that sort of life, he would long ago have lost all trace of conscience. But clearly he felt far from confident that he had got the better of me and he continued assiduously to unearth proof of his moral (or amoral) superiority. An example of his trying to present such proof was a call he made late at night about six months after we parted.

'Listen, mate!' he said, in the old hoarse voice, but without the least hint of its former warmth, as if I had been insulting him constantly over the past six months (no doubt I had been insulting him in the sense that I had made no attempt to ask for my money back, clearly indicating that I felt it wasn't even worth asking someone like *him*).

There was no knowing whether or not he would ever forgive me.

'Listen, mate!'

Then he informed me that he had got everything he had promised, and the very best quality Finnish stuff too. It was all there at the warehouse. I was to bring 'one and a half K' to the restaurant straight away and make sure I didn't go out the next day. Obviously it would have been throwing good money after bad, but what I could not understand was why he was trying it on with me a second time. Of course, it may have been simply that he thought he could get away with it, but then again, perhaps not; there must have been more to it than that. On second thoughts, perhaps not. It was more than likely he had nagging doubts that I doubted his loyalty to his friends and might not be wholly convinced of his honesty. These doubts probably drove him mad. The wish to prove his complete integrity, coupled with the usual need to steal, contributed more than anything else to the tragedy of his life.

However, there must have been a grain of decency in him if he still had something to prove. He was trying to prove his honesty to me in particular – none of the people he dealt with could care less about that sort of thing. Then I turned up. Who knows, I may have been the one bright star in the dark night of his life; I may have represented a final chance for him to save his soul. He probably hoped secretly that his relationship with me would enrich him spiritually, while in actual fact I enriched him in a material way only and was happy to settle for that.

Certainly he had a tough exterior – whenever he met with suspicion he would resort to insults, when attacked he would reply with savage blows and when accused of something he would respond with much more serious accusations. If there was a way of getting to his heart and soul, it could only be by getting him on the end of a particular hook. That hook – the only one by which he might be lifted from where he was – was the hook of true friendship, of friendship that knows no bounds. Admittedly, by and large he had pulled down on that hook, towards himself, but he might also be pulled up on it.

In any case, something must have been gnawing away at him, considering that more than a year later he suddenly pulled up and stopped his Zhiguli car on the pavement beside me.

'Well, you old brute, where have you been?' he said, flinging open the door and baring his teeth.

They were all gold now. 'Good for you!' I thought.

There was a bloke in the back, looking pretty uncomfortable. He was well dressed, but not pretentiously so.

'Klim!' he said, introducing himself in a deep voice and squeezing my hand.

'He's just turned up from Siberia,' said Phil laughing.

So, apparently Phil needed to show off his friends, because he hadn't come to terms with what had happened: otherwise, of course, he could have driven by without stopping.

'I fixed him up with a hotel reservation, but when we arrived – there was bugger-all there for him!' said Phil huskily.

'Well, there we are, never mind ... I'll go back home,' said the deep-voiced Klim.

'What about my place,' I said suddenly, to my surprise.

'Valery, mate!' Phil shook me by the shoulders.

And I thought to myself: 'Not again?!'

Translated by James Doyle

SERGEI DOVLATOV

The Fifth Compromise

('Soviet Estonia.' November 1975)

A MAN HAS BEEN BORN. The annual holiday of Liberation Day is widely observed in the republic. Factories and mills, collective farms, machine-and-tractor stations – all report to the government on the high statistics attained.

And still another milestone has been reached in the last few days. The population of the Estonian capital has reached four hundred thousand. In Tallinn Hospital No. 4, a baby has been born to Maya and Grigory Kuzin – their long-awaited firstborn. It's this little boy who is fated to be the four-hundred-thousandth inhabitant of the city.

'He'll be an athlete,' says Chief Doctor Mikhkel Teppe, smiling.

The happy father awkwardly tries to hide his callused hands. 'We'll call our son Lembit,' he says. 'Let him grow like the folk-hero of that name!'

The famous Tallinn poet Boris Shtein addresses these verses to the happy parents:

> In factories, in the deepest mines,
> On planets strange and far,
> I see four hundred thousand heroes,
> And your firstborn, too, I see there!

One remembers the words of Goethe[1]: 'A man is born – an entire world is born!'

---

1 Author's note: The fantasy of the author. Goethe did not write this.

I do not know what you will grow up to be, Lembit! A lathe operator or a miner, an officer or a scientist. Only one thing is clear: a man has been born! A man condemned to happiness!

Tallinn is a small city – intimate. You meet a friend on the street and hear, 'Hi, I was just looking for you,' as though you were in a company cafeteria. The point is, I was surprised to learn just how many people live in Tallinn.

It was like this. Turonok called me in and said, 'A constructive idea has turned up. It might make for some effective reporting. Let's discuss the particulars. Just don't get crude with me.'

'Why should I be crude? It's useless . . .'

'Actually, you've been crude already,' Turonok said, turning gloomy. 'You're always being crude, Dovlatov. You're even crude at general meetings. The only time you're not crude is when you're not around for a long time. You think I'm so dull? Think I read nothing but newspapers? You should drop in on me at home sometimes. You should see my library. By the way, I've got some pre-revolutionary editions –'

'Why,' I asked, 'did you call me in?'

Turonok was silent for a moment. Then he straightened up sharply, as if to change a lyrical pose to a businesslike one. He began to speak with confidence and precision. 'Next week is the anniversary of Tallinn's liberation. The day will be widely observed everywhere, including the pages of this newspaper. We'll cover all its various aspects – economic, cultural, human-interest . . . Every department is working something up. There's a job for you, too. To be specific: according to the data issued by the Bureau of Statistics, the city has around four hundred thousand inhabitants. This figure is somewhat relative, just as the city limits are. So here's what it comes down to. We talked it over and decided: the four-hundred-thousandth inhabitant of Tallinn is about to be born on the eve of the jubilee.'

'There's something here I don't quite understand.'

'Go to the maternity hospital. Wait for the first newborn. Get the measurements. Interview the happy parents, the doctor who delivered the baby. Naturally, get photographs. The story will run in the jubilee issue. The pay – I know this is not without significance to you – is double.'

'You should have said so in the first place.'

'Mercantilism is one of your more unpleasant traits,' Turonok said.

'Debts,' I said. 'Alimony.'

'You drink a lot.'

'It happens.'

'Let's cut this short. The general idea is, a happy man has just been born. I'd even put it this way – a man condemned to happiness!' This foolish phrase pleased the editor so much that he repeated it twice. 'A man condemned to happiness! In my opinion, not bad. Maybe we'll use it as a headline: "A MAN CONDEMNED TO HAPPINESS."'

'We'll see,' I said.

'And remember' – Turonok stood up, closing our conversation – 'the infant has to be publicizable.'

'Which means?'

'Which means meeting all requirements. No damaged goods, nothing gloomy. No Caesarean sections. No single mothers. A complete set of parents. A healthy boy meeting all the social requirements.'

'It has to be a boy?'

'Yes, a boy is somehow more symbolic.'

'Genrikh Frantsevich, about those photographs. If you think about it, newborns can look pretty awful.'

'Choose the best one. You can wait. There's time.'

'We'd have to wait at least four months. Any earlier, it will hardly look human. Some people still don't after fifty years.'

'Listen,' said Turonok, turning angry, 'don't give me that demagoguery! You have an assignment. The material has to be ready by

Wednesday. You're a professional journalist. Why are we wasting time?'

He's right, I thought. Why indeed?

I went down to the bar and ordered a gin and a sandwich. I noticed Zhbankov, the photographer, not very sober, and I waved to him. He sat down next to me with a wineglass of vodka and broke off half of my sandwich.

'You should go home,' I said. 'The office is full of bosses.'

Zhbankov emptied the wineglass and said, 'You know, I've already made a mess of things. Did you see the shot I took for Fedya's piece?'

'I don't read newspapers.'

'Fedya had a piece in *Young News*. More exactly, a sketch, "Three against the Storm". About divers. How they search, you know, for valuable sunken cargo. With a storm moving in, no less. So that was my photograph. Two big guys sitting on a log. And a hose sticking up out of the water – that's one of their buddies keeping busy on the bottom. So naturally I go out and shoot it, tie up the rowboat, and forget the whole thing. But then, as I walk through the port, I hear laughing. What's going on, you know? It turns out to be quite a story. It seems there's a fellow down there named Mironenko, chief of the auxiliary shop. Earlier that day he happens to walk out of the lunchroom and light up a cigarette by the third mooring. Et cetera, et cetera. Throws away the cigarette. Gets ready to spit, pardon the expression. And spits out his teeth. His false ones, naturally. And he's got about eight hundred roubles' worth of gold in them. So he runs to the divers. "Comrades, help!" And they yell back, "We'll get them after work." "I'll make it worth your while." "Stand us a bottle each?" "What a question!" So they finish work and start diving around. And now Fedya comes by from another assignment. Takes in the scene. "What are you doing there?" he says. Makes himself important, you know. And the divers get a little shy. "Your mother, such-and-such," they answer, "some valuable cargo has sunk." And Fedya asks like an idiot, "What's your name? What's your name?" And these guys give him all the right answers. "What do you like to do in your rare moments of leisure?" "Music," they say, "painting . . ." "And why are you working so late?" "A storm is coming in, we're in a hurry," they say. Fedya calls me at the newspaper. I show up and shoot some pictures without asking around. The main thing was, it was some kind of man-made harbour. No storm could ever get there.'

'You should go home,' I said.

'Wait, the main thing wasn't even that. Later I found out how the whole business ended. The divers did find the guy's dentures. Mironenko was in bliss up to his eyebrows. So he herds them all to a tavern. Orders vodka. Has a few shots. Starts to demonstrate his dentures to everybody. "I want to thank these kids," he says, "who saved my life and found them. Eagles," he says, "heroes of labour, Stakhanovites." Shows them his dentures at one table, then another. The doorman comes up to take a look, the trombonist from the band. The waitresses shake their heads in amazement. And Mironenko opens the sixth bottle with the divers. Suddenly he does a double take – no dentures. Somebody took them. He yells, "Give them back, you bastards!" Fat chance. Now even the divers can't help.'

'Fine,' I said. 'I've got to go.'

I didn't feel like going to the maternity ward. I find the atmosphere in hospitals depressing. The rubber plants get me down.

I dropped by the office to see Marina. She said, 'Oh, it's you. Sorry, I'm busy.'

'Has something happened?'

'What could happen? There's a lot of work.'

'What kind of work?'

'The jubilee and all that. After all, we're dull people. We don't write novels.'

'Why are you in such a bad mood?'

'And why should I be in a good mood? You're always disappearing somewhere. One moment you're madly in love, then you're gone for a week, playing around.'

'What do you mean, "playing around"? I was on assignment near Saaremaa. I'm all bitten up from the bedbugs in the hotel.'

'Those aren't bedbug bites,' Marina said, squinting suspiciously. 'Those are from some women. Some revolting little tarts. What do they see in you, I wonder. Never any money, always with a hangover ... I'm amazed you haven't caught some infection already.'

'What can you catch from a bedbug?'

'If only you'd stop lying! Who was that tall, fidgety redhead? I saw you from the bus this morning.'

'That was no fidgety redhead. That was the metaphysical poet Vladimir Erl. He's letting his hair grow.'

Suddenly I realized that she was about to burst into tears. Marina always wept despondently, bitterly, with little yelps, holding nothing back — like an actress after a performance.

'I beg you, calm down. Everything will be all right. Everyone knows how attached I am to you.'

Marina got out a tiny rose-coloured handkerchief and wiped her eyes. She began to speak more calmly. 'Can you be serious for a moment?'

'Of course.'

'I'm not so sure. You're completely irresponsible, like a skylark. You have no address, or possessions, or ambitions. You have no deep attachments. I'm just a random stopping point in space. But I'm already pushing forty. I have to put my life in some kind of order.'

'I'm also pushing forty. More exactly, I'm over thirty. And I don't know what that means, "to put your life in order". You want to get married? But what will that change? What will that idiotic stamp give us? It's a horse-brand. While things are good, I'm here. When I get tired of them, I'll go. That's the way it will always be.'

'I don't plan to get married. Anyway, what kind of husband would you make! It's just that I want to have a child. Otherwise it will be too late.'

'So have a child. But think of what's in store for him.'

'You always paint things in such dark colours. Millions of people live and work honestly. Anyway, how can I have a child alone?'

'Why alone? I'll . . . participate. And as for the material side of the question, you earn three times as much as I do. Which means, practically speaking, you don't need me to support you.'

'I was talking about something else.'

The telephone rang. Marina picked it up. 'Yes? . . . Well, that's great. He's right here.'

I waved my hands no.

Marina nodded understandingly. 'I mean, he just left . . . No, I have no idea. He's probably off drinking somewhere.'

Well, I thought, the little bitch.

'Tsekhanovsky is looking for you. He wants to pay you back some money you loaned him.'

'What's wrong with him?'

'He got paid for his book.'

'A *Caravan to the Skies*?'

'Why "*Caravan*"? The book is called *To Be Continued*.'

'It's the same thing,' I said. 'Fine. I've got to go.'

'Where are you off to? If it's no secret.'

'Picture this – the maternity hospital.'

I glanced at the tables heaped with newspapers, caught a smell of cigarette smoke and glue, and felt such a strong pang of boredom and bitterness that even the hospital didn't seem so bad.

Outside the door I realized that Marina had shouted out, 'Well, get lost, you pitiful drunk!'

I got on a bus and headed for Karl Marx Street. In the bus, I fell asleep unexpectedly and woke up, after a minute, with a headache. Crossing the hall of the maternity hospital, I caught a glimpse of myself in the mirror and turned away.

A woman in a white smock came towards me. 'Unauthorized visitors are not permitted.'

'How about authorized authors?' I asked.

The nurse froze in confusion. I held out my press pass and

climbed to the second floor. A few women in shapeless white coats were smoking on the landing.

'Where can I find the doctor?'

'One flight up, across from the lift.'

Across from the lift means that the doctor is a modest man. Across from the lift it must be noisy – doors slamming.

I walked in. An Estonian of about sixty was standing in front of an open window doing exercises.

I can spot an Estonian right away, and I'm never wrong. Nothing raucous or flamboyant about them. Invariably, the tie and the crease in the trousers. A rather poor line to the chin and a calm look in the eyes. Anyway, what Russian does exercises alone?

I held out my ID.

'Dr Mikhkel Teppe. Please have a seat. How can I be of help?'

I told him what I was there for. The doctor was not surprised. In general, no matter what the press comes up with, it's hard to surprise the average reader. He's used to everything.

'I don't think it should be difficult,' Teppe said. 'The clinic is enormous.'

'Are you notified about every birth?'

'It can be arranged.' He picked up the receiver, said something in Estonian, then turned to me. 'Are you interested in the actual labour?'

'God forbid! All I want to do is write up the data, take a look at the baby, and talk with the father.'

The doctor made another call and once again said something in Estonian. Then he said to me, 'There's a woman in labour right now. I'll check again in a few minutes. I'm sure everything will be all right. The mother is such a big, healthy blonde.' The doctor was getting carried away.

'And you yourself,' I asked, 'are you married?'

'Of course.'

'Do you have any children?'

'One son.'

'Do you ever wonder what's in store for him?'

'Why should I wonder? I know exactly what's in store for him. He's in for a strict-regime labour camp. I consulted a lawyer. They've already got from him a written promise that he won't leave town, which means they must be about to arrest him.' Teppe spoke calmly and simply, as though we were talking about the most natural thing in the world.

I lowered my voice and asked in a confidential tone, 'The Soldatov case?'

'What?' the doctor said, not understanding.

'Your son – did he take part in the Estonian Spring?'

'My son,' Teppe said distinctly, 'is a black marketeer and a drunk. And I can only stop worrying about him somewhat when he's locked up.'

We were both silent.

'At one time I worked as a medic on the islands. Then I served in the Estonian Army Corps. I was given a high position. I don't know what we did wrong. His mother and I are people with a positive outlook, while our son has a negative one.'

'I wouldn't mind hearing his side of the story.'

'It's impossible to listen to him. I say to him, "Yura, why do you despise me? I've obtained everything I have through hard work. I haven't had an easy life. Now I have a high position. Why do you think they made me – a humble medic – a chief physician?" And he says, "Because all your smart colleagues were shot." As if I shot them.'

The telephone rang.

'Speaking,' Teppe said. 'Excellent.' Then he changed to Estonian. The conversation was about centimetres and kilograms.

'There we are,' he told me. 'A birth in the ninth ward. Four kilos two hundred grams and fifty-eight centimetres. Want to see it?'

'No, thanks. Babies all look the same.'

'The mother's last name is Okas. Khilia Okas. Born 1946. Works as a regulator in the Punane Factory. The father's Magabcha.'

'What does that mean – "Magabcha"?'

'That's his last name. He's from Ethiopia. He's studying at the Merchant Marine Academy.'

'Black?'

'More like chocolate.'

'Listen,' I said, 'this is interesting. We could play up international-ism. The friendship of nations. Are they married?'

'Of course. He writes her notes every day and signs them, "Your carob bar."'

'Can I use your telephone?'

'Help yourself.'

I called the office. Turonok came to the phone.

'Yes? Turonok speaking.'

'Genrikh Frantsevich, a little boy has just been born.'

'What? Who is this?'

'It's Dovlatov. From the maternity hospital. You gave me an assignment.'

'Oh, yes. I remember.'

'Well, a little boy has been born. Big, healthy. Fifty-eight centi-metres. Four kilos two hundred grams. The father is Ethiopian . . .'

An uneasy silence.

'I don't understand,' Turonok said.

'An Ethiopian. He comes from Ethiopia. He's a student here,' I said. 'A Marxist,' I added for some reason.

'Are you drunk?' Turonok asked sharply.

'How can you say that? I'm on assignment.'

'On assignment. When did that ever stop you? Who vomited all over the Regional Party Headquarters last December?'

'Genrikh Frantsevich, I can't tie up the line for long. A little boy has just been born. His father belongs to a friendly nation.'

'You mean to say he's black?'

'More like chocolate.'

'That is, a Negro?'

'Naturally.'

'What is there natural about this?'

'Isn't an Ethiopian a human being?'

'Dovlatov,' Turonok said, in a voice choked with torment, 'Dovlatov, I'll fire you . . . for attempting to discredit the very best

. . . Leave your sodding Ethiopian in peace! Wait for a normal – do you hear me? – *normal* human baby!'

'Fine,' I said. 'I was only asking.'

The line went dead. Teppe looked at me with sympathy.

'It won't work,' I told him.

'I had doubts right away, but I didn't want to say anything.'

'Well, fine.'

'Would you like some coffee?' He took a brown jar out of a cabinet. The telephone rang again. Teppe talked for a long time in Estonian. Obviously it had nothing to do with me.

I waited till he finished and then unexpectedly heard myself ask, 'Could I use your bed to take a nap?'

'Of course,' Teppe said without surprise. 'Would you like to put my raincoat over you?'

'This is all right.'

Behind a screen I took off my shoes and stretched out on the bed. I had to concentrate. Otherwise the contours of reality might become hopelessly lost. Suddenly I saw myself from the outside, distracted and absurd. Who am I? What am I doing here? Why am I lying behind a screen waiting for God knows what? And how stupidly my life is going.

When I woke up, Teppe was standing over me.

'Excuse me, I'm sorry if I startled you, but your acquaintance has just given birth.'

Marina, I thought, with a light flash of terror. (As everyone knows, fear can be felt in even slight degrees.) Then, pushing this crazy thought aside, I asked, 'What do you mean "my acquaintance"?'

'A journalist from *Young News* magazine. Rumyantseva.'

'Ah, Lena, the wife of Borya Shtein. Of course. That's why I haven't seen her since May.'

'She gave birth five minutes ago.'

'This has possibilities. The editor will be happy. The father is a famous Tallinn poet. The mother is a journalist. Both are in the Party. Shtein will undoubtedly write a ballad for the occasion.'

'Very glad for you.'

I called Shtein. 'Greetings,' I said. 'You're to be congratulated.'

'It's still early for that. I get the answer on Wednesday.'

'What answer?'

'About whether I'm going to Sweden or not. They tell me I have no experience travelling in capitalist countries. But how can I get experience if they won't let me out? Have you been to any capitalist countries?'

'No. I couldn't even get permission to go to a socialist country. I applied to go to Bulgaria.'

'But I've even been to Yugoslavia. Yugoslavia is practically capitalist.'

'I'm calling from the clinic. Your son has just been born.'

'Your mother!' Shtein shouted. 'Your mother!'

Teppe handed me a scribbled sheet.

'Height,' I said, 'fifty-six, weight three kilos nine hundred grams. Lena feels fine.'

'Your mother!' Shtein could not stop. 'I'll be right there. I'll take a taxi.'

Now I had to call the photographer.

'Call him, call him,' Teppe said.

I called Zhbankov. His wife answered.

'Mikhail Vladimirovich is not well,' she said.

'What – drunk?' I asked.

'Like a pig. Was it you who got him drunk?'

'Nothing of the sort. Anyway, I'm at work.'

'Well, sorry.'

I called Malkiel. 'Come over and take a picture of a baby for the jubilee issue. Shtein has a new son. The pay is double, by the way.'

'You want to write about that baby?'

'Why not?'

'Why not? Because Shtein is a Jew. And every Jew has to be submitted for approval. You're fantastically naïve, Serge.'

'I wrote about Kaplan and didn't submit him for approval.'

'Tell me more. Tell me how you wrote about Gliksman. Kaplan

is a member of the Regional Party Bureau. He's been written up hundreds of times. Don't start comparing Kaplan with Shtein.'

'I'm not comparing them. Shtein is much nicer.'

'So much the worse for him.'

'I get the point. Thanks for warning me.'

I said to Teppe, 'It seems that Shtein won't work, either.'

'I had my doubts.'

'Then who woke me up?' I asked.

'I woke you up. But I had doubts.'

'So now what?'

'Very soon another woman will finish labour. She might have given birth already. I'll call right now.'

'I'll just take a little walk outside.'

Cats were prowling around the dreary hospital courtyard. The leafless poplars made harsh scraping sounds. A skinny, slouching boy in his teens passed by, rolling a serving cart with a coffee urn on it. His faded blue attendant's smock made him look like an old woman.

Shtein appeared from around the corner.

'Ah, congratulations,' I said.

'Thanks, old man, thanks. I just dropped off a basket of food for Lenka. I'm in a fantastic mood. We should have a drink to celebrate.'

Some drinking one can do with you, I thought. It's bound to end badly.

I didn't want to disappoint him. I didn't want to tell him that his baby was a reject. But Shtein already knew that something was up.

'You're writing an article about the jubilee?'

'I'm trying to.'

'And you want to make my family famous?'

'The trouble is,' I said, 'we need a worker-peasant family. And you're intellectuals.'

'Too bad. I already wrote some lines in the taxi. Here's how the poem ends:

In factories, in the deepest mines,
On planets strange and far,
I see four hundred thousand heroes,
And my firstborn, too, I see there!'

I said, 'Why firstborn? You have a grown daughter.'

'From my first marriage.'

'Ah,' I said, 'then that's all right.'

Shtein thought for a while and suddenly said, 'This means that anti-Semitism really does exist, doesn't it?'

'Looks like it.'

'How could it appear in our country? Here, in a country where it seems —'

I interrupted him. 'In a country where the "founding corpse" has still not been buried. A country whose very name is a lie.'

'You think everything is a lie!'

'There are lies in my journalism and in your lousy poems! When did you ever see an Estonian in space?'

'That was a metaphor.'

'A metaphor. There are dozens of euphemisms like that for lies.'

'So you're the only honest man left. And who wrote that long article about the Baikal-Amur Main Line? Who praised that KGB man, Timofeev?'

'I'm quitting this business. You'll see, I'll quit.'

'Wait until then to criticize anyone else.'

'Don't be angry.'

'You've spoiled my mood. I'll see you.'

Teppe met me at the door.

'Kuzina in the sixth ward has just given birth. Here's the information. She herself is Estonian, a trolley-car driver. Her husband is a turner in a shipyard, Russian, Party member. The child is within all bounds of the norm.'

'Thank God. I think this will work. I'd better call in just to make sure.'

Turonok said, 'Now, that's excellent. Arrange for the child to be called Lembit.'

'Genrikh Frantsevich,' I begged, 'who would call their child Lembit? It's so old-fashioned, you only see it in folklore –'

'Let them call it Lembit. What's the difference to them? Lembit has a good, manly, symbolic ring to it. In the jubilee issue it will catch everyone's eye.'

'Could you call your own child Bova? Or Mikula?'

'Don't give me any of your demagoguery. You have an assignment. The material has to be ready by Wednesday. If they refuse to call it Lembit, promise them some money.'

'How much?'

'Twenty-five roubles or so. I'll send a photographer. What's the newborn's last name?'

'Kuzin. Sixth ward.'

'Lembit Kuzin. Sounds beautiful. Now get on with it.'

I asked Teppe, 'How can I find the father?'

'There he is. He's sitting down there on the lawn.'

I went downstairs.

'Hello,' I said, 'are you Kuzin?'

'I'm Kuzin, all right,' he said, 'but what good is it?'

Evidently Comrade Kuzin was in a philosophic mood.

'Allow me to congratulate you,' I said. 'Your baby turns out to be the four-hundred-thousandth inhabitant of our city. I am from the newspaper. I would like to write about your family.'

'What is there to write about?'

'Well, about your life.'

'What about it? We don't live badly. We work, like everyone else. We broaden our horizons. We use our leadership abilities.'

'We should go somewhere to talk.'

'You mean, have a drink?' Kuzin brightened. He was a tall man with a granite chin and childlike, innocent eyelashes. He got up from the lawn energetically and brushed off his knees.

We headed for the Kosmos, and found a table by the window. The hall was still uncrowded.

'I've got eight roubles on me,' Kuzin said, 'plus a bottle of poison.' He pulled a bottle of Cuban rum out of his briefcase and hid it behind the curtain. 'Shall we start with three hundred grams apiece?'

'And beer,' I said, 'if it's cold.'

We ordered three hundred grams of vodka, two salads, and a chopped-meat cutlet each.

'Would you care for a plate of smoked fish?' asked the waiter.

'Relax!' Kuzin said to him.

The hall was deserted. On a raised platform four musicians had taken their places – piano, guitar, bass, and drums. The oak music stands were decorated with tin lyres.

The guitarist furtively wiped his shoes with a handkerchief. Then he walked to the microphone and announced, 'By the request of our friends, who have just returned from the resort town of Vasalemma . . .'

A significant pause.

'. . . we will now play the lyrical song "Raindrops are Falling on My Kisser".'

An unimaginable din began, heightened by the amplifier. The musicians shouted something unintelligible in chorus.

'Do you know what Vasalemma is?' Kuzin asked, amused. 'It's the biggest prison-camp town in Estonia. Maximum-security prisons, transit stations, strict-regime camps . . . Well, let's have one!' He raised his glass.

'To you! To your son!'

'To our meeting! That it may not be our last!'

Two couples danced, aloof, between tables. The hall was filling up. More and more waiters in black-and-white outfits appeared, carrying trays of glasses and carafes and plates of food.

'Another round?'

We drank again.

Kuzin took a few quick bites of food and began to talk. 'The way things went with us – it's pure theatre. I was working at the shipyard, living alone. Well, I met this woman, also alone. Not exactly bad-looking, and quiet. She started coming by, doing the laundry, ironing – that sort of thing. We got together around Easter. No, I'm wrong – around Ascension Day. Before that, what did I have after work? A vacuum. How much can you stuff yourself? We lived together about a year. How she happened to get pregnant I don't know. She used to lie there like a codfish. I'd say, "You can't fall asleep?" And she'd say, "No, I can hear everything." "Not much heat in you," I'd say. And she'd say, "There must be a light on in the kitchen." "Where'd you get that idea?" "Listen how the meter's clicking." "You could take some lessons from it." That's how we lived for a year.'

Kuzin reached behind the curtain for the bottle of rum and tilted it invitingly. We drank again.

The guitarist straightened his jacket and shouted, 'By the request of Tolya B., sitting by the door, we will now sing . . .'

A pause, while the volume became greater.

'. . . we will now sing the lyrical song "What's the Poison You Gave Me to Drink?"'

'Are you married yourself?' Kuzin asked with interest.

'I was.'

'And now?'

'Now, it seems, no.'

'Do you have any children?'

'Yes.'

'Many?'

'Many. A daughter.'

'Maybe you'll have some more?'

'I doubt it.'

'It's the kids I feel sorry for. The kids aren't to blame. I call them Flowers of Life. Shall we have another?'

'I'm all for it.'

'With beer.'

'Naturally.'

I knew that three more glasses and it would all be over. It's nice to drink early in the day with this thought in mind: Once you're drunk, the whole day is free.

'Listen,' I said, 'call your son Lembit.'

'Why Lembit?' Kuzin was surprised. 'We wanted Volodya. What on earth is that – Lembit?'

'Lembit is a name.'

'What is Volodya – not a name?'

'Lembit is from folklore.'

'What's that – folklore?'

'The art of the people.'

'What does the art of the people have to do with it? My own private son I want to call Volodya. What he'll be called later is another problem. For example, I was named Grisha, and what happened? Who did I grow up to be? Guzzler. That's what they should have called me in the first place. Bottoms up.'

We now drank without bothering to eat anything.

'We could call him Volodya,' Kuzin proposed, 'and get God knows what. Of course, much depends on upbringing –'

'Listen,' I said, 'call him Lembit temporarily. Our editor has promised to lay out some dough, and then next month you can change the name when you register him.'

'How much?' Kuzin was interested.

'Twenty-five roubles.'

'That's two half bottles and some snacks. In a bar, of course.'

'At least. Wait here, I'll call.'

I went downstairs, found a pay telephone, and called the office. The editor happened to be right there.

'Genrikh Frantsevich! Everything is *OK*! The papa is Russian, the mother is Estonian. Both work at a shipyard.'

'Your voice sounds funny,' Turonok said.

'It's the pay phone. Genrikh Frantsevich, send Khubert over right away with the money.'

'What money? What are you talking about?'

'The bait. So they'll name the baby Lembit. The father has agreed to twenty-five roubles. Otherwise he says he'll call it Adolf.'

'Dovlatov, you're drunk!' Turonok said.

'Nothing of the kind.'

'All right, let's settle it. The material has to be ready by Wednesday. Khubert will leave in five minutes. Wait for him at Town Hall Square. He'll give you the key.'

'The key?'

'Yes. The symbolic key. The key of happiness. Present it to the father with the proper ceremony. The key cost three-eighty. I'm deducting it from the twenty-five roubles.'

'That's not fair,' I said.

The editor hung up.

I went back upstairs. Kuzin was napping, his head on the tablecloth. Under his cheek a bread dish stuck up sideways.

I shook Kuzin by the shoulder.

'Hello,' I said, 'wake up! Khubert's waiting for us.'

'What?' he said, startled. 'Khubert? You said Lembit.'

'Lembit is something else. Lembit is your son. Temporarily.'

'Yes, I've had a son.'

'His name is Lembit.'

'First Lembit, then Volodya.'

'And Khubert is bringing us the money.'

'I've got money,' Kuzin said. 'Eight roubles.'

'We have to pay. Where's the waiter?'

'Hello! Smoked fish, where are you?' Kuzin yelled.

The waiter appeared with a dreary expression on his face. 'One plate has been broken,' he announced.

'Aha!' said Kuzin. 'That was me hitting my head on the table – bang!' Sheepishly he took some bits of broken crockery out of his jacket pocket.

'And one toilet stall is a mess,' the waiter added. 'You should have aimed more carefully.'

'Get the hell out of here!' Kuzin shouted suddenly. 'Do you hear? Or I'll polish your bald spot!'

'I don't advise you to try it while I'm carrying out my duties. You might find yourself in jail.'

I slipped some money into his hand. 'Pardon us,' I said. 'My friend here has just had a son. He's a little upset.'

'If you have to drink so much, at least conduct yourselves decently,' the waiter said, backing off.

We paid and walked out. It was raining. Khubert's car was parked near the Town Hall. He signalled and opened the door. We climbed in.

'Here's the money,' Khubert said. 'The boss is worried that you might start drinking.'

I took some bills and change from him in the dark.

Khubert held out a heavy box.

'And what is this?'

'Something he picked up in Pskov.'

I opened the box. Inside was an electroplated key the size of a small balalaika.

'Ah,' I said, 'the key of happiness!'

I opened the door and threw the key into a litter bin. Then I said to Khubert, 'Let's go have a drink.'

'I'm driving.'

'Leave the car and we'll all go.'

'I have to take the boss home.'

'He can get home himself, the fat slob.'

'Look, they promised me an apartment. If it weren't for that –'

'Live with me,' Kuzin said, 'and I'll send my woman to the country. To Usokhi, near Pskov. They haven't seen margarine there since summer.'

'I've got to go,' Khubert said.

We went out into the rain again. The windows of the Astoria Restaurant shone invitingly. A street lamp picked out from the darkness a multicoloured puddle by the door.

Is it worth going into what happened next? How my companion climbed on to the stage and yelled, 'They've sold out Russia'? And hit the doorman so hard that his cap rolled into the closet? And how we were taken to the police station? And how they let us go, thanks to my press pass? And how I lost my note pad with all my notes? And how I then lost Kuzin himself?

I woke up in Marina's room in the middle of the night. A pale light filled the room. The ticking of the alarm clock was unbearably loud. I smelled ammonia and damp clothes.

I touched a swelling scratch on my temple.

Marina sat next to me, sad and a little drawn. She was stroking my hair softly. She kept stroking and saying, 'Poor boy . . . poor boy . . . poor boy . . .'

Who's she talking to, I thought. Who's she talking to?

Translated by Anne Frydman

SASHA SOKOLOV

The Anxious Chrysalis

For Irina Ratushinskaya

> ... Everything was going
> To plan, was it not so, Lord? Beneath a cold heaven
> He raved about all lands, mixing up fact and fiction.
> ....
> If only we could know – why us, God? for what?
>
> *Irina Ratushinskaya*

What a slip-up! Instead of being born and bred in unequalled
Buenos Aires, where instead of '*¿Cómo está usté?*' everyone asks
everyone else '*¿Cómo están los aires?*' and everyone answers '*Gracias,
gracias, muy buenos,*' where the paper boy from the *¡Oye!* newspaper
shows off by reading it without the help of a dictionary and rides
with no hands into the bargain, and where a conductor, an ordinary
tram conductor, recites to passengers passages from Octavio Paz by
heart – that is, instead of appearing there amongst the well-read and
the refined and becoming a citizen called Jorge Luis Borges; but no,
wait; in Uppsala, indescribable Uppsala – or somewhere thereabouts
– in the land of gloomy Gothic wisdom, how about not just passing
for Professor Lars Bäckström, but being him; selflessly weaving, in
the name of delightful Aurora from the glorious Borealis clan, one's
spells called *svensk poesi*; or, seeking neither Rome nor Athens, how
about in inexpressible Jerusalem, oh radiant childhood on Dolorosa
Street, amidst fetters and legends – O Lord, it needn't even be
Jerusalem, let's leave it in peace until some future date, it can be
elsewhere in the region: in unprepossessing Bethlehem say, with its
smell of falafel, or if not there – in Afula full of its past grandeur

and mules, or if not there – in merry Sodom, in lifelong conversation with mates in the language of Ecclesiastes, as if nothing extraordinary had happened, how about qualifying as a master craftsman of the guild of Amos Oz: in a word, instead of *anything* from the above list or something else in that sublime and strange spirit, a spirit not of these parts – you have to make your appearance and live the devil knows where, babble, mutter, talk rubbish, become a hack writer and even fall in love, even rave in the most ordinary Russian. Suddenly, before you know it, you find yourself being who knows who, whoever you like, or more accurately, no one but yourself. Scandalous! When you realize what has happened, you feel as if you're a victim of a chance link, a link caused by the selfishness of circumstances and times. It is as if you are completely surrounded by a sticky cobweb, you've become entangled in a kind of gluey interlacing, in a certain thread. The accursed Parcae. Look how swaddled and cocooned I am. Let me out immediately. This is an outrage. Where indeed is that celebrated *noblesse* of yours? Am I a fly? Do you hear? Evidently not. In any event – no response. This is unheard of. On the whole, not a bundle of laughs. You used to joke like this in your youth. That is, not you, but they, the others. You couldn't even think of jollity now that you'd realized what had happened and how unattractive it all was. Quite the opposite: passing time in the snares of a predestined dialect, you sank into sullenness. And if you smiled sometimes, it was only out of politeness, and the smile was sardonic. But life goes on. Trying to overcome depression, you managed, thanks to a poster with a *postscriptum*: *Those of a nervous disposition need not apply*, to get a job in a morgue. Having begun as an assistant to a hospital attendant, you rose to the rank of laboratory assistant. Your duties included the shaving of clients and assistance at post-mortems. To say that a post-mortem is aesthetically displeasing is to dissemble, to hide affectedly behind a veil of litotes. From an abstract humanist's viewpoint, the only difference between it and unbridled desecration of the deceased is the existence of a code of conduct. Nevertheless, this posthumous operation, as the cynics call it, is undergone by everyone who passes away in the hospital. The rule is sacred: exceptions are made only when powerful patrons intervene. The unfortunates' lack of rights was reminiscent of your own. Together you were slaves of two disconsonant elements. You were a slave of your natural language; the clients – of a lethal speechlessness. 'Living is vulgar and very bad for you,' you complained to beautiful ladies in nightingale orchards. Though death is not a solution either. For even death does not guarantee us freedom of will. And you entrusted to them lines oozing with professional melancholy. And in the hall – over icy enamel – waltzed a skeleton at midnight – from a yonder orange-pale – there flowed a pensive light. The torments of a broken talent provoked complete and utter exaltation in the ladies. Touched by their sympathy, you whispered what was called for and received what was desired. Oh, what balm was granted in those nights for the sonorous Russian Open Sesame! How the lilacs flamed along the shores of the dawn, and how in its rays the ears of cats, inexorable like fate, turned pink around the aquariums as they lay in wait for the jewel-like fish. Yet despite this you felt you'd been cheated of your fair share. You longed for other shores, where different passwords are in use. *Ich liebe dich, S'agapo, te amor*, the heroines of your day-dreams kept repeating. But the day-dreams sometimes turned into nightmares. Stop! Excuse me, but what about a choice? you say to someone wearing a mask and something like an inquisitorial mantle. You speak feverishly, with your whole being, like Dostoevsky confessing all on Freud's couch. No choice is given, he answers with cold arrogance. But there is no freedom without choice, and no happiness without freedom, is that not so? Possibly, but why do you assume that you have the right to happiness? The right? I was told that one doesn't need the right to happiness, that if a butterfly is born to fly, an individual is born to be happy. You are not an individual, he intones, you are the larva of an individual. How dare you – how tactless of you, et cetera. Meanwhile his mask slips. The strong-willed face of an usurper. The sorrowful, hoary eyes of a basilisk. The unsmiling mouth of an executioner. A quivering and bifurcated, iguana-like tongue. Even trifurcated. Quadrifurcated. Endlessly divided. Be so good as to tell me, who are you? Я am the unspoken Word. Я am the Word which was at the beginning of the beginnings. Я am the German yes and the English R in mirror-writing. Я am Я. Я am He Who affirms: I am who I am. I am who I am, confirm those who champion the cause of the interrelatedness of all things. I am your enemy. I am a scourge. I am slavery, vale of tears, lily of the valley and forget-me-nots in valley mists. I am she loves me, she loves me not. I am that which you learn to live with, then to love, and when you do, then you will soar. And when you've soared above the vale, you'll begin to dissect existence, to extract from it its steamy bleeding essence. Don't feed it to the fowl of the air: they have been sated on the Firethief's liver. But drop by drop, piece by piece, transubstantiate it into living prose. Be patient and work hard. For I shall give you both stylus and wings. For I am your language. By virtue of the law of osmosis and of solutions, substances and statuses finding their levels, dream and reality imperceptibly flowed into one another from their former states, fusing and getting into a state of confusion, like in the Oblonsky household, when the remarkable Russian dreamer Oblomov used to swagger in off the cuff and without cufflinks, taking liberties. He drank, stamped his feet, whistled, swore and shouted down with the Baroque, and long live the Rococo. An example worthy of imitation in every respect. But there was no welcome for you at the Oblonskys', and there was really nowhere else for you to go following in your idol's footsteps. So, cancelling ambitious plans, you acted in accordance with what your tongue had said: you were patient and worked hard. This took place within the limits of A to Я and from here to there. Treading the boards of high society, you didn't eclipse the giants of that puppet-booth show for the sole reason that you played only small parts. To make up for it, however, you were the wizard of the fleeting moment, the virtuoso of brief episodes. No Olivier could have been so adroit at helping people on with their coats, at stumbling and tipping over a tray. There was an excess of episodes. Your stage wardrobe could have dressed the whole carnival bareness of Copacabana. In your moments of leisure you would open your much-respected wardrobe and carefully would run through the costumes hanging there, just as a sentimental memoirist turns over the leaves of the ledger of his own works. With a kind of sadness. Apart from your lab assistant's smock one could note the following: the frock-coat of an office clerk, the uniforms of a circus cleaner and the chief of a theatre fire brigade, the sleeveless jacket of a boiler man and a tail coat of a chimney sweep, a jockey's costume and a market trader's apron, a game-keeper's uniform, and the padded jacket of a dog trainer, damaged by the dogs, a private's overcoat and a strait-jacket. You treasured the last-named as a relic. It's paradoxical: that drab apparel symbolized your gradual emancipation from socio-political prejudices. For it was precisely in this outfit that you made the first step towards becoming one of the citizens of the world and chairmen of the globe. It was in that jacket that one Tolstoyan gloomy morning you were transferred from the loathsome army barracks to the freest of all the fatherland's institutions. A carriage which had been decorated with a red cross was brought up to the edge of the parade ground where guards were being drilled. And, led through the gauntlet of its guard of honour, you shouted to the loyal subjects, inspiring in them good spirits and pride in their king: Down with the Rococo and the Baroque, long live Surrealism! And in that very same strait-jacket seven hundred and twenty-nine injections later you appeared before the highest commission. Well, now at least do you realize, my dear chap, that you're no Dali? the military Aesculapians said to you. Yes sir, now I am an amazing chrysalis, developed from an ordinary midnight larva. What a marvellous metamorphosis. Look, I am completely cocooned. Rodin's *Balzac* and no mistake. I thank you. I am pleased with this set-up. I don't need anything else. And somewhere inside, in the focal point, where it used to hurt, I now feel infinite; or more to the point, infinitely comfortable. But on the whole – I'm all anxiety. Has Salvador himself been informed about what has happened? A telegram must be sent. Urgent! Saying, It gives me great honour. I have been transfigured. And sign it: The Anxious Chrysalis. See to it, if you'd be so kind. Only I am afraid that the maestro will not be able to endure such a loss. Alas, for we were as one, he and I. He weeps. The strait-jacket grows dark from tears before the eyes. And it was in precisely this jacket as a mark of protest against the conquistadorial policies of late medieval Spain and Amerigo Vespucci himself that you marched through your unloved town soon after your discharge. You took that shirt in secret. You stole it from the madhouse like a hero scout captures a banner from enemy headquarters. That was the banner of the moral majority, waging an undeclared war against the Artist. By this act of heroism you significantly weakened the Hydra. However, there was at the very least one more cause for rejoicing. In the appropriate document one could read that much desired formula: Discharge – totally flat-footed and useless. The grounds: the dissident ravings of a dishon-ourable nonentity against a background of sluggish megalomania. And you rejoiced. And you appeared in your strait-jacket amidst the half-beaten geniuses of fine arts, amidst aesthetes who'd dared to spread sedition in huddled-up squares and languorous salons. And in the hall – across the slippery enamel – out of the distances orange-pale. Oh strait-jacket! In this very jacket you burned out your youth, like burning a hole with a cigarette. Ah, right through. How thoughtless. Surely it's clear that such objects need to be handled with care. It is a relic after all. Remember, it was in this very jacket that you seethed to excel in your best episodes, working as a bouncer, a swapper of rocks for hard places, as a nude model, an eternal student, and other Clever Toms and Dicks peeping for the state. In it, being patient and working hard, you grew into a typical representative of your extra-class – the class of men superfluous and without profit in their own fatherland. Wearing it, you joined the ranks of *milites gloriosi* (unacknowledged) in the Most Glorious Order of Little Tin Drummer Boys, Cymbal Tinklers, Cockleshell Heroes and Old Soldiers for the Retired Goat. The order of the uneasy and rebellious, of those hearing a different drummer, of the restless and maladjusted, of seekers of justice and fools holy for the sake of an *idée fixe*, where Señor Quixote was magister. A natural drummer, a drummer to the marrow of your bones, you were an open enemy of everything you didn't like. Never mind that because of your pupated state you weren't too handy at beating the drum. Forget the problems. To make up for it you became an outstanding theorist of the drum, its courageous ideologist. And, fighting for the just cause of the Sacred Goat, you drummed not with drumsticks on her tanned skin, but with your heart on ribs, with blood – on temples, with the same blood – on your own ear-drums, and with a wail – on other people's. That is why you will be able to say before you die: Hand on heart, I wasn't a bad drummer before God. So bury me with honours. But don't put yourselves to needless expense – don't sew a cerement. Get me up in a strait-jacket – and that will do. In memory of the period once upon a time when I lived, fought and played the drum. And, if you like, when I thought. You thought as a chrysalis. As an individual. As a generation. As a class. Because there were so many yous. A lot more than there were clothes in your wardrobe. And a lot more than there were episodes. One day you looked back and realized exactly what the great American dreamer Walt Whitman had realized a century before, namely, that you are large, you contain multitudes. There were so many of you that it would be enough for a battle scene in an epic movie. Forget the crowd scene: enough for a good hecatomb. And you realized that almost every one of you is cocooned in your image – dressed in the same sackcloth. And you were struck with horror for your ill-fated people, born in a strait-jacket. And its tongue tasted bitter to you. Because what had seemed in a young nonentity's ravings to be the Grand Inquisitor's mantle, turned out to be in reality that very same red straitening thing, like yours and like everyone else's. And what had been foretold by the Grand Inquisitor in the terrifying visions of one's early years came to pass. Grieving for him, you shared his troubles and came to love him. He dissolved in your blood and became pollen on your wings. Because it was at that time that you left your chrysalis and soared. Not however in the imago of a bewitching Nabokovian butterfly, but as a grey, gloomy, grubby night moth, inspired and given wing by never-ending anxiety. True, it is better to soar gloomily and greyly than not to soar at all. Acting in the way already indicated, you realized that you were a tiny but free-flying moth of your native dialect, and you strove to soar higher and higher. But on the whole the language – as before – dragged itself along down below, in the ashes of the hated vale of tears, or lay there like a hospital corpse deprived of rights – the victim of a lethal dumbness. And coarse, stupid, wingless lab assistants in scarlet Russian-style shirts kept on desecrating it, mockingly. O unfortunate, impotent, cocooned and fooled Russian language, you kept saying to yourself, paraphrasing Ivan Turgenev. And you prayed. O Lord, preserve and have mercy on our natural tongue, for we have no other. Preserve and have mercy on us, its anxious moths, fluttering helplessly around the light of the world and glimpsed fleetingly among other tongues and nations. From Uppsala to Buenos Aires. On us, grim and grey, carrying on our wings the ashes of its alphabets and annals, the dust of apocrypha, the soot of lamps and candles. On us and on all those who seek release from the strait-jacket of circumstances, in order to soar in our wake. And on those who do not seek. And on those who will not soar. Look on us, and on them. Speak to us in Your sublime Esperanto. Give us a sign. Strengthen us. Set us on the right path. Confirm that I am what I am, and that this is no longer a dream, but reality. And my dream – wake me up, dream, and reveal yourself. Only to me, a small butterfly. To me, a moth. To me, rust and dust. Whisper in my ear. Rustle like a falling leaf – a manuscript leaf, perhaps – a bamboo grove:

for what?

Translated by Olga Pobedinskaya and Andrew Reynolds

EVGENY KHARITONOV

The Oven

Tuesday. Going into the village for bread, I have a rear view of him up on the mound, even say to little Lennie, 'Look at that boy waiting for someone.' He really gets to me, guitar strap round his neck, leg thrust forward. Coming back, what do you know, he's still there. I see his face, ask for a light. He comes straight over without a word. Why doesn't he answer, or is it just his hard street manner? He walks over, lends me the matches, and asks a cigarette in return. I think, 'Now it's bye-bye and I never see him again.' Moving off, what can I do? Sudden thought, go back and ask him to play the guitar. Lennie is useful cover. He starts straight in (his voice has just mended), songs boys sing in courtyards. He runs out of songs, I run out of excuses, make it home in a daze and have no one to tell about him. Head for the Rainbow rather than sit here alone. Half-way through the village I see him coming towards me. A miracle! Perhaps not so surprising, though, if he's living here. I'm just out for a stroll, could join him if he's at a loose end. He nods. I feign interest in playing the guitar, which strings to press. We walk a lot, say little. He's still at school, final year coming up, a special school for mathematicians which draws from the entire surrounding region, highly selective. Not your average boy in the street. A thoroughbred. He was waiting on the mound for friend Sergei, champion wrestler, due back from town. While we're supposedly drifting aimlessly past plywood holiday homes we meet a couple of girls his age. They're going to speak. I'm to one side, out of the way. It gets dark. He says, 'Let's go over to the sportsmen.'

'Sure,' but I tell him, of course, I don't know them, or anyone here. Conversation stalls on cars or some song they all know. He has passed advanced swimming. I realize it must have been him I saw about three weeks ago walking down the street between the dachas with an aqualung and flippers under his arm, surrounded by girls his own age, or children. It struck me then how beautiful he is. Heartless eyes because of that. I only caught a glimpse before they were past, but now I know it was him. It's dark. We're sitting on a bench outside one of the houses and he's strumming the guitar and singing in that street voice of his, sentimental songs from the criminal underworld, about love. A woman from one of the houses asks him to stop, and we move to the open-air veranda at the Rainbow. In the middle of the café a low, dim light they leave on all night is casting long shadows; an old woman on duty, cigarette in her mouth; the two girls we saw; and a lad we'd also seen. He asks Misha, 'Any birds?' Misha laughing. He hands over the guitar and this Tolya starts singing comically and emotionally in his Ukrainian accent, not like Misha at all, and every second word's a swear word. Tolya sends the girls off for a pack of cards. I'm thinking, 'Good. Four of them. No need for them to find out I don't play.' The girls live in the dacha next door, maybe daughters of the café manageress. By the time they get back Tolya is busy singing. They go off to one corner to play patience with the woman in charge. Misha and I listening to Tolya, laughing, brought closer by the song. Tolya's songs: homeless urchin goes up to ticket window, tries to steal a ticket, gets arrested, says, 'How cruel you are, citizens, cruel and heartless. I am but a homeless boy. Why pick on me?' Or, man in rags kills sailor in low dive in a brawl over a pair of pretty eyes, bends over the corpse, recognizes his own brother, kills the woman too. Or ornate schoolboy songs about love, which Tolya sings so seriously and sincerely they get to you. The recital ends. We see Tolya back to the tents and get an uninhibited account of his amorous exploits. He assures us he's already popped four cherries, while other people want all their lives to get married and can't find a virgin. Telling us how affectionate girls are towards him. All this addressed mainly to me. Misha is preoccupied with the guitar, perhaps because he's heard it all before. Anyway, I'm a good listener. Misha and I walking home together, and he tells me about a murder, reminded about it because I have to go on through the woods. A few days ago a boy was beaten to death hereabouts with motorbike chains. Parting of the ways. 'Goodbye, then.' 'Goodbye.' Then he adds, just as a matter of form, I know, but still: 'See you tomorrow.' When I spoke to him on the mound I thought even getting to know him was too much to hope for, yet here we are, having spent the whole evening together, talking. I know he lives here, he knows my name, I know his is Misha, and he's going to see me tomorrow.

Next, Wednesday. I'm off early to the village and down to the tents, find Tolya of the Ukraine on his own by the gully. 'Hi!' 'Hi!' 'Seen Misha?' 'No.' 'Good,' I think. 'When he comes he'll just happen to find me here.' He won't see I've been looking for him, and anyway I'll be with Tolya, as if to say, 'I'm Tolya's friend too, now.' I won't be a solitary figure lying in wait for him. The sportsmen come and lie down next to us to play cards. Their leader or trainer comes to dish out vitamins, and they give me some too. I see him coming. 'Hi!' 'Hi, let's go to the river.' Tolya of the Ukraine has something else to do. On the way Misha tells me a horror story about sitting at a table in his school hostel, leg wedged between the table and the wall. A sudden pain below his knee, worse and worse until he realized the noise on the other side of the wall was somebody drilling just where his knee was. There was no way he could pull free in time: the drill was already in his knee, and it was stuck fast between the table leg and the wall. He couldn't even move the table. It was only when he screamed through the wall that they stopped and a workman came in to see what was up. Misha pulled his leg free, but he'd already been drilled to the bone. He says that, speaking mathematically, the probability of the drill entering his knee like that was zero. We come to the place where they swim. His swimming trunks are brown, with yellow stripes down the sides; he shows me the scar the drill left. He has no idea how beautiful he is. Girls may have told him, but he could look at himself in a mirror and not see it, and his friends are just as blind. For them he is just their friend. He suggests swimming out to the island. There and back will be pushing it, but I don't let on. We get to the island, and have only been sitting there for a moment before he wants to swim back. I say, 'Let's dry off first.' Even so, the last few metres are a real struggle. We climb out. I play for time. We are talking like old friends, and there is always the guitar. Naturally I ask him to teach me his songs and how to play it. He shows me how to strum and play the chords. His sister is at college and sings before film shows at the Andrei Zhdanov Culture Club. Or maybe it was yesterday he mentioned his sister. Tolya of the Ukraine comes back and they teach me together. Eighth position, seventh position, I'm really getting the hang of it. Tolya suggests flicking me on the head the relevant number of times. It's supposed to help you remember. They want to go for another swim, but I say I'll just sunbathe this time. I'm dead beat. Another thing: Tolya has already had lunch, so when it's time for Misha's lunch Tolya won't be going with him. So that I can, without it seeming too deliberate, I pave the way by saying I'll have to go for lunch in a minute, so that when Misha wants to leave I can go with him without seeming to be tagging along. It all takes planning. We walk all the way to his turning together. I ask, in fact really just say, 'Come swimming again later?' He says, 'Uh-huh.' This time I'll know where to look for him, and in only an hour's time. He even lends me the guitar over lunch-time to practise. When I get home Vanya has come to see me. I want to tell him about some poems and give him a chance to see Misha. I wonder whether he too will recognize a boy in ten thousand when he sees one. We go down to the river. Misha turns up half an hour later. It helps having someone from my own circle to talk to. I'd be hard pressed to stay animated and keep an interesting conversation going with Misha on his own, but through Vanya he can listen to me talking, and laugh, and get caught up in what I'm saying, and take to me a little. Also I don't want him thinking I'm a complete loner. He can see now I have friends of my own. We spend maybe three hours together before Vanya has to go back to town and I see him to the bus. Misha asks, 'You coming back afterwards?' He is being polite, of course, but still it means we are friends now, we can walk down the street together. I would never have dared hope for as much on Tuesday when I saw him on the mound. Talking to Vanya on the way to the bus, he doesn't share my predilections, confirms everything I have thought about Misha. I'm tired, what with the island and so much walking in one day. I won't go back to him. It's a good idea not to show up now and again. Let him think I have a life of my own to live rather than just being some loner hanging around him all the time. The guitar is a godsend: everything can be put down to wanting to learn his songs and how to play it. Another thing, that first evening he said he wanted to enrol at a college in Moscow next summer and he'd be spending the holidays there this winter. I thought I'd make sure he left this village with my address in his pocket.

Thursday. Wake up feeling pleased with myself for not imposing myself when I wasn't needed. Not a mistake I am likely to make, but you have to be on your guard. I trek a full kilometre and a half to the café and the same again to the swimming place without seeing him. I want to go round and look him up in his dacha. He mentioned yesterday it was No. 32, and I even shouted 'Misha' when I was going past with Vanya after lunch. I thought then he must have been back at the river, but it was just that he hadn't heard me. Because I shouted to him yesterday and, more to the point, because I didn't put in an appearance yesterday evening when he was expecting me, I decide I can allow myself to look in on him now. I can see grandma laying the table, and don't need the number to tell me his is the dacha with the flippers and aqualung by the door. 'Is Misha down at the river?' I ask. 'He's still asleep,' she says. 'I'm just now getting breakfast.' No welcome in her voice. People suspect anyone their children meet, let alone an older man. A glimpse through the door of the end of a camp bed, feet protruding from the sheet. I decide to go to the river and doze on the grass for an hour to kill time, where I was lying yesterday morning, so that when he comes along he will be the one to find me. An hour goes by, or maybe half an hour that seems like an hour. I can't wait any longer, go back to the dacha, feeling all the time some neighbour has started taking an unwelcome interest. At last he comes out, shirt knotted over his tummy. I say, 'I came round to see you. Let's go to the river.' I make a point of mentioning looking in earlier. His grandmother is bound to have told him and I don't want him thinking I have some reason for keeping it quiet. He goes to get the guitar back from the dacha opposite, someone he lent it to yesterday. Halfway there he is hailed by robust, ugly Sergei in a vest; the same Sergei, I immediately guess, that he'd been waiting for to come back from town the first evening. No introductions. Quite right. We've only gone swimming together a couple of times, and I can perfectly well introduce myself if need be. Misha promised to borrow the book Sergei had written his songs in for me. Next the three of us go down by the river and they swim to the island. No, that's not right. Sergei doesn't undress, he is sitting with his clothes on. He taught Misha how to play the guitar. He's allowed to tease him, about his playing, for instance, although Sergei isn't that hot himself. He'd keep his end up at a party but that is about it. A bit of horse-play, Sergei gets to put his arms round Misha and give him a bear hug. This day, or the day before, I ask Misha how long I have for learning the guitar. He tells me he is leaving around the twentieth. This day is the eighth. Their slang: words like 'bona' (good); 'slag' (a girl you've slept with); and 'skin' (a jacket). I know not to don an 'older friend' smile, put an arm round his shoulders and ask him what 'slag' or 'squelch' mean, placing myself in a different category rather than being one of the boys, with the privileges of friendship between equals. We come to Sergei's and they stop by an upturned boat. Even before that Misha asks him for the book. What matters isn't that he has remembered and that I am pleased he has, but that now he has an explanation for why I am going around with him. Sergei brings the book out. Masses of mistakes. 'Cheers,' I say. 'I'll let you have it back this evening.' Again, being too polite would be counter-productive. I know when not to try too hard, but also not to be too different. I type the songs out and just want to be with them again as soon as possible. They invited me back when I left: 'We'll be here. See you.' I trail all the way to the swimming place. No luck. Walk back and see him coming in the distance, and show the book so he can see I'm on business. 'I've typed it out but forgotten where Sergei lives.' We go to Sergei's, whistle for him, and all sit down on the boat as if simultaneously overcome by ennui, Misha inseparable from the guitar. Sergei tells him, 'You've given me a headache with that guitar, cocksucker.' I sit down on the grass opposite, all the better to see him. When it is time for me to go, Misha says, 'We'll be at the camp-fire, over with the sportsmen.' I come to him a third time that evening, find him by the sound of the guitar in the house by the café the girls had gone to to fetch playing cards that first evening. Through the window I can see the girls with Misha and Sergei. I wonder about clearing off, two boys, two girls and all that, but they are obviously just sitting in there together. They let me in. 'Did you hear the guitar?' 'Yes.' I sit next to Misha on a bunk with no mattress. He never stops playing and humming. The mother of one or both of the girls comes in and straightforwardly asks us to go home. We go to the camp-fire. The sportsmen have been drinking, and one calls out, 'Hey, come over here. Give us a song.' Misha suddenly shows his special directness; he starts straight in singing for them with no fuss. Nobody with any taste could say he plays well. He is trying to sing like Tolya of the Ukraine yesterday, having evidently liked the accent. When it is time to head back he says, 'I'll probably go into town tomorrow. I don't suppose you need to, do you?' He is asking me! 'Yes,' I say, 'I do, actually.' We will take the bus together. We're walking home, the three of us, late at night. By luck Sergei's house is halfway and we walk on, the two of us together. That's when I tell him about the murder. Misha told me on Tuesday the boy had been beaten to death with chains, but on Wednesday Lennie told me they hanged him with the chains. I pass on Lennie's version, but he just laughs. Everybody's got their own story. We agree he will call in for me tomorrow morning as he'll pass my dacha on the way to the bus anyway, and he lends me the guitar. 'Want it for tonight?' I walk on, practising his way of strumming. Tomorrow we're going to town together.

Tomorrow is Friday and I wake up around seven. He'll be looking in just after nine. I sit on the veranda playing his guitar to kill time. He arrives wearing a white shirt and tells me he heard the guitar in the distance. I grab some translations. They don't mean anything to him, of course. No talk as we walk along, and even in the bus he is quietly strumming the guitar. At first we are both standing, then I sit down and he stays standing up, refusing a free seat. Then he has to change buses. He tells me he may come back that evening, or perhaps the following morning. He is going to the mathematical school. I wonder if he just wants to show me how clever he is, but maybe not. At all events I can't now arrange for us to phone about when he'll be coming back. He heard me shouting as I left the dacha that I'd be back at four. Suppose he did ring up, it would seem I'd been waiting specially. Perhaps he didn't hear when I said I would be back, or perhaps he's forgotten, but it just can't be done without looking too deliberate. I'd been looking forward since yesterday evening to travelling back with him. Friday night is dance night. Friday, Saturday, Sunday. I travel back to the village and go straight to Sergei. I plan to get closer to him, so that when I am with them Misha should not twig, before I am ready. Or Sergei, who might point out to Misha the reason I am hanging around them is Misha. A cool day, but Sergei is wearing swimming trunks. The holiday-makers we meet are fully dressed and give him odd looks. I ask if he is cold, but he just laughs and says he is a sportsman. We don't talk much. I fill in the silence by whistling. Sturdy but not much of a looker. I noted that on Wednesday when I saw him side by side with Misha. Conversation tricky when we get on to tennis or badminton. This time I don't have my trunks on, which gives a good excuse for not going in the water, except that I had gone to invite him to come to the river. I am walking along and thinking I can't get out of swimming. He has even brought the flippers so I can try swimming with them too. Before we get to the river we see a drunk sportsman belabouring a pine tree with a big stick. 'Oy, you!' he shouts at me. 'Stand on the end of this.' There are two of us, Sergei built like a wrestler. I walk past without a word and he doesn't try anything. A bit later we hear a bicycle falling over. He has stuck the cudgel in front of the wheels of a boy of fifteen or so who was riding along. The boy picks his bike up, knowing better than to say anything. The sportsman is having the time of his life. As we career down the slope to the river, Sergei says, 'Why haven't you taken your sandals off? You'll get them full of sand.' I've made several slips. I really ought to go into the water too, when I suggested coming here in the first place. He'd been sitting at home reading a book, now here I am not wanting to swim. I say, 'I'll just sit here for a bit.' We have, of course, brought the flippers and there is only one pair, so it could be his turn to go first. Then he invites me to swim to the island, but I haven't forgotten how tired I got last time, and I was on a high then, and besides now it is cold. He thinks I am the same as him, only without the swimming certificates. He swims out to the island, and I really am going to have to get into the water. I don't know what to do. First I wash the sand off my feet so as not to get his flippers dirty. As I start I see how dumb this is since I will be going into the water anyway. Perhaps he hasn't noticed, or thinks it is just a quirk I have. Anyway, he is only seventeen and I am from Moscow and for all he knows that may just be the way these things are done. It is difficult going into the water in flippers. Just before I do Sergei light-heartedly tells me most people who drown are wearing flippers. He says you should walk in backwards. He does some diving too. We walk back beneath the steep river bank. When I called for him I brought the news that Misha will be back this evening or, more likely, tomorrow morning. As we are walking along the water's edge he tells me that when the weather was like this last year (he noticed earlier when we were walking along the top of the gully that the water level has risen – no, fallen – judging by the shoreline of the island opposite), anyway, when the weather was like this two girls archly invited a sailor to come swimming who they knew couldn't swim, for a laugh. The sailor didn't rise to the bait, and the girls went swimming alone and drowned. When the water level rises you get whirlpools. He tells me too about the time he and some other boys were out in a boat when the Young Pioneers were having their open day for parents. One of them was diving, pretending to be searching for something, and another shouted, 'Any luck?' He shouted back, 'Not so far,' so somebody would ask them from the bank what they were looking for, and they could reply, 'Some Pioneer's got drowned.' There were two Pioneer camps, and the next day each was saying a Pioneer had been drowned in the other. We come back to the murder. To keep the conversation going I say I heard from my neighbour's boy Lennie that the boy hadn't only been beaten with the chains, but hanged with them too. Lennie said it happened at night and two kilometres away, but Sergei says actually it happened in broad daylight in the middle of the village. I wipe the egg off my face and ask Sergei why they did it. 'The usual. No reason. They were pissed.' Sergei knows who did it: two boys from town, and it was a boy from town they killed. He was seventeen. The police aren't going to find the body. Sergei's house. I say goodbye. Am I coming to the dance? We'll meet at ten. At first, talking about it on the way to the river, I said I'd come round for him. I don't remember whether I said I didn't know where they hold the dances. He is going to explain, so now I say I know, so he shouldn't wonder how come someone living in the village could not know where the dances are held. In any case I have a fair idea, I've heard the music. I go along in the evening, intending just to put in an appearance. It was good at home. Some pies cooking nicely in the oven. The dance is in full swing, and there is Misha, back from town, in the grey sweater he wears when it is cold. 'Oh, you're back. When did you get here?' 'Oh, such and such a time. How about you (me)?' 'I came back this afternoon.' Sergei says he didn't think I would come. Everybody is excited. Terrifying youths lurking, looking for somebody to beat up. Girls have to be joked with, and Misha and Sergei do. The music makes you sad, and everybody enjoying themselves while you're not part of that life. They dance, you don't, and you've got the murder on your mind. Misha's fourteen-year-old girl cousin, wearing a leather jacket. His 'slag' beside her (the girl he says he has slept with). Perhaps he is fibbing, although he has been living in the school hostel for a year. Sergei is trying to get me to dance. 'Go on. You must be freezing. Show us how you do it in Moscow.' They discuss whether to go looking for girls. Boys are prancing about with boys. Misha invites me to dance with him. 'No, Misha, I'll just stand here.' I am cut off from them, the music making me sad. Always having to pretend to be interested in how they dance or how Misha plays the guitar. Another opportunity: a girl called Olga arrives with a young man. Misha's sister, evidently. Now I can pretend I want to hear her sing. She has hosts of admirers, little girls, Lucy the Waitress. Misha in his element. You can believe he needs a friend like Sergei to mind his back. What a family, Misha, his sister and the cousin in her leather jacket. The singing sister is very pretty, though she doesn't have Misha's face. Immediately the centre of attention. Her man is a Jew, good looking but not in the competition. Those girls, though, and Misha! I think at the time the cousin is another sister and don't pay much attention to her, but Olga and Misha . . . I know she is his sister the moment she starts singing with such assurance. Then Misha asks the man I had taken to be her husband what his name is, not because he wants to be introduced, but because he wants to ask him for something. He says it is Slava. Sergei clears matters up later by telling me he isn't her husband, who is away competing in some championship or other. Also Sergei points out two thuggish looking youths, one of whom murdered the boy whose body the police are never going to find. Perhaps it isn't all true, but what a picture: these princes of bloodshed here, taking their ease; and the royal children in the robbers' camp blissfully unaware of their own identity. How Misha dances! Of course, he doesn't know how, but he is quite without inhibition, just as when he sang for the sportsmen yesterday. Big sister and her lover make moves to leave: I imagine them going back and sleeping together in grandma's house. Misha and Sergei do not, in the event, go looking for anybody, it was all talk. The three of us, Misha, Sergei and I, go off through the woods. Lots of people with their arms round each other in the bushes. One old man who isn't actually all that old, forty-seven, he tells me, and very lively with it, is mixing with everybody, listening to the young, basking in their warmth. He makes himself useful, organizing the boys to get firewood, chaffing himself for being so old and wanting to be with them all, and they laugh at him too, a bit, but not unkindly. He is nineteen years older than me, an old man compared to them, and behaving like one. I am twelve years older than Misha. A good feeling round the camp-fire. It gets warm. I grow tired of standing, but the ground is damp and I find a log to sit on. Misha and his pal don't grow tired and stay standing. I find myself at Misha's feet. He lends someone the guitar until tomorrow; somebody else has one. The old man is having a great time and nobody minds him wanting to feel good among young people like them. Someone who looks as though he's just a little boy starts singing in a quavering, almost childish treble. His voice is weak, straining at the top of his range and he is constantly having to transpose what proves to be a very long song. Just as it seems about to end he keeps starting up again. When others join in they are singing slightly at odds with him so that he is syncopating in the chorus, but he sticks to his guns not to be put off his beat. Some other boys take the guitar off him and Misha and Sergei get ready to leave. While he was singing I was looking at Misha and laughing at the singer's tribulations, and my emotion communicated itself to him. The next day I tell Misha how much I liked his sister's singing, and I say the boy's singing was certainly in a class of its own, and later Misha uses my exact words himself. They are leaving and ask if I am coming, but I am not going their way and if I were to go with them I would seem to be seeing Misha home again; and if I get up and go home on my own, again it will show I only wanted to stay while Misha was there; so I say I will stay a bit longer. When they have gone I get up and leave too.

Saturday. I have to go into the village for cigarettes, and want to get in some extra to see me over Monday and Tuesday when the store will be closed. I forget there is Sunday tomorrow. I do not see him, only Olga the Singing Sister and the young cousin who was wearing leather the night before, among the roadside trees. Again I trek to the swimming place. No Misha. Still asleep perhaps. I know my next move: get hold of some money and go drinking with the boys. Much more fun, and if you go too far it gets blamed on the drink. Time to take some risks and make some headway. My white bag has gone off back to Moscow, so I ask Anya to lend me some money. I meant to go drinking with them before, but the store only sells wine by the glass. Anyway, now seems a good time to get one or two inside me and bump into the boys slightly wrecked. I pay for a glass of wine, some cucumber to eat with it, and sit down to drink on the steps of the store on the off chance he may go by. He doesn't. I drink up and leave. Ah, that's when I see Olga and her cousin behind me among the trees, because I keep turning round. I decide to ask Anya for some more money when the wine has taken effect. I shall just be nicely tipsy. I have a warming up session with Anya to get myself in a talkative mood for the café. It will close for lunch in half an hour. Slava the Lover-Boy is there. We exchange nods and then, just as I am getting nicely oiled drinking on the veranda with no one else about, wine in one hand and a cucumber in the other, starting to feel at peace with the world, I see him riding towards me on his bike. 'Fancy a drink?' He declines. Had I stayed on long last night? This is when he describes the singer using my words. He wants to go and put in an hour on his Chemistry, which he hasn't taken. With only one day between it and the preceding exam, a lot of candidates have chosen to put it off. We are on close enough terms now for me to say, 'Come on, it's Saturday. You should rest on the Sabbath!' He says, 'I know, but I can't. I made a vow.' No, I've got that wrong. This is when I am downing my first glass. Then I talk to Anya for half an hour and walking there and back takes another half hour, and that is the hour he is doing his Chemistry. After I drink the second glass I am hoping to see him in the street or at the river, and ask Sergei to join me. Two glasses with an hour between don't have much of an effect. I only have enough money left for one glass for Sergei and one for me, but then the café has a beer delivery. I reserve a place in the queue behind Slava the Lover-Boy. Very trendy and flaunting his stubble. He remembers me sitting with them at the dance, listening to Olga's singing. Now I am wearing my good shoes and my body feels quite different. Slava seems to be about my age. We haven't been introduced, but Misha called him that. From his manner he is closer to the circles I move in than, say, Sergei; relatively, at least. Slava starts unloading beer crates with another man in the queue and I help, Sergei too. The vendor slams her window in our faces and starts stock-taking. 'I'll let you buy some in a minute, boys,' says she. The man behind asks her to sell him some too. I give Slava a rouble to buy some for me and go off to sweet-talk Lucy into giving us glasses. A new experience for me, buttering her up the way all the other customers automatically chat up the waitresses and cashiers. She is at the till. I take the bottles from Slava and spot Misha in the street. I point to Sergei as if to say, 'Sergei's here. Come and join us.' He doesn't want to drink the beer; says he doesn't like things that taste bitter. Sergei and I drink up, and Misha finishes off what is left in the bottle. He is very well-mannered, even pretended he was refusing the beer because there was no glass for him. He probably felt himself he hadn't quite got it right, because you can always drink out of the same one. He hasn't been doing Chemistry, he's been busy with his bike, and wants to go back now to his studies. We try to talk him round and I think he agrees not to, but has to pop home to sort something out. He says he will come and find us after that. After that Sergei and I are hidden just thirty yards from Misha, behind the roadside trees. You can't see us through the bushes. Sergei climbs a cherry tree and says there are wild raspberries too. I am lying on the ground. A drunk has been lying not far away behind the bushes for ages and a woman who comes past asks if he is with us, evidently convinced he must be a friend of ours since I am lying in the grass too. Soon we hear Misha give the agreed whistle. As he is coming along he can only see Sergei up in the tree and asks where I am. We do not have long together. I can't remember how we part afterwards. First we go towards our swimming place and there is table tennis set up near the tents. They have a game, which Sergei wins by miles. On the way there I think about Olga. I must use her to tell him how beautiful he is. The table tennis: I pretend to be watching them play from the grass. I don't understand a thing: my thoughts are all over Misha. I only hear them saying the score is twenty to three, rather a walk-over for Sergei. I gather up the dented table-tennis balls lying in the grass. I don't remember whether it is Sergei or Misha who asks if I am going to set light to them. They like setting them on fire. Misha squats down beside me and lights them and they flare up. I've forgotten how we part. We are walking, the three of us together as usual. Sergei turns off at his place, and Misha and I go on to the parting of our ways. But also, when we went to the table tennis the sportsmen were there, including the one Misha lent his guitar to the day before, but when we went back to collect the guitar he had gone. And also, when the three of us were walking along Sergei told me about one time last year when they had been out of cigarettes and he and Misha saw some packs of cigarettes through a window. Misha poked the window and broke the glass, all in broad daylight, and I asked if you wouldn't get your hand hurt, but they said not if you pushed it in. They picked out the broken glass and Misha climbed in because he was thinner. Sergei was on the look-out when he heard Misha laughing inside. The cigarette packets were all just full of nails. Also, when Misha and I were walking alone he told me he had had a little sister who died before he was born, and I said, 'Good, otherwise your parents wouldn't have bothered to make you,' and I had been made in just the same way. So there is the game of table tennis, and burning the ping-pong balls, and them telling me those stories, but I can't remember parting or what happened after that. When I get home my crowd have returned and that's when I put on the shoes I asked them to bring. But I definitely remember enjoying walking around on the veranda at the café with a glass of wine in one hand and a cucumber in the other, and sitting down for a moment at an empty table. No, I haven't forgotten anything, because I definitely remember walking as far as the fork with Misha. When we were saying goodbye I said, 'See you at the dance, then,' and he said, 'Come early.' So I am on my way there. It is a long way, but it is still light and I am going towards the table tennis but don't meet him. I go back to the volleyball pitch, which is where the outcome of this whole thing will finally be decided. Also I had thought it would be best for the boys to find me there, but they don't come. I go in to find Sergei because his house is next to the pitch. He is wearing a smart shirt. We meet Misha or go in to get him, or Sergei whistles for him to come out. We did go in one time together. I went in, Sergei was standing beside me, Misha had the guitar. We walk for a bit before he says he'll go back and leave the guitar, and Sergei tries to talk him out of it but he goes back anyway, and then comes on and catches us up. Sergei is wearing my jacket. It comes down to his knees and he asks Misha how it suits him. It is too early for the dance but we go anyway as we won't have long to wait. Dances are a different world. Everyone accepts you so readily. We arrive before anyone else, and for the people who come next we are the people who arrived first. On the way the boys are saying there is always one particular record playing when they arrive at the dances, only today it is a different one. They are laughing about it. People do not recognize Sergei in my jacket. We sit there, people arrive, Olga and her Slava, and also some other friend and the fourteen-year-old cousin. Everything is familiar. Misha's sister sits beside me, obviously interested. We are out of cigarettes and Slava finds us some. Each time Olga inhales she passes the cigarette over to me; each time she finishes dancing she comes and sits beside me. She has obviously found out all about me from Misha. I ask her to sing, and she gazes into my eyes as she does so. Then it is young people's talk, with Slava and his friend bandying book titles not entirely à *propos*, but it is still a circle of friends, and I am wearing these shoes with the instep support, and have sussed the way they dance here. I get up to dance with Olga. She was just waiting to be asked. I tell her we will dance when the beat is right. I start feeling good just before that, when the three of us are standing together, Sergei and Misha, and I. I am freezing without my jacket, and to keep myself from shivering, mostly from excitement, I remember you can make your blood run faster by tensing yourself. Anyway, Misha is bumping his knees together in time to the music without thinking. I start too, just for something to do. Sergei keeps on asking me to show him the latest dances in Moscow. He is constantly expecting me to come up with something amazing and immediately starts taking an interest. He even says, 'Look, Misha. He's really got sent.' I get excited and pick up the rhythm from him very strongly. I can feel it in my legs. I have been hoarding it. I can feel it in my shoulders. I tell Olga when something starts that has this beat we will get up and go, but the trouble is, I can't tell whether what is starting has that beat. They all have slow introductions, and then roar off into The Shake, and while I am trying to make my mind up somebody else will ask Olga to dance. During one of these long introductions Olga reaches over to me with a cigarette in her hand. I think she wants me to finish smoking it but she is throwing it away and inviting me to dance. Also, I talk about the dog-end of a cigarette. They don't understand at first, stare at me in amazement, and then laugh with delight. They call it a butt. They love having a Muscovite in their party who even speaks a different language. Olga and I are dancing together and I have a feeling of freedom. When we were dancing some slow shuffle before that I told her she should pack it all in here and come to Moscow as a singer. She says, 'What sort of a singer am I!' It doesn't go with her panache. With luck she could be a star, surrounded by young male admirers and girls who would give their eye teeth to have her caprice and brio. Slava probably isn't her lover anyway. She just needs an entourage she can rely on in order to show herself to advantage. That is quite beyond Sergei and Misha. It was Misha told Sergei Slava was her lover. Sergei laughed and said, 'The minute her old man goes off to the championships . . .' Whether he is or whether he isn't, what she needs most is a retinue of admirers whose admiration will communicate itself to people who do not know her. Then Olga, her Slava, his friend and the little cousin decide it is time to go. Olga asks if I will walk home with them, and as we walk along she puts her arm round Slava the Jew or round his friend, acting up for the benefit of her little cousin too, and keeping an eye on me to make sure I am entering into the spirit of things. Without a lot of wine, though, I won't be overstepping the mark. Again, she takes my arm so as not to trip, or runs over to kiss Slava the Jew, or ask his friend to kiss her. The young men give as good as they get. The friend is Shurik. He asks the little cousin to kiss him and goes into ecstasies; then Olga kisses him and he makes a great show of spitting and everybody laughs. We come to the tents. Lucy the Waitress is with us. I danced a waltz with her. She said so seriously, 'Hold me tighter. When we whirl round I'll let go.' Lucy had been crying earlier in the evening, and Olga took her to one side, comforting her like a little girl. You could tell she was enjoying the part. We come to the tents and there is a small tent for two which, it transpires, Slava the Jew is sharing with his pal Shurik, so Olga will be going home to grandma on her own. She continues her recital by the tent. She sings at length from *The Queen of Spades*, singing all the vocal parts and filling in for the orchestra as well. They are clearly all children from good families. Shurik is lying with his head on Olga's lap and says, 'Olga, when did such and such a girl find out who I am?' 'Good gracious,' I think, 'so that's who he is!' You can tell from his voice. Slava the Jew isn't a bit like that. It is a quite different picture from yesterday's. Lucy keeps saying to Olga, 'Let's go home. It's past my bedtime.' In the end she gets fed up and goes off through the woods on her own. Nobody bothers to go with her. Olga and the little cousin get up too, and Olga asks me rather stiffly if I am coming. I have been sitting next to her and haven't put my arm round her all evening, or held her hand. I don't on the way home either. When we are saying goodbye she invites me to meet her at the tent tomorrow. I go from her dacha to find my way back to my young friends but get lost. I shout, 'Slava!' but nobody hears. Then I spot the tent. They answer the second time I call, even though I was only a couple of yards away from them the first time. When we were breaking up and I was going off with Olga and her cousin, Slava said gaily, 'It's bedtime for me and Shurik too. We're going to fuck.' I wondered if he was joking. I thought they wouldn't be in bed yet, and I could sit with them for a while and listen to them talking. They had been polite, asking me what was happening in Moscow, but now I have tracked them down Slava says from inside the tent, 'We're in bed. Can you find your own way back?' 'Oh, you're in bed. Yes, of course.' So that is that.

On Sunday morning we have rain for the first time. Again I can't find their tent and don't like to shout out for them. I go to Misha's dacha and am admitted. Grandma is baking scones. Misha takes me through. A lot of cigarette smoke, and the four of them sitting in a room together. Olga is playing cards with the two young men, and the little cousin is in bed. I thought during the night I would regale them with the poem about the emperor trembling in his bed, sensing his end approaching fast, and manfully holding himself in hand until he made it come at last. I make it seem I had prepared it for them yesterday. They laugh. During the night I have been thinking up ways of getting Olga to come to Moscow to seek her fortune, and thinking too of how I will work on Misha, and certainly get him to come and stay with me over the winter holidays. Misha's little sister appears. A lot of Misha in her, and she looks set to grow into a real beauty, except that her little teeth are all decayed from eating too many sweets. Olga starts kissing her and telling her how much she loves her brothers and sisters and aren't they beautiful? Then Slava the Jew asks me if I think he should try to come to Moscow to study. Yesterday when I was seeing Olga home she told me Slava was a journalist and that Shurik was studying to be a doctor. So Slava doesn't already have a degree in journalism, he is just working on a newspaper. I realize he must be a good seven years younger than me, even though we both look the same age. I can tell he would make an excellent journalist. Very up on current affairs, with a superficial grasp of everything that's going on. Misha starts showing me his textbooks on chemistry and physics, something about surface tension, and telling me how good they are. Then Olga adds a new touch to the picture by mentioning their surname. Small world! Their father is a famous professor my family know. How everything is coming together! From being children I knew nothing about . . . I say loudly through the curtain to grandma, 'There now. We already know each other through our parents,' hoping she will be less frosty next time I drop by for Misha. Their father has the resoundingly Jewish name of Lev Moiseevich. I ask Misha how it is he talks about the Jews in such a detached way, and he explains his father is Russian, and only one quarter Jewish. Anyway, Misha says, it is all the same to him whether someone is Jewish or Russian. Their mother must be Russian. I find out later the father is half and half. They all want to go into town, including Misha. He wants to put in three days there on his chemistry. I am to go with them. Olga's husband is back, so we shall meet at the flat of Shurik the Medic. From behind the curtain grandmother tells Misha he shouldn't go, but needless to say he ignores her. When we set off for the town he says rather unkindly that his grandmother and grandfather get up his nose and he hopes they will die soon. On the way to the bus I suggest a diversion to my place for a snack; they refused when grandmother suggested they might want something to eat. I settle them all down at my house with tea and find there is nowhere left for me to sit. Slava or Shurik wants to take cups off one of the chairs, but I tell them not to bother and sit on the floor, and Misha says, 'Don't worry. That's what he likes.' And to me he says, 'I noticed you like sitting that way.' Then he sits down in just the same way. As we are going for the bus they change their minds about meeting up today. Slava suggests I could go back home and join them tomorrow for the party, but I say no, I will come with them anyway as I have some things to do in town. I walk part of the time with Olga, and part of the time I manage to walk with Misha, since Olga has her friends with their arms round her a lot. It is some distance. The forty-six bus drives off under our noses and we have to walk on to the stop for the twenty-six. There is a big puddle at the terminus, with a tree stump in the middle. I jump up on it. Misha pauses at the edge, and the rest go over to a bench. I should join them. It is obvious Misha will not stand where he is forever, and then he and I would be sitting together, but he goes and joins them on the bench and then it is too late for it not to be obvious to everyone that I am going over to be beside him. So I sit on my own until the bus comes. A lot of people pile in, and I manage it so there is no empty seat beside Olga. She is with Slava and Shurik, and Misha and I sit together at the front. He suddenly thinks he has forgotten his bag just as the bus is about to move off. There is a rare Russian translation of a foreign chemistry book in it. He starts making for the exit. I keep his seat for him, afraid somebody may sit there or that the bus may leave without him. His cousin shouts from behind the other passengers, 'Misha, the bag's here.' He comes back and we set off. I suggest turning to face the window so as not to have to give our seats up, but Misha says, 'I can't do that. I always give my seat up.' I don't quite catch what he said. 'You don't give your seat up?' He says, 'No. I do.' And I say, 'Of course you do. Quite right too.' When I made the suggestion I thought it would please him. There are no elderly people near us anyway, as it happens. Nearer town there are fewer people standing. I look round at Olga occasionally, so she shouldn't feel I have all I need sitting with Misha. We arrive and get out at the same stop, Olga, Misha and I. Their friends have further to go. Misha asks me just before the stop, 'Do you stay on here?' It makes better sense for me to go on, but I say, 'Of course not. I'll get out here with you and have a bit of a walk.' Possibly Misha puts it down to Olga. The three of us get out and I can't think of anything to say to her. She is constantly expecting me to come out with something. She hasn't a clue what is going on. Anyway, the party is off, and I suppose she will put my silence down to the fact that she is going to her husband, or that all that hugging of her friends on the way to the bus has put me in a bad mood. It is heavy going until we get to their turning. 'I'll be off then,' I say. 'I'll go back to the village tomorrow morning, but I'll come back for the party in the evening,' although I am thinking I won't bother. What is the point of turning up and having nothing to say all evening? When we were on our way to the bus in the village Olga said she would phone me, and I gave her my phone number in town. She repeated it. Shurik the Medic, our putative host, gave me his phone number and showed me how to memorize it from the symmetrical numbers at each end. Now we are saying goodbye she has forgotten my number. When I am drunk I decide to phone her from where I am staying. I want her to know I have been drinking, and anyway without that I would not know what to say to her. I ring. 'Olga, let's get together!' She says, 'I can't. Arkady's home. See you tomorrow.' I ring another four times or so, but either get no reply, or somebody says she isn't home or tells me I've got a wrong number. Then I start openly asking for Misha, as if I want to get him to call Olga to the phone, or so he and she might think.

The next day, Monday, I go back to the village, too late if I had been intending to be back in town that evening. I am sure Misha won't get to go to the party. To Olga he is just her kid brother, and much younger for her than he is for me. I can see the weather has broken for the first time this holiday, with no prospect of it clearing. I set off to Misha's dacha to borrow his guitar. I asked him yesterday if I could borrow it for the two or three days he would be in town. He didn't take it with him, so as not to be distracted from his studies. Suddenly I see the back of his grey sweater going away from the house into the depths of the garden. So he's here. By the time I have spotted him I am already asking at the open door whether I can come in. His grandfather replies, 'Yes, yes. Is that you, Arkady?' When he sees me he says, 'What can I do for you?' 'I'm looking for Misha,' I say. I have already found Misha, but it is too late to take the question back. He says, 'Misha is loading up the car before they leave.' I catch up with him just as he is carrying out the guitar along with some other things. 'You're leaving,' I say. 'I've already heard. I was just coming to borrow your guitar, like we said.' There is a dark blue car behind the fence and his father standing beside it. This is the first time he has seen me in the role of a friend of his children. I say, 'Good afternoon, sir.' He answers drily, 'How do you do,' and turns back to the car boot. In the past I have always got a benevolent 'hello' and a smile from him. He goes off to the house. Misha says they are taking all their things and leaving because the weather has broken. He also asks if I am not feeling cold. It is raining, although just at that moment it isn't too heavy. I say, 'That's it, then.' He says, 'No, of course not. We may come back.' But it is obvious the season has changed once and for all, as was long overdue, and as it has been threatening for the last few days; the rain yesterday was the beginning. Somehow it is also clear, as it has been all along, only now it is glaringly obvious, that Misha is still just a child. He does not decide anything, it is all decided for him by the grown-ups. Just listen to the way his father talks down to him. After all his father doesn't see him as an Antinous, a boy in a hundred thousand: for him he is just a sixteen-year-old son who has to be kept on a short leash. I say to Misha, 'Your father doesn't seem too pleased to see me.' Misha says, 'He's just in a bit of a hurry.' I can see that for myself, and I'm never wrong about these things. I don't know whether grandma and grandpa have told him Olga has been gallivanting about with a crowd of young people for the past two days and coming home at two in the morning, and that I called round yesterday. I even gave my name, so grandma will have associated me with all that, and then there were yesterday's phone calls. He may have heard that someone kept trying to ring Olga. And Misha. Four times. Of course he isn't to know who it was, but I am one of the young people Olga has been running around with. That much he will have gathered from grandma. She now knows who I am, and I have been coming round to see Misha, and anyway what am I doing making friends with a sixteen-year-old? Perhaps half of this is paranoia but I seem to detect it all in that frosty 'How do you do?' While Misha and I are standing his father is carrying things out beyond the fence, then he asks Misha to take something a couple of times, and each time I make to help him, only Misha gets there first. I'm not pretending, although it looks as if I am. Another touch: I tell Misha I have come to borrow his guitar because I don't want him to feel it is goodbye, and he holds out the guitar to me. 'Here you are.' So I can play it while they are loading the car. How I love him! The next thing is, out pops grandma and I don't manage to say hello properly to her either. First she is so far away I would have to shout to make her hear, which would seem ridiculously overdone, but she seems in any case to be making a point of not looking in my direction. Perhaps she is being so odd towards me because she has told Olga's father about her behaviour. Yesterday she had at least been talking to me, but today she seems to have quite a different attitude, and so has father. They are in a hurry, of course, but even so . . . Then I find myself alone with little sister with the bad teeth. Everybody has gone off to collect their things and in order not just to sit there in silence I give her a nice smile and ask what medal that is she is wearing. I read the inscription, 'Every Day is a Rainy Day'. She puts me right: 'Every Day is a Rainbow Day'. Equally nonsensical. She tells me she has won a race here. Running? I have no idea what she is talking about, so I give her another nice smile. Misha comes back bearing belongings. 'She won a race, you know.' 'So I hear.' 'Has she been boasting from the minute you met?!' 'That's not fair. I asked her what the medal was for.' I have a little more time with Misha, or perhaps it was earlier, since grandma went by. He asks, 'Do you know my phone number?' I say I do. 'Misha,' I say, 'I'd rather you phoned me. Have you got anything to write the number down with?' He finds a piece of paper but no pencil. 'Look it up in the phone book, then.' I should just tell him the number. As a mathematician he could easily memorize it. Also, I think I ought to mention phoning yesterday. He must have been at home and heard the phone ringing so many times. Even if he wasn't, he will have been told. 'Actually,' I say, 'I phoned you yesterday, only I was drunk. I asked if Olga was in, then I asked if you were.' 'You were drunk?' he asks me back, so he probably does know about the calls, and I've just given him an explanation for the absurdity of ringing four or five times in a row. Or perhaps he is just asking.

They get in the car and his father says, although without looking at me, 'Goodbye.' I say goodbye very respectfully, and stand watching them drive away. Misha is in front with his father. His father takes a long time turning the car. Also I think it is a mistake to be walking home. They will drive past me on the way and see this figure walking in the rain, and it will be very obvious I am going back to my dacha and had only come out to see Misha. It is a mistake, and I will really feel very sad. It is too late to turn back, but it would have been better if I were going in the opposite direction, as if I were going to lunch at the café, but then I see the car turn to go back beyond the fence and along the street of dachas, so they won't see me anyway. Also, when Misha and I were talking he asked me if I was going back into town today, and I said most likely I was and we agreed to meet up at the boys' party. I can't make up my mind whether to go or not. He says Arkady won't be there. When they have gone I walk after them to the bus stop. Just like yesterday the forty-six drives off in front of my nose and I walk on miles to the stop for the twenty-six. Our evening get-together doesn't happen. I ring Shurik and he tells me Olga can't come because of her husband. I ask where it is and how to get there, but have no intention of going. I don't see him for a week. He doesn't ring, of course, and in the meantime I get on with my work, trying not to phone him so as not to spoil things. And another thing: I think I will only allow myself to ring after I have finished everything, and that the writing will act as a delaying mechanism and keep me from being in too much of a hurry. Even so I ring a couple of times, but one time, I think, nobody is home, and the other a voice says Misha is not home but can they take a message and I say, 'No, but thank you. I'll ring again later.' After I have hung up I realize it was Olga and that she had recognized my voice. That is why she asked, with a catch in her voice, whether she could pass on a message, just to prolong the conversation, but I hadn't realized it was her, hadn't prolonged the conversation, and now it is too late. I am puzzled. I rang in the morning thinking she would be at work. I hold myself back for a week by writing. Then I ring up and ask for Misha and a woman's voice, not Olga's and not an old voice like grandma's, the mother, I imagine, says what I take to be, 'Just a minute.' I think she has gone off to get Misha but somebody hangs up. I am so impatient I rashly dial again. Again mother answers. 'Misha isn't home, I told you. Who's that calling?' I tell her and explain I misheard the first time and thought she had gone to get him. 'No,' she says, 'I told you the first time he isn't home.' I was right all the same to ring back, otherwise I would have thought she had hung up deliberately, and that perhaps Misha had even asked her to. It is Friday, the day they hold the dances, and the weather is good. I think he must be at the village. I go there, to his dacha, as fast as I can. Everything is shut, the blinds drawn, only an empty tea caddy has been left on the window sill inside, some old shoes standing by the door, a broom. Everything just as when they drove off. I come back for the first time in those next three days, see this picture, and know he isn't back yet. The next day, Saturday, Misha does not come, and he does not come on Sunday. I am back in town, of course, early on Monday morning and phone him. I wait till ten. Any earlier he might still be sleeping: any later he will have gone out. Nobody answers the first time. The second time Misha answers the phone himself. I think he probably heard it ringing the first time while he was half asleep and maybe guessed it was me, but never mind. 'When are you going back to the village?' I ask. 'Tomorrow, or more likely the day after, Wednesday.' I say, 'I'm just coming over to your district. I've got some business. Why don't you come down to the street if you haven't got anything better to do.' 'Right,' he says. 'See you in our courtyard.' He tells me the number of the apartment block and what it looks like. I say, 'I'll be there in forty minutes or so on my way back.' I look into his courtyard on my way out, thinking it would be good to take him on my errand with me, to show I really do have business in his district, but he isn't there. I go, collect the keys I have to get, and go back to see him. He whistles to me from a first floor flat. It is exactly a week since I last saw him. When I close my eyes I find I can't remember exactly what he looks like. His features have started to blur, and now when I see him it is as if we have been apart for a very long time. He comes down and says, 'Did you see Arkady? He was walking right behind you. Olga's husband.' 'No,' I say, and regret not having been more observant. It would have been interesting to see what sort of husband she has. 'Shall we go to a film?' he asks. 'Great,' I say. 'Only let's go to a cinema in the centre of town.' 'Well,' I ask, 'have you finished revising your chemistry?' meaning, 'Are you free to come out with me now?' 'No,' he says. 'I haven't got down to it. Yesterday I went to the dacha where Olga and Arkady are staying. It was much more fun than staying here.' He says it is boring in our village with only a few dachas to it. Where he was yesterday there are a thousand. What struck me as a bustling little society had struck him as the back of beyond. He starts going through the films which are on in town. This one he's seen, but *Rash Marriage* might be worth going to. We don't talk much in the bus, get out at my stop. 'You go up,' he says. 'I'll wait down here.' That's their way. They meet each other in the streets and that's where their life is centred, well away from the eyes of their parents. That's why they are so keen to get a place in residences or go to study in Moscow. We do go up to my flat, to look through the newspaper and see what is showing. He has seen most of the films already, and what he hasn't seen doesn't start for a couple of hours. I am afraid he will change his mind, and when we are leaving I say it was the Sunday paper and the programmes are different on Monday, although I know perfectly well it has the next week's programmes too, and that he has looked through them. Everything is fine, only he wants to ring home from a phone box on the way to say where he is, and neither of us has the right change and he decides to phone without putting a coin in. He invites me into the phone box with him to see how it's done. Unfortunately that telephone isn't working, so I don't get to hear who he speaks to or what he says to them. When we get some change I no longer have an excuse for joining him in the phone box. Also he tells me as we go along that Arkady has a solid gold cross the size of your hand on a chain down to his waist which his grandmother has given him. She has lots of valuables and lives alone in a large flat, but it would never occur to anyone to rob her. The film is about a man who drowns wearing a rucksack full of gold. The old lady has her gold stashed away in jars and he fancies trying to rob her. Arkady and his amazing gold cross have really caught Misha's fancy, but it is only too obvious in the hour before the film, and when we are walking around the town centre after it, that I have nothing to interest him. I just don't know any interesting things, and there is no basis for our friendship to flourish. Why would he have phoned me? He has pleasures enough of his own, and what have I to offer? He and a friend had gone out on a Java motorbike and ended up in the ditch when the road suddenly turned into a dirt track. Lots of people come off there, and there had even been a fatal accident shortly before. I have no Java for him to ride. He says he will be going back to the village on Wednesday, perhaps even Tuesday. I don't write my address in Moscow down for him, as I have been planning to all week. I have no pencil and paper on me, and I know if I ask, neither will he: he is wearing an open-necked shirt. My invitation will have led nowhere and have to be repeated later, when it needs to be issued just once, without any suggestion of urgency. I remembered I didn't have a pencil when I was leaving home this morning, but I thought if I did prudently take one it would be tempting providence and I wouldn't get through to him on the phone. Our relationship is exactly where it was that first day when an incredibly beautiful boy I did not know was standing on a mound playing a guitar. For him I was and am a passer-by whom there is no point in knowing. There is nothing in what I say or do to engage his attention, no matter how hard I try.

Tuesday. I go to the village. He said he would be here on Tuesday or Wednesday. All I want now is to let him have my Moscow address, since otherwise the end of the thread will be lost forever. The blinds of his dacha are drawn down just as they were before, and the tea caddy still stands on the window-sill. The broom and the old shoes still stand by the door. I go over again around

seven in the evening. That leaves Wednesday. On Wednesday I
come by in the morning and afternoon, and at around eight o'clock
in the evening. Then I walk over to see Sergei. He looks out in
some perplexity because he is having dinner. He has a friend staying
and they are just going over to the volleyball pitch to play badminton. He seems almost embarrassed that I have turned up when he
cannot keep me company. I walk back below the gully so he should
not see that I am going home again and had only come over this
way to see him. Misha is obviously not coming on Wednesday
either. The next day I go over to look in at his dacha just on the
off-chance, and suddenly from the garden fence I can see the white
curtained window is now black. I can't believe my eyes. I go closer.
No broom, no shoes, no tea caddy. My heart starts pounding. I
think, he's here. He's still asleep, or somebody from his family is in
the house and he's gone for a walk. I look in the window. There is
nobody there. Everybody has left for good. The season is over and
his dacha is empty. You can look straight through it from one
window to the other. Late yesterday evening, when I couldn't be
bothered to come round late in the evening, Misha was here.
Perhaps he went this morning, in the car with his father. He could
hardly have carried the curtains and mattresses back to town in his
arms. They have gone for good, and now I can never write my
address down for him. I can't phone and invite him to Moscow. It
would have quite the wrong effect. In three days' time I shall have
to return to Moscow myself, and there is no chance they will come
back here. Again, just like the last time I said goodbye to him after
those sunlit days, the rain is pouring down as if on purpose to make
everything sad. The days that followed that goodbye were sunny.
When we went to the cinema on Monday it was positively hot, but
now it is raining and I am alone. The village is empty. It isn't just
that people are staying indoors, they have gone for good. When
Misha and I used to walk this way together there was an empty
dacha. I always looked at my reflection in its windows, and Misha
would stop to do the same. I thought the twelve years dividing us
were not quite so visible in that dark mirror. Now I think the dacha

was a prefiguring. They are lived in only until the autumn, and then they empty one by one. Now it is the turn of Misha's dacha. I walk the street from end to end, right to the place where they went to swim. For a moment I even dare to hope he might be there. Yesterday it almost hadn't hurt, but today, when I have missed him so ridiculously, walking miles only to miss him when he did come, today it is like that last time. In town this evening I have another reminder, a young man whistling to his friend from the balcony of his flat using exactly the same signal as Misha and Sergei. A call-sign, evidently, from some Western song they all know.

Translated by Arch Tait

VYACHESLAV PIETSUKH

The Central–Ermolaevo War

The enigma of the Russian soul is actually very easily explained: the Russian soul encompasses everything. By way of comparison the German soul or, say perhaps, the Serbo-Croat soul . . . Not that we have any grounds for supposing their souls to be in any wise shallower than ours; indeed they may well in some respects be more thorough-going, more compositionally sound if you like, as a bowlful of stewed fruit containing fruit is more compositionally sound than a bowlful of fruit consisting of fruit, vegetables, spices and minerals. That said, however, there is no getting round the fact that certain things they do lack. They may, for instance, be brimming with constructiveness but quite hopeless at negating the universe. They may be bursting with entrepreneurial flair, but lack any trace of that eighth note of the octave, that sense of 'let's watch the whole lot go up in flames'. Again they may be long on national pride, but quite hopeless at building castles in the air. The Russian soul has the lot: constructiveness, negation, flair, pyromania, national pride and castles in the air. Building castles in the air is, in fact, a particular strength. Imagine for a moment that a Russian, from having nothing better to do, has dismantled a shed he actually very much needs, explained to his neighbour why Russia was victorious in the war against Napoleon, and given his wife a good thrashing with the kitchen towel; he then sits back on his veranda smiling peacefully at the loveliness of the day, and is suddenly struck by the thought that it's perhaps time he invented a new religion.

No doubt this feature of the Russian soul results from a whole raft of unexpected causes. Some possible candidates may perhaps raise an eyebrow here and there and have admittedly been little researched but seem, to the present author, for all their apparent naïvety, no less germane than, say, the high incidence of goose-foot. We have in mind such factors as toponymy, climate and topology.

Toponymy has an obscure but, as it were, electric significance for the lives of Russians. There is no two ways about it, if a Russian has been born in a town called Golden Reaches, or an urban settlement called Third Left Riverbanks, or the village of Afrikanda, or on Robespierre Street, he is marked for life. This is all the more evident if we go on to discover that Golden Reaches boasts a wire factory and the entire town is ankle deep in sunflower seed husks expectorated by the local inhabitants; that the launch visits Third Left Riverbanks rather less than daily; that the English teacher is the only person in Afrikanda who knows what 'subjective idealism' means; and that there are no street lights on Robespierre Street. The impact of toponymy can doubtless be exaggerated but everybody knows that Muscovites differ from Leningraders in just the same way as the words 'governor' and 'governess', despite their shared roots.

We must admit straight away that the influence of toponymy on human activity in the locality where the Central–Ermolaevo War broke out in July 1981 was marginal. Assuredly there is a town in the region called Orgwork, but Ermolaevo derives its name from Fyodor Ermolaev who dynamited the local church in 1922, thereby unwittingly writing his name in Russian geography. Before that the village had been known as Little Harvest, and local lore would have it that this was the dispiriting Little Harvest mentioned in the writings of Nikolai Nekrasov. Why the urban settlement of Central should have been called Central is a mystery.

If we turn now to climate, we find its influence in the locality does indeed tend towards divisiveness. If, for example, a perpetual motion machine were to be invented in Central, the people of Ermolaevo would hear about it no sooner than after the successful completion of one of the two current road mending sagas. This result of the climate does, however, have a significant cultural impact which is the direct opposite of what might have been expected. The fecundity of the local temperament, universal secondary education, and the lack to hand of one essential after another means that the people of Ermolaevo are constantly inventing things. Even Ermolaevo's shepherd Pashka Egorov, who is in some ways a relic of times past, has invented a new way of cracking a whip which produces a note so fearsome as to cow even Frigate the Finnish bull. Add to this the interminable winter evenings relieved only by the dismal mutter of the television or the clatter of a sewing machine, or the winter sprite who periodically howls in the flue, vitamin deficiency in the spring, and the curtain of water vapour which hangs dully in the air as the water table rises in the autumn, and we can appreciate that climate does, to say the least, exert a significant influence on the psychology of the local people.

Finally, topology. Ermolaevo is entirely surrounded by fields. Hard by the eastern gate into the village is an abandoned stable, beyond which a field is bounded by a stream with the somewhat workaday name of the Handwash. Further on is bird cherry scrub, then again a field pitted with ravines which, although not deep, are very damp, and where hemlock, stinging nettles and gigantic burdocks riot. Beyond that is a field, flat as a bench, then one with edges skewed somewhat like the cap of a pine mushroom; and only in the far distance, almost at Central itself, do the woodlands begin. Beyond the right gate there are more fields.

Ermolaevo is, then, a wholly unexceptional village of some fifty households with the wholly unexceptional features we would expect to find: a windowless structure of uncertain purpose alongside which a length of rail hangs from an old lime-tree, the local *veche* bell for summoning the citizens; log-lined wells with a boggy smell; a cartwheel lying by the village hall, perhaps dating from the conflict on the China and Oriental Railway; and metal hydrochloric acid casks overgrown with goose-foot: in a word, all those features which relate the hamlets of central Russia to each other more intimately than a shared womb links twins.

Central for its part is also a wholly unexceptional urban settlement; less than exceptional, indeed, in that it does not even have a clubhouse of its own, although it does have a bus station, café, repair workshops, and a large flower border outside the soviet council offices with a silver-painted plaster footballer in the middle of it. Little pink flowers line up artfully round him to form a slogan reading, 'He who does not work, neither shall he eat'.

The topology of the locality is, then, nothing special, your average, unassertively picturesque landscape. That said, it does insistently prompt one to the positively Gogolian insight that such landscapes leave you with a sense of obligation. What that obligation might be is anyone's guess, but that you are under it there is no gainsaying. Lake Geneva is said not to leave people feeling under any obligation. The Apennines, 'breath-taking wonders of nature, crowned by breath-taking wonders of art', don't place people under any obligations either. This near-desert, however, surely does, even if you can't work out what to. At the very least, it obliges you to rack your brains as to what obligation you are being placed under, and surely that is not so little.

This near-desert region of Russia does also periodically stir a man to devilry when he wants to laugh and cry and set the world on fire all at the same time. There is thus nothing too surprising in the fact that in July 1981 the youth of Ermolaevo and Central should have gone to war with each other for no very obvious reason at all.

The immediate causes of the war remain unclear. Perhaps, indeed, apart from such fundamentals as toponymy, climate and topology, the Central–Ermolaevo conflict was a war without causes, and we may pass over this traditional preoccupation without more ado. Of the forces drawn into this internecine strife we may say at the outset that they were far from numerous: virtually all the young men in both communities were involved, some forty souls in all; and Police Inspector Svistunov, Semyon Ablyazov the vet, Alexander Samsonov (a tractor driver), and a certain clerk in the regional office of the State Grain Procurement Agency were all to play a part. At the head of the forces of Central stood an eighteen-year-old repairs mechanic known as Papa Carlo, while the kingpin of the Ermolaevo faction was a twenty-two-year-old driver, Pyotr Ermolaev, grandson of the dynamiter.

As is more often the case than not, the spark which ignited the Central–Ermolaevo war was a mere nothing. On 17 July 1981 Pyotr Ermolaev drove into Central on his motorbike to buy volume six of the *Medical Encyclopaedia* for his uncle. When he came out of the bookshop, shoving the tome inside his blue nylon anorak, he found Papa Carlo standing by his motorbike and gazing pensively at its rear wheel.

'Ciao!' said Papa Carlo. 'How much is the bike?'

'I won it in the lottery,' Pyotr Ermolaev replied, 'but in the shops it would cost five hundred roubles.'

'Tell you what, Petro, I give you five hundred and fifty. Can't say fairer than that.'

'No, Papa Carlo, I'm not selling it. Winning something in a lottery is like being given a present.'

Pyotr Ermolaev refused so categorically that Papa Carlo could see he had no prospect of getting the motorbike and, somewhat riled, he decided to wind its owner up.

'I heard a hunter came across a herd of wild cows twenty kilometres from your Ermolaevo,' he said. 'Perfectly ordinary cows they were, Sentimenthalers, only wild.'

'Get away,' Pyotr Ermolaev resisted.

'Incidentally, the cows were from the Ermolaevo collective farm,' Papa Carlo continued, paying no attention to his interlocutor's interjection. 'The hunter said they must have wandered off into the woods foraging. There you are in Ermolaevo stuffing yourselves with sausage and you leave your cattle to graze on pine needles. A right bunch of country bumpkins you lot are, aren't you.'

Pyotr Ermolaev was dumbstruck because, in the first place, although Central was designated on maps as an urban settlement, its inhabitants had never previously had pretensions to being town-dwellers; and in the second place, it had been generally acknowledged from time immemorial that the people of Ermolaevo were distinguished solely by their far from rustic characteristics of brazenness and lack of self-control.

'You watch your tongue!' Pyotr Ermolaev said, striking his knuckles on his forehead in mock amazement. 'Think yourself a real townie, don't you! You're a turnip head, Papa Carlo, and a wurzel-picking turnip head at that!'

Now it was Papa Carlo's turn to be dumbstruck, because his justly renowned very nasty temper had ensured that no one had directed a remark of this kind, or anything remotely resembling it, at him for a very long time.

'How you like your teeth in the back of your head?' he inquired chillingly. 'How about it, fella?'

Papa Carlo, despite his youthfulness, was a sturdy, powerfully built lad endowed by nature with fists like hams, and Pyotr Ermolaev had no illusions regarding the likely outcome if their exchanges were to become physical. He gazed thoughtfully, indeed soulfully at this man who reviled him, as people do when resolved to commit some particular moment of time to memory for the rest of their lives. Then he started his motorbike, climbed into the saddle, jabbed the accelerator pedal and took off in a cloud of yellow dust.

'Yokels like you,' Papa Carlo shouted after him, 'only ever do win in lotteries!'

This parting shot was even more impossible to shrug off, and Pyotr Ermolaev vowed to even the score at the first available opportunity.

This presented itself on 19 July, Field Husbandry Day, two days after his contretemps outside the bookshop. Visitors flocked to the festivities in Ermolaevo from miles around, some of them from far-off Orgwork and some from villages the people of Ermolaevo had never even heard of. The urban settlement of Central was represented by the night shift from the repair workshops, under the leadership of Papa Carlo, and a garland of unruly maidens.

At about three in the afternoon the right bank of the River Handwash began filling up with people. The men arrived wearing dark suits, each with a comb in its breast pocket. They wore white shirts, most with all the buttons done up, and sandals. The women wore cheap and cheerful dresses and muslin kerchiefs, tied in a manner suggestive of renunciation of worldly desires, as if aware they had nothing left to hope for unless, perhaps, a miracle. The younger generation affected studied casualness.

Shortly afterwards the buffet arrived on a truck, a loudspeaker was installed, and the dance began. In the first interval a representative of the village soviet made a speech about the importance of grain; in the second, he awarded certificates of merit; and in the third, a girl from out of town climbed on the back of the truck and performed the following catchy song:

> All the boys from Vologda
> Are hooligans and thieving gits
> They jumped a peasant carting dung
> And robbed and left him in the shits.

Then the visitors went round the village visiting, the Ermolaevo Amateur Dramatics Circle gave a short performance, and dancing resumed. In short, Field Husbandry Day was a great success. Admittedly, Alexander Samsonov did try to disperse the crowd with a bulldozer. He was shown the error of his ways, but not crippled, and sent to sleep it off out of harm's way. Towards evening, however, when with twilight falling the dance transferred to the clubhouse, or to be absolutely precise, just after Semyon Ablyazov, the vet, had put 'The Drum Dance' on for the fourth time, a major disturbance broke out behind the clubhouse. It was instigated when Pyotr Ermolaev went up to Papa Carlo, took him to one side and said:

'How's it going, Papa Carlo. Enjoying yourself with us?'

'Not a lot,' Papa Carlo answered, and spat on the floor.

'It's going to get worse,' said Pyotr Ermolaev.

He thereupon took a broad swing and punched his detractor in the face. Papa Carlo merely grunted and headed for the exit, scowling like Frigate the bull.

Behind the clubhouse some five men of Ermolaevo were waiting for Papa Carlo with fists and staves, but the night shift from the repair shop hastened to his defence, preventing them from evening the score to their full satisfaction. It could, however, be claimed in good conscience that Papa Carlo had got his comeuppance and that the first battle had been lost by Central. The mechanics were beaten, albeit not too bloodily, but to the accompaniment of those humiliating jibes which are more wounding than mere sticks and stones.

It was this that caused mortal offence to the lads from Central, impelling them to the judgement that an immediate counterblow must be struck. Returning to their community on a passing truck, they roused the morning shift, three drivers, one or two pupils from the secondary school, and returned to Ermolaevo, again on a truck, only this time one attached to the repair shop, to take revenge.

It was not all that late, about eleven o'clock or a little after, but already a large barn padlock hung on the clubhouse door. The village street was empty and there was no sign of life beyond the dogs morosely barking in people's yards. In the distance, however, by the abandoned stables, the intriguing glow of a campfire was to be seen. The lads from Central were feeling very upset, as if they had been cheated of something large and important, but now the surmise that it might be none other than the enemy lurking by that distant midnight campfire restored their spirits.

Around the half defunct campfire sat a group of small boys from Ermolaevo, baking potatoes in the embers and talking among themselves about the things small boys do talk about on such occasions. Incensed as the lads from Central might be, they could not stoop to taking it out on the small fry. They therefore confined themselves to debagging the small boys and throwing their trousers on the fire. To complete the act of vengeance, and in order further to relieve their spleen, they stood round in a circle and urinated on the embers, the potatoes, and the smouldering trousers.

The following morning the small boys of Ermolaevo told their big brothers about the outrage perpetrated by the mechanics, and it was unanimously agreed that a riposte was needed. On the night of

21 July the men of Ermolaevo crossed into Central, inflicting appreciable losses on the settlement. They broke the street lights at the bus station, wrecked the flower border outside the soviet, beheading the plaster footballer in the process, gave a good thrashing to a tipsy mechanic they encountered, broke down Papa Carlo's gate, and removed the carburettors from two Belarus tractors.

On the way home the men of Ermolaevo sang songs, and from time to time their leader shouted into the wind, 'This is living, eh lads? This, I reckon, lads, is life!'

Both sides in the Central–Ermolaevo war were now obliged to dig in, while continuing actively to gather intelligence. This was caused by the temporary relocation to Ermolaevo of Police Inspector Svistunov. As evening was falling on 24 July, the lads of Central loaded themselves into a bus and set off towards Ermolaevo with the intention of inflicting a decisive defeat on the rustics, but on the bridge across the River Handwash they unexpectedly encountered Svistunov and decided on a rapid tactical retreat. Svistunov was not, as it happened, in full uniform. In fact he had on only his peaked cap, a vest, police breeches, and a pair of domestic slippers, but Papa Carlo nevertheless suspected a subterfuge. Most likely the men of Ermolaevo had chickened out and referred the conflict to Authority. That evening Papa Carlo prevailed upon his men to withdraw.

Upon regaining their home patch they argued noisily over whether the men of Ermolaevo had deliberately enticed the inspector to their village or whether his appearance was down to chance. They were, needless to say, unable to reach agreement, and as the discussion proceeded they became so embittered that had it not been for Semyon Ablyazov, the vet, having had a few drinks at his sister's wedding in Central, the war would assuredly have developed on a less strategic and more cruelly direct plane.

Ablyazov was unexpectedly discovered sleeping on his feet, like a horse, by the bus station ticket office, snorting and sighing periodically as if to emphasize the resemblance. The mechanics grabbed him under the arms and dragged him off to Papa Carlo's, with the firm intention of extracting an unambiguous answer from him the following morning as to the cause of Police Inspector Svistunov's appearance in Ermolaevo.

Semyon Ablyazov was locked in the bathhouse behind Papa Carlo's house. The following morning he awoke at daybreak and puzzled at length as to where he might be and why. That he was sitting in a bathhouse was clear, but in whose, and why he should be sitting in a bathhouse at all, was a mystery. He yelled and yelled, and then fell silent.

It was after seven in the morning when Papa Carlo came into the changing room, sat down on the bench, lit up a cigarette, and said:

'What you got Svistunov snooping around in Ermolaevo for?'

'Is this an interrogation?' Ablyazov inquired sluggishly.

'Yup,' Papa Carlo replied.

'In that case I refuse to answer.'

Papa Carlo recognized with annoyance that he had made a bad start and that Ablyazov would probably have responded better to entreaty than bullying. It was, however, too late. His prisoner had, as they say in Central, locked horns.

'How you like us to torture you? How about it, fella?' Papa Carlo asked, his eyes becoming fierce predatory slits.

Ablyazov began to throw off his torpor, evidently considerably intrigued by this suggestion.

'And how exactly,' he said, 'would you be thinking of torturing me?'

'I bet you sing like a canary if we give you nothing to drink but water. Or perhaps you prefer a pair of red-hot combination pliers . . .'

Ablyazov didn't believe the bit about the pliers for an instant, but he was so thirsty he could see fiery rings floating in front of his eyes.

'Right,' he consented. 'Go ahead and torture me, but start with the water.'

Papa Carlo spat and went outside. He wandered round the bathhouse for a time before sitting down on a pile of firewood to try to work out how to get the vet to talk. He suddenly heard an incomprehensible mumbling emanating from the bathhouse.

'Hola, Semyon,' Papa Carlo called out. 'What you muttering about in there?'

'Eh?' came the voice from the bathhouse.

'I said, what you muttering about in there? You dying or what?'

'I'm writing a poem. I've got this habit. I write poems while I'm regenerating after a hangover.'

'Right. Well then, what you written?'

'This. Listen:

> The more you sing and make a racket
> The less you worry how much you get in your wage packet.'

'Well!' said Papa Carlo. 'That's a real poem, sinuous, politically literate. You ought to be writing poetry for the newspapers, Semyon, not inseminating heifers. You tried sending any of them to the papers?'

'Of course I have,' came a long sigh from the bathhouse. 'They won't publish them, the sods. They say my commas are all over the shop.'

'They're lying to you. The reason they won't publish your poetry is you've got a mean personality. The minute anyone publishes you you'll be demanding a state grant for the rest of your life. You're like that all the time. For example, someone asks you in a perfectly friendly way why Svistunov is snooping around in Ermolaevo and heaven only knows what you imagine.'

The bathhouse was a tomb.

Several of the mechanics came round to Papa Carlo shortly afterwards in search of news. As he had no news, his lads considered the matter and decided to resort to the pliers. Papa Carlo went off to the shed to get them while the mechanics stoked up the stove in the summer kitchen. When the pliers had been heated to a raspberry red radiance, making their greasy handles give off an acrid smoky smell, the whole unit piled into the bathhouse.

Seeing the red-hot pliers and the mechanics' resolute expressions,

Ablyazov realized things were turning nasty. His face fell because, although he would now have been only too glad to answer any question they might care to ask, not only did he not know why Svistunov was snooping around in Ermolaevo, he hadn't even known Svistunov was there at all. His ignorance was, in a sense, a blessing, since he was delivered of the temptation to behave dishonourably. He grimaced in terror, and even smiled, but they seared his arm in two places all the same.

Getting no sense out of Ablyazov, the lads from Central freed him around lunch time to go in search of beer and began considering their next move. After a time it occurred to Papa Carlo that he had a secret agent he could send to Ermolaevo. This agent, a certain clerk in the regional office of the State Grain Procurement Agency, was Papa Carlo's brother-in-law. He was due in any case to go to Ermolaevo on business, and was charged with making inquiries regarding the presence of Inspector Svistunov, which he faithfully did.

For their part the men of Ermolaevo were so discomfited by the enemy's inaction that they asked Alexander Samsonov, who was on his way to Central to have the piston rings on his tractor changed, to sniff out whether some new and terrible act of vengeance was being prepared. Samsonov, however, provided no information on his return, since the mechanics gave him very special piston rings and he ground to a halt a bare two kilometres outside Central. After drowning his sorrows he returned to base in no state to tell anyone anything.

The clerk from the State Grain Procurement Agency, meanwhile, conscientiously reported that Police Inspector Svistunov was in Ermolaevo solely to visit his cousin, that he would be departing on the morning of 29 July to spend a lengthy period in Orgwork, and that on that evening the youth of Ermolaevo would be assembling in the clubhouse to rehearse a play by Medical Orderly Serebryakov entitled *Home Remedies Spell Trouble*.

The twenty-ninth of July was therefore set as the date for a switch from trench warfare to open battle, and this was duly implemented. In the morning of that historic day men of Ermolaevo beat up the driver of a Central truck who was transporting food from Orgwork and had imprudently stopped by the River Handwash to take a break. That evening the Battle of Ermolaevo was fought.

At about five in the evening the lads of Central boarded their bus armed with bike chains, lengths of hose-pipe, and a hessian covered cardboard box. Some time after six the bus stopped by the river bridge. The lads had been over-eager and had now to await the coming of dusk, since they were to strike under cover of darkness. To kill time they bathed in the Handwash, then lit a fire, settled round it, and began telling dirty stories. At last the first star of evening twinkled in the deep blue of the sky. The lads from Central put out their fire and filed off towards the enemy village.

At just this time the youth of Ermolaevo was, as had been promised, rehearsing *Home Remedies Spell Trouble* under the direction of the author himself. Serebryakov was sitting on the billiard table, holding a roll-your-own between his fingers, and saying, 'You have to appreciate, comrades, that what we have here is drama, almost tragedy. Because this, this *free-thinking* results in someone's becoming even more ill instead of recovering. One could weep, comrades, but you are hamming it up mercilessly. Now do let's start this scene again from the beginning. Cue, Vetrogonov . . .'

Vetrogonov, played by a puny lad with a quite unrustic pallor, snivelled purposefully and delivered his line:

'I believe solely in folk remedies. For example, a hundred grams of pepper to a tumbler of vodka.'

'Cue, Pravdin,' Serebryakov interjected.

'You'll never have enough money for that sort of medicine,' Pravdin volunteered on cue (the part was being acted by Pyotr Ermolaev). 'Unless, of course, you are going to print it yourself.'

'Excellent, Pravdin.' Serebryakov gave him a thumbs up. 'Now Vetrogonov again.'

'I have no need to print money. I always have some stashed away from my wife.'

'No, no,' Serebryakov interrupted the little lad. 'That won't do at all. Do try to say these words, how should I say, lasciviously, perhaps. Because in the section "Dramatis personae" we have a note, "Roman Vetrogonov, young agricultural engineer, proponent of marital freedom". The way you say the lines it sounds as if you are apologizing. Once more, please.'

'I have no need to print money. I always have some stashed away from my wife,' Vetrogonov repeated, affecting such an inane expression that other members of the cast concealed their mirth with difficulty.

'Those are absurd words,' Pravdin said. 'Everything in the family should be mutual, with the full agreement of both parties. Because family happiness is very fragile. It comprises three categories: the spiritual, the physical and the material. The material basis of family happiness is not by any means the least, and for this reason you should always put your wages in the same place as your wife. The stronger the family, the stronger our fatherland!'

'Right,' said Serebryakov. 'Now we have the sound effects: "Cows mooing, sheep bleating, a bull bellowing." Pashka? What's happened to Pashka?'

'I'm here,' Pashka Egorov responded. The young shepherd had been entrusted only with the sound effects because he wasn't very bright.

'Sock it to us, kid,' muttered one of the men of Ermolaevo rather unkindly.

Pavel dutifully imitated what was required.

'Right,' said Serebryakov. 'Exit Pravdin. Vetrogonov on stage solo. "Ah, perhaps I should take some more medicine now." "Takes the glass,"' Serebryakov read the stage direction, '"tips in pepper, camomile, rhubarb, vanilla. Pours vodka over it, stirs it, raises it to his lips." Then voice off again.'

'*Home Remedies Spell Trouble*,' Pashka intoned in a sepulchral voice, peeping out from behind the walnut finish rostrum and bursting into affected laughter.

'Ooh, who's that talking?' Vetrogonov asked, fairly naturally. 'Is it a ghost?'

'Only old women and fools believe in ghosts,' Pravdin replied, emerging from the wings. 'You heard the voice of reason . . .'

Even as he was speaking the words 'You heard the voice of reason', the forces of Central, their infiltration of Ermolaevo undetected, completed taking up position in a broad semi-circle round the clubhouse and Papa Carlo began unpacking the cardboard box. It proved to contain Molotov cocktails prepared by the local genius, who was known as Mad Mendeleev. Taking their bottles, the lads from Central readied themselves and froze into immobility.

Meanwhile the lights in the clubhouse were switched on and the windows threw huge, pale rectangles on to the grass outside. In the distance a calf called pitifully, plaintively. The voice of Pyotr Ermolaev could clearly be heard denouncing folk remedies. A boy came out on to the porch, his cigarette glowing like a tiny star, drew on it several times and disappeared inside again.

'Go, go, go!' shouted Papa Carlo, and the Molotov cocktails sailed through the clubhouse windows. Glass tinkled, a neurotic shriek followed by the sound of stampeding feet was heard. Oily black smoke began billowing from the windows, the lights went out, and the club interior was lit up by an eerie glow as the fire took hold.

Contrary to Central's expectations, the men of Ermolaevo were not thrown into disarray by the surprise and novelty of the attack. Rushing from the clubhouse straight into the waiting lads from Central, they recovered their composure almost immediately and dealt the enemy a merciless rebuff. For a quarter of an hour the situation was impossible to read. There was no telling who was giving ground and who, on the contrary, was coming out on top: there was only the eerie sound of bicycle chains whistling in the air, heavy breathing on all sides, wild shouting and cursing. Pyotr Ermolaev furiously dispatched the mechanics, his blows accompanied by the cry of Alexander Nevsky: 'He who comes to us with the sword . . .!' For some reason he did not go on.

Papa Carlo battled in silence.

When it had become so dark it was impossible to tell friend from foe, the lads from Central were forced back, first to the abandoned stables, and then to their waiting bus by the River Handwash.

Having flushed the enemy from the village, the men of Ermolaevo returned to the clubhouse to count their losses. These were exclusively material, if we except grazes, bumps and bruises. The clubhouse windows had been smashed and the billiard table destroyed in the fire, as had the trunk containing the New Year decorations and two chairs of little significance. These remarkably light losses were taken very much to heart nevertheless, and the men of Ermolaevo, grimacing from the acrid fumes, immediately began considering ways of again avenging themselves on Central. The suggestions made were: to dust the settlement's apiary freely with insecticide (it was constantly being brought up to take advantage of Ermolaevo's buckwheat crop); to totally dismantle Papa Carlo's hut; and to blow up the repair workshops. None of these suggestions was, however, to be taken up, because a cosmic occurrence unexpectedly terminated the civil war between Central and Ermolaevo.

Early the following morning, almost before the *veche* rail had ceased to reverberate and half-awake people set off for work, Alexander Samsonov was spreading a curiously unsettling piece of news. The last total eclipse of the sun in the twentieth century, it seemed, was expected on 31 July.

For some reason this news threw the village into a state of unrest. Old men became disagreeably animated, evidently anticipating the fulfilment of biblical prophecy; middle-aged men glanced at the old men unnerved; and the youth of Ermolaevo set industriously to manufacturing pieces of smoked glass. This labour they persisted in from morning till night, devoting their every leisure hour to it. Pyotr Ermolaev went even further. He stayed off work and sat down to create a small telescope from a kaleidoscope, two magnifying glasses, two mirrors from ladies' compacts, and an old rustic lathe holder found behind a roll of pitched roofing paper in the attic.

Early in the morning of Friday, 31 July the entire population of Ermolaevo congregated in the street. Rage as the collective farm brigade supervisor might, trying to drive his farm hands to their work, they stood silently beside their homes awaiting the promised eclipse. It was an affecting sight: early morning; the air still cool; the street with some one hundred and fifty people of Ermolaevo, their heads thrown back, looking up with the most touching expressions into the sky; complete silence. You might have thought some unprecedented misfortune was about to be-fall the human race, or that on the contrary great and universal happiness was at hand. You felt it would be positively odd if nothing fell out of the sky; and to cap it all, there was Pyotr Ermolaev up on his roof with his telescope, looking so much like a priest preparing to commune with the heavens that it fair made your flesh creep.

For some time the sun showed no sign of the expected eclipse and impatient voices were raised. Suddenly, however, the right hand rim of the fiery disk seemed to become shrouded, as if the place had been slightly doused. The crowd gasped and grew still as something apocalyptic began, like a flu-induced dream. Everything grew gradually darker and darker. There was a sudden total silence. The very grasshoppers in the fields fell silent, and only Frigate the bull bellowed wildly in the farmyard. A little later the stars twinkled, not so much shining as welling up like tears. Night fell abruptly. A light wind ran over the Earth, startling as an unexpected touch, and cold and musty as the breath of a dungeon. A black sun looked down from above like an empty eye socket at a golden peep-hole. The horizon burned with an other-worldly light, and a hush des-cended, cosmic and unearthly.

The people of Ermolaevo were completely thrown by the eclipse, particularly the young people. It made so deep an impression that Alexander Samsonov, for example, vowed to give up drinking. The young people were quieter and less assertive for a time, like children after a good telling-off. Nobody really understood what exactly had happened, but that something had happened nobody was in any doubt.

There's nothing so surprising about the extent to which we are influenced by toponymy, climate and topology. It just seems to be the case that nothing so stirs us Russians, affecting our very lives, as completely extraneous and apparently peripheral circumstances. There have been times, as in the early seventeenth century, when arid winds have jeopardized the very existence of the Russian State. Ungovernable expanses and epidemics have determined the direction of our literature. Tailed comets have so deranged our rulers as to incite our neighbours to intervention. And what of our rivers in flood sweeping away whole churchyards? Or the blessed roads of Russia, whose great contribution since history began has been to protect us from our enemies? Or the grammar of our language, which compels us to such strenuous mental effort? What, finally, of the high incidence of goose-foot? In short, it would not be too far-fetched to suppose that the way in which the solar eclipse made melancholy the young people of Ermolaevo had a lot in common with the way that even a complete waster who meets a funeral procession becomes a human being again. For a time at least.

It can, of course, also be quite logically argued that what matters is not celestial mechanisms, arid winds, or the grammar of the Russian language at all, but that a fundamental law of life creates multi-talented characters, men with top-heavy destinies, and all sorts of peculiar goings on in which the spirit of the Mongol Horde is palpable. This is all rather dubious, however, because it really is highly debatable whether a farmer in Oklahoma is any more morally developed than an agricultural engineer from Tambov; or whether life in Ostavkovo district is somehow less full than life in the State of Maryland. Yet for all that, young country people in America do not strip their souls bare as ours do; so that the answer must after all lie in the fact that the Russian soul encompasses everything, and it encompasses everything because for some reason it is completely open to nature, which encompasses everything. What really tells, then, is precisely celestial mechanisms, arid winds and the grammar of the Russian language.

But we digress. Immediately after the solar eclipse of 31 July 1981, hostilities in the Central–Ermolaevo conflict unexpectedly ceased. Peace was formally concluded on 4 August in Panteleevka, a village on the road to Orgwork, which was celebrating its local Festival of the Angelic Thrones and to which once again everybody from miles around had flocked. Pyotr Ermolaev and Papa Carlo ran into each other just as the dance was beginning. Papa Carlo was already reaching towards his back pocket for the adjustable spanner he had prudently brought for just such an eventuality, but noticed that his enemy appeared to be in such a sunny and peaceable state of mind that he confined himself for the time being to glowering at him murderously. Pyotr Ermolaev came up to him confidently, proffered a cigarette, lit a match, and asked:

'Did you see the eclipse?'

'Maybe I did,' replied Papa Carlo.

'Impressive, wasn't it?'

'Maybe it was.'

'Look, Papa Carlo. Let's make peace.'

Papa Carlo glanced round at his mechanics standing at the ready nearby and said:

'We're not against making peace any time.'

'And to show I really mean it,' Pyotr Ermolaev went on. 'You can have the motorbike. After all, I only won it in a lottery.'

Papa Carlo blushed and at first flatly refused to take the motorbike, then on principle offered to pay one and a half times the price, but in the end was forced to give in.

'If I offended you, sorry,' he said in conclusion.

'And I'm sorry if I offended you,' said Pyotr Ermolaev.

As a Russian 'sorry' differs from all the world's other sorries in having a weight of its own, usually out of all proportion to the event which prompted it, the peace which now broke out proved just as unbridled as the war which had preceded it. The sworn enemies became sworn friends, and it was even decided to stage a joint production of Medical Orderly Serebryakov's new opus, *Beware of Botulism!* Alexander Samsonov did, however, warn his young fellow villagers that their goodwill might yet prove premature, since a total eclipse of the moon was to be expected the following January, and there was no predicting what the consequences of that might be.

Translated by Arch Tait

EDWARD LIMONOV

The Night Souper

I am a solitary man, my amusements those of a solitary man. Even when living with women I have been and remain solitary.

Flying into New York some ten years after first landing there, I stayed out of interest at the same Latham Hotel where I spent my first night on the North American continent, the night of 18 February 1975. I walked its corridors, somnambulistically savouring the past. I did not ring up old friends. Warm feelings towards them were alive deep in my heart, but I did not feel like seeing them. I like the personages from my past to stay in their proper place and not get under my feet by suddenly turning up in the wrong place, like the present.

Back again in the city of my second youth, I did partly regress to old habits, perhaps not fully aware of doing so. My routine became fragmented and jerky and chaotic, as it had been then. I would wake suddenly at two in the morning, dress, go down to New York, and wander the streets until dawn. At dawn I would buy a pack of beer in a supermarket, an n-shaped Polish sausage, and return to the hotel. I would switch on the telly, climb into bed, drink the six-pack, consume the sausage. I suspect this supposed sausage was in fact a hundred per cent hormones; at all events when you bit it open it was a pinkish colour as venomous as the pinks and greens on the screen of the clapped out television.

Sprawling in the Latham with my beer, television and Polish *kiełbasa*, I discovered to my deep satisfaction that I was completely happy. The stupid soap operas I had known and loved were still being shown or repeated, and I had no trouble in working out within a few days who was who in the new ones. That the soaps were stupid in no wise prevented them from prompting me to thoughts both serious and profound. Looking at the plump physiognomies of their heroes, I reflected without resentment that Americans look like visitors from outer space. They have far fewer wrinkles than Europeans. If a European face is a veiny piece of meat ramifying into bags under eyes, hollow cheeks, pouches at the mouth and ears, the American physiognomy is a piece of meat less defined, more *généralisé*. It is a bare and unashamed plaster *moulage*, unchipped by history, uncrazed by the delicate patina of culture. I was reminded of *Invasion of the Body Snatchers* where aliens from outer space are clones of people rather than real people. If you look closely at the actors in *Dynasty* or *Dallas* (which I mention here not as an opinionated intellectual intent on disparaging them, but because these are soaps known to the entire world, so that everybody can share my perception), you easily notice the inhuman smoothness of their faces, hair inhumanly healthy and flawless such as is found only in wigs or in the coats of well-fed, neutered dogs. Again, the tele-Americans remind you of mental patients doped to the eyeballs with insulin. (I lived among such placid homunculi many years ago during my incarceration in the Kharkov mental hospital, so know what I am talking about: a topic for research.) Our American cousins look like people, but were we to dismantle, say, an arm or a leg (as the robotic Arnie Schwarzenegger 'repairs' his own arm in *The Terminator*), would we not discover the mechanical architecture and printed circuits of a computer? Happily, the actual denizens of urban and small town America are less bland than the tele-Americans.

It was hot all 'that' day, but cooled towards evening and, with the falling of darkness, became cooler still. A wind blew the warm clouds away from the skies over New York, a large moon appeared, and all nature composed itself into a likeness of autumn. This coolness was unseasonable: usually early September in New York is hot and muggy. It left me feeling restive. About midnight I found myself in a bar on midtown Broadway. Seated at the piano, a jazz singer was performing.

In the semi-darkness I downed several Guinnesses in a row and tried chatting up the singer, only to be rebuffed. This occurrence will not be going off in my last act like Chekhov's rifle, but it set the tone for the evening and night to follow. Feeling symbolically rejected not only by the singer but by New York itself, I blazed with a desire to be taken once more to the bosom of my native city. Whither this desire was to lead you will shortly see. The singer explained her grounds for turning me down so frankly that I shall allow myself to quote our brief exchange. When I asked what time she finished and whether I might buy her a drink in a different bar, my leggy interlocutor took a pair of red-framed spectacles from her handbag (it was during her break), put them on, and said seriously, unsmilingly, bespectacled, 'Sorry, but no. I already have plenty men in my life: one steady boyfriend and three occasional. Now, if you were in show business you could help get me out of this crummy hole,' she tapped her heel on the sawdust of the floor, 'but you're not even American. I'm sure you're a great guy, but I'm tired of men.' She removed the spectacles and returned them to her handbag. I told her I only wanted to invite her for a drink because I so admired the brilliant way she, a white girl, performed Billie Holiday's repertoire. 'Yeah, sure. The repertoire ends in bed every time,' she said wearily. 'Somebody must have done something very bad to her in bed,' I thought, 'for her to be so down on bed now.'

I left the bar and instinctively turned uptown. I had lived further up Broadway in 1977. My feet customarily took me to the Embassy Hotel without having to be asked, and I had been there once this time already. I knew that a perfectly nice, decaying, reeking hotel which had accommodated several hundred poor people (all of them blacks except for Limonov) had been bought up by the Japanese who had turned it into a plush, stupid apartment development called Embassy Tower. When I reached 72nd Street I came to a halt on its east side and, having halted, concluded there was no point in trekking on up Broadway, that I needed a beer at the very least, and most probably a half ring of *kielbasa* too. To tell the truth, one Guinness in a piano-bar was out of my league, let alone three. Settling now for beer and sausage might not balance the budget, but would at least halt a process of ruinous extravagance. I could go back down Broadway a few streets to Anzonia Post Office Station where there was an all-night I and P supermarket. Or at least there used to be.

The supermarket was still there and still open with its cheery yellow panes of dull, bulletproof glass. Greatly moved, I entered my old friend. The familiar insanitary odours wafted in my face. How many times had I come here of a night to buy 'my menu' of *kielbasa*, beer, the cheap, vile hamburger mash, and bread the consistency of cotton wool ... There was the same fat Mexican security guard with his baton (Could it really be him? It could indeed.) gossiping with the black woman at the check-out; the same grey-green-faced manager walking around straightening the trolleys, his sagging belly pushing out the same trousers. The same bright red forcemeat was sweating under its plastic and offering itself up for hamburgers. A superabundance of cheap, unhealthy food, crudely packaged ... a poor man's paradise. Chickens frozen like blocks of ice, dirty water flowing over tiles from beneath the meat counter. Oh, *supermarché* of my youth in New York, not reconstructed like the Embassy, you remain the same scruffy, unhealthy institution you always were. In days gone by, at this time of night my fellow-residents from the Embassy, alcoholics living on welfare, would have been lurching among your cheap wonders, selecting a 'Malt Liquor' with a venomous blue label. Now a more prosperous stratum of the population streamed to the banks of Broadway at Anzonia Post Office Station. There were fewer black faces. The supermarket would soon be refurbished and rendered sterile, and the prices would go up.

Finding no *kielbasa* I took some tinned pork and a pack of buns. They sold hard liquor now, in a separate enclosure, practically behind bulletproof glass. In my time only beer and the homicidal malt liquors were on offer to the discerning customer. I wondered in passing about the bulletproof windows. Did the guys from Harlem raid all-night supermarkets for alcohol? Improbable. I bought a bottle of port and left, absently fitting my purchases into the shop's sturdy brown bag.

The night moved on into the small hours. I thought of the forty long blocks separating me from the Latham Hotel, resolutely brushed aside as unappealing the hypothesis of travelling on the subway, and turning the bottle of port in the brown bag, squashed the buns and their packaging and decided to organize myself an open-air night supper, a picnic. But where? If I made the effort I could turn off Broadway to Central Park, dispose myself excellently on the greensward, and sup beneath a poetic New York moon, mulling nostalgically over the far-off days of my youth.

Here I shall allow myself a historical digression on my relations with Central Park. New Yorkers are properly afraid of the park at night time and shun it after dark. The northernmost part, bordering Harlem, is visited rarely or not at all by the white man even by day. But I am different. I know fear, as everyone does, but always feel an urge to break taboos. I feel an urge, too, to prove to myself and others how brave I am. What prompted me to cross Central Park at night for the first time was not, however, bravado but dog-tiredness. I had drunk epically with my friend Bakhchanyan on East 83rd Street, and did not have the fare for the bus or subway. Usually I would return home from this friend's, whom I visited frequently in those years, by skirting Central Park, walking down the east side to 59th Street, also known as Central Park South, striding westwards, and then walking up Central Park West to the Embassy. This time I thought, why not? I clambered over the stone park wall (I could have entered by one of the entrances, which were always open, but preferred to go in over the wall as befitted a cutthroat, just in case anyone was watching) and headed for the West Side, doggedly progressing from tree to tree, bush to bush, openly, noisily, as a bandit, or aborigine, or master on his own territory should. Inwardly I kept telling myself, 'You, Edward, are yourself the fiend, the gaunt figure in the night heedlessly bestriding your territory. You are yourself the most fearsome creature of the night, your purposes unknown or unpredictable. It is for others to be afraid of you . . .' A belated cyclist, possibly taking my conjurations seriously, veered away from the side of the road in fright and, attaching himself to a convoy of taxis crossing the park from East to West, pedalled off for all he was worth. Perhaps I really was someone to be afraid of in 1977. I was in crisis and had nothing to lose, not as yet having found anything. Growing in brazenness, I took to traversing the park every time chance led me at night to or from upper East Side. Each time I experienced a degree of fear, but I got hooked on this twenty- or twenty-five minute thrill.

Recalling past glories and smiling at my own recklessness, I now came to the park in the vicinity of 70th Street. Clutching my brown bag, clad in white jeans, boots and a light-coloured jacket, I walked unhesitatingly over to a bench without so much as a backward glance, stepped up on to the seat, then on to the back spar, and from there on to the wall of Central Park. I leapt resolutely down. The wall was not high on the street side, but fell away a couple of metres on the park side: further than I had expected. To my good fortune the turf on which I landed proved as well-padded as the average American midriff.

It was great: the moon, the pungent scent, despite the all-pervading smell of city dust and gasoline, of plant life beginning just slightly to decay, a masked ball of trees, the shadow of each deep and impenetrable. I scuffed my feet boldly through the grass.

I did not, however, go in too deep, preferring to stay on familiar territory. I could hear the sound of drums from the direction of 72nd Street. (On the corner of Central Park West and 72nd Street towers the fortress-like Dakota apartment building where John Lennon lived, and beside which he was zapped.) In my day the local dog-owners and joggers sat by the brightly lit park entrance at 72nd Street, joking or swearing at each other. We, the Embassy set, hung out there too. It was our people who came with drums and put on nights of African music. Who was beating the drums tonight? Could old friends, resettled now way out somewhere in the 150s, be coming back to our patch with their drums? I felt I really needed the beat of those tom-toms as an accompaniment to my night supper. 'Are you by any chance afraid, Edward?' I asked myself, moving in under an unusually spreading pine tree. 'Have you perhaps moved up to a higher social class and now fear the amusements of your former class so much that you skulk beside the exit?'

The pine tree was growing on a slope, and part of its crown bowed down like a separate tree, trailing powerful boughs over the grass, protecting me from the front from possible idle glances. Breathing in the piny scent, I put my brown bag down on the grass. I wanted to luxuriate in the pininess, and broke off a small branch, pricking myself in the process. I rubbed some of the needles between my fingers and sniffed them. Wonderful! I felt like a holiday-maker at his dacha and laughed out loud.

With my first swig of port I felt even better.

I made a mess of opening the tin. I pulled the ring too hard, with the result that the metal skin only partly came away, opening a small chink which gave access to the contents. I had to pare the needles off my branchlet and use it to root the pork out in sticky lumps. It was sweet. Never a glutton, I have nevertheless always enjoyed my food.

I tired of digging out pork, splitting buns and chewing. I put the tin to one side on the brown bag, gulped down a whole lot of port, and leaned back against the tree trunk. Automobile herds were lowing somewhere far away; distance mitigated the wailing of police sirens; a rural peace and quiet reigned in this collective of bedraggled shrubs. Through the branches of my pine tree drops of moonlight dappled the brown bag, the mutilated pork tin, and the buns. When the wind swayed the crown of the tree, the drops splashed down a little to one side, on to the grass.

Naturally I was visited by memories. They always come when I am comfortably sprawled, usurping the present. Memories came down on me like pink clouds, invisible as radioactive fall-out. I wended my way in spirit to the drums, and from them along

Central Park West to 71st Street. I had worked there for several days with old Lenya Kosogor, installing an X-ray machine for a doctor whose name has been chewed and swallowed by time. Once we had installed it we had to line the walls of the X-ray room with thick lead sheeting. Why should this memory have come back to me? Memory had latched on to metals and sought out that lead. Across the years I saw the heavy sheets, their structure, the scratches on them. The broad round wooden mallet fell rhythmically on the black sheeting, kneading it to the surface of the wall. Memory next admired Lenya himself. Tall and round-shouldered, he was doing up the buttons on his quilted Moscow overcoat. We were walking down 71st Street towards Broadway, to the McDonald's. The interior of McDonald's on Broadway, Kosogor eating in his shirt sleeves, picking out the French fries with his fingers, calling me 'Cuntface', lovingly . . . He looked after me like a father. He was old enough to be my father and all. Where is he now? I remembered Kosogor's cavern in the basement of the Astoria, his tools. I must ring him. He's a good old boy. I took another swig of the port, planted the bottle down on the grass, and saw, screened from me by the branches, a figure standing there, blocking the moonlight . . .

Terror is not extremity of fear. It is a special condition. You do not experience terror in a café on Place de la République when, in the course of a gradually escalating quarrel, your antagonist suddenly pulls a knife on you. To experience fear is natural. The character with the knife may turn out to be seriously weird and end up stabbing you in the belly, or he may just put it away. Around you, however, there are other human beings; the *patron* may intervene; you don't really believe the character is going to use the knife. In any case you may manage to throw a glass at him, or a chair at his foot. You do not want to compromise your masculine dignity; you shout at him, he insults you . . . You may be frightened, but you do not feel terror. Or another situation: war. You are lying with other soldiers waiting for the signal to attack. You are holding a sub-machine-gun, its hardness reassuring. If the next moment a bomb were to score a direct hit on your regiment, you would not have time even to be frightened. A third situation: you have been taken prisoner by some organization which has imprisoned you in a cellar, chaining you to an iron ring. You feel fear (it is unusual, but not unknown, for hostages to be killed), physical discomfort, humiliation; but your masked kidnappers bring you food, you can even talk to them. When everything, or nearly everything, is clear the preconditions for terror simply are not present. Terror is possible only under the following circumstances:

1. An almost complete lack of information about the nature of the threat;
2. A situation which prevents the obtaining of information on the nature of the threat;
3. An element of *mystery*: unpredictable, irrational behaviour on the part of the threat (a wild animal, dragon, Frankensteinian monster, Sick Mind) which is prosecuting some inhuman purpose.

What I felt was terror. He, the threat, stood there wordless. He was wearing light trousers, a white shirt, and holding a knife. (Why should he have an unsheathed knife in his hand? What was his purpose?) It was large, theatrical somehow, emphatically symbolic, like the scythe of the Grim Reaper in an engraving. It would glint in the light of the moon or the stars or a distant streetlight, then almost disappear in darkness. He was holding the knife close to his hip in his left hand and drawing back a branch with the other. When he had drawn it back, he stood there staring at me.

Perhaps it was some brash businessman with an odd sense of humour who had slipped out into the night from one of the expensive apartment buildings on Central Park West for a little dangerous entertainment? Not very likely. Anyway, what difference would that make? I froze like a catatonic, the port bottle at chest height, barely removed from my lips.

There he stood, wordless, holding back the branch, the knife in his hand. He was white, in all probability even a blond, although it was also entirely possible that his blondness was an effect of the green light reflecting from the grass and trees. With the moon behind him I could see nothing of his facial features. His height was average and he was hefty, or perhaps he only seemed to be because of his loose-fitting shirt and trousers. I watched him, mesmerized, like a rabbit before the open jaws of a boa. Only because I could not see his eyes was I able to find the strength to ask him loudly whether he would like to have a drink with me. I straightened the arm holding the bottle towards him. I immediately recognized that it would be very foolish indeed to actually give him the bottle, my only weapon against his large knife.

He released the branch, turned, and quietly rustled off through the grass into the depths of the park. He did not want alcohol. He had not demanded money. He belonged to the most frightening category of all: he was an idealist of the moonlight. Oddballs who want neither to take your money nor to rape you most probably want to eat you. Why otherwise would he need a knife that size? He wanted to kill and eat me, as I myself had just eaten the jellied pork, and he wanted to do it under this very tree. I felt like a caged rabbit whose master has sized it up before, for some reason, not choosing it for his dinner. Watching the departing silhouette, I put the bottle to my lips, drinking in as much as I could of the sweet, strong liquid. I tried to think whether I had ever been in a similar state in my life. I had to go back to when I was nine, to the age of earliest consciousness. In a great, loud thunderstorm I had suddenly sensed that my parents would some day die and that I would be left alone. The lot of mortal man came to me in that thunderstorm. I remember I burst into tears, hiding my head in a dark press in a corridor inside our flat. We kept old blankets in it and things we never or rarely needed. The heavens above the outskirts of Kharkov were shaken by thunder, and my mother came from the kitchen to comfort me. Why should I have been visited by terror during just that thunderstorm? It was, however, in any case terror of quite a different kind, terror at the lot of man, terror of future death, at the very idea of death.

The smell of smoke was drifting from 72nd Street. Had somebody lit a bonfire? With that same billow of air the drums came nearer. I took up the can and sank my fingers into the pork. The sticky jelly made the meat difficult to catch hold of. A fork would have made all the difference. I chewed and swallowed the sweet meat, wiping my fingers on the grass. They smelled unexpectedly, when I sniffed them, of fish. The September grass must have combined with the bicarbonates, or hydrochlorides, or whatever in the jelly to produce the smell of fish. Central Park quivered tremulously, its depths, its light spots and dark, all its shades of green from pale lettuce to dark fir; all its distances, its geometrical shapes, or more exactly shapeless-nesses. I could feel a breeze blowing at ground level, over the grass, on my feet, as if somewhere doors had been left open, like a draught in a huge flat which extended fifty blocks from north to south, and ten from east to west, such a chill draught, perhaps the wind of death? The oddball was plainly off his rocker. What was he doing wandering around with an oversized knife which looked like it belonged on the stage or in someone's kitchen? Why was he showing it off when he should have been hiding it? Black or Puerto Rican muggers like thin knives with a blade which springs out from inside, or a folding knife flicked open by a spring at the edge of the blade. Puerto Ricans' knives are like Puerto Ricans, slim and agile. Is it because I am myself diminutive that I warm to Puerto Ricans? Perhaps. Oddball was no Puerto Rican, his silhouette was all wrong. He was a stark raving white loony with all the wires in his head mixed up. They had connected at random, unnaturally, and lit up he was wandering the park at night without purpose, a switched on, hoofed Minotaur. Some of the wires in his brain were short circuiting, that was all. It was enough . . .

Behind my back, on the slope, I heard a crunch. Somebody had trodden on a twig in the grass, a branch, an empty packet of . . . My back peeled from the pine tree of its own accord. Without standing up, I swivelled deftly on my heels like the Prince in *Sleeping Beauty*, and saw *him*. He was now standing over me in the same pose, one hand drawing the pine branch back from his face, the other holding the stagy knife. My feet went cold, and I could feel the sweat on my calves. Sweating calves?! I took this strange biological phenom-enon as a final warning from an organism deeply concerned for its self-preservation. I saw myself as a machine on the verge of blowing up. All the needles on the pressure gauges were at the red line, quivering and jerking. It was time to get the hell out of there. I got up and, lifting the bottle, came unhurriedly out from beneath the pine tree, parting its crown which trailed over the grass. I knew that if I hurried (my back was acutely registering the pressure of his stare) towards the exit at 72nd Street, the oddball with the messed up wires in his head would come for me, because his pupils (or whatever part of his eyes he used) would register fear in my back. His reactions were triggered by fear. A certain intensity of heat, a certain level of fear would turn him on, and then he would hack, and grind his teeth, and cut out my liver and gorge himself on it, cut out my heart and gorge himself on that too. For some reason I recalled that Captain Cook got eaten when the natives decided he wasn't God. I thought, too, that the doomed victim taken to the Minotaur in his labyrinth, must have felt something like what I was presently feeling: completely alone with a malevolent (alien) brain, surrounded by cliffs, and rocks, and trees. Man seems monstrous to a rabbit, a hen, a sheep, a cow. For them Man is the Evil One. The Minotaur seems monstrous to man.

Brandishing my bottle, I headed off unhurriedly into the depths of the park, into the dark, where a labyrinth of tarmac paths gradually lead the wanderer a length equivalent to thirteen blocks to Central Park South, a street of plush hotels and stretch limousines. My father had firmly drummed into me in childhood that you should never run away from dogs. Oddballs with the nerve wires joined up in their heads all wrong must be subject to the same instinctive laws as large dogs, hunting instincts.

The first few minutes were heavy going. When his stare was no longer directly on my back, attenuating with distance and as my back became partially shielded by branches, shrubs, even rocks and the edges of rocks (Central Park is located on a basalt plateau striated in pre-human times by a glacier), I felt easier. *He* had not followed me, because in his programming the Prey, the Quarry had different characteristics. It should dart about nervously, shrieking, squealing, trying to run away. The sounds and movements I made did not trigger him. I am quite sure of this. I am quite sure too that if I had reacted otherwise, if my fear had been picked up by his sensors, I would have ended up lying beneath that pine tree, my fingers covered in pork jelly, birds jumping up and down picking at the remains of the rolls. The bottle of port would have rolled down to the tarmac path, my sound, healthy blood would have soaked the earth and glued the grass into filthy densely matted tufts, as chocolate mats the hair of a child.

Coming out towards Central Park South, still noisy and bright in the night, I felt suddenly sick. Leaning against the park wall I threw up all the poisonous pork, and the port, and the buns irradiated by the stare of a Sick Mind.

There is a scientific theory to the effect that events can take place only within a strictly defined period of time. If we explain the incident in Central Park in this light, we shall have to say that I forcibly invaded a new period with an action which belonged to an earlier one, and that the incompatibility all but destroyed me. As I wandered through night-time New York in 1977, I had given off a different biological field, potent and threatening. The power of my present-day field, that of a writer from Paris, for all my daring and experience, had barely sufficed to deflect a Sick Mind. In 1977 the Minotaur would have been afraid to come close to me. One Minotaur to another Minotaur.

Translated by Arch Tait

EVGENY POPOV

How They Ate the Cock

For a long time Nikolai Efimych, together with his wife, lived at my aunt Ira's place in her little wooden house on Zasukhin Street. As a lodger, paying for his living space in ready cash once a month.

Sad, troubled, precarious and uncertain is the life of those people who do not possess some square metres of their own space, or of some they share with somebody else. Vague urges and suspicions eat away at them, they keep wanting to move from one place to another, changing their line of business and work. They want to be happy, so they go to the cinema, and then they want to be happy all over again.

Take Nikolai Efimych, for example. A remarkable master of his trade. A metal worker. All his life long riveting or casting or soldering something. Grinding.

Only he didn't grind all his life, you know. Before that he landed himself in Siberia for some insignificant post-war crimes, and in 1953 he was amnestied.

There were thousands of amnestied people wandering the streets of our town in those years. They wandered around, ate, and slept in garrets and cellars. And on account of these ex-cons the life of the town-dwellers got more complicated in many ways. It was rare for any peace-loving bold spirit to venture out of the house on a late winter's evening, because everybody knew that on one occasion a lady had gone out for five minutes at nine o'clock one evening, and she ran into some people wearing sleeveless coats who relieved her of all her outer clothing and her watch. That was in Tarakanovka near the meat-processing plant. She dashed off towards Surikovsky Bridge, having seen that the street lights were on there and that some other people were standing there. She shouted to them:

'Citizens! I've been stripped! Oy! Over there! They ran off over there. I can remember what they look like.'

'Can you?' they asked.

'Yes, I saw them! I saw them! They took my winter coat and my astrakhan hat.'

'And if you saw them again, you'd recognize them?'

'Yes, I would, I would! No two ways about it,' answered the woman, without scenting any trouble.

And they promptly swiped her across the eyes with a glove, and her face turned the colour of blood, seeing as there were razor blades stitched into the glove. Well then, the woman, all covered in blood, groped her way on to Peace Avenue, collapsed and there, so the story goes, a couple of people saw her. The woman was blinded, and the gang got away. The 'Black Cat' gang. Siberia '53.

Or there was another story they used to tell – how some children were captured, hung up in the woods, cut open with knives, and their blood drained off into laboratory retorts.

'What for?'

'So that their blood could be handed in at the blood transfusion centre in exchange for vast sums of money.'

'Rubbish!'

'I'll give you "rubbish". I'm telling you, they caught some children, hung them up in the woods, cut them open with knives and drained off their blood into retorts.'

But Nikolai Efimych didn't do things like that, he wasn't interested and didn't take part in such things. Good Heavens! Quite the contrary, if he were to hear or see something like that, he'd immediately raise the alarm and call the police himself.

In fact, he wasn't interested in anything at all. It was the opinion of Nikolai Efimych that he'd landed up in the camps completely by accident, since he was innocent. I don't know. I don't know. To my mind guilt is such a slippery, uncertain concept, that on the question of Nikolai Efimych's guilt or innocence, I just can't say one way or the other, since I don't understand and can't profess. The important thing is that after the amnesty was granted he became a very placid person, he wanted to be happy and he went to work in a factory, wishing to apply his golden hands there.

And he had a wife, who worked as a saleswoman on a manufactured goods stall in the collective farm market. Elena Demyanovna. Nickname – Demyan.

She herself was deaf, that is to say, she could only hear a little and only when it was shouted right in her ear in a loud voice.

She sometimes concealed her deafness, pretending that she could hear everything – whether it was shouted at her in a loud voice or said in a soft voice.

The concealment somehow amused Nikolai Efimych. He used to swear at her for a joke. For a joke. And seeing as she couldn't hear anything, it all worked out fine: Nikolai Efimych swore at her, Demyan couldn't hear, she chatted about this and that, and he chatted away, and as soon as she turned her back, he'd swear at her.

To describe the outer appearance of the couple you would need neither skill nor inspiration. And you wouldn't require high artistry either. I can still see them, even after the passage of so many years, as if it were yesterday.

He was of average height. A man no different from any other. His clothes were undistinguished, grey. Whatever everyone else was wearing, that's what Nikolai Efimych wore. Just what everyone wore – tarpaulin boots, a sleeveless coat. And if they had their trousers tucked in their boots, that's the way Nikolai Efimych wore them. And when they started selling drain-pipe trousers in 1955, and a lot of people bought them, then Nikolai Efimych acquired some too.

Ordinary clothes, undistinguished, grey. An ordinary person – grey, undistinguished.

And as regards Demyan, you could also put it very simply and say that seeing as she was deaf, she didn't particularly put herself about. She wore the pick of everything that was on sale in her manufactured goods stall, and she didn't believe in the existence of the hearing aid. She considered such a device to be a piece of trickery, made up by the newspapers and magazines.

They brought my aunt Ira some advantage. In the first place, as lodgers who paid for their living space, and in the second place as people who had some access to goods in short supply. For example, Elena got me some size 4 tarpaulin boots from her shop. At the time I wore size 4 boots and I was in the second year of the Surikov primary school.

They didn't get on very well, but they always slept together. They were used to it, and anyway they didn't have any choice, since their living space consisted of an area screened off with plywood, measuring two by three, equalling 6 square metres all told. True, the plywood went right up to the ceiling. You can't argue with that.

But they didn't get on very well. Apparently because they took offence at the different nasty habits that each of them had.

Nikolai Efimych himself was very fond of squatting down on his haunches, propping up the wall and puffing away at his *makhorka* coarse tobacco. And also getting pissed with all those who agreed to get pissed with him. Which was why he usually drank his way through all their earnings.

To get her own back, Demyan wouldn't give him anything to eat, and if she did give him something to eat, then it was only slops, made of flour, potato, water and millet. And with some stinking yellow pork fat added to it. Nikolai Efimych got the pork fat regularly enough from somewhere, but it was of poor quality.

Stomach-churning aromas floated around the kitchen when Demyan was in the process of preparing the family meals.

Obviously, this offended Nikolai Efimych.

It also irritated him that his deaf wife loved dancing shamelessly to the gramophone, when she'd had a drop of vodka: kicking up her legs and showing the edge of her lilac knickers. It irritated him, but not as much as the stinking food. Apart from that, he resented the fact that his wife got money on the side through the shop, and kept it stashed away in a secret account and wouldn't show him the savings book. She pretended that it, the money on the side, just, as it were, didn't exist.

'It would serve a serpent like her right, if there were another currency reform like there was in 1947,' mumbled Nikolai Efimych. Not understanding that a savings book was guaranteed against all reforms. And so Elena's money, if she had any, would never disappear.

And so they lived. And on occasion frightening explosions of intolerance were to be observed between the couple.

At New Year, 1956, Nikolai Efimych said:

'Demyan, let's boil a chicken.'

But she didn't hear.

'Let's booiil the cheeekeeen?!' shouted Nikolai Efimych.

She didn't hear.

'Boil the cock for me, you old cow! Let's at least stuff ourselves for New Year!' he yelled in her ear.

Not a glimmer of a response from her.

She was quiet for a bit, and then she declared:

'I'm not giving it to you. It's going to be New Year, and we've got to have something to eat throughout the New Year.'

At these words red blotches broke out all over Nikolai Efimych's mug and he took a swing at Elena with a stool.

Now, this conversation was taking place in the kitchen. The small, nimble Demyan jumped agilely away towards the stove, grabbed a boiling kettle and gave Nikolai Efimych an almighty bash on the head with it.

The scalded man charged about, swearing. He smashed up the kitchen furniture and yelled. He crashed into corners and kicked walls.

'Agh, I'll kill you!' bellowed Nikolai Efimych.

But Demyan gave him the slip nice and quiet like, and was hidden by my aunt in the cellar. They shifted a chest of drawers over the trapdoor to the cellar as camouflage. Demyan saw in New Year of 1956 amid potatoes and barrels half full of cabbage.

And Nikolai Efimych kept roaming around the flat, repeating plaintively that as soon as he found her he was going to kill her on the spot.

His face was wrapped up in cotton wool and bandaged with gauze. He mooched about, peeping through the slits of his eyes to try and catch a sight of Elena. You would have thought he was a performer in a dumb show.

Demyan stayed in the cellar, stayed put. Only how long could she stay there? you might ask. But she stayed there. And she waited until 2 January 1956, when Nikolai Efimych went off to work. And she decided, damn him, that she would boil the cock after all. She didn't go to her shop.

Now they had a cock. Or rather, to start with, they had a hen and a cock. Demyan thought that, with the cock, the hen would produce some chicks for her. The chicks would grow up, and start laying eggs. And Demyan would become the proud owner of hen's eggs. If she felt like it, she could eat them. If she felt like it, she could sell them as surplus at the collective farm market.

She'd reckoned it up carefully. Yet unfortunately, it didn't work out. Because, in the first place, the cock turned out to be somehow not right, a weakling. He didn't go for hens, but just sat on his perch all day, preening himself.

Then in the November, the hen went and died all of a sudden, from no known causes. It walked around and around the hen-house, and then one day – flat on its back. It twitched, writhed and started to go blue. It's really astonishing how quickly the hen died!

Demyan, of course, had her suspicions. In particular, concerning my auntie or me. But she didn't come out with them. And she didn't come out with them because she herself couldn't fathom it: who would need to poison her hen, and why?

And all that was left was the cock, which Nikolai Efimych kept asking to have for dinner, but which Elena wouldn't give him. Thus it was that on 2 January 1956 she none the less decided to boil the cock, and she set about boiling it. Nikolai Efimych by then had gone off to work, to the factory where he did his metal work.

There he took a ring bearing, cut it open, straightened it out, hammered it, tempered it, and made some final adjustments. After that he spent all day scraping away at the erstwhile ring with a file.

'Nikolai Efimych, you're not making yourself a pen in the firm's time, are you? Instead we ought to be having a hair of the dog after the holiday,' his workmates said to him.

But Nikolai Efimych, frowning, made no reply and continued his zealous filing.

'Pack it in, Nikolai Efimych. Don't sharpen it. You're sharpening that knife and you'll be on the receiving end of it,' urged one level-headed man whose prescience was so sound that he was forever afraid that he'd be given one in the mug at any minute.

But with an enigmatic smile Nikolai Efimych just set off for home. He stood for a while near the snow-covered porch, looking around.

'Goodbye freedom,' mumbled Nikolai Efimych and strode into the house.

And there he found that, at home, behind the plywood wall, there was no stink of fried yellow pork fat, and that there, behind the plywood wall, it was all nice and clean. There, behind the plywood wall, it was light. There, behind the plywood wall, there was a bottle of vodka on the table, the tail of a herring, sausage meat and cucumbers. And there was a saucepan, and out of the saucepan there rose the smell of a cock.

And this smell told Nikolai Efimych that he had won a complete and resounding victory over his wife. That, possibly, even the savings book would be his, if, of course, it existed. And as for his scalded face – that was neither here nor there, a trifle.

Frowning, he sat down at the table and yelled:

'Demyan!'

She was there in an instant, just as if she had popped out of the ground.

'Here. I'm here.'

Quiet, shy Elena.

'Sit down! Let's have it! Let's have a drink!'

And indeed they sat down, and indeed they had it. They had a drink. Yes indeed – they sat, and drank, and ate. They finished a half-litre and started drinking a second. And eventually they got to the cock. It was duly removed from the saucepan. And it was splendid.

Then Nikolai Efimych got the knife out of his pocket, showed it to his wife and explained what kind of a threat she was under. His wife behaved towards the ominous object with a degree of sincerity and deference which Nikolai Efimych found pleasing. He gave the knife to his wife, and she started cutting off first one leg from the cock, then the other, first one wing, then the other, then the neck and the parson's nose.

And they were scoffing the cock till midnight, and by the time it struck twelve, the couple were completely drunk, and they fell into bed without even undressing.

Both of them are old now, and they can barely walk. They don't live with my auntie any more. My aunt's house was pulled down, and all the people were rehoused in various flats. Demyan and Nikolai Efimych were given a one-room flat in the Fifth district. I sometimes see them. They can barely walk along, holding each other up.

And anyway, these days, of course, life isn't like it was: the old houses have all been pulled down, it's tower blocks all round now, gas all round, lighting, colour, lifts, tiled bathrooms, balconies and hot water. The cellars and basements have all disappeared, no one keeps cocks and hens in town, there are goods on sale in the shops instead, there's asphalt all round. You can walk the streets freely in the evening, see your friends and acquaintances.

Yes, and I sometimes see them. They can barely walk along, holding each other up.

And that's how they ate the cock . . .

Translated by Robert Porter

TATYANA TOLSTAYA

The Poet and the Muse

Nina was a marvellous woman, an ordinary woman, a doctor, and it goes without saying that she had her right to personal happiness like everyone else. Of this she was well aware. Nearing the age of thirty-five after a lengthy period of joyless trial and error – not even worth talking about – she knew precisely what she needed: a wild, true love, with tears, bouquets, midnight phone vigils, nocturnal taxi chases, fateful obstacles, betrayals and forgiveness. She needed a – you know – an animal passion, dark windy nights with streetlamps aglow. She needed to perform a heroine's classical feat as if it were a mere trifle: to wear out seven pairs of iron boots, break seven iron staffs in two, devour seven loaves of iron bread, and receive in supreme reward not some golden rose or snow-white pedestal but a burned-out match or a crumpled ball of a bus ticket – a crumb from the banquet table where the radiant king, her heart's desire, had feasted. Well, of course, quite a few women need pretty much the same thing, so in this sense Nina was, as has already been said, a perfectly ordinary woman, a marvellous woman, a doctor.

She had been married: it was as if she'd done an interminable, boring stretch on an intercity train and emerged – tired, dispirited, and yawning uncontrollably – into the starless night of a strange city, where the only kindred soul was her suitcase.

Then she lived the life of a recluse for a while: she took up washing and polishing the floors in her spotless little Moscow apartment, developed an interest in patterns and sewing, and once

again grew bored. An affair with the dermatologist Arkady Borisovich, who had two families not counting Nina, smouldered sluggishly
along. After work she would drop by his office to see him. There
was nothing the least bit romantic about it; the cleaning lady would
be emptying out the rubbish bins and slopping a wet mop across
the linoleum while Arkady Borisovich washed his hands over and
over, scrubbing them with a brush, suspiciously inspecting his pink
nails and examining himself in the mirror with disgust. He would
stand there, pink, well fed and stiff, egg-shaped, and take no notice
of Nina, though she was already in her coat on her way out the
door. Then he would stick out his triangular tongue and twist it
this way and that – he was afraid of infection. A fine Prince
Charming! What sort of passion could she find with Arkady Borisovich? None, of course.

Yet she'd certainly earned the right to happiness, she was entitled
to a place in the line where it was being handed out: her face was
white and pretty and her eyebrows broad, her smooth black hair
grew low from her temples and was gathered at the back in a bun.
And her eyes were black, so that out in public men took her for a
Moldavian Gypsy, and once, in the metro, in the passageway to the
Kirovskaya station, a fellow had even pestered her, claiming that he
was a sculptor and she must come along with him immediately,
supposedly to sit for the head of a houri – right away, his clay was
drying out. Of course she didn't go with him; she had a natural
mistrust of people in the creative professions, since she had already
been through the sorry experience of going for a cup of coffee with
an alleged film director and barely escaping in one piece – the
fellow had a large apartment with Chinese vases and a slanted garret
ceiling in an old building.

But time was marching on, and at the thought that out of the
approximately 125 million men in the USSR fate in all its generosity
had managed to dribble out only Arkady Borisovich for her, Nina
sometimes got upset. She could have found someone else, but the
other men who came her way weren't right either. After all, her
soul was growing richer as the years passed, she experienced and

understood her own being with ever greater subtlety, and on autumn evenings she felt more and more self-pity: there was no one to whom she could give herself – she, so slim and black-browed.

Occasionally Nina would visit some married girlfriend and, having stopped off to buy chocolates at the nearest shop for someone else's big-eared child, would drink tea and talk for a long time, eyeing herself all the while in the dark glass of the kitchen door, where her reflection was even more enigmatic, and more alluring in comparison with her friend's spreading silhouette. Justice demanded that someone sing her praises. Having finally heard her friend out – what had been bought, what had been burnt, what ailments the big-eared child had survived – and having examined someone else's standard-issue husband (a receding hairline, tracksuit bottoms stretched at the knees – no, she didn't need one like that), she left feeling dismayed. She carried her elegant self out the door, on to the landing, and down the staircase into the refreshing night: these weren't the right sort of people, she should never have come, in vain had she given of herself and left her perfumed trace in the drab kitchen, she had pointlessly treated someone else's child to exquisite bittersweet chocolate – the child just gobbled it down with no appreciation; oh, well, let the little beast break out in an allergic rash from head to toe.

She yawned.

And then came the epidemic of Japanese flu. All the doctors were pulled out of the district clinics for house calls, and Arkady Borisovich went, too, putting on a gauze face mask and rubber gloves to keep the virus from getting a hold on him, but he couldn't protect himself and came down with it, and his patients were assigned to Nina. And there, as it turned out, was where fate lay in wait for her – in the person of Grisha, stretched out completely unconscious on a bench in a caretaker's lodge, under knit blankets, his beard sticking up. That was where it all happened. The near-corpse quickly abducted Nina's weary heart: the mournful shadows on his porcelain brow, the darkness around his sunken eyes, and the tender beard, wispy as a springtime forest – all this made for a magical scene. Invisible violins played a wedding waltz, and the trap sprang shut. Well, everybody knows how it usually happens.

A sickeningly beautiful woman with tragically undisciplined hair was wringing her hands over the dying man. (Later on, to be sure, it turned out that she was no one special, just Agniya, a school friend of Grisha's, an unsuccessful actress who sang a little to a guitar, nothing to worry about, that wasn't where the threat lay.) Yes, yes, she said, she was the one who'd called the doctor – you must save him! She had just, you know, dropped in by chance, after all he doesn't lock his door, and he'd never call for help himself, not Grisha – caretaker, poet, genius, saint! Nina unglued her gaze from the demonically handsome caretaker and proceeded to look the place over: a large room, beer bottles under the table, dusty moulding on the ceiling, the bluish light of snowdrifts from the windows, an abandoned fireplace stuffed with rags and rubbish.

'He's a poet, a poet – he works as a caretaker so he can have somewhere to live,' mumbled Agniya.

Nina kicked Agniya out, lifted her bag from her shoulder, and hung it on a nail, carefully took her heart from Grishunya's hands and nailed it to the bedstead. Grishunya muttered deliriously, in rhyme. Arkady Borisovich melted away like sugar in hot tea. The thorny path lay ahead.

On recovering the use of his eyes and ears, Grishunya learned that the joyous Nina meant to stay with him to the bitter end. At first he was a bit taken aback, and suggested deferring this unexpected happiness, or – if that wasn't possible – hastening his meeting with that end; later, though, softhearted fellow that he was, he became more complaisant, and asked only that he not be parted from his friends. Nina compromised for the time being, while he regained his strength. This, of course, was a mistake; he was soon back on his feet, and he resumed his senseless socializing with the entire, endless horde. There were a few young people of indeterminate profession; an old man with a guitar; teenage poets; actors who turned out to be chauffeurs and chauffeurs who turned out to be actors; a demobilized ballerina who was always crying, 'Hey, I'll call our gang over, too'; ladies in diamonds; unlicensed jewellers; un-attached girls with spiritual aspirations in their eyes; philosophers with unfinished dissertations; a deacon from Novorossisk who always brought a suitcase full of salted fish; and a Tungus from eastern Siberia, who'd got stuck in Moscow – he was afraid the capital's cuisine would spoil his digestion and so would ingest only some kind of fat, which he ate out of a jar with his fingers.

All of them – some one evening, some the next – crammed into the caretaker's lodge; the small three-storey outbuilding creaked, the upstairs neighbours came in, people strummed guitars, sang, read poems of their own and others, but mainly listened to those of their host. They all considered Grishunya a genius; a collection of his verse had been on the verge of publication for years, but a certain pernicious Makushkin, on whom everything depended, was blocking it – Makushkin, who had sworn that only over his dead body . . . They cursed Makushkin, extolled Grishunya, the women asked him to read more, more. Flushed, self-conscious, Grisha read on – thick, significant poems that recalled expensive, custom-made cakes covered with ornamental inscriptions and triumphant meringue towers, poems slathered with sticky linguistic icing, poems containing abrupt, nutlike crunches of clustered sounds and excruci-ating, indigestible caramel confections of rhyme. 'Eh-eh-eh,' said the Tungus, shaking his head; apparently he didn't understand a word of Russian. 'What's wrong? Doesn't he like it?' murmured the other guests. 'No, no – I'm told that's the way they express praise,' said Agniya, fluffing her hair nervously, afraid that the Tungus would jinx her. The guests couldn't take their eyes off Agniya, and invited her to continue the evening with them elsewhere.

Naturally, this abundance of people was unpleasant for Nina. But most unpleasant of all was that every time she dropped by, whether during the day or in the evening after her shift, there was this wretched creature sitting in the caretaker's lodge – no fatter than a fork, wearing a black skirt down to her heels and a plastic comb in her lacklustre hair, drinking tea and openly admiring Grisha's soft beard: a person named Lizaveta. Of course, there couldn't possibly be any affair going on between Grishunya and this doleful aphid. You had only to watch her extricate a red, bony hand from her sleeve and reach timidly for an ancient, rock-hard piece of ginger-bread – as if she expected any moment to be slapped and the gingerbread snatched away. She had rather less cheek than a human being needs, and rather more jowl; her nose was gristly; in fact, there was something of the fish about her – a dark, colourless deepwater fish that slinks through the impenetrable gloom on the ocean floor, never rising to the sun-streaked shallows where azure and crimson creatures sport and play.

No, no love affair, there couldn't be. None the less, Grishunya, the beatific little soul, would gaze with pleasure at that human hull; he read poems to her, wailing and dipping on the rhymes, and afterwards, deeply moved by his own verse, he would blink hard and turn his eyes up towards the ceiling as if to stanch his tears, and Lizaveta would shake her head to show the shock to her entire organism, blow her nose and imitate a child's sporadic whimpers, as if she, too, had just been sobbing copiously.

No, this was all extremely unpleasant for Nina. Lizaveta had to be got rid of. Grishunya liked this brazen worship, but then, he wasn't picky; he liked everything on earth. He liked swishing a shovel about in the loose snow in the morning, living in a room with a fireplace full of rubbish, being on the ground floor with the door open so anyone could drop in; he liked the crowd and the aimless comings and goings, the puddle of melted snow in the vestibule, all those girls and boys, actors and old men; he liked the ownerless Agniya, supposedly the kindest creature in the world, and the Tungus, who came for who knows what reason; he liked all the eccentrics, licensed and unlicensed, the geniuses and the outcasts; he liked raw-boned Lizaveta, and – to round things out – he liked Nina as well.

Among the visitors to Grisha's part of the house, Lizaveta was considered an artist, and indeed she did exhibit in second-rate shows. Grishunya found inspiration in her dark daubings, and composed a corresponding cycle of poems. In order to concoct her pictures, Lizaveta had to work herself into an unbridled frenzy, like some African shaman: a flame would light up in her dim eyes, and with shouts, wheezes, and a sort of grubby fury she would attack the canvas, kneading blue, black and yellow paint with her fists, and scratching the wet, oily mush with her fingernails. The style was called 'nailism' – it was a terrible sight to behold. True, the resulting images looked rather like underwater plants and stars and castles hanging in the sky – something that seemed to crawl and fly simultaneously.

'Does she have to get so excited?' Nina whispered to Grishunya once as they observed a session of nailism.

'Well, I guess it just doesn't happen otherwise,' dear Grishunya whispered back, exhaling sweet toffee breath. 'It's inspiration, the spirit, what can you do, it goes its own way.' And his eyes shone with affection and respect for the possessed scrabbler.

Lizaveta's bony hands bloomed with sores from caustic paints, and similar sores soon covered Nina's jealous heart, still nailed to Grisha's bedstead. She did not want to share Grisha; the handsome caretaker's blue eyes and wispy beard should belong to her and her alone. Oh, if only she could become the fully empowered mistress of the house once and for all, instead of just a casual, precarious girlfriend; if only she could put Grisha in a trunk, pack him in mothballs, cover him with a canvas cloth, bang the lid shut and sit on it, tugging at the locks to check: are they secure?

Oh, if only . . . Yes, then he could have whatever he wanted – even Lizaveta. Let Lizaveta live and scratch out her paintings, let her grind them out with her teeth if she wanted, let her stand on her head and stay that way, trembling like a nervous pillar beside her barbaric canvases at her annual exhibitions, her dull hair decked out with an orange ribbon, red-handed, red-faced, sweaty, and ready to cry from hurt or happiness, while over in the corner various citizens sit at a rickety table cupping their palms to shield against inquisitive eyes as they write their unknown comments in the gallery's luxurious red album: 'Revolting,' perhaps; or 'Fabulous'; or 'What *does* the arts administration think it's doing?' or else something maudlin and mannered, signed by a group of provincial librarians, about how sacred and eternal art had supposedly pierced them to the core.

Oh, to wrest Grisha from that noxious milieu! To scrape away the extraneous women who'd stuck to him like barnacles to the bottom of a boat; to pull him from the stormy sea, turn him upside down, tar and caulk him and set him in dry dock in some calm, quiet place.

But he – a carefree spirit ready to embrace any street mongrel, shelter any unsanitary vagrant – went on squandering himself on the crowd, giving himself out by the handful. This simple soul took a shopping bag, loaded it with yogurt and soured cream, and went to visit Lizaveta, who had fallen ill. And of course Nina had to go with him – and, my God, what a hovel! what a place! yellow, frightful, filthy, a dark little closet, not a single window! There lay Lizaveta, barely discernible on an iron bed under an army blanket, blissfully filling her black mouth with white soured cream. Bent over school notebooks at a table was Lizaveta's fat, frightened daughter, who bore no resemblance to her mother but looked as though Lizaveta had once upon a time bred with a St Bernard.

'Well, how are you doing here?' asked Grishunya.

Lizaveta stirred beside the dingy wall: 'All right.'

'Do you need anything?' Grishunya insisted.

The iron bed creaked. 'Nastya will take care of everything.'

'Well then, study hard.' The poet shuffled about and stroked fat Nastya on the head; he backed into the hallway, but the enfeebled Lizaveta was already dozing, a stagnant lake of unswallowed yogurt apparently frozen in her half-open mouth.

'She and I should really, er, hook up or something,' Grishunya said to Nina, gesturing vaguely and looking the other way. 'You see what problems she has getting a flat. She's from way up north, from Totma, she can only rent this storeroom, but what talent, no? And her daughter's very drawn to art, too. She sculpts, she's good – and who can she study with in Totma?'

'You and I are getting married. I'm yours,' Nina reminded him sternly.

'Yes, of course, I forgot,' Grishunya apologized. He was a gentle man; it was just that his head was full of a lot of nonsense.

Destroying Lizaveta turned out to be as hard as cutting a tough apple worm in half. When they came to fine her for violating the residence permit in her passport, she was already holed up in a different place, and Nina sent the troops over there. Lizaveta hid out in basements and Nina flooded basements; she spent the night in sheds and Nina tore them down; finally, Lizaveta evaporated to a mere shadow.

Seven pairs of iron boots had Nina worn out tramping across passport desks and through police stations, seven iron staffs had she broken on Lizaveta's back, seven kilos of iron gingerbread had she devoured in the hated caretaker's lodge: it was time for the wedding.

The motley crowd had already thinned out, a pleasant quiet reigned in the little house in the evenings, and now it was with due respect that the occasional daredevil knocked at the door, carefully wiping his feet under Nina's watchful gaze and immediately regretting that he had ever come by. Soon Grishunya would no longer be slaving with a shovel and burying his talent in the snowdrifts; he would be moving to Nina's where a sturdy, spacious glass-topped desk awaited him, with two willow switches in a vase on the left, and, on the right, from one of those frames that lean on a tail, Nina's photo smiled at him. And her smile promised that everything would be fine, that he'd be well fed and warm and clean, that Nina herself would go to see Comrade Makushkin and finally resolve the long-drawn-out question of the poetry collection: she would ask Comrade Makushkin to look over the material carefully, to give his advice, fix a few things, and cut up the thick, sticky layer cake of Grisha's verse into edible slices.

Nina allowed Grishunya a final goodbye to his friends, and the innumerable horde poured in for the farewell supper – girls and freaks, old men and jewellers. Three balletic youths with women's eyes arrived prancing on turned-out toes, a lame man limped in on crutches, someone brought a blind boy, and Lizaveta's now nearly fleshless shadow flitted about. The crowd kept coming; it buzzed and blew around like rubbish from a vacuum cleaner hooked up backward; bearded types scurried past; the walls of the little house bulged under the human pressure; and there were shouts, sobs and hysterics. Dishes were broken. The balletic youths made off with the hysterical Agniya, catching her hair in the door; Lizaveta's shadow gnawed her hands to shreds and thrashed on the floor, demanding to be walked all over (the request was honoured); the deacon led the Tungus into a corner and questioned him in sign language on the faith of his people, and the Tungus answered, also by signs, that their faith was the best of all faiths.

Grisha beat his porcelain brow against the wall and cried out that fine, all right, he was prepared to die, but after his death – you'll see – he'd come back to his friends and never be parted from them again. The deacon didn't approve of such proclamations. Neither did Nina.

By morning all the scum had vanished, and, packing Grishunya into a taxi, Nina carried him off to her crystal palace.

Ah, who could possibly paint a portrait of one's beloved when, rubbing his sleep-filled blue eyes and freeing a young, hairy leg from beneath the blankets, he yawns with all his might. Entranced, you gaze at him: everything about him is yours, yours! The gap between his teeth, and the bald spot, and that marvellous wart!

You feel you're a queen, and people make way for you on the street, and your colleagues nod respectfully, and Arkady Borisovich politely offers you his hand, wrapped in sterilized paper.

How fine it was to doctor trusting patients, to bring home bags full of goodies, to check in the evenings, like a solicitous sister, to see what Grishunya had written during the day.

Only he was a frail little thing: he cried a lot and didn't want to eat, and he didn't want to write neatly on clean paper but, out of habit, kept on picking up scraps and cigarette packs, and doodling or else just drawing flourishes and curlicues. And he wrote about a yellow, yellow road, on and on about a yellow road, and high above the road hung a white star. Nina shook her head: 'Think about it, sweetheart. You can't show poems like that to Comrade Makushkin, and you should be thinking about your book. We live in the real world.' But he didn't listen, and kept on writing about the road and the star, and Nina shouted, 'Did you understand me, sweetheart? Don't you dare write things like that!' And he was frightened and jerked his head about, and Nina, softening, said, 'Now, now, now,' and put him to bed. She fed him mint-and-lime-blossom tea, infusions of adonis and motherwort, but the ungrateful man whimpered and made up poems that offended Nina, about how motherwort had sprouted in his heart, his garden had gone to seed, the forests had burned to the ground, and some sort of raven was plucking, so to speak, the last star from the now silent horizon, and how he, Grishunya, seemed to be inside some hut, pushing and pushing at the frozen door, but there was no way out, there was only the pounding of red heels in the distance . . . 'Whose heels are those?' demanded Nina, waving the piece of paper. 'I'm just interested – whose heels are they?'

'You don't understand anything.' Grishunya snatched the paper.

'No, I understand everything perfectly well,' answered Nina bitterly. 'I just want to know whose heels they are and where it is they're pounding.'

'Aaa-agh!!! They're pounding in my head!!!' screamed Grishunya, covering his head with the blanket, and Nina went into the bathroom, tore up the poems, and scattered them into the watery netherworld, the little domestic Niagara.

Men are men; you have to keep an eye on them.

Once a week she checked his desk and threw out the poems that were indecent for a married man to compose. And once in a while she would rouse him at night for interrogation: was he writing for Comrade Makushkin, or was he shirking? And he would cover his head with his hands, lacking the strength to withstand the bright light of her merciless truth.

They managed this way for two years, but Grishunya, though surrounded by every care and concern, did not appreciate her love, and stopped making an effort. He roamed the apartment and muttered – muttered that he would soon die, and the earth would be heaped over him in clayey, cemeterial layers, and the slender gold of birch coins would drift over his grave mound like alms, and the wooden cross or pyramid marker (whichever they didn't begrudge him) would rot beneath the autumn rains, and everyone would forget him, and no one would visit, only the idle passer-by would struggle for a moment to read the four-digit dates. He strayed from poetry into ponderous free verse as damp as pine kindling, or into rhythmic lugubrious prose, and instead of a pure flame, a sort of white, suffocating smoke poured from his malignant lines, so that Nina coughed and hacked, waved her hands about, and, choking, screamed, 'For heaven's sake, stop writing!'

Then some kindhearted people told her that Grishunya wanted to return to his little house, that he had gone to see the caretaker hired in his place – a fat woman – and bargained to see how much she would ask for handing him back his former life, and the woman had actually entered into negotiations. Nina had connections in the Municipal Health Department, and she dropped hints that there was a wonderful three-storey building in the centre of town, it could be taken over by an institution, hadn't they been looking for something? Municipal Health thanked her, it did suit them, and very soon the caretaker's lodge was no more: the fire-place was torn out, and one of the medical institutes settled its faculty there.

Grisha fell silent, and for about two weeks he was quiet and obedient. Then he actually cheered up, took to singing in the bath and laughing – but he completely stopped eating, and he kept going up to the mirror and pinching himself. 'What are you so cheerful about?' Nina interrogated him. He opened his identity card and showed her the blue margins freshly stamped with fat lilac letters reading 'Not Subject to Burial.' 'What does that mean?' asked Nina, frightened. Grishunya laughed again and told her that he had sold his skeleton for sixty roubles to the Academy of Sciences, that 'his ashes he would outlast, and the worms elude', that he would never lie in the damp ground, as he had feared, but would stand among lots of people in a clean, warm room, laced together and inventoried, and students – a fun crowd – would slap him on the shoulder, flick his forehead, and treat him to cigarettes; he'd figured it all out perfectly. And he wouldn't say another word in answer to Nina's shouts; he simply proposed that they go to bed. But she should keep in mind that from now on she was embracing government property and thus was materially responsible before the law for the sum of sixty roubles and twenty-five kopecks.

And from that moment on, as Nina said later, their love seemed to go awry, because how could she burn with fully-fledged passion for public property, or kiss academic inventory? Nothing about him belonged to her any more.

And just think what she must have gone through – she, a marvellous, ordinary woman, a doctor, who had indisputably earned her piece of the pie like everyone else, a woman who had fought for her personal happiness, as we were all taught to do, and had won her right in battle.

Despite all the grief he'd caused her, she was still left with pure, radiant feelings, she said. And if love didn't turn out quite the way she had dreamed, well, Nina was hardly to blame. Life was to blame. And after his death she suffered a good deal, and her girlfriends sympathized with her, and at work they were kind and gave her ten unpaid days off. And when all the red tape was done with, Nina made the rounds of her friends and told them that Grisha now stood in the little house as a teaching aid, tagged with an inventory number they'd given him, and she'd already gone to have a look. And everything was actually just as he had wanted: the students joke with him, they tug on his wrist to make him dance about, and they put a white cap on his head. The place is well heated, at night he's locked up in the closet, but otherwise he's always around people.

And Nina also said that at first she was very upset about everything, but then it was all right, she calmed down after a woman she knew – also a lovely woman, whose husband had also died – told her that she, for one, was even rather pleased. The thing was that this woman had a two-room apartment and she'd always wanted to decorate one room Russian style, just a table in the middle, nothing else, and benches, benches all around the sides, very simple ones, rough wood. And the walls would be covered with all kinds of peasant shoes, icons, sickles, spinning wheels – that kind of thing. And so now that one of her rooms was free, this woman had apparently gone and done it, and it's her dining room, and she always gets a lot of compliments from visitors.

Translated by Jamey Gambrell

Description of Objects

Introduction

The aim of this collection has been to give precise descriptions of the objects in terms of their most recognizable characteristics, while at the same time attempting a demystification of the said objects by drawing upon the ancient socio-culturo-spiritual experience of mankind as well as the latest scientific data.

The objects have been selected on the basis of their significance and widespread occurrence in all of man's social, industrial and cultural activity. The particular descriptive methodology which we have devised will facilitate an extension of the work at some future date and lead to an eventual exhaustive inventorization of the entire surrounding world.

No. 1: The Egg

Comrades! The egg is one of the objects most frequently encountered in all of man's social, industrial and cultural activity.

It forms a complex curved sealed surface with a complex organic filling; it may vary in length between 20 mm and infinity. It can be symbolized by cupping both hands and placing them together. Its everyday uses include being given as feed to all kinds of farm animals and man, either raw or in the form of fried eggs, omelettes, boiled eggs and suchlike. The historical emergence of the egg has been linked with the appearance on the earth of the first egg-laying creatures; this, however, is incorrect, since much earlier naturally occurring eggs are being discovered.

The image of the egg has frequently been used as a religio-mystical symbol representing the primeval atom (or cosmic egg); however, from a scientific viewpoint this is absolutely incorrect, since it would be more correct to consider the origin of the world as a creative act of the Demiurge which lasted seven days.

The image of the egg has sometimes been associated with the concept of social class as a substance and an inflexible form of class ideology; however, from a Marxist viewpoint this is incorrect, since the mechanism governing the interaction of class and ideology is fundamentally different.

In view of the complexity of the curved sealed surface and the thinness of the shell, this object is virtually impossible to reproduce. For these reasons its very existence is held to be highly improbable.

No. 2: The Cross

Comrades! The cross is one of the objects most frequently encountered in all of man's social, industrial and cultural activity.

It forms an absolutely perpendicular intersection of two narrow planes; it may vary in length between 20 mm and infinity. It can be symbolized by placing one finger of each hand against each other at right-angles. Its everyday uses include crucifixion, wearing round the neck, fixing on buildings of a religious designation, drying clothes, setting out systems of coordinates and suchlike. The historical emergence of the cross has been linked with the emergence of the institution of law in ancient Rome and with the practice of crime prevention; this, however, is incorrect, since much earlier naturally occurring crosses are being discovered.

The image of the cross has frequently been used as a religio-mystical symbol representing the world as a tree; however, from a scientific viewpoint this is absolutely incorrect, since it would be more correct to consider the pillar to be the symbol of the world tree.

The image of the cross has sometimes been associated with the concept of the irreconcilability of the will of the individual and that of the state; however, from a Marxist viewpoint this is incorrect, since the mechanism governing the interaction of the individual and the state is fundamentally different.

In view of the complexity involved in achieving a perfect perpendicular intersection of two planes, this object is virtually impossible to reproduce. For this reason its very existence is held to be highly improbable.

No. 3: The Pillar

Comrades! The pillar is one of the objects most frequently encountered in all of man's social, industrial and cultural activity.

It forms a perfect cylindrical shape positioned vertically relative to the earth's surface; it may vary in length between 20 mm and infinity. It can be symbolized by pointing upwards with the tip of one finger. Its everyday uses include supporting electric power lines, fences and gates, marking the centres of places and suchlike. The historical emergence of the pillar has been linked with the emergence of the commune-type social structure; this, however, is incorrect, since much earlier, naturally occurring pillars are being discovered.

The image of the pillar has frequently been used as a religio-mystical symbol (of the phallic variety) representing male sexual potency; however, from a scientific viewpoint this is absolutely incorrect, since it would be more correct to consider it a representation of the androgynous mechanism of sexual energy.

The image of the pillar has sometimes been associated with the concept of the role of the personality in history; however, from a Marxist viewpoint this is incorrect, since the mechanism governing the role of the personality in history is fundamentally different.

In view of the complexity involved in achieving a perfect cylindrical shape and absolute perpendicularity in its positioning, this object is virtually impossible to reproduce. For these reasons its very existence is held to be highly improbable.

No. 4: The Pillow

Comrades! The pillow is one of the objects most frequently encountered in all of man's social, industrial and cultural activity.

It forms two strips of material sewn together and containing a filling, and strikes a perfect balance between mouldability and elasticity; it may vary in length between 20 mm and infinity. It can be symbolized by placing the palms of each hand against each other. Its everyday uses include being placed under heads, elbows, sides, backs, buttocks and suchlike. The historical emergence of the pillow has been linked with the stratification of primitive society; this, however, is incorrect, since much earlier naturally occurring pillows are being discovered.

The image of the pillow has frequently been used as a religio-mystical symbol representing the female sexual energy of the female sexual organs or womb; however, from a scientific viewpoint this is absolutely incorrect, since it would be more correct to consider the earth as the proper representation of the womb.

The image of the pillow has sometimes been associated with the concept of the decay of society within the framework of obsolete labour relations; however, from a Marxist viewpoint this is incorrect, since the mechanism governing the interaction of labour relations and the decay of society is fundamentally different.

In view of the complexity involved in achieving a perfect balance between mouldability and elasticity this object is virtually impossible to reproduce. For this reason its very existence is held to be highly improbable.

No. 5: The Scythe

Comrades! The scythe is one of the objects most frequently encountered in all of man's social, industrial and cultural activity.

It forms a wooden handle hafted with a strip of iron, one edge of which is tapered to a width of absolute zero; it may vary in length between 20 mm and infinity. It can be symbolized by positioning the open palm at an angle to the axis of the forearm. Its everyday uses include scything, cutting, sharpening, brawling, waging civil war and suchlike. The historical emergence of the scythe has been linked with man's transition to a settled existence of rearing livestock; this, however, is incorrect, since much earlier naturally occurring scythes are being discovered.

The image of the scythe has frequently been used as a religiomystical symbol representing one of Death's attributes; however, from a scientific viewpoint this is absolutely incorrect, since it would be more correct to consider Death as a river with a ferryman.

The image of the scythe has sometimes been associated with the concept of the dictatorship of the proletariat in the period of transition from capitalism to socialism; however, from a Marxist viewpoint this is incorrect, since the mechanism governing the dictatorship of the proletariat is fundamentally different.

In view of the complexity involved in achieving a width of absolute zero this object is virtually impossible to reproduce. For this reason its very existence is held to be highly improbable.

No. 6: The Wheel

Comrades! The wheel is one of the objects most frequently encountered in all of man's social, industrial and cultural activity.

It forms a perfect circle and is made of wood, iron or other material; it may vary in length between 20 mm and infinity. It can be symbolized by pressing together the tips of the thumb and index finger. Its everyday uses include forming part of a cart, a car, a locomotive, a steamer, an aeroplane and suchlike. The historical emergence of the wheel has been linked with the beginnings of man's social and industrial activity; this, however, is incorrect, since much earlier naturally occurring wheels are being discovered.

The image of the wheel has frequently been used as a religiomystical symbol representing the nature of this earthly life; however, from a scientific viewpoint this is absolutely incorrect, since it would be more correct to consider life as a light shining in the darkness.

The image of the wheel has sometimes been associated with the never-ending goods-money-goods-money-goods-money cycle of exchange; however, from a Marxist viewpoint this is incorrect, since the mechanism governing the goods-money-goods cycle of exchange is fundamentally different.

In view of the complexity involved in achieving a perfect circle this object is virtually impossible to reproduce. For this reason its very existence is held to be highly improbable.

No. 7: The Ape

Comrades! The ape is one of the objects most frequently encountered in all of man's social, industrial and cultural activity.

It forms the very final stage in the evolutionary chain which sets man apart from the world of all the other animals; it may vary in length between 20 mm and infinity. It can be symbolized by clenching the hand into a fist and moving the middle finger slightly further forward than the others. Its everyday uses include serving as an exhibit in zoos, a subject of scientific research, a basis of name-calling and suchlike. The historical emergence of the ape has been linked with the process of the immediately preceding biological species evolving into it; this, however, is incorrect, since much earlier naturally occurring apes are being discovered.

The image of the ape has frequently been used as a religio-mystical symbol representing the arbitrary, deceptive and low-down nature of life; however, from a scientific viewpoint this is absolutely incorrect, since it would be more correct to consider the transitoriness of life as maya, or the illusoriness of the real world.

The image of the ape has sometimes been associated with the conversion of the progressive social classes of today into the reactionary ones of tomorrow; however, from a Marxist viewpoint this is incorrect, since the mechanism governing regression of social classes is fundamentally different.

In view of the complexity involved in determining the final stage in the evolutionary process this object is virtually impossible to reproduce. For this reason its very existence is held to be highly improbable.

No. 8: The Woman

Comrades! The woman is one of the objects most frequently encountered in all of man's social, industrial and cultural activity.

It forms the totality of all the ideal characteristics of femininity; it may vary in length between 20 mm and infinity. It can be symbolized by placing two fingers (to represent the legs) on any surface. Its everyday uses include love-making, child-birth, house-keeping, dancing and suchlike. The historical emergence of the woman has been linked with the period of the emergence of the human race; this, however, is incorrect, since much earlier naturally occurring women are being discovered.

The image of the woman has frequently been used as a religio-mystical symbol representing love; however, from a scientific viewpoint this is absolutely incorrect, since it would be more correct to consider love as an impersonal all-pervasive energy or field.

The image of the woman has sometimes been associated with the amorphousness of the masses; however, from a Marxist viewpoint this is incorrect, since the mechanism governing the amorphousness of the masses is fundamentally different.

In view of the complexity involved in achieving perfect femininity this object is virtually impossible to reproduce. For this reason its very existence is held to be highly improbable.

No. 9: The Hammer and Sickle

Comrades! The hammer and sickle is one of the objects most frequently encountered in all of man's social, industrial and cultural activity.

It forms a perfect, indissoluble combination of a hammer and a sickle; it may vary in length between 20 mm and infinity. It can be symbolized by crossing the two arms, one of which is clenched into a fist, the other having an open palm. Its everyday uses are those of a hammer and sickle. The historical emergence of the hammer and sickle has been linked with the rise of an awareness of the unity of the worker and peasant classes; this, however, is incorrect, since much earlier naturally occurring hammers and sickles are being discovered.

The image of the hammer and sickle has frequently been used as a religio-mystical symbol representing eternal mutability; however, from a scientific viewpoint this is absolutely incorrect, since it would be more correct to consider eternal mutability as a god dying and coming back to life.

The image of the hammer and sickle has sometimes been associated with the mechanical uniting of the interests of workers and peasants; however, from a Marxist viewpoint this is incorrect, since the mechanism governing the uniting of the interests of workers and peasants is fundamentally different.

In view of the complexity involved in achieving perfect indissolubility this object is virtually impossible to reproduce. For this reason its very existence is held to be highly improbable.

Translated by Mark Shuttleworth

The Six-winged Seraph

1 Angels can vary terribly.

2 God, what a family!

3 A serious conversation.

4 A serious conversation (continued).

5 Yes or no?

6 Georgy Nazarych.

7 Anxiety is never unfounded.

8 Long farewells mean extra tears.

9 Unforeseen circumstances.

10 In Moscow.

11 What a pleasant surprise to find you here!

12 With fingers light as sleep . . .

13 There's no harm in trying.

14 Moreover, you're no Pushkin.

15 Those accursed questions again.

16 The ghost of Hamlet's father.

17 Farewell, free element.

18 Father.

19 A new face.

20 Senka–Samurai.

21 The ebb and flow.

22 There is a chance.

23 So near and yet so far.

24 Alarm in the night.

25 In the graveyard.

26 A song without words.

27 I'm mixed up, totally mixed up.

28 Let him leave first.

29 A truce.

30 It comes down to where you're coming from.

31 One more test.

32 I can't cope with so much sweating!

33 Unsuccessful wooing or love for corn
    wotsits.

34 One hundred and eighty over ninety.

35 Mama! He's come!

36 Don't leave – I'm terrified.

37 Three more of them – and all with their
    sleeves rolled up.

38 Nor did the morning bring relief.

39 The ferryman's tale.

40 The ferryman's tale (continued).

41 Both funny and sad (The conclusion of the
    ferryman's tale).

42 Don't be surprised, it's me.

43 How can one achieve something on one's
    own?

44 His parents' son.

45 Changes are in the pipeline.

46 What will become of us all?

47 Forget, if you can.

48 *Vox clamantis in deserto.*

49 A man with a secret.

50 Lyovushka, come to us!

51 Waiting.

52 Along the very edge.

53 Separation, O separation.

54 A completely ordinary visit.

55 Nothing but weariness.

56 Missed again!

57 Then the bad news.

58 A strange individual.

59 Misha, supper's on the table.

60 Igor Andreevich's unexpected revelations.

61 What's done is done.

62 See to it that I don't have to see him any
    more.

63 The torment of the soul or chasing shadows.

64 Once again pet answers and evasions.

65 Once again insomnia and anxiety.

66 A tempting offer.

67 From Friday to Sunday.

68 No, now would you please shut up.

69 An unpleasant duty.

70 Alexander Markovich, we've come to see you!

71 An evening of telephone calls.

72 Happiness is seeking us, but can't find us.

73 Jean-Paul makes his choice.

74 Alekseev had good reason to be worried.

75 Anna Arnoldovna gives a warning.

76 The people in Paris are human too, you know.

77 This cat would eat fish, but doesn't want wet feet.

78 No need to see me home, I don't have far to go.

79 Is it possible that we'll have a summer?

80 It's simply a question of who drank the milk.

81 We creep up with cat-like stealth,
    exuding sepulchral stench.

82 You're getting ideas above your station,
    Rozvalnev.

83 Granddad's condition worsened.

84 Poetry is all around you, my friend!

85 Something between a wedding and a funeral.

86 Oh these damn contradictions.

87 Until you are completely sure, keep your
    opinions to yourself.

88 From the lips of babes.

89 She's not quite Missie, but there's something
    of her about her.

90 As if the wind were blowing from all four
    quarters.

91 If you don't keep an eye on him he'll
    definitely end up in trouble.

92 There are more different situations,
    Heaven and earth's creations,
    Than we've dreamt of, friend Horatio.

93 Same place, same time.

94 Prophet, see and hearken.

95 'It's not true, you don't love and you've
    never loved him,' said Kuzmin unexpectedly,
    who had kept silent all this time. 'You
    invented all this to torture both yourself
    and him . . .'

96 'You all know what you can do with your
    attempts to console me!' exploded Nadya, and
    one could see that all the bitterness and pain,
    all the terrible tension of the past few days . . .

97 'You've got nowhere to hurry to. That is the
    last place anyone will be expecting you,
    believe me.' Micky stood up, lit a cigarette,
    went to the window, and without looking
    back repeated: 'You've got nowhere to hurry
    to.'

98 'Oleg, I've been looking for the chance to
    have a talk with you for some time. Tell me
    what's happened? You've become sort of . . .
    Well sort of . . . I don't know – sort of not
    yourself.
    What are you thinking about all the time?
    All the time I keep catching myself feeling
    that you're here of course, and yet you're not
    here.
    What's the matter with you? I'm worn out
    with worry. I'm lost in conjectures. You're
    hiding something from me. Do you think
    that I can't see that?
    What happened? Well, what happened?'
    Sveta walked right up to him, placed her hands
    on his shoulders, and looked into his eyes.

99 'Lads! Let's go and catch some crayfish!'
shouted Vadka sonorously, the youngest of
the Vedenyapins.
'Don't shout! Can't you see?' The sensible
Slavik sharply put him in his place. Although
he was only a year and a half older than his
brother, nevertheless he considered himself a
responsible adult and the head of the
household.

100 'Vera, hey Vera!'
'Wot you want?'
'Vera, how about it now, eh?'
'What a fool!'
'But why not, Vera?'
'Just leave me alone. Can't you see my hands
are covered in soap?'
Vera turned away, hiding a smile.
'What a fool,' she repeated tenderly. But
quietly this time.

101 'And if you didn't please her one way or
another you'd get a further kick in the teeth.
She used to pinch you all over your body.
She was a playful one, God rest her soul.'
Granny Katya made the sign of the cross and
was about to add something, but changed
her mind and fell silent for a long time.

102 After a few days a particular level of mutual
understanding was established between us in
which questions seemed unnecessary, and
silence seemed highly significant and not at
all awkward.

103   Despite himself he cried from the sudden pain,
And, turning on to his back, grew quiet . . .
And everything around grew quiet. Nothing broke
The silence, apart from drops of rain
And the voices of those by the river crossing
Haggling with the ferryman, who was demanding,
Because of the bad weather, extra dosh.
Other voices quarrelled with him. And it seemed
That these cross words would never ever end.
And then he lost consciousness once more.
And whether he lay there for a minute or a week,
A year or a century, no one could even say.
But the sun was shining,
When he opened his eyes once more and understood
That he'd been born again . . .

Translated by Andrew Reynolds

ANATOLY GAVRILOV

The Story of Major Siminkov

... There is a certain general idea which at times imparts to all these grim individuals gathered together the beauty of genuine greatness – the idea of self-renunciation.

Alfred de Vigny, 'The Bondage and Greatness of the Soldier'

It is very unlikely that the story of guards officer Nikolai Ivanovich Siminkov, which I am about to relate, created at the time even the slightest stir among the upper circles of the élite officers' corps of the rocket forces, yet now, with the passage of years, it seems to me to be both highly instructive and very sad.

In the mid-sixties when, with the rank of Captain, I commanded the mining and defence-works company in our rocket battalion, a young and slightly foppish officer called Nikolai Ivanovich Siminkov joined our battalion. Everything about him – the excellently tailored suit, the genuine leather suitcase, the silver cigarette case monogrammed with the emblem of the rocket forces, the 'Hercegovina Flor' cigarettes, the subtle aroma of expensive cologne, his gait and manner of speaking – everything bespoke a man of the world, infatuated with himself, a man out of the ordinary.

At this point I may permit myself a few brief words concerning our battalion's disposition and its manner of life.

We were stationed in a marshy forest, surrounded at its perimeter by the tangled threads of a signal system, a steel cobweb of traps and electrified wire netting, and we were billeted with families in the village of Glyboch, forty kilometres away from the battalion.

The battalion commander at the time was Fyodor Stepanovich Suprun, a regular soldier who had travelled the difficult road from company sergeant to colonel, a man of the most stern character and,

309

as they say, somewhat given to extremes. He wouldn't think twice about keeping the division out in the rain and snow for several hours, issuing an order to conduct political education classes in gasmasks or humiliating an officer in front of the men ... He compensated for the deficiencies of his technical education – and our equipment was by no means simple – with a fanatical zeal in matters of order and discipline. A family man, he might not leave the battalion for weeks or months at a time, while he got to the bottom of every petty matter. But then, the soldiers seemed to love him, and he, probably recalling his own beginnings, loved them too, after his own fashion.

Officers, however, he could not stand, especially young educated officers who attempted in any manner to demonstrate an independence of judgement or viewpoint, and he referred to them contemptuously as 'ballerinas'.

And so, in view of our somewhat monotonous way of life and Colonel Suprun's character, it was with a certain lively curiosity that we presented ourselves at headquarters for the formal introduction of the new boy, whose appearance and manner placed him, beyond the slightest doubt, in the category of 'ballerina'.

Unfortunately, I can no longer recall the details; all I can say is that young Siminkov bore his first test worthily. Not a single muscle in his handsome face so much as twitched in response to the commander's crude remarks and insults. 'A dandy, but tough,' we thought. 'But what will happen next?'

Next, as we should have expected, there came other tests. The young and inexperienced officer was appointed to command the section that was the very worst in every respect – the fuelling section of the fifth launching company. Colonel Suprun's thinking was simple and easy to understand: Now we'll see what fancy capers you can cut, ballerina!

From then on there was probably not a single day when Suprun did not call in on the fifth company to crow over Siminkov because of one set of shortcomings or another – and there were certainly more than enough of them. The commander of the fifth company at that time was Viktor Petrovich Naumchik, a man given to imbibing excessive amounts of pure spirit, for which reason he was quite incapable of taking Siminkov's part.

Siminkov's own imperturbability merely poured oil on the flames, and one day when we two were left alone at the lunch table, I advised him not to irritate the old man, but to mollify him somehow or other.

'*Vous comprenez, mon cher,*' Siminkov replied, tapping a cigarette on the lid of his remarkable cigarette-case, 'the service regulations are my protection, and therefore I have not the slightest intention of pandering to Suprun's insults, and – please believe me – I find squabbling with him an infinite bore ... The Supruns of this world are on the way out, but we are here to stay. I see my duty in serving the fatherland, and everything else is simply not worth a rotten damn, *n'est-ce pas, mon cher?*'

Here I should explain that Siminkov was an alumnus of one of the most prestigious secret military institutions, at which the inmates were furnished with both a brilliant education and the very finest of prospects, and when we learned of this, we were more than a little surprised that such an officer should have been posted to our remote parts. Rumours and guesses of the most varied kinds circulated in our battalion, but the most persistently repeated explanation was that he had been exiled here ... for being a mason. Siminkov himself never revealed his secrets to anyone, he held himself aloof and apparently took no interest in anything but military service.

After some time he succeeded in getting his section up to scratch, and then the 'Black Cat' himself – the divisional commander Lieutenant-General Bondarenko – took notice of him during exercises, and from then on, his career advanced on the nod from above, against Suprun's will and despite his wishes.

After six months he was appointed assistant commander of the fifth equipment company, and a year after that he was already a captain and commander of the entire company in place of the luckless Naumchik, who at this stage, completely ruined by drink, had been transferred to the quartermaster's platoon: and all of this took place, as I have already mentioned, over Suprun's head.

Suprun was in a state of constant fury, but it was now a helpless fury – there was no way he could countermand the will of the 'Black Cat' . . . So then he switched from direct to indirect assault – at which he was also a past master. Siminkov, however, maintained his former *sang-froid* and adhered with emphatic strictness to the letter of the regulations, further arousing admiration by the fact that never once in any way did he emphasize his privileged position under the light of the general's star . . .

His inheritance from Naumchik was no easy one: the fifth company was distinguished both for its slack discipline and its sybaritic licence, and yet none the less, in an extremely short period of time, Siminkov succeeded not only in taking the company in hand, but in making it exemplary. The red challenge pennant took up long-term residence in his relaxation room, and the room itself was so completely transformed under him that it could serve as a model of advanced military design, political maturity and almost domestic comfort. Furthermore, the barracks and its depots, store-rooms and adjoining territory were all in gleaming good order. And the political instruction sessions that Siminkov gave! Always in his own words, without any of our usual cribs or any straining or stumbling over words. It was a real joy both to watch and listen to him, which we did by inviting ourselves to his sessions . . .

With the men he was unfailingly affable, although I do think that behind this affability they could not but sense a certain coldness native to his character, and they could hardly, therefore, have loved him: most likely they were somewhat afraid of him. I can well believe that something about a commander of this type might irritate them, or even at times provoke their hatred, such as the term 'my lad' which he unfailingly employed in addressing them, and which might very easily be followed by a dressing-down or punishment. This same phrase, incidentally, annoyed Suprun extremely, reducing him to a state of pure frenzy, and often served as the pretext for all manner of investigations and even appeals to higher levels of command, all of which, however, remained without any serious consequences for Siminkov . . .

As for other matters, I should observe that our hero was a bachelor and our ladies demonstrated a certain curiosity about him, but that he responded with the standard compliments, by no means entering into those relations with them which we officers referred to among ourselves as 'waxing the thread'.

I do recall that on the day of the regiment's anniversary, at the concert in which our ladies participated, political instructor Tkachevsky's wife winked at the major and at the instructor . . .

I believe I have already mentioned that Siminkov led a somewhat solitary life, didn't join in our usual drinking-bouts, and shunned jokes and bawdy stories. In the mornings we were frequently crumpled, sullen and irritated, all the more so in the face of a jolting ride of thirty miles over a ruined road that was laid in our forest God knows when by some prisoners or other, but he always came walking cheerfully up to the bus at exactly the same time, skipped lightly into it, gazing round with a smile at our morose company, and never failed to ask: '*Qu'est-ce que c'est*, my friends?'

Once, when I was on duty and had drunk a fair amount with Captain Postoi, I confused the doors in our officers' hostel and found myself in Siminkov's room – he was standing duty that week as well. There was nobody in the room and, taking it for my own, I was all set to hit the hay when my glance suddenly fell on the lighted desk and I realized immediately that I was in someone else's room. On the desk there was a cigarette-case with the monogram 'SNIr', meaning 'Siminkov Nikolai Ivanovich, rocketeer', a plaster ashtray in the form of a skull, made by our division handyman, the enlisted man Prokatov, and a thick book, on the cover of which, as I approached the desk, I read the word 'Bonaparte'. 'So that's what it's all about. Well, well, well!' I thought, swiftly sobering up and withdrawing from this alien room.

Siminkov didn't remain a battery commander for long, either; in combat exercises his company displayed exceptional coordination and mastery, and when the nominal enemy had been nominally destroyed with a nominal nuclear warhead, the 'Black Cat' patted Siminkov affectionately on a shoulder which shortly thereafter bore the gleaming star of a major, and following that he was appointed our battalion chief of staff, to replace Viktor Mitrofanovich Korzhuk, who had retired.

We were no longer surprised at how rapidly the young officer advanced, indeed we fantasized about his rise to even more exalted spheres, and the more farsighted among us had long been seeking his friendship, even flattering him in an attempt to curry favour, and only Suprun was morose, assuming, not without reason, that Siminkov's next promotion would be to his own position of commander.

Obviously, he was now obliged to abandon even his indirect sallies against Siminkov, and only his furtive glances of disdain and hatred betrayed his feelings concerning the young man's advancement, seeming to say: it's not over yet . . .

Siminkov, however, behaved simply and naturally with him, addressing him with formal politeness and apparently bearing no grudges, although behind all his simplicity one could sense a certain condescension towards the old man – Suprun felt it, and with every day he grew still more morose.

In his new position Siminkov once again showed himself to advantage, and we were already awaiting his next promotion with some impatience, when the sudden fall came.

In uttering this word and investing it with a certain symbolic meaning, I none the less in the first instance have in mind Siminkov's actual fall on the parade ground during a ceremonial parade, in the presence of the top army command led by the 'Black Cat' himself, Lieutenant General Bondarenko.

It happened as follows. After three days of exercises and the drawing of provisional conclusions, in which we were assessed very positively, the division was fallen in on the parade square for the changing of the guard. It was foul weather, with heavy clouds slithering along above the autumnal forest, pouring down first rain, then snow, then hail; the three days had thoroughly exhausted us and we were eagerly anticipating warmth and a tasty officers' luncheon at which, in consideration of our efforts, Lieutenant-General Bondarenko might unofficially permit us to relax over a heartening glass or two. A glimpse of the re-enlisted man Brui from the quartermaster's platoon on the porch of the dining hall, carrying his sacred jerrycan, had already lent us greater strength and hope. Meanwhile, the ceremonial changing of the guard was proceeding as usual: commands rang out, reports were received, the flag was slowly run up the flagpole to the strains of the anthem, following which the battalion performed a right turn and set off to the sound of a bravura march, one battery at a time, eyes left past the tribune, where the 'Black Cat' sat among his entourage, distinguished by his heavy astrakhan hat and his blazing eyes, and at a little distance to his left sat the gloomy, hunched Suprun.

The battalion was led by Nikolai Ivanovich Siminkov, and let me tell you that for his erect figure, carriage and stride he was without equal, not only in our battalion and regiment but, I am sure, in the entire division. His ceremonial step was an astonishing combination of military precision with aristocratic lightness and elegance, it was a step of the highest class, a step which would grace a parade of any rank, even the very highest: it was sad to realize this and see this step going to waste in our backwoods – as sad and painful as it would be to catch sight of a beautiful young village girl surrounded by emaciated collective-farm women in their dirty boots and overalls in a corn-field flattened by bad weather . . .

But to return to our theme . . . Stepping out with his fine stride, Siminkov led the battalion after him, then suddenly, right in front of the tribune, having assumed the eyes left position, he staggered, flung his arms in the air and collapsed on to his backside . . . Whether he slipped, or his limbs were convulsed by a sudden cramp, whether it was the fatigue of three days of exercises taking its toll or he had caught an accidental whiff of rocket-fuel fumes somewhere, God only knows . . . a loud gasp ran through our ranks, General Bondarenko turned away, and a grin of malicious delight flitted across Colonel Suprun's gloomy face.

The fall, however, was over in a matter of seconds; Siminkov immediately jumped to his feet, drew himself erect, and strode firmly on, but from that very moment we noticed that something in him was broken . . .

On that ill-starred day he was so distressed that he did not even turn up for a luncheon with Ukrainian bortsch, excellent meat balls with mashed potatoes and an unofficial ration of pure spirit, later reinforced by a cherry liqueur drawn from Private Brui's finest stock.

That same evening, at home in Glyboch, on answering a ring at the door I was astonished to see Siminkov standing there. His face bore an expression of extreme embarrassment, and he was holding a large bottle of Stolichnaya vodka. I hastily invited him into the house, told him to make himself at home, and apologized for my appearance, since my wife and I had just settled down in front of the television to watch the news, and we were not dressed to receive guests. Our dining-table was immediately extended and covered with the best tablecloth, hors-d'oeuvres appeared, and my dear Nina, realizing the unusual nature of this visit, was particularly affable and attentive. After a while, when I had recovered from the surprise and adapted to the role of confessor assigned to me by Siminkov, I did my best to calm and reassure him, and even reminded him of what he himself had once said to me in the mess, that the most important thing was to serve the fatherland, and all the rest was not worth a rotten damn – so why should he distress himself over a ridiculous accident that everyone had already forgotten! As an example I told him how, before he arrived in our division, on the morning of an inspection following a night spent in devotions to Bacchus, Captain Pridybailo had been unable to report his own name to the inspecting officer. 'But it didn't matter, he's still in the army!' I said. 'He could even be made a major soon!'

I took up my guitar, my Nina spread her luxuriant wavy hair across her shoulders and sang a romance for us, I paid attention to keeping the glasses full, and I recalled a few funny stories – that is, I tried my very best – and gradually Siminkov grew livelier, he cheered up and laughed, calling my Nina Lyudmila Zykina, and he even felt like dancing ... As I saw him off in the middle of the night we walked along arm in arm and sang loudly, something by Vysotsky, I think it was ...

The event which I am about to relate here brought about a decisive change in Siminkov's fortunes, and even we, the officers of the division, who were not directly connected in any way with the event, were badly shaken and completely perplexed by it.

It happened as follows. Immediately before the anniversary of the October Revolution, Siminkov was summoned to regimental head-quarters to collect some papers of particular importance. In the morning he set off for headquarters with the requisite escort and in the early evening he returned safely to the division, hid the bundle of papers in the safe and sealed it. It is difficult even to guess now how it happened that next morning, as he checked the papers against a list, he discovered that one was missing. According to instructions he should have immediately reported the incident to regimental headquarters, but he did not do this, realizing only too well that the call would be enough to seal his fate. In those days in the rocket forces a blind eye was turned to many things and many sins were granted absolution, but there was one thing which was punished rigorously and without mercy – a breach of security. They never went easy, they simply threw the book at you. In general, a stain of that nature was regarded as indelible and equivalent to the loss of an officer's honour. I think it was less serious to be found drunk or caught stealing: I would not claim all that was accepted as a matter of course, but none the less it was forgotten with time, somehow wiped away – but a breach of security made an officer a pariah in the eyes of his superiors, and even of his friends and fellows. It could be hard even to shake such a man's hand.

It is easy, therefore, to understand Siminkov's confusion and despair. He would probably have shot himself, if not for the fear of blackening still further his good name and his memory, for in that case he would have been suspected not only of cowardice, but of possible links with foreign intelligence.

Defending his honour and finding the lost document were now the only aim of Siminkov's life. His self-control suffered to the extent that he immediately gave a bloody beating to the headquarters' military clerk, Romashko, whom he suspected of tampering with the bundle of papers. Then he put the battalion on alert and all day long, divided into squares, we worked without once straightening up our backs, rummaging through every nook and cranny, raking through rotten leaves, ash, garbage and old scraps of food, carefully inspecting every piece of paper. And even though it was quite obvious that we would not find the lost document, Siminkov persisted in his insanity, rousing murmurs among the men and even among us, his well-wishers.

By evening he turned his attention to the latrines and ordered a mobile generator, searchlights and a pump to be brought up. We opened the tank, lowered the pump hose into it and began pumping out and sifting the contents. Siminkov personally checked the slurry as it passed through the mesh of the filter, picking out each scrap of paper and inspecting it in the beam of the searchlights.

By midnight, when we were all quite literally dropping from exhaustion, he ordered the boom for an 8-U 208 rocket fitter to be brought to the tank, robed himself in a protective suit for inspecting rockets, pulled on a gas-mask and had himself lowered to the bottom of the tank in the cradle of the boom, in order to make quite sure for himself that everything had been pumped out and the ill-starred piece of paper was not there.

Up above, the moon illuminated the autumnal forest; down below, in the blinding beams of the powerful searchlights, the luckless Siminkov staggered between concrete walls oozing green slime. He tried to give us some commands from inside the tank, but the only sounds that reached us were pitiful moans and groans. Suddenly he stopped, tore off his gas-mask and gazed with a hunted expression around and above him. At that moment, I remember, the thought suddenly came to me that in an atomic war this tank could serve as a good shelter, but the same moment, glancing at Siminkov, I rejected the idea with revulsion. We hurriedly hoisted

Siminkov out of the tank, washed him off with firehoses in the beams of the searchlights, and carried him, half-crazed at this stage, over to the officers' hostel.

He fell into a fever. For about ten days afterwards he lay in our divisional infirmary under the care of our kindly physician Styopa Pynzar, a great fancier of the female sex and teller of humorous stories. Even here in the medical unit he had managed, God knows through what fair means or foul, to have the object of his passion employed as a medical instructor. She walked about among us in a tight-fitting khaki skirt, appointing each of us in turn her cicerone. The two of them, Styopa – that is, Senior Lieutenant Pynzar – and the lovely Lyubasha, nursed our Siminkov back to health.

For a while he was very poorly, he pined and kept repeating that he should have searched the bunker more thoroughly.

It was during those days that I was transferred to *N* unit and left before these sad events reached their conclusion. From there I retired with the rank of major and moved away permanently to the small seaside town of *N—k*. For many years I heard nothing of Siminkov and even I began to forget him amongst the daily cares and family squabbles of my new civilian life.

Then last summer, when I was in the capital, jostling with the crowds in GUM in the hope of buying some cotton stockings for my wife, I suddenly bumped into Lyubin, formerly our battalion's billiard player, poet and free-thinker. He recognized me first, we embraced and shed a few tears.

'Hey, do you remember Siminkov?' he asked suddenly, and told me how the story ended.

After the loss of the document, not only was Siminkov not jailed, he was not even reduced to the ranks, but simply demoted. An investigation by special officers from army H Q lasting several days established that all that had been lost was the instructions for a potato-peeler for the soldiers' mess, but even so there was no way he could remain on the regimental staff after that, and he returned to his old fifth company as battalion commander. However, according to Lyubin, he was no longer the same Siminkov: he was somehow slack in command and even began drinking and swearing, and the only bitter reminder of his brilliant past was his remarkable cigarette-case with the emblem and monogram.

At the first possible opportunity he applied for a discharge, and the district authorities offered him a job as director of a new pig-fattening complex, but he rejected this offer point-blank and left the district for ever.

'Would you like to see him?' Lyubin asked.

I looked at him in amazement.

'He's right here in Moscow, in Sokolniki Park! Running one of the fairground attractions – the shooting gallery! He's put on weight, mellowed a bit and he doesn't object to a glass or two. Why don't we call in for a chat about old times over a beer?'

But, saying I was a bit under the weather and pressed for time, I declined his insistent invitation and quickly changed the subject.

Translated by Andrew Bromfield

Next Item on the Agenda

Vitka Piskunov arrived at the factory's social club some time after eight. Two lamps were already on, and some lads were milling around imposing ten-metre high columns from which the paint had peeled away. When they spotted Vitka they stopped chatting, and turned their drunken faces towards him:

'Hi, Piskun.'

'All right . . .'

'So, all prepared then?'

'Yeah. Be prepared like. Morally and physically.' Vitka took out a cigarette, went over to a broad-faced lad: 'Give us a light . . .'

The lad took his cigarette out of his mouth and held it out to Vitka:

'They're all there already. You're keeping them waiting.'

'To hell with them.' Vitka lit up.

'That's all very well, saying "to hell with them", but they'll make you sweat, that's for sure.'

'So why're you worrying then? I'm the one who's going to have to sweat, not you.' Vitka threw back his head, and sent a puff of smoke into the air. He looked up at the stars above him.

'Hey I'm not worried, I just said it for something to say.' The lad put out his dog-end on the column. A second lad, tall and hook-nosed, bared his teeth and slapped Vitka on the shoulder:

'Don't worry, boys, they won't have Vitka for breakfast! He'll make mincemeat of them! That's right, innit Vitka?'

Piskunov carried on smoking in silence, slumped against the column.

'You've had one drink too many this time, Piskun,' said another lad with a shake of the head. 'I don't envy you.'

'That'll do, Zhenya, don't upset him . . .'

'And what's this idea of theirs, having it in the club?'

'The hall's being repaired.'

'Aha . . . I get it.'

Piskunov finished his cigarette, threw his fag-end into a flower bed, and, pushing aside the broad-faced lad, moved towards the door.

'Are you coming to the disco afterwards?'

'Dunno . . .'

'Actually, Vitka, you owe us a bottle for this one,' tutted hook-nose back to Vitka's.

'A bottle?' Vitka, who'd already opened the door, turned round. 'You know where you can stick your bottle. You'll provide the bottle, you still owe me one from the football . . . And you won't go grey waiting for me to pay up, have no fear . . .'

And with a slam of the door he entered the vestibule.

It was empty inside. There was no light in the box-office window. A cleaner's overall, three overcoats and Klokov's grey raincoat were hanging in the cloakroom.

'Knew he wouldn't miss this,' thought Piskunov, walking through the vestibule. 'Nothing he likes better than sitting on his arse in a meeting, that one.'

The door into the main hall was open. Piskunov entered. A few people were sitting on a poorly lit stage, directly underneath a huge portrait of Lenin. They occupied the middle part of a long table covered with red baize.

'May I come in?' asked Piskunov quietly. His voice echoed in the empty hall.

'Enter, enter,' Simakova replied. She was sitting in the centre of the table and was going through some papers.

'He can't even be on time for this meeting,' said Khokhlov, who was sitting next to her, as he looked at his watch. 'Quarter past eight.'

'He's made a habit of it,' laughed Klokov. 'It's in his blood. Every day the same old story. Who's late – Piskunov. Who's drunk – Piskunov. Who was rude to . . .'

'Sergei Vasilievich, let's put Piskunov on the back burner for the moment,' interrupted Simakova. 'Let's finish dealing with the holiday allocations first. As for you, Piskunov, just sit and wait for a while.'

Vitka walked unhurriedly past rows of seats and sat down at the end, closer to the door.

'If we award the forge shop a hundred and the smelting shop a hundred and ten, as Starukhin is suggesting, then the machine-assembling shop will only get eighty-four places. And the garage a mere twelve . . . that is, fourteen,' said Khokhlov, shuffling his papers.

'And that's how it should be,' said Zvyagintseva calmly, tapping her pencil on the table, 'the machine-assembling shop never fulfils its plan, it always lets the factory down. The forge shop and the smelting shop give one hundred and ten per cent, and then the assemblers put the brakes on everything: they say their lathes are broken, or else they haven't got enough workers, et cetera . . . That's why the factory as a whole gets treated so badly: no flats, orders, trips.'

'Well, that's not the only reason why there aren't enough flats,' said Klokov gloomily. 'The builders are having some problems. But there will be flats. The foundations of three blocks of flats in Yasenevo, and two in Medvedkovo, have been laid. And you have to see it from the assemblers' point of view as well. They've got greater responsibility and more difficult conditions, and they aren't paid well either.'

'Oh come off it!' Zvyagintseva straightened up, which made the two medals attached to her grey jacket jingle slightly. 'They aren't paid well! Everyone gets the same. They have to work harder. Fulfil the plan. Then they'll be paid better, and there'll be orders, and trips. The whole factory loses out thanks to the assemblers! The whole factory!'

'But you have to understand that it's much harder to work on the assembly line, and for one hundred and forty roubles no one is exactly losing sleep over not wor —.'

'See if you can understand him sitting over there, go on, understand him!' Zvyagintseva pointed her pencil into the semi-dark hall, where Piskunov's head could just about be made out between the round seats. 'He's one of your bods, from the machine-assembling shop, try to understand him! He's on the bottle all the time, skips work, and yet we're supposed to show him a little understanding!'

'Tatyana Yurievna, leave it for now,' said Simakova. 'Let's divide up the trips. I have to give a report to the All-Union Central Council of Trade Unions tomorrow, I'll be up all night as it is . . . So basically it's a case of either giving them all the same number, or doing as Starukhin suggested.'

'We mustn't divide them equally,' interjected Urgan. 'Tatyana Yurievna is right. The smelters are the best workers, so they should get more than the others. Whereas the assemblers should go to tourist hostels in less clement climes. For example last year I went to one near Saratov, it's a wonderful place. The food was fine, and you're next to the Volga. Not any worse than the Black Sea.'

'Very true,' Zvyagintseva turned towards him, 'let them go there. They all seem to think they deserve a trip to the Black Sea. Piskunov probably applied to go south too. Am I right, Piskunov?'

'Me?' Vitka raised his head.

'You, yes you. I'm asking you.'

'Wot, to Yalta, you mean?'

'Yes.'

'Why would I want to go to Yalta? I'm better off staying at my aunt's in Obninsk. Take it easy like.'

'He's politically aware,' grinned Zvyagintseva, '"take it easy"! If only they were all like that, "taking it easy, no fuss!" But look at this!' She tapped a mountain of papers with her finger. 'Four hundred applications!'

'So we've decided then to split them up as Starukhin suggested, yes?' Simakova asked.

'Of course.'

'Let's do that . . .'

'Simple and fair.'

'And the important thing is that there's an incentive. If you work hard you'll get a trip.'

'That's right.'

'Are we going to vote on it?'

'There's no need. It's clear what we think anyway.'

Simakova jotted something down in her notebook.

'Oksana Pavlovna,' Khokhlov said, leaning forward, 'we have in our workshop one woman, a mother of three, politically and socially very active, very public-spirited. From an old working-class family. I'd very much like her to get a trip.'

'I've also got two I'd like prioritized. They're young, but they're both good social activists,' added Klokov.

'All the activists, war veterans and invalids will get trips, as always,' answered Simakova, 'but we'll sort all that out later, comrades. The main thing is that we've made the basic allocation between the various shops. You can sort out the small print among yourselves later. Now let's deal with the next item on the agenda: the problem of Piskunov. Stand up, Piskunov! Come here.'

Vitka got up slowly and approached the stage.

'Come on, come on up.'

Vitka walked up the wooden stairs on to the stage and stood next to the rostrum. For a minute those sitting behind the table scrutinized him closely.

'Couldn't you find a better pair of trousers?' asked Klokov.

'No, I couldn't.' Vitka was looking up at the huge knot on Vladimir Ilyich's tie.

'You could at least have cleaned them. Look how filthy they are. After all, it isn't as if you've come for a disco or gone to the wine shop.'

'You're wrong, he'd have found a different pair to go dancing,' interposed Zvyagintseva, 'smarter trousers and a smarter shirt. And he wouldn't have forgotten to put a tie on either. And he would have knocked back a whole bottle of vodka with his friends.'

Simakova put two sheets of paper in front of her.

'The factory committee has received two memos. The first is from the foreman of the machine-assembling shop, Shmelyov, the second is from its trade union cell. In both memos our comrades request that the factory committee look into the behaviour of Viktor Ivanovich Piskunov. I shall read what they say . . . So, this is what the foreman writes:

> I am bringing to the attention of the factory committee of the trade union that Viktor Piskunov, who works in my brigade, is guilty of systematic infringement of the industrial code of conduct, that he shows up at the place where he works drunk, and that he doesn't fulfil the required industrial production norm, and that he is rude to his bosses, to his fellow-workers, and to me. Since June of this year Piskunov has taken to the bottle again, he appears in the factory visibly shaking, and also uses the most obscene language. I personally have warned him many times before, I've asked him nicely and even shouted at him, but it's all like water off a duck's back, he carries on drinking, swearing, being rude and acting like a hooligan. On the 16th of June, while working on his milling lathe and milling the butt-ends on some bodies, he attached one of the parts the wrong way round, with resultant serious collateral damage to the lathe. And when I shouted at him, he took another part and hurled it at me, but I managed to swerve and went straight to the boss of the workshop. Even before that date Piskunov hadn't looked after his lathe properly, he scratched swear words on its relay, and alongside he scratched an obscene picture. And when I asked him to erase it, he said he needed some kind of stimulus, an incentive. And on the 10th of July in the cloakroom he beat up Fyodor Baryshnikov so badly that he required medical attention. Because of Piskunov our brigade has never fulfilled the plan, since he has never milled more than two hundred bodies, whereas the norm is three hundred and fifty. On numerous occasions I've told the administration about this, but they say there's staff shortages as it is, so education, not dismissal, is what's called for.

And whenever I tear Piskunov off a strip, he takes out his pen and says: 'Give me a piece a paper, I'll write my letter of resignation, and you can stuff your works.' And he speaks badly about his colleagues in our work's family. And he swears. I've worked at our factory for twenty-three years, and as a Party member I demand that effective measures be taken against Piskunov, and that a very serious talk should be had with him, a good and proper, effective talk. After all he's been sent before a meeting of the factory committee on two previous occasions, but it didn't affect him one little bit. Our whole collective joins with me in demanding that a serious, meaningful, effective talk be had with Piskunov.

Foreman Andrei Shmelyov.'

Through the half-open door a cleaner carrying a bucket and brush entered the hall. Having put the bucket on the floor, she took the floor-cloth off the brush and started washing it in the bucket.

Simakova picked up a second sheet.

'And this is from the trade union cell . . .

The members of the workshop's trade union committee request that the factory committee look into the behaviour of Viktor Piskunov. During the last month Piskunov has regularly infringed industrial discipline by appearing at work in a drunken state and by not fulfilling the required industrial production norms. On the 16th of June Piskunov caused serious damage to his lathe while being in a state of intoxication, and thereby held up the work of the whole brigade for an entire day. Depriving Piskunov of his bonuses has had no influence whatsoever on him – as before he continues to infringe discipline and is offensive to both the workshop administration and to his comrades.'

Simakova put the sheet to one side:

'Yes, Piskunov. You've been working here for less than a year, but everyone knows you already. Not as a shock-worker, however, but as a scrounger and an alcoholic.'

'So I'm an alcoholic now?' Piskunov raised his head.

'Well how else would you describe yourself?' asked Klokov. 'You're a genuine, hundred-per-cent-proof alcoholic.'

'Alcoholics are laid up in hospital for treatment, whereas I work. I'm no alcoholic.'

'Of course! Of course he's not an alcoholic!' agreed Zvyagintseva, with mock seriousness. 'How can you call him an alcoholic? He has a glass of vodka in the morning, a glass at lunch and half a litre in the evening! Surely that doesn't make him an alcoholic?' The table laughed as one.

The cleaner finished wringing the cloth, put it on the brush and started to wipe the aisle between the chairs.

Simakova sighed. 'Do you realize, Piskunov, that working when you're drunk is dangerous not only for you and for your lathe, but for those around you too? Do you understand?'

'I understand.'

'So how come then you understand, yet go on drinking?'

'I don't drink, right . . . It only happened once, they've blown it up out of all proportion' – Piskunov swayed a little and shook his head – 'like I was at it every day, but in actual fact it only happened perhaps once, I'd been at my brother-in-law's, on his birthday . . .'

'How can you look us in the face and say that, you bare-faced liar?' yelled Zvyagintseva. 'Have you no sense of shame? You're stewed to the eyebrows every day, every day! Look,' she nodded towards Klokov, 'your trade-union organizer's sitting here, you could at least have been ashamed about lying before him!'

Vitka looked at Klokov and only now noticed that sitting next to him was Seryozha Chernogaev, a drillman from the brigade next to his. Seryozha was looking at Vitka nervously and guardedly.

'Perhaps once,' repeated Klokov, 'perhaps once he was sober during the whole period! I see him every morning in the cloakroom, I look into his eyes – Brahms and Liszt again. And his eyes are red like a rabbit's.'

'What's all this red rubbish? My eyes ain't red.'

'They're red. Red. And a face as white as a sheet. And swaying from side to side.'

'When was I swaying from side to side? Why do you have to go and lie all the time, huh?'

'Don't you get stroppy with me, my friend!' Klokov slapped the table. 'I'm not one of your boozing partners. I'm not Vaska Senin! Or Petka Kruglov! You can talk to them like that, but not to me! And stand properly! Why are you propping up the rostrum! You're not at the bar you know!'

'Stand normally, Piskunov,' said Simakova strictly.

Vitka moved away from the rostrum reluctantly and squinted as he straightened up. The cleaner finished wiping the floor and, leaning on her brush, looked at the stage with interest.

Zvyagintseva looked at Piskunov with disgust, and shook her head.

'Yeees . . . I feel sick just from looking at you, Piskunov. You're a pitiful creature.'

'So how come I'm pitiful now?'

'Every alcoholic is pitiful,' chipped in Starukhin. 'And you're no different. You ought to take a look at yourself in the mirror. You're all puffed up. Your face is a purply colour, it's in a hell of a mess . . . Not a pretty sight.'

The door creaked, and into the hall came a tall militiaman carrying a cello case. All those who were seated looked at him. Having stamped up and down on the spot, the militiaman walked slowly down the aisle and sat down at the end of the fourth row. He rested the black case against the next seat, took his cap from his balding head and hung it on the case.

'That's shut him up a bit,' muttered Klokov, casting a sidelong look at the militiaman. 'But you should see what he gets up to in the workshop and in the cloakroom.'

'When did you see me getting up to something?'

'You've been told not to answer back!' Simakova said, leaning forward. 'You'd better tell us how you beat up Baryshnikov. Or perhaps Klokov made that up too?'

Piskunov let out a miserable sigh, and put his hands behind his back. The militiaman was looking at him with screwed-up eyes. The cleaner left her bucket and brush in the aisle and sat down near the militiaman.

'Why don't you say something? Tell us about it.'

'There's nothing to tell . . . He started it. He was swearing at me, threatening me . . . And I was tired, out of sorts.'

'And drunk as well, yes?'

'Well, maybe just a little bit . . . I'd had some beer in the morning.'

'And the effect still hadn't worn off by evening?' asked Klokov. 'That's some beer!'

The members of the factory committee laughed.

The cleaner shook her head and adjusted the scarf which had fallen down over her eyes.

The militiaman, squinting as before, was looking at the stage. Simakova took a pencil and, fiddling with it, asked:

'So, you took your bad mood out on your comrade?'

'But he started it. He called me names.'

'Don't lie, Piskunov,' Klokov butted in. 'He didn't pick a fight with you, you started it, you got as drunk as a skunk in the cloakroom with Petka Kruglov and started hassling everyone. And Baryshnikov brought you down a peg or two. And you beat him up. Look – we have a witness here,' he nodded in Chernogaev's direction. Everyone looked at the witness. Chernogaev blushed. Vitka looked at Sergei's red face and turned away.

'No further questions, eh? I see. The truth hurts. You should be grateful to Baryshnikov that he didn't report you to the militia. He had the right to. You would have got fifteen days in clink for that bruise you gave him for sure.'

'And why didn't he go in fact to the militia?' asked Urgan.

'Well it just so happened he's a good lad. He brushed it off, as if it were nothing.'

'You were lucky, Piskunov.'

'His sort have all the luck.'

'Exactly, exactly. They have all the luck!' The cleaner got up from her seat. 'I beg your pardon, of course, but the thing is, you know,' she threw up her hands, 'I've got a neighbour just like him, just like him! I just don't know how the earth can tolerate such parasites!'

She left the seating area behind her, ran up to the stage and started counting out on her fingers: 'He doesn't work anywhere! He's drinking every day! He drags tarts home, he's a real hooligan, he fights and nothing happens! But no one's going to throw him out! I've been to the militia, been here, there and everywhere – but no! He drinks as much as ever!'

The members of the factory committee shook their heads sympathetically. The cleaner sighed and sat down in the first row. Simakova looked at Piskunov: 'This is after all the third time you've been dragged before the Factory Committee, Piskunov. Surely you've got some conscience left? You are after all letting the collective down and bringing disgrace upon the works. Even if you don't think about yourself, think about others. The brigade doesn't fulfil the plan because of you, so no one gets any production bonuses or any other bonuses. Or don't you care? Why don't you answer?! You don't care, is that it?!'

'It really is all one to him, Oksana Pavlovna,' sighed Zvyagintseva. 'He's had a drink – he's happy. He's had a fight – he's happier still. He's skipped work – he's in paradise. And he couldn't be less interested in the brigade.'

'Do you know, Piskunov, how much the damage to your lathe cost the state? Can you guess?' asked Klokov.

Vitka shook his head.

Klokov raised himself off his seat, and, leaning on the table, said: 'If it were up to me, I would dock it all from your salary. That would teach you! Then you'd know how much it cost! But as it is he broke the lathe and couldn't give a damn – he sits there smoking in the gangway. What are you doing, Vitya? I'm having a smoke. While others are repairing the lathe. He could at least have helped the adjusters? No, he couldn't give a damn! And in general you couldn't give a damn about work, about the workshop, about his comrades. Here's Chernogaev, a worker, in the same workshop as him, come on, tell us, tell us what his comrades say about Piskunov! Tell us! We're all ears.'

Chernogaev got up uncertainly, swaying. Everyone was looking at him. 'Well I . . . well you know . . .' He passed his hand over his forehead.

'Hey, don't be nervous, Seryozh, tell it just as it was,' Klokov said, trying to encourage him.

'Well, um, comrades, I work in the same workshop as Piskunov, so I see him, I mean, every day. He and I work in different brigades, but I see him every day. Both in the cloakroom and in the dining-room. Yes. Well, you know, most of it's been said already. He drinks. He gets drunk regularly. He is drunk in the morning and he is drunk in the evening. I mean. Yes, indeed. I see his lathe too. It's dirty, not tidied up properly. I walk past after work, and there's shavings on his lathe. And the brush is lying on the floor. And practically every day the same old story. And overall he behaves badly, he's rude. Beating up Baryshnikov, for example.'

'How did that happen?' asked Simakova.

'Well, I mean, Piskunov and Petka Kruglov left for the cloakroom before everyone else did. Oh yes. It wasn't even six, but they'd already called it a day. And when the others began arriving, and when I got there, they were already sitting there drunk, swearing and smoking. But he and Fedya had had a run-in before. Fedya had really torn into Piskunov because Piskunov had mucked up the brigade's chances of fulfilling the plan. So now as soon as Piskunov saw Fedya, he started looking for trouble, obviously. "Hey," he says, "our Stakhanovite shock-worker, come over here, I'm going to give your face a good working over."'

'Why you lying, Chernogai, I never . . .'

'Shut up, Piskunov! Go on, Chernogaev.'

'Well then. And Fedya says to him – behave properly, he says. And Piskunov started swearing. And Fedya, I mean, says that there'll be a meeting and, he says, I'll tell them all about you and we, he says, will report you to the factory committee. Well, at this point Piskunov attacked him. We managed to break it up. Fedya's face was all smashed in. The lads took him to the first-aid centre. But Piskunov stayed sitting in the cloakroom for a long time afterwards. Swearing all the time. He was badmouthing the works . . .'

'I never said nothing bad about the works!'

'Don't interrupt, Piskunov. No one's asking you.'

'But why's he lying?'

'I'm not lying. He said that everything here is bad, that the pay is bad. He said there was nothing to buy and nowhere to go and nothing to do.'

'Naturally! After all, apart from the wine shop he doesn't go anywhere else! And he doesn't buy anything apart from half-litre bottles of vodka!'

'How's that I don't go nowhere?'

'Because! Because you're an alcoholic! An immoral person!' Zvyagintseva shook her head.

Chernogaev continued:

'And he also said that here at the works everything is bad, there's nothing to buy, the food is bad. And that's why, he says, you don't even feel like working.'

Everyone stared in silence at Piskunov.

'Just how . . . just how could you have the nerve to say such a thing?!' The cleaner got up from her place and approached the stage. 'Aren't you ashamed? How could you, how could you dare to say that, eh?! You . . . You . . .' Her hands were clasped to her breast. 'So who raised you?! Who educated you, gave you free schooling?! During the war we ate bread made with wood shavings, worked for nights on end so that you'd have a shirt like that on your back, have sweet food to eat and know no cares! So how can you? Eh?!'

'You're fouling your own nest, Piskunov!' interjected Khokhlov. 'You're spitting into the well from which you yourself drink!'

'And from which others drink,' added Simakova. 'You spit on everyone. On the brigade, the works, your motherland. Watch out, Piskunov,' she tapped her finger on the table, 'one day you'll spit once too often!'

'Spit once too often!'

'Just fancy, he's unhappy with things! One has to work, then things will be fine. But loafers and drunks will find things tough anywhere.'

'But then such people are unhappy wherever they are. Let someone like that into a Communist world – even there it wouldn't suit him.'

'Yes. You're a rotten individual, Piskunov.'

'Are you a member of the *Komsomol*?'

'No.' Vitka looked wistfully at the portrait.

'And you have no intention of joining?'

'It's too late now. I'm twenty-five . . .'

'We don't need his type in the *Komsomol*.'

'Too true! Such people don't belong in the working class as a whole.'

'Brought before the factory committee for the third time, and it's all like water off a duck's back! What a new generation we've brought up to replace us, and no mistake! And it's all because of our softness. We are still trying to educate them!'

'That's certainly the case, Oksana Pavlovna,' Zvyagintseva turned to Simakova. 'I mean what on earth is this? We're not some kind of two-bit operation! We're the factory committee! So is he simply going to listen to us for a while, then go off, spit in the corner, and tomorrow at eleven o'clock be at the bottle again? We are the factory committee after all! The factory committee of the trade union, comrades! Trade unions are the foundry of Communism! Those are Lenin's words! So why then are we using kid gloves with them, why are we so soft on such people?'

'Too true. It's time to stop being on their side!' contributed Starukhin. 'At the end of the day we're in charge of industry here, Soviet industry! And we have to answer to the Motherland for the effectiveness of our works! The special bonus has been taken away – that hasn't worked! The end of year bonus has been taken away – that hasn't worked! We can't sack him, so therefore we have to look for some other ways of doing things! Some new measures! And no more of the human touch! We're going too far with our humaneness!'

'Absolutely, Oksana Pavlovna, you have to be tough with people like Piskunov. Tough and determined! The softly-softly approach doesn't work with them!'

'Giving him all these reprimands – it's like flogging a dead horse!'

'But what other alternatives are there apart from taking away his productivity and other bonuses? After all we can't sack him . . .'

'Then what's the point of having any sittings?! It makes a mockery of the trade union.'

'A complete mockery . . .'

'And we set a bad example, lose all our credibility. Today he's drinking, and tomorrow, perhaps, the whole brigade'll be at it.'

'But, at the end of the day, what can we do about it?'

The militiaman sighed, stood up and straightened his uniform: 'Comrades!' Everyone turned in his direction. He waited for a moment and then started to speak: 'I, of course, am an outsider here, so to speak. And I don't have any connection with this case. But as a Soviet citizen and as a member of the militia I should like, so to speak, to share with you some of the simple fruits of my experience. Comrades, I have been working with youths such as this for almost nineteen years. I've had to deal with them since I was twenty. These people – scroungers, alcoholics, hooligans and other more serious, so to speak, hardened criminals all work on the same assumption – that we will go soft, so to speak, on them. As soon as we start being softer and nicer to them, they immediately get worse. They feel our weakness straight away! And they draw the obvious conclusions, and become a greater danger to society. I've been sitting here, listening, and on the whole, I can see how it all is. I understand your position very well, comrades. And in my opinion, you shouldn't be afraid of taking new, radical measures. After all, at the end of the day you are responsible not for yourselves, but for the works. You're always thinking about the works. You're its most loyal supporters. It should be safe in your hands! And your factory fully deserves its state award for industry! Fully deserves! You must remember that.'

He sat down and put his hands together.

'That's correct!' said Urgan. 'Our comrade here, even though he doesn't work at our works, is entirely right. By encouraging people like Piskunov, we wreck our works! We harm our works, and we harm ourselves! So then, it would appear, that literally we ourselves are to blame, would it not?'

'Of course we're to blame!' echoed Zvyagintseva. 'No need to look any further! Because of our short-sightedness the factory suffers too!'

The cleaner once more half-raised herself from her seat: 'If I had the choice, well, with people like this, like him here, well, I just don't know what I'd do! They just make life impossible! Every day, from morning to evening, they're drinking and fighting and making a racket outside our very windows!'

'Then again, what can we do? We are after all an ordinary factory committee, our powers are extremely limited.'

The militiaman sighed: 'Comrades, you haven't understood me. What I said was that you shouldn't be afraid of taking new, more effective measures. After all, you shouldn't be putting yourselves first, correct?'

'No of course, that's correct,' responded Simakova, 'but the fact remains that we, comrade militiaman, really don't have any powers . . .'

'Comrades!' the militiaman slapped his knees, 'it makes me angry just listening to you, honestly it does! You don't have the powers! And whose fault is that?! Why, yours! Everything depends on you, on your initiative! If you had some concrete proposals, you'd have the powers as well. So I suppose you think that laws just fall from the sky? No! The people create them! Everything depends on you, on the people. As it is, you've made obstacles for yourselves, and now you're waiting for someone to come and hand you powers and authority on a plate. That's just childish. You won't get anything waiting around like that. And people such as this,' he pointed his finger at Piskunov, 'certainly won't give you a second chance, won't leave you in peace! And no powers will be able to help you then. But now, while there's still time, make some suggestions! Give it a try! What are you afraid of? Are you really planning to use fine words and persuasion and little chats in your struggle with lads like this? A fatal error. There's no point in trying to persuade them. You have to try a different approach. But which exactly – that's for you to decide. And the initiative has to come from you. If you show initiative, and if there are suggestions, then, obviously, the powers will follow also. But without radical initiatives, and without practical, so to speak, suggestions, then of course there won't be any powers either.'

He sat down, pulled out his handkerchief and mopped his sweaty brow.

There was a minute's silence. Then Klokov sighed, hunched his shoulders, and said: 'Well, in general, I have, that is we have . . . well, on the whole one suggestion has been made . . . Concerning Piskunov. True, I have to say . . . well I don't know how it . . . well . . . how. On the whole, I'm not sure whether I, I mean we, will be understood properly . . .'

'No need to be afraid,' the militiaman said encouragingly, putting away his handkerchief. 'If it is a practical suggestion, a concrete suggestion, so to speak, then, you know, people will understand. And approve.'

Klokov looked at Zvyagintseva. She gave him an understanding glance in return.

'Well, in general, we suggest . . .' Klokov was examining his hands, 'in general, we . . .'

Everyone looked at him expectantly. He licked his lips, raised his head and said with a sigh:

'Well, in general it has been suggested that Piskunov should face a firing squad.'

Silence hung in the hall. The militiaman painstakingly scratched his temple and grinned:

'Heeey . . . comrades . . . now you're just being silly. What have firing squads got to do with any of this?'

Those gathered there looked uncertainly at one another. The militiaman started to laugh even louder, stood up, picked up his case and, still laughing, moved towards the exit.

All eyes followed him attentively. He stopped right next to the door, turned around, and, putting his cap on the back of his head, said quickly:

'My advice to you, Piskunov, would be to listen to some good, classical music more often. Bach, Beethoven, Mozart, Shostakovich, Prokofiev, a bit of classical music, that sort of thing. You can't imagine how music ennobles man. And the main thing is, it makes him purer and more aware. You, for example, don't know anything other than boozing and dances, and that's why you don't feel like working. You should try going to the conservatory just once, have a listen to the organ. You'll find a lot of things become clearer to you straight away . . .' He was silent for a moment, then sighed and continued: 'And you, comrades, instead of wasting your time with such pointless meetings, you'd do better to organize a club for devotees of classical music here in the works. Then the young people would have something to do and absenteeism and drunkenness would decrease . . . I'd have been happy to go on about this at greater length, but I'm already late for my rehearsal, so I hope you'll forgive me . . .'

He walked out through the door.

The cleaner gave a sigh and, lifting up her bucket, made as if to follow him. But before she could even reach for the door, which had just swung shut, it flew open again as the militiaman burst into the hall with a wild, inhuman roar. Pressing his case to his chest, he knocked the cleaner off her feet and on half-bent legs ran towards the stage, his head thrown back. Having run as far as the first row of seats, he stopped sharply, threw his case on the floor and froze on the spot, roaring and leaning backwards. His roar became more hoarse, his face turned a dark crimson, his arms dangled at the sides of his contorting body.

'Pene . . . pene . . . penetenter . . . penetenter . . .' he roared, shaking his head and opening his mouth wide.

Zvyagintseva rose slowly from her chair, her hands started shaking, and her fingers with their brightly painted nails became bent. She dug her nails into her face and scraped her hands downwards, leaving bloody furrows the whole length of her face.

'Penetenter . . . penetenter . . .' she croaked in a low chesty voice.

Starukhin stood up sharply in his chair, placed his hands on the table and then smashed his face against the table with all his might.

'Penetenter . . . pene . . . penetenter . . .' he uttered as he rolled the top half of his body along the table.

Urgan shook his head and started muttering very rapidly, scarcely managing to enunciate the words: 'Well if we're talking about in the context of technology penetenter, about the sequential order of assembly operations, about the interchangeability of parts and why at the end of the day everything's so penetenter, why then there is at once more rejects of interrepublican and more obvious also penetenter on a local scale well we're not provided with guaranteed supplies with funds and raw materials for any other business for welding but they don't give cash in hand and pressurizing us into self-financing . . .'

Klokov shuddered, jumped from behind the table and collapsed on the stage. Turning on to his stomach, he began making jerking movements, crawled to the edge of the stage, and toppled into the stalls. There he started to toss and turn and sing something quietly. Khokhlov burst into loud sobs. Simakova led him out from behind the table, Khokhlov leaned forward, hiding his face in his hands. Simakova grabbed him firmly from behind by the shoulders. She vomited over the back of Khokhlov's head. When she'd finished spitting and coughing, she shouted in a shrill, powerful, piercing voice:

'Penetenter! Penetenter! Penetenter!'

Piskunov and Chernogaev leapt off the stage and, each imitating the other's strange movements, strutted with mincing gait towards the entrance. When they reached the cleaner who was lying motionless, they grabbed her by the legs and lugged her down the aisle towards the stage.

'Penetenter! Penetenter!' roared the militiaman hoarsely. His body bent back even further, so that his red face was staring up at the ceiling. His body was shaking.

Piskunov and Chernogaev dragged the cleaner up to the steps

and pulled her on to the stage. Zvyagintseva removed her hands from her bloody face, leaned right forward and approached the cleaner who was still lying on the floor. Urgan also came up to the cleaner, muttering: 'Well if it's a case of the technology penetenter, citizen foremen, they never provided high-voltage supports or added bitumen oxidizers, when the polishing process is essential for the crucial business and decisions we're responsible for, and the strange alternation of junctions of packing gland and mech-conductors . . .'

Chernogaev, Piskunov, Zvyagintseva and Urgan lifted the cleaner off the floor and placed her on the table.

Starukhin raised his smashed, bruised face slightly: 'Penetenter,' he pronounced distinctly through his swollen lips. Simakova let go of Khokhlov and, still making her piercing cries, walked towards the table.

Khokhlov fell to his knees, touched the floor with his forehead, and started raking the piles of vomit, which had formed pools on the floor, towards his face. Chernogaev, Piskunov, Zvyagintseva, Urgan, Starukhin and Simakova surrounded the cleaner who was lying on the table, and set about tearing off her clothes. The cleaner came to and muttered quietly:

'Sa it's peneten . . . sa it's peneten then . . .'

'Penetenter! Penetenter!' shouted Simakova.

'Penetenter . . .' croaked Zvyagintseva.

'But penetenter by technically proven and economically based principles of the lubrication of shafts . . .' muttered Urgan.

'Penetenter!' roared the militiaman.

Soon all the clothes had been stripped from the cleaner's body.

'Sa at it . . . Sa at it . . .' she kept muttering, lying on the table.

'Procto! Procto! Procto!' screamed Simakova.

The cleaner was turned face-down and pressed against the table. 'Procto . . . sa at it . . .' wheezed the cleaner.

'Punctera! Punctera!' roared the militiaman.

Piskunov and Chernogaev, who were dropping curtsies and making rapid circular movements with the palms of their hands, jumped off the stage, picked up the case lying at the militiaman's feet, carried it over and placed it on the edge of the stage.

'Pusshyin! Pusshyin!' roared the militiaman.

Piskunov and Chernogaev opened up the case. Inside it consisted of two compartments, separated by a wooden partition. In one half lay a sledgehammer and several short metal pipes; the other half was full to the brim with worms wriggling in a brownish-green slime. Under the writhing sea of worms the remains of half-rotted flesh could be seen.

Chernogaev grabbed hold of the sledgehammer and Piskunov took the pipes. There were five pipes.

'Perfavorate! Perfavorate!' roared the militiaman and shook even more.

'Nipples, perforating nipples and fixed giving head couplings of general human values State All-Union Standard 652, article 58 not inventoried,' muttered Urgan, as he joined the others in pinning the cleaner's body to the table. 'Length four hundred and twenty centimetres, diameter forty-two millimetres, bevel three by five.'

Piskunov carried the pipes up to the table and tipped them on to the floor.

'Perfavorate . . . so then it's perf . . .' muttered the cleaner.

Piskunov took one pipe and positioned it, sharpened end down, against the cleaner's back.

'Keela! Keela!' roared the militiaman.

'Keela! Keela!' echoed Simakova.

'Keela . . . keela . . .' repeated Starukhin.

'Keela . . .' croaked Zvyagintseva.

Piskunov wrapped both his hands around the pipe to hold it steady. Chernogaev started hitting the butt of the pipe with the sledgehammer. The pipe went clean through the cleaner's body and came to rest in the table with a thud. Piskunov took the second pipe and positioned it on the cleaner's back. Chernogaev hit the butt of the pipe with the sledgehammer. The pipe went clean through the cleaner's body and came to rest in the table with a thud. Piskunov took the third pipe and positioned it on the cleaner's back.

Chernogaev hit the butt of the pipe with the sledgehammer. The pipe went clean through the cleaner's body and came to rest in the table with a thud. Piskunov took the fourth pipe and positioned it on the cleaner's back. Chernogaev hit the butt of the pipe with the sledgehammer. The pipe went clean through the cleaner's body and came to rest in the table with a thud. Piskunov took the fifth pipe and positioned it on the cleaner's back, Chernogaev hit the butt of the pipe with the sledgehammer. The pipe went clean through the cleaner's body and came to rest in the table with a thud.

'Pulleat ... Pulleat ...' muttered Khokhlov into the pile of vomited bits he had scraped together.

'Pulleat! Pulleat!' yelled Simakova and grabbed one of the pipes sticking out of the cleaner's back with both her hands. Starukhin helped Simakova and together they pulled out the pipe.

'Pulleat! Pulleat!' roared the militiaman.

Starukhin and Simakova pulled out the second pipe and threw it on the floor. Urgan and Zvyagintseva pulled out the third pipe and threw it on the floor. Piskunov and Chernogaev pulled out the fourth pipe and threw it on the floor. Urgan and Zvyagintseva pulled out the fifth pipe and threw it on the floor. Blood started flowing freely from beneath the cleaner's body.

'Poro! Poro!' screamed Simakova.

Streaming quickly over the red baize, the blood poured on to the floor and formed three big pools.

Khokhlov crawled on all fours to the open case.

'Larda! Filla! Decanta!' roared the militiaman.

'Stiffed vermas! Stiffed vermas!' yelled Simakova and everyone apart from the militiaman, and Klokov, who was still lying in the stalls, moved towards the case.

'Stiffed vermas!' Starukhin said over and over again. 'Stiffed . . .'

'Stiffed in accordance with technological blueprints produced on a state basis and done number ones after economic calculations in real terms for the third quarter,' muttered Urgan.

Everyone who had approached the case took a handful of worms and carried them to the table. On reaching the cleaner's corpse, they started to push the worms into the holes in her back. No sooner had they finished stuffing her with worms, the militiaman stopped bending up and down, ceased roaring, took his handkerchief out and started to wipe most painstakingly his sweaty face.

Klokov got up from the floor and set about brushing down his suit. Piskunov and Chernogaev gathered up the pipes which had been hurled all over the floor, and the sledgehammer, placed them in the free half of the case and started locking it up.

'So wot is you mucking about wif there?' asked Klokov in annoyance. 'A right to-do's we 'as 'ere . . .'

Chernogaev and Piskunov locked the case, lifted it up and stepped down into the hall. Everyone, with the exception of Khokhlov, followed them. Khokhlov disappeared into the wings.

'Why is you 'anging around there?' Klokov called out to Chernogaev and Piskunov. 'Chuck it, chuck it!'

'I would appreciate it if you didn't shout,' said Chernogaev, looking Klokov in the eye. 'Kindly deport yourself in a more fitting manner.'

Klokov shook his hand in irritation and turned away. Chernogaev and Piskunov swung the case and hurled it into the centre of the hall, where with a crash it disappeared between the chairs.

A bent-in-two Khokhlov re-emerged from behind the wings. On his back he had a large cube made of a semi-transparent, jelly-like material. The cube wobbled at every step he made. Khokhlov crossed the stage, descended the steps into the hall with great care, and made for the exit.

'Stop!' said the militiaman.

Khokhlov stopped. The militiaman walked up to him and said something in a whisper.

Zvyagintseva opened up her brown handbag and took out a pistol. The militiaman whispered something to Khokhlov. Khokhlov nodded his head, which caused the cube to quiver slightly.

Zvyagintseva took the gun barrel in her mouth and pressed the trigger. A muffled shot rang out and blew the back of her head away, splattering Starukhin and Urgan with blood and brains. Zvyagintseva fell backwards.

The militiaman again whispered something to Khokhlov. Khokhlov sighed and said: 'I should like to make an announcement to all the ladies and gentlemen who have suffered so much. The thing is . . . the thing is . . . that I . . .' He stumbled over his words. The cube on his back quivered.

'Go, go, go!' the militiaman raised his voice at him.

Khokhlov moved towards the door, pushed it open with his head and left. The militiaman left in his wake. Klokov ran to the door and disappeared through it.

'Go on, run, run, you bastard,' said Chernogaev contemptuously.

'So, shall we be off then?' Simakova took out her cigarettes and lit up.

'Let's go,' nodded Chernogaev, and they all made for the exit.

Translated by Andrew Reynolds

IGOR YARKEVICH

Solzhenitsyn, or a Voice from the Underground

If I was Alexander Isaevich, Galina Vishnevskaya and Mstislav Rostropovich would let me live in their dacha, and then as all the ordinary folks go walking past, they'd say:

'He's a martyr!'

Sometimes, right out of the blue, I'd be approached by delegations of tender-hearted Jews who'd suggest I could emigrate to Israel, but I'd reply that a writer's place is by his people's sick-bed, and everyone would be left with a slightly sour taste in their mouths. At night I would dream of oranges in Jaffa and the bitter scent of the desert, but in the morning I wouldn't regret a thing.

If I was Solly, Tvardovsky would come to Ryazan to see me and take away my manuscript to Moscow, and I'd be published there and accepted into the Union of Writers, but the way things are a miserable wanker like me just gets the boot from the lefties and the righties, even though I feel for the people's woes just as deeply as Solly. Lots of famous people – not just Galina and Slava – would be proud to know me, but the way things are everyone just tries to forget a miserable wanker like me as quickly as possible. When it came down to it, if I was Solly, Russia would pay heed to my voice, and when the vicious neurasthenics tried to slander me (Solly, that is), the answer they'd get would be:

'Hands off, this is holy. He was the first one to cross all the t's and dot all the i's.'

Nobody loves me, but if I just happened to be Solly, then young girls with their breasts not fully formed yet and their bums sticking out on both sides would go to sleep with my books under their pillows, and when the phone rang and they were asked out, they'd say:

'I can't, I'm busy, I've got . . .' and they'd sigh mysteriously down the phone, the poor little nanny-goats.

If I was Solly, I'd be friends with Heinrich Böll and the two of us would frown disdainfully at the acronym 'KGB', and hate totalitarianism in all its manifestations, even the latent ones. Thousands of dissidents – and every one of them a complex figure – would seek the Way in my books, and every time they got drunk (every day) they'd call me the Leo Tolstoy of our era.

If I was Solly, I'd have a son and he'd be christened in the church on Kropotkinskaya Street, and afterwards lots of the people walking by would whisper:

'That's the place!' and point. And then they'd go into the metro and forget about it, but it would still mean something anyway.

If only I was Solly, I'd be nominated for a prize, and whether I collected it or not, there'd be no doubt it was a big event. But the way things are, when I was a child and I won a table-tennis tournament, no one was even pleased for me, they even insulted me afterwards, they said:

'So the wankers have beaten the honest kids again.'

Now if I was Solly, lots of young writers, still with roses in their cheeks, would bring me their first works to look at. Lots of people would come to see me, women and men, and everybody would have something to say to me, and I'd have an answer for every one of them. And afterwards they'd go away uplifted. And meanwhile the whole place would be surrounded by KGB agents.

But the way things are, sometimes I don't hear a word from a living soul for a week at a time.

One word of truth can outpull a team of horses.

If I was really Solly, I'd write a letter to the Congress of Russian Writers, and then the authorities would rebuke me and say I was shit. In fact, it would be them who were shit, the authorities, because all of Russia would be languishing, with no democracy anywhere, the tyrant's heavy tread would be firm on every side, every free word would be strangled [. . .]

If I was actually Solly, historical parallels and all sorts of others would converge around me – stolypin lenin etc. – they'd all be there beside me all the time – masons, lieb-masons and all the other filth who'd lined their nests in our Russian field! [. . .]

And then if I was Solly, I'd be able to take a look around myself and regard things with a fresh eye, an eye that had picked up all sorts of things, that had seen all sorts of things [. . .] – and then the very simplest of things, all screwed up tight inside since the beginning of time, nourished on blood and yielding blood and become blood would be revealed to me – oh, and then at last I'd understand them. [. . .] Ah, now I've got carried away, miserable wanker that I am! I haven't got worked up like that for ages, and all because the August nights are so sultry and it's impossible to sleep, and my dear friend Petya Blyudsky in the next room is tumbling this way and that and tumbling his broad this way and that, and she's half-asleep already and doesn't respond to anything . . .

In the morning Petya will say:

'You miserable wretch, what d'you mean by raising your hand to our sacred Solly?'

But then, Petya, my little angel, it doesn't matter what I raised it to, the important thing is what I grabbed with it and how it all ended.

If I was Solly, Petya, I wouldn't be scared by those fat greasy fingers, and I wouldn't be afraid of cold tea. In the evening, when the house feels sad, with nothing but a broken clock and burnt-out matches on a cracked saucer – even such a still life wouldn't frighten me, for something clarifying and illuminating would be revealed to me, not the way things are now. Oh God, don't abandon me, abandon anybody else, but not me! Every crack in the place is filled with the sound of diabolical rock and jazz music, the cunning tempter . . . Oh Lord, why have you abandoned us miserable wankers?

If I knew I was Solly and not a lousy cockroach, I'd probably grow a beard – the way things are I cut myself every day with my rotten razor and blunt blades, and I haven't got any money to buy a decent one – where would a poor man get money? [. . .]

If I became Solly, I'd write lots of large-format works with heavyweight content, and in among these masterpieces there'd be *One Day in the Life of Ivan Denisovich* – the first swallow of the beginning of the approach of the anticipation of the end. Then I'd see quite different things from lots of other people in the world around me, and I'd know how things stand – where the truth is, and where it isn't, and what to do so there would be truth, and how to carry on in general – but the way things are I'm just a miserable wanker who doesn't know a thing and got everything confused ages ago.

If I was really and genuinely Solly, Petya Blyudsky wouldn't turn up at my place with his broad, he'd bring an interesting book and we'd talk at length of the salvation and rebuilding of Russia, but the way things are – they're in there tumbling about. Or else we'd all tumble about together. But the way things are, I'm beyond redemption, and I haven't got a son, and nobody loves me, not a single man or woman, and no one takes any joy in me, not a single man or woman, and I've no hope left, and all because I'm not Solly. Ah, if only I was him, then I could stack all the volumes of my collected works under the backside of that girl in there with Petya, and work her over good and proper in the name of all the ruined and tormented people I know and all the ones I don't know! And then forgive everybody everything . . .

If I was Solly, I wouldn't have to hide anything from people. But the way things are I have to hide absolutely everything, because I'm a miserable wanker.

If I was Solly . . . Hm . . . I wonder – perhaps it's possible to be Solly and a miserable wanker at the same time?

Translated by Andrew Bromfield

VICTOR EROFEYEV

Zhenka's A to Z

'Tacitus is right.' I saw Zhenka in my mind's eye. 'Instead of childhood, *bracie*, a living death. They're man-haters, not man-lovers. They can't stand any signs of initiative: the only thing that matters is to die by the Good Book. My aunt loved pulling my ears. She pulled them for anything and everything. That's why they stick out so. For my edification.' 'Come on, Zhenka, surely you can't judge them all by that zealous old maid?' 'She was a simple soul: she gave the whole Christian game away. It's submission, humility, worship and ear-pulling.'

For this relief much thanks. A couple of Americans had turned up from Warsaw with warmest greetings from Evgeny – Zhenka for short. My thanks sounded hollow. Why's that? wondered the Yanks (of Polish origin, incidentally). Poland's unreciprocated love for America.

The fact that history (with a capital H) had as good as ended for me, irrespective of its possible progress elsewhere, and the fact that I will not now be signing up for any other history (with a capital H), the fuel gauge is on zero, go some way to explaining why I was sitting there miserable and bored.

One could gather from what they said that Zhenka was thriving and had multiplied. Evgeny had engendered four little girls. Not a single boy. Why is it that these Americans are so wearisomely willing and so full of good cheer? A common cause, a universally acknowledged truth is a guaranteed source of energy and good cheer. But your propeller will break soon too.

The Polish Americans and I had struggled together once. I, evidently, was even beautiful in some respect in the hopeless struggle, insomuch as she, despite the fact that they were very happily married, always pressed herself close to me in a special way, giving herself up utterly to the unpunishable minimalism of our kisses of greeting and valediction. And then they were leaving for ever: we cried, which is a sure sign of life.

Meanwhile, dressed up to the nines, but tastefully, she correctly diagnosed my boredom, my worldweariness from the symptoms, and started blabbering on about how I was on Olympus, whereas their name was legion. But I'm not taken in by such flattery these days: bathing in the chill and bitter water of Biarritz, I let the war's final battle from the old song slip by me, I let my last historical chance pass, lying in the peaceful August sands of the topless beach, a beach which ignored events back in Russia, unless you count the international family of flags stretched taut above the heads of the girls selling ice-cream. At least I got my good spirits and energy back as I acquired once more a common cause, something to rally round; but it all stopped almost before it started, and everything got screwed up into a ball again. History got taken short.

My boredom, misleadingly, smacked of arrogance, so with pangs of conscience I said that my Olympus was, so to speak, not even Pelion, but a pile of shit, and that my Parnassus wasn't the top of the world, but more of an arsehole. This perplexed everyone and set everyone thinking, myself included. We played dead, like tiny lizards.

So what about Zhenka then? How is he? I hear that he's no longer an actor but a writer, indeed he'd tried his hand at writing before, he told me about some of his ideas.

What a right little bastard, I thought to myself with a tinge of admiration, what a complete and utter bastard.

In a slipshod Warsaw journal I'd run across his (as it was proclaimed) *sensational* novella. In other words, a novel about

Warsaw's luscious whores. A dirty pile of slang, a sewerage melt-down, a bastardized *Decameron*. The whores miss their clients on New Year's Eve and slag off the holiday, because they're lying idle, waiting to break their luck, and talk business. The poverty of authenticity, I announced to the startled Americans. And it's more than that. I don't like the trade in jaded, washed-out genitals.

For some reason, it seems that there are a hell of a lot of Poles spread all around the world. I didn't even know why I'd bothered to phone. There's no point in spending your time in Paris in the company of Poles. I am splendidly indifferent to Polish culture. I don't know the first thing about it, though I make out I do. I haven't read anything, I don't know their history, I don't know how to spell King *Batory*, or what he's famous for, I'm just not interested. I used to go to Warsaw in the days when you weren't allowed to go anywhere else, to rummage in the slagheaps of Europe, which seemed to me to be rich veins full of valuable deposits.

Now it's highly amusing to observe their difficulties. But back then, in the days when Zhenka went round in a denim jacket, his bare chest sticking out, and wearing a Mao-Tse Tung badge, I couldn't even have dreamed that such things were possible. Through the conduit of Zhenka a few things trickled through to me. Weakly, of course, hardly at all, but something got through to me. Through his large stupid badge.

He was once more wearing a denim jacket, but he was no longer bare-chested, and he was a lot broader. He had been thin as a rake in the old days – with a badge. A memento of childhood rickets. But now he looked like his father. This even made me feel a bit queasy. Back then he'd had a nervous tic – he'd been struggling to get his big break. He ordered two beers in atrocious French, then two more, rummaging in his pocket for crumpled francs. I'd also put on weight since that time. In the light, if you'll pardon the expression, of *glasnost*. The café was noisy and cramped. He shouted across the little table that he lived in the suburbs, that all his children were girls, Ewka didn't work, but they didn't go without, he wasn't planning on returning to Warsaw, because Poland was shit. It was shit before and it was shit now, even shittier, in fact, and there was no point in being there. I agreed tactfully, showing restraint, and yelled in answer that I was just passing through Paris, that I was flying to New York, and then from there to Los Angeles for a month, on all sorts of business. It thus transpires that I'm a real man of the world, just like him – a true international.

Overjoyed for some reason, indeed in raptures over our meeting as a whole, Zhenka pulled out a thick notebook and gave me a load of numbers starting with 213. They were the numbers of some Poles or other in and around Hollywood, who had elbowed their way into the newspaper and cinema businesses, whom I didn't phone, because I threw the numbers into a Parisian litter bin, having no desire to see Poles in Los Angeles either. I didn't really want to go to Los Angeles for that matter, that profound Eden of oranges, I had forebodings, but that's another story. OK, then, I shouted amiably, how's your big-breasted Ewuniya? Immediately Zhenka started trying to drag me to the outskirts of Paris, but why should I bother? A man gets tired and lazy from life in Paris very quickly, he walks little and travels little. And certainly not out to the suburbs.

It had also been a New Year's Eve, in a Warsaw flat, when Ewa's tits had burst upon the world of God and man. But it was her own fault, or rather, it wasn't her fault, but simply what she wanted. There's a certain type of Polish woman. Incredibly fuck-hungry. Praying for it. Perhaps the most fuck-hungry of all the white races, I can't speak for the blacks. They're on heat all the time, just dripping for it, their flesh wet and willing. But Zhenka, simple as a bull, with his Mao-Tse Tung, simply saw red.

We were sitting on the floor singing the local protest songs. In those days Polish youth was really something else, not just in the fucking department. They were two generations ahead of our cack-handed wankers, or to be more accurate, two centuries. The fact that Russia never experienced the Renaissance really made itself felt.

The portals of Europe began in the centre of the bridge spanning the bald river Bug. On their side, with their cottage-industry jeans rolled up to their knees, children looked for tiddlers. On our side the boy-soldiers with their tommy guns played hide and seek.

> Mr Procurator's speech needs no corrections:
> We Poles enjoy our free elections . . .

At midnight the whole gang crawled under the tree for the presents. Ewka, who was sitting next to me, received a pack of Danish playing-cards. At that time Denmark was a great power in that particular respect, and Ewka was thrilled by the full-colour beastliness. I don't know Mickiewicz very well, but I get the feeling that he's just a little bit brighter than his Russian chum Pushkin. On the other hand, the Poles are not a talented people, they're exhausted, as if by self-abuse, by an unfortunate geopolitics.

Ewka's daddy, a party big-wig with regulation crew-cut, advised Zhenka to go to university, as he saw in his future son-in-law a first-class fighter against the Hydra of the Roman Catholic Church (95 per cent believers, if not more). Ewa used to gobble Russian caviare and had her own Beetle. I've screwed eighty-three women, confessed Zhenka. I was struck by his openness.

Even in Poland it seemed as if the Kingdom of the Reds was without end. Ewka daintily showed me a Danish card with a teenager licking away as if her life depended on it, covered in sweat and come. 'Just imagine what you'd have to do to bring that Danish tart to such a state . . .' I thought to myself. 'And do you like it *like that*?' she asked me even before she knew my name. The soft contours of the Polish countryside soothe one's nerves. Storks. Weeping willows. Storks. Ewka was no exception. Despite the close cosiness of the Communist family, she didn't know any Russians and was afraid of them. The fact that she'd married the half-Russian Zhenka was no mean feat in Poland.

In her question there was much warmth and joy from the vodka she'd drunk, a joy unknown in the lands to the east of the Bug. 'And what about you?' I asked, at once directly and evasively, a *real* Russian bastard. 'I love it,' she nodded, with no sign of embarrassment.

Blood throbbed in my temples. 'I'm also Russian,' Zhenka said to me in Polish. He was thin and nervous, the usual promising actor. His way of walking was not at all Russian, nor were the movements of his body, nor his bulging chest. Noting my doubts, or my indifference perhaps, or, at the very least, my extremely limited interest, Zhenka announced to me that he was searching for his Russian father, that he'd been searching for him for many years.

With glasses of *jarzębiak* in our hands we went into the kitchen. We downed loads of this rowanberry vodka, and Ewka, squeezing herself in behind the fridge, in a most friendly manner showed me her smooth tits, which I, with her approval, handled with care. A little later I tried to tempt her in the direction of the staircase, the basement, the street, where there was hardly any snow to speak of, not a patch on our snowdrifts, no need for felt boots, where the smell of petrol in the damp air was different from that same smell at home. Zhenka expertly covered up Ewka's tits and dragged her away into the john. Twenty minutes later she glided out smoothly, glowing blessedly. I didn't try to get in the way.

Zhenka and I decided to become friends.

Leaning on a curved counter in a bar haunted by trendy actors, he told me all about his miserable childhood. She had turned up at the funeral like a Fury, taken one look at Zhenka, sighed, and carted him away in disgust. To her dying day she was convinced that her sister had died on purpose, in order to burden her with a little three-year-old bastard.

I asked intelligent Polish people who they would prefer their daughters to marry: a German, a Jew or a Russian (all these nations are unloved, and represent alien religions). The Russian came a poor third: they would even prefer their daughters to marry a Jew.

She used to lock him up in a stinking toilet. She used to commit all sorts of dumb acts against him. Forced him to learn prayers. If he couldn't recite them by heart she would smear his cheeks and neck with excrement. He grew up to be full of initiative, enterprising. His aunt loved cleanliness and simple darned clothing, she despised other people's luxuries, she was a believer in charitable works, hated the so-called people's government.

So therefore, *bracie*, Communism is better. At least you can shoot yourself if you don't like it, simply cease to be, whereas here with us suicide is forbidden, all your thoughts are on display and can be seen from above, there's no hiding-place.

'Be a bit more careful about what you're saying,' I said with a shiver.

Pani Kasia refused to serve us any more vodka.

'No more vodka for you gentlemen! Just listen to yourselves speak, you're already talking in Russian!'

'We are Russian,' I tittered.

'Give me strength!' *Pani* Kasia said, losing her temper, such a kind and greasy *Pani*.

'It's useless,' said Zhenka, good-naturedly giving her up as a bad job. 'My aunt got me into such a state that in the end I started to enjoy finding juicy bits to read about how they tortured the early Christians, especially the bits about the torments undergone by the early Christian women. I was particularly keen on the sufferings of the great martyr Anastasia. Have you heard of her?'

'What do you think?' I asked earnestly.

'She was a rich and beautiful bitch! Though in fact they were all rich and beautiful . . . Many and varied were the methods,' declaimed Zhenka in his best actor's voice, 'used to encourage her to renounce her faith, but they all met with failure. Then she was sentenced to a most terrible death . . .' He slowed down, his little eyes staring into mine. 'She was to be spread-eagled between four stakes, a fire was to be lit under her, and she was to be burnt alive.'

We walked through the night along Nowy Świat. The low-key Socialist neon lights were shining. The endless decapitations were sometimes totally tasteless, and Zhenka's imagination chewed on them without any relish, as if they were carrot cutlets from a third-rate canteen, but sometimes he received lip-smacking titbits:

'Strengthened by prayer and by their mother's exhortations, the three maidens, the eldest of whom was only twelve years old . . .' Wet dreams tormented the life out of Zhenka.

Zhenka put down roots in Ewka's family: he recovered from his childhood. He wanted me to set about looking for his father. I promised, but did nothing. He had this uncontrollable itch: he had to find his father.

Tell me then, I asked him in Paris, have they found out who killed Ivan Sergeevich? They'll never find out, he said confidently. Write about your father, I said, that's much more interesting than prostitutes. Zhenka made a wry face. My memory is playing tricks on me as far as Ewka goes. She had just put the girls to sleep. Zhenka was being filmed somewhere. A new, tiny flat with a dark kitchen, despite dear old Daddy. We drank tea. I think I tried to grab hold of her hands, but nothing, I think, came of it. Showing me the door, she affectionately stroked my cheek. Thanks to his Soviet contacts Ewka's crew-cut Papa tracked down, through diplomatic channels, Zhenka's father. Zhenka was hurriedly bought a place on a tour, starting in Leningrad.

A warm, leaden night. The Polish consulate, offering shelter to Zhenka on the crew-cut's recommendation, was locked and bolted. The only sign of life was a sleepy militiaman, slumped in his sentry box, half standing guard. Wheezing heavily, Ivan Sergeevich drew near to the railings. The militiaman rushed on swollen feet to bar his way. 'Don't hurt him!' yelled Polish Zhenka. Frightened Poles have a hundred eyes. As far as Russia is concerned they always exaggerate everything on account of an acute historical gnosis. Two weeping shades, their fingers entwined through the railings, they stood there until morning, kissing each other's hands.

Grabbing Zhenka's thin rucksack, as happy as newly-weds, they took the first available train to Moscow.

The infant placed a miraculous ring on her finger and said to her: 'Know not an earthly bridegroom.' Ekaterina awoke with an indescribable joy in her heart.

From the pack of fathers and forefathers Zhenka'd been dealt not an operetta-, opera- or even ballet-type joker, not a brilliant mind or a fool, he'd been dealt a real horror, kick-in-the-teeth, 100 per cent-proof prick of a father to show that they meant business: rudely, crudely, persistently, full-frontal, in your face. Like a pup, Zhenka had been hurled to Leningrad for someone's sport and amusement, and later, in Moscow, the stakes got higher; after a supper with crystal, cognac, cured fillet of sturgeon, marinated mushrooms, salmon pie (Ivan Sergeevich, the masterchef, baked it himself) and plenty to drink – on the very first evening (why waste time?) his father's confession was served up for dessert.

As I remember, Augustine said: 'I want to recall my past foulnesses, and the carnal corruption of my soul, not because I love them, but that I may love Thee, my God.'

He captivates me so much even now that, at the risk of harming my chance (in essence) narrative, I shall quote the rest of his thought, which quietly and gradually assumes the intonation of a prayer: 'Grow sweet unto me O Lord, a sweetness undeceitful, a sweetness happy and serene, and gather me up from the dispersion where I was broken in pieces after I had turned away from Thee, the One Good, and lost myself in many vanities. At one time in my youth my heart burned to take its fill of hell, and my soul was not afeared to grow thick with the tall weeds of shadowy loves, my beauty was consumed away, and I became rotten in Thine eyes.'

After each encounter with Augustine I always get, how can I put it, yes, the English word: *dizzy* (I don't know whether anyone will understand me). But that's not important. In contrast to the Bishop of Hippo, the 'rotten' Russian recalled all his past foulnesses with great fervour.

He hunted the partisans, the 'forest brothers', in Lithuania after the war, and butchered them.

'I was a god!' yelled Ivan Sergeevich, red in the face. 'I did everything: I tortured and tormented people, forced them to do all sorts of things, recruited spies, raped virgins, judged, sentenced, tortured some more, then carried out my death sentences.'

He used what was almost a hand-picked selection of all the verbal exceptions to the rules of human morality.

It should be noted however that there was some sort of booby-trap here: the confession was just too abstract, unsupported by evidence, just one long line of verbs. It went out of its way to avoid elegant literary language. He couldn't even give a decent account, Zhenka complained afterwards, of any details worth remembering. The only thing that was clear was that he'd been quite a butcher.

The fact that the story was told in such a completely talentless way struck me as a disturbing piece of evidence. The story lacked colour not because, I reflected, there was no colour in what actually happened in reality, but because those whose aim it was to teach Zhenka a lesson, *to bring him to book*, were not up to the art of lying. The whole apparatus of torture seemed to be offered more in edification than as a reflection of life – and as a result, failed to convince.

The logic behind the story demanded an explanation of how Evgeny was conceived. According to Ivan the Ripper's account, the ghost of vengeance was soon to raise its head. In the middle of taking by storm some hut full of partisans (bearded, as partisans tend to be) he finally received his come-uppance in the form of a bullet in the stomach.

If one can be bothered, one can picture his surprise, his staring eyes: he clasps his stomach, he's in shock, he doesn't understand a thing, driven by his own absurd momentum he charges with his bayonet, hoping to take them by the beard, blood on his hands, etc. He came to in hospital.

The next stage is the nurse, a Pole for some reason, a faded, wan country girl, cowed, pro-Soviet, but despite that ending up in Poland when pregnant.

Who let her go there, or why did she want to move there, if according to his so-called father's statement they loved each other? Of course, in the presence of his son he made much of the fact that it was love, though for a man is love anything more than a weak, though fairly steady, preferring of one woman to the rest?

In short, our butcher doesn't die. Zosia nurses him. Zosia stinks of disinfectant like an old Aeroflot jet. Somewhere there in the room where the laundry was stored, or even perhaps almost under the rotting porch, they have their love affair, and Zhenka's father revels in his superiority over his recuperating comrades who have no one to milk them dry.

When Ivan Sergeevich was well on the road to recovery, he was put on the road to Siberia. In any event, on parting, he and Zosia shed a few tears, according to one version, while another claims that they didn't even say goodbye.

He said nothing about his time serving as a camp guard (O God, yet another well-worn theme!) – though for that matter no one asked him about it – but, evidently, they had a file on him, and no sooner had Stalin died than he was kicked out of the state security service. However, it's not clear whether it was for his dissident contact with a foreign woman – his fellow soldiers shot full of holes must have grassed on him in reality, if of course reality has anything to do with any of this, unable to stand his success with this faded, of course, but still not so old cunt – or whether it was for the brutal acts of violence committed against the Lithuanian population or, then again, perhaps it was for both these crimes of equal seriousness.

In later life he was given the post of government inspector and was engaged in the struggle against the pilfering, embezzlement and misappropriation of state property; and he therefore lived the life of Riley, since he was a dishonourable man, though he kept his wealth firmly under wraps (his flat in stinking Koptevo seemed to me to be a dark fortress crammed with furniture, unpacked chests, refrigerators, luxury food items. And not forgetting the diamonds, added Zhenka).

Coming to the end of his far from artistic confession before his newly acquired son, Ivan Sergeevich unexpectedly and suddenly changed to a weeping voice and went to the other extreme.

'Will you forgive me, my son?'

'I will, *tato*!' Zhenka, who was by now thoroughly pissed off, quickly replied.

'But how on earth is it possible to forgive me as simply as that?'

said Ivan Sergeevich in annoyance, clasping his hands under the strain of emotion. 'I used to stuff revolvers up the cunts of tubby Lithuanian girls and shoot off my mad load . . .'

'Horrible, just horrible!' Zhenka held his hands to his head. 'But that's what the times were like, *tato*. It was war.'

'Our cause was just, my son.'

'*Rozumiem.*'

'I used to smash open the heads of Lithuanian infants against fences!'

Zhenka cleared his voice. 'And what was the reason for that, *tato*?'

'To help in the struggle against Fascism.'

'*Tak-tak, rozumiem.*'

'I herded innocent peasants into the gas chambers!'

'Surely the Commissars didn't have any gas chambers?' said Zhenka in astonishment.

'We had everything,' said Ivan Sergeevich sadly.

'*Tato*,' said Zhenka, 'no matter what you were like, I'm glad that I found you.' With tears in his eyes he kissed his father's right hand.

'Then let us pray together before the icon,' said Ivan Sergeevich, his eyes flashing, and he dragged Zhenka into the adjoining room, where he got down on his knees, and also tried to force Zhenka to kneel alongside him. Zhenka, tainted by Catholicism, refused.

As a result of a certain incongruity, a lack of correspondence which hadn't been bargained for and which destroyed, according to my guess, the basis of the plan of divine retribution (perhaps Zhenka's good nature was the stumbling block?), a moment's hesitation followed, a sort of time-out, a pause for thought about how best to continue. When time started moving again after this fermata, Zhenka was standing there in open-mouthed astonishment.

'My inheritance,' his father said proudly. 'This is the only woman I love.'

Staring at Zhenka, in the form of a priceless Russian icon, was a *Matka Boska*, the Mourning Virgin, the image of grief. The gold framework was covered with precious stones, and shone like the celebrations marking a church's patron saint's day.

'Which century?' I asked Zhenka.

'Fifteenth.'

'Are you religious, father?'

'Extremely,' came the quiet answer.

'Forgive him,' Zhenka passionately implored the Russian Ortho-dox Madonna, getting down on his knees. 'Forgive this sinful old man.'

Zhenka had always dreamed about getting rich. Ivan Sergeevich tempted Zhenka by agreeing to allow him to take *her* out of the country. I occasionally travelled on an official business passport to raise the standards of Polish teachers of Russian, teachers who bred otters, mink and rabbits. Father and son started a frantic campaign to soften me up by spooning black caviare into my mouth.

I didn't say no, but I'd made up my mind not to. In the meantime they were walking hand-in-hand through the Aleksandrovsky Park by the Kremlin wall and visiting the Tretyakov Gallery.

After looking round the Exhibition of Economic Achievement of the USSR on the third day, Zhenka's father, standing before the icon prior to retiring to bed, dropped his trousers.

The folds of his stomach were covered with uneven scars, crenellated imprints left by elastic. Near his belly-button another button had made its mark, a clear impression, like a prehistoric bird on a stone. His face suddenly took on a mischievous look.

'Why don't you join me!'

Zhenka fell silent at the suggestion. 'It's true,' the thought flashed through Zhenka's head, 'we're right to say in Poland that with the Germans you lose your freedom, but with the Russians you lose your soul.'

'Let's do it together!'

'I don't want to.'

'So you think this is blasphemy?'

Now, many years later, it seems to me that I understand the long-term thinking behind this question. If Zhenka had just yelled out 'Yes', most probably everything would have turned out all right.

But instead, his utter revulsion made him feel, to his intense shame, sexually aroused.

The mischievous, oedematose government inspector, communing with the divinity in his own manner, could not fail to see this. A government inspector's eyes have it. Having decided that discretion was the better part of valour, Zhenka rushed to hide in the bathroom. Ivan Sergeevich hurriedly began declaring his love for him.

OK, he masturbates ... so what? ... In any event, Zhenka offered this amusing story to me precisely as a curiosity, no more.

And then ... what happened then? Then, without further delay, the crucial move was made. The following evening they got very drunk. They tripped over the rugs, bumped against the furniture and doors.

'Hey, let's make up,' suggested Ivan Sergeevich.

'Fair enough,' said Zhenka.

'But what are you?' asked Ivan Sergeevich.

'You know yourself,' answered Zhenka.

'No I don't,' retorted Ivan Sergeevich stubbornly.

'What is it you want?' asked Zhenka.

'Love,' was Ivan Sergeevich's reply. He burst into tears. 'You think that I begrudge you the icon? She's yours. Go on, take her. But don't forget me either. Surely that's not too much to ask?'

'I won't forget,' stammered Zhenka, growing cold.

Well, of course, like any promising young actor Zhenka was ambidextrous. He had his small amount of experience of which he, quite naturally, was proud. And, on the other hand, one could sell it and begin to live. In short, he answered his father not limply exactly, but not very firmly either ('What's with you? Are you totally nuts?'). And I, for my part, not being particularly sure that this drunken dialogue took place, or that the rugs from Dagestan on which they tripped or even the earlier ejaculation before the icon ever existed, not sure of anything, I find it painful to go on ...

With this inoffensive refusal serving as his answer, and still dreaming of the icon, Zhenka went to bed, and during the night his father came to him.

Having sobered up a bit, but with the bad smell of an old second-hand body, his father made his appearance.

And yet, how much nicer it would have been to write about a different meeting, let's have a different one! A man unbroken by the Gulag, with his camp tattoo 'Slave of the USSR', a man firm in his faith, who finds his sceptical son. The son is converted. A tear-jerking, honest, theologically correct story, a story with a reward for the spirit's steadfastness, and why on earth weren't those joyful, martyred women, who'd entered the canon, big-hearted enough (if I've understood anything) to beat the swords of revenge into that love which Zhenka so longed to share, to *multiply love many-fold?* who can answer me that? No one, never (I understand that the forces aren't equal, and that I look stupid, but I can't contain myself).

Zhenka was woken by a strange feeling. Ivan Sergeevich, wearing glasses and, for some reason, bookkeepers' elbow-protectors was attentively jerking him off and, seeing that Zhenka had stirred, said quietly:

'Wait a sec, you're just coming.'

Zhenka decided that he was dreaming all this, and sat up with a jolt, in order to drive away this impossible, unbearable dream, but the moment he sat up he came and woke up completely. Ivan Sergeevich was rolling his tongue over his lips. The skin on his face was sagging, he was a sick man. Zhenka understood everything in an instant and mercilessly kicked his heel into his father's lips, and leapt up, grabbing his clothes. His father ran after him, shouting through his smashed-in mouth:

'The icon's yours!'

In the hour before dawn Zhenka grabbed a taxi and came tearing to the one and only friend he had acquired in this terrible Russian city. He couldn't calm down for a long time. He paced up and down the flat, brewed coffee in the kitchen, smoked and moaned.

Now isn't that a nasty little incident. He slept right through his unsavoury orgasm.

In the morning Ivan Sergeevich telephoned: Zhenka had disappeared. He wasn't with me by any chance? The bruised sensualist talked in an anxious, sickly sweet voice. Zhenka grabbed the receiver and started screaming obscenities at him, mixing up Russian and Polish words, as Poles usually do.

'He'll take his revenge on you,' said Zhenka, and he wasn't wrong. Ivan Sergeevich spread as widely as possible the rumour that we'd shacked up with two whores from the city of Gorky and were devoting ourselves to group debauchery. I pretended to them that I was Polish and then had great difficulty in keeping up the accent. We fed them with supplies from my fridge which were, for the most part, presents from Zhenka's father.

The small one had nifty little tits like prawns, the second had nice big breasts which she covered with a dark-blue scarf (with white, friendly inscriptions) to hide her embarrassment. Zhenka immediately tore all his clothes off and started jumping up and down on one leg; they started giggling. It's not size that matters but what you can do with it, explained Zhenka. And you've got nothing to fear from him, he said, referring to me. He's impotent, but he's able to pass himself off as a good fuck. Show them what you've got strapped to your ankle. The young tarts burst out giggling once more. I was shocked by Zhenka's sense of humour, I took umbrage, and didn't show them straight away.

They phoned someone. A third girl appeared from somewhere or other. She too was soon persuaded to take her blouse off, but the second girl asked me not to do anything else to her, as she was still little. The third stared and stared at the dances from her armchair and said: that's different . . . She was someone's sister, the second girl's, I think. Then the young ladies went into the bathroom and came out wearing towels. Then the towels were removed. The third didn't budge an inch from the armchair. By this time Zhenka was drunk. He and the first girl left the room, and then he returned and fell asleep on the couch. Then girls number one and two started caressing each other's breasts, examining them with undisguised interest. Then all of us, apart from the sleeping Zhenka, touched the third girl's tits, but no more. Then the third girl grew exhausted with all this debauchery, she couldn't stop yawning, her little face grew all wrinkled, and she quickly fell asleep in the armchair. Girl number two and I went into the bedroom and did everything, but didn't screw. Then the first girl knocked on the door, and asked to sleep on the bed, and no funny stuff. In the morning the tall, thin girl from Gorky and I woke up lying next to one another, I was pleased to see her, and she me and, like lovers, we got down to serious business on her narrow and dark pubes, all the time going further and deeper into the interior. The first girl lent a helping hand: she sighed languorously and squeezed and stroked my balls, until I discovered that we all had blood on us. At this point the thin girl was forced to admit that this was only her second time, and that the first time it hadn't worked out. She had become a woman with a pseudo-Pole, a pretender whose accent had gone with the wind the next morning, just like it happens in films, and this fact surprised no one. But on the other hand the thin tart's virginity inspired me, and I wanted to say something nice to her, to give her an appropriate present, or simply shout out something. When she went off with her bloody belly for a wash, I decided to get to work on the first, but at the critical moment number one announced that she wanted to have a piss, went out and didn't come back, I found the girlfriends in the bath, my broken Braun electric razor was lying on the floor, and the third girl had in fact left very early, having managed to figure out the lock for herself. In the bath the thin girl wore a look of total triumph. We fried six eggs and ate them with gusto, a group of friends making plans for life together. Zhenka got up late, with a headache, complaining, but we didn't encourage him, ignoring his aimless wanderings around the flat.

Somewhere in Nizhny Novgorod, formerly Gorky, lives a girl with a bloody belly. Or have you gone away, darling? Where are you now? After the fried eggs she and I parted for ever. The first girl's pissing, or perhaps her pity, saved me.

Zhenka picked up syphilis and was treated in Warsaw. His father found out about the syphilis and blamed me for everything. He spread the most awful lies about me. Ewuniya also decided that I was the guilty party and across the miles broke off our friendship once and for all.

When Zhenka had been cured, he came back to Moscow and visited Koptevo to smash Ivan Sergeevich's face in for him as repayment for the phone calls to his wife. In addition, he demanded the icon as compensation for what he'd suffered. His humiliated father agreed to the damages, but said that he needed some more time. Zhenka lived a quiet life at my place, he'd been given a scare by his recent brush with syphilis, and waited for the icon. His father used to visit us. He would take his boots off in the hallway and would perch on the edge of the armchair, his legs and his raspberry-coloured socks crossed under him. He used to bring us gifts, boxes of chocolates and bottles of cognac. We accepted the tribute with good grace. But we wouldn't sit down to drink with him: the very thought turned our stomachs.

Zhenka offered me dollars in exchange for taking *her* out of the country. I didn't want to hear about this. I was a bit frightened of dollars *per se*. Then one day, still in his boots, Zhenka's father said that his place had been done over during the day, while he was at the office, and that the icon had been taken. Zhenka laughed out loud, not believing a word of it. Ivan Sergeevich, tears in his eyes, suggested that we should go and see for ourselves. The shock will kill me, he kept whispering throughout our journey. The door had been broken down. The crockery was smashed into bits. Slivers on the floor. The diamonds were missing. The icon had gone. 'I've lost everything!' We were silent. 'Someone must have put them on to me,' said Ivan Sergeevich grimly. 'Someone close to me.' 'You haven't got any friends,' said Zhenka. 'So cut the crap.' His father stayed silent. 'You arranged this yourself, you son of a bitch!' Zhenka suddenly howled wildly. He couldn't control himself. His father started crying, as if he'd been offended. Zhenka shrugged his shoulders. We left.

I went with him to Sheremetievo airport to see him off. He'd already come to terms with the fact that the icon had slipped through his fingers, but he was all gloom. This fucking country's got a curse on it, he said on parting, it's even worse than Poland.

It was about six months later that I was summoned to a meeting by an investigator, who immediately set about using, as only they know how, the pressurizing techniques based on the psychologism of the last century. The fosterlings of Russian belles-lettres. I don't like that line of questioning. I don't like that line of business. I thought it was something to do with the black icon. I guessed wrong. My telephone number had been found in the notebook of Zhenka's father, who had been thrown from a train in the Northern Caucasus. He'd been there doing his rounds as an inspector. The mere mention of the Northern Caucasus gave me heartburn, I don't like people whose eyes become bloodshot so easily. I don't like their golden smiles.

The investigator knew nothing about the break-in at the flat. He was a shady character, as far as I can judge, I noted. He agreed. I got by with a few general observations, without going into any of the details I did know about. At the end of the day, I was supposed to be Zhenka's friend. The investigator waited patiently for the information to trickle out of me. It didn't. 'Do you like it?' asked the investigator, who'd noticed that my eyes kept returning to his small antique 'Remington'. 'A real classy object.' 'One journalist offered one thousand two hundred for it.' Two lads chewing on loaves of bread clattered into the room without knocking. The investigator made a nervous grab for the pistol in the holster under his arm. 'We wish to make a statement,' said the lads, chewing. 'Get out!' roared the thin investigator (for some reason nearly everyone in my story's thin), hiding his weapon. The lads departed, chewing. I also left, with the 'Remington' under my armpit, well-pleased. 'Perhaps he threw himself from the train?' I offered as my parting shot. 'Fuck only knows,' the investigator replied.

We are sitting in a noisy, cramped café in Montparnasse.

'Have your children been christened?'

'Yes, why do you ask?' Zhenka was surprised by the question.

'So Tacitus was wrong then?' I said with a smirk.

'Which Tacitus is that? Ah, Tacitus! Well, naturally Ewka wanted them christened.'

'But what about Tacitus?'

'This is a different world, *bracie*. This is Paris. No time for those accursed Russian questions.'

Now that he'd grown brown and bald he'd started to look like his father, though he lacked his father's Soviet uncouthness. 'Have they found who killed him?' I continue the Russian line of questioning. 'Found who killed him? They'll never find out who killed him,' says Zhenka, twisting his lip. 'What about the icon?' 'I bought myself a flat here, *bracie*, on the strength of that icon. But fifteenth-century – don't make me laugh! I had great difficulty selling it. Shall we go to my place? Ewka will be pleased.' 'I have to fly to America tomorrow,' I say. 'I need my full eight hours' sleep.'

Then he gave me the telephone numbers of some Poles in Los Angeles, and I jotted them down, and then we embraced in the street outside the bar.

'Do you want a surprise?' asks Zhenka.

'Go on, surprise me,' I say, without any particular enthusiasm.

'Do you know who did the old man in?'

'Who?'

'Go on, guess,' he laughs.

'No,' I say.

He looks at me provocatively, almost aggressively.

'You still don't get it?'

'Stop telling fairy stories,' I say. 'You weren't even in the Soviet Union at the time.'

'I would shut my eyes and see my sperm dripping from his lips. Every night. That wasn't nice, *bracie*. I had to be free of that.'

Translated by Andrew Reynolds

Biographical and Explanatory Notes

VARLAM SHALAMOV was born in 1907 in Vologda, the son of a priest. In 1926 he entered Moscow State University to study Soviet law, and was arrested in 1929 for disseminating Lenin's 'Anti-Stalin Testament' and sentenced to three years in a labour camp. He returned to Moscow in 1932 and for a while worked for magazines, but was arrested again in 1937 and sent to the Kolyma camps for five years. In 1943 his sentence was extended for a further ten years for the crime of 'anti-Soviet agitation' (calling the Russian *émigré* writer Ivan Bunin a classic Russian writer). In 1946 he was given the literally life-saving chance to train to be a paramedic in the camp hospital. He was released from the camps in 1951. After his rehabilitation in 1956, Shalamov lived in Moscow and worked for the journal *Moskva* as a freelance correspondent. Due to his bad health he was put in an old people's home in 1979, where he died in 1982.

Although books of Shalamov's poetry appeared in Russia during his lifetime, his prose was not and could not have been published there. In the sixties his *Kolyma Tales* were distributed through *Samizdat*, and from 1966 onwards appeared in the New York journal *Novy zhurnal*. A complete edition was published in Russian in London in 1978 by Overseas Publications Interchange. English translations of selected stories from *Kolyma Tales* have been published in two volumes, *Kolyma Tales* (translated by John Glad, W. W. Norton, New York 1980) and *Graphite* (translated by John Glad, W. W. Norton, New York 1981); these two volumes are available in a one-volume edition, *Kolyma Tales* (translated by John Glad, Penguin Books, Harmondsworth 1994).

Solzhenitsyn wrote in *The Gulag Archipelago*: 'Shalamov's experience in the camps was longer and more bitter than my own, and I respectfully acknowledge that to him and not to me was it given to touch those depths of bestiality and despair towards which life in the camps dragged us all.'

'Typhoid Quarantine' ('*Tifozny kvarantin*') was first published in Russian in *Kolyma Tales* (London 1978). It was first published in the USSR in *Novy mir*, no. 6, 1988. The *Novy mir* text, which contains some additional passages, is the one translated here.

VIKTOR ASTAFIEV was born in 1924 in the village of Ovsyanka, Siberia and orphaned at an early age. He volunteered for the army in 1942 and was seriously wounded two years later in Poland. He is one of the leading 'village prose' writers in contemporary Russian literature.

His most important works are the novellas *The Pass* (1959), *Shooting Stars* (1960) and *The Shepherd and the Shepherdess* (1971), and the novels *Last Respects* (1967), *The Tsar-Fish* (1975), and *A Sad Detective Story* (1985). His works have been translated into many languages; English translations include the volumes: *The Horse with the Pink Mane* (translated by Robert Daglish, Progress Publishers, Moscow 1978) and *To Live Your Life and Other Stories* (Raduga, Moscow 1989).

'Lyudochka' was first published in *Novy mir*, no. 9, 1988. There is another translation of 'Lyudochka,' by David Gillespie, in the journal *Soviet Literature*, no. 8, Moscow 1990.

p. 22   The translation omits the Russian text's epigraph, which is taken from a poem by Vladimir Sokolov:

> '*Ty kamnem upala,*
> *Ya umer pod nim.*'
> ('You fell like a stone,
> I died under it.')

p. 22   *What's in a name? My name too soon will die*   The first verse of a 1830 poem by Pushkin written in response to Karolina Sobanskaya's request that he inscribe his name in her album.

p. 45   *Komsomol*   The Young Communist League.

p. 63   '*I sired you with this, I shall slay you with it too!*'   In Gogol's story, Taras Bulba's last words to his son before he slays him, are: 'I gave you life, I will also kill you.'

p. 64   *Genius and villainy* 'Genius and villainy are two things that are incompatible' from Pushkin's *Mozart and Salieri*.

p. 69   *Kutya* Boiled rice with raisins and honey, eaten at funerals.

ABRAM TERTS (ANDREI SINYAVSKY) was born in 1925 in Moscow. He worked in the Gorky Institute of World Literature in Moscow and became one of the leading literary critics working for the liberal journal *Novy mir*. Realizing that there was no chance of publishing his own prose in the USSR, Sinyavsky had two books and an article on Socialist Realism published in the West under the pseudonym Abram Terts: *The Trial Begins* and *On Socialist Realism*, with an introduction by Czeslaw Milosz (Engl. trans. by Max Hayward and George Dennis, University of California Press, Berkeley 1960) and *Lyubimov* (published in Russian in Washington, DC 1964; translated as *The Makepeace Experiment* by Manya Harari, Pantheon Books, New York 1965 and Harvill Press, London 1965). The Russian texts of these works were published in *The Fantastic World of Abram Terts* (Inter-Language Literary Associates, New York 1967). In 1966 he was sentenced to seven years in a strict-regime camp for 'slandering the Soviet Union'. Upon his release he emigrated and has been living in Paris since 1971, where he is Professor of Russian literature at the Sorbonne.

While imprisoned he wrote the books *Strolls with Pushkin* (published in Russian by Overseas Publications Interchange, London 1975; Engl. trans. by Catharine Theimer Nepomnyashchy and Slava I. Yastremski, Yale University Press, New Haven 1993), *A Voice from the Chorus* (published in Russian by Stenvalley Press, London 1973; Engl. trans. by Kyril Fitzlyon and Max Hayward, Farrar, Straus & Giroux, New York 1976 and Harvill Press, London 1976; Quartet Books, London 1994) and *In the Shade of Gogol* (published in Russian by Overseas Publications Interchange, London 1975). Since he left the Soviet Union he has written *V. V. Rozanov's 'Fallen Leaves'* (Sintaksis, Paris 1982), the autobiographical novel *Goodnight!* (Sintaksis, Paris 1984; Engl. trans. by Richard Lourie, Viking, New York 1989), *Ivan the Fool* (1991), *Soviet Civilization: A Cultural History* (translated by Joanne Turnbull, with Nikolai Formozov, Little, Brown & Co., New York 1990).

'The Golden Lace' ('*Zolotoi shnurok*') was first published in *Sintaksis* (a journal founded by Sinyavsky and his wife), no. 18, Paris 1987.

FRIDRIKH GORENSHTEIN was born in 1932 in Kiev. His father, an Austrian Communist who had emigrated to the Soviet Union, was arrested in 1935 and died in the camps. His mother, evacuated with her young son in wartime, died during the journey. Gorenshtein ended up in an orphanage, where he spent most of his childhood. After working as an engineer he studied in Moscow to become a scriptwriter. Five of his screenplays have been made into films; among them are Andrei Tarkovsky's *Solaris* and Nikita Mikalkov's *Slave of Love*. His literary debut, 'The House with a Little Tower', made his name, but it turned out to be the only significant work he was able to publish in the USSR. After being involved in the Samizdat almanac *Metropol* (Ardis, Ann Arbor 1979; Engl. trans. *Metropol*, edited by Vasily Aksyonov, Victor Erofeyev, Fazil Iskander, Andrei Bitov, Evgeny Popov, W. W. Norton, New York 1982), he emigrated to Vienna. He has been living in West Berlin since 1980. He has been married twice, and has a son.

His works include the novellas *Winter of 1953* (published in the journal *Kontinent*, nos. 17 and 18, Paris 1978 and 1979), *Steps* (1979; Engl. trans. in *Metropol*, 1982), *Atonement* (Hermitage, Tenafly, NJ 1984; part of this book first appeared in the journal *Vremya i my*, no. 42, Tel Aviv 1979), the plays for reading *Arguments about Dostoevsky* (*Teatr*, no. 2, Moscow 1990) and *Berdichev* (*Vremya i my*, nos. 50 and 51, Tel Aviv 1979 and 1980), and the novel *The Psalm* (Munich 1986). His best-known novel, *The Place*, was published in Moscow in 1991.

'Bag-in-hand' ('*S koshelochkoi*') was first published in *Sintaksis*, no. 10, Paris 1982. The first publication in the USSR was in the journal *Ogonyok*, no. 35, Moscow 1990.

p. 95 *Rouses kindly feelings* An allusion to a line from one of Pushkin's last poems, '*Pamyatnik*' ('Monument') (1836), his version of Horace's '*Exegi monumentum aere perennius.*'

YURY MAMLEEV was born in 1931 in Moscow. He graduated from the Moscow Technical Institute for Forestry. In the sixties he became one of the best-known *Samizdat* writers, and a major figure in the Moscow literary underground. In 1974 he emigrated to the USA, where he taught at Cornell University, but moved to France in 1983.

He is the author of the novel *The Vagrants* (written 1966–8); a shortened version of *The Vagrants* (using the Russian title of the work, *Shatuny*) is available in English translation, along with some short stories, in *The Sky Above Hell and Other Stories*, trans. by H. W. Tjalsma (Taplinger,

New York 1980). In Russia his works began to be published in 1989. At present he divides his time between Moscow and Paris.

'An Individualist's Notebook' ('*Tetrad' individualista*') was first published in Russian in a collection of Mamleev's short stories, *A Living Death* (Tret'ya volna, Paris 1986).

VENEDIKT EROFEEV was born in 1938 in the small railway station of Chupa on the Kola peninsula. His father, the station master, was arrested soon after his son's birth and spent sixteen years in labour camps. Erofeev had many jobs including watchman, stoker and construction worker, and was expelled from no fewer than five Russian universities for his unorthodox behaviour. He became a father in 1966, a grandfather in 1988. He died in 1990 from cancer of the throat.

He wrote his first major work, *Notes of a Psychopath*, at the age of seventeen. In 1970 two typed copies of his 'epic poem' in prose, *Moscow–Petushki* (translated as *Moscow to the End of the Line* by H. W. Tjalsma, Taplinger, New York 1980; and as *Moscow Circles*, by J. R. Dorrell, Writers and Readers Publishing Co-operative, London 1981) appeared and it became a *Samizdat* 'bestseller' almost overnight. It has since been published in numerous languages.

'Through the Eyes of an Eccentric' ('*Vasily Rozanov glazami ekstsentrika*') was first published in the almanac *NRL* (*Neue russische Literatur*), Salzburg 1978. The work was first published in Russia in the almanac *Zerkala*, edited by Alexander Lavrin, Moscow 1989.

p. 129 *Vasily Rozanov* Vasily Vasilievich Rozanov (1856–1919) was a writer, philosopher and literary critic. In 1880 he married Apollinariya Suslova, fourteen years his senior, who had been at one time Dostoevsky's mistress. His most famous works include *Dostoevsky and the Legend of the Grand Inquisitor* (1894), *Solitaria* (1912) and *The Apocalypse of Our Times* (1917–18).

VALERY POPOV was born in 1939 in Kazan. Since 1949 he has lived in Leningrad (St Petersburg), and he graduated from the Electro-technical Institute in 1963 and the All-Soviet Institute of Cinematography in 1970. He is married and has one daughter.

The author of novellas and short stories in the main, he has published books for children and adults; they include *Normal Speed* (1976), *Two Trips to Moscow* (1985) and *A New Scheherazade* (1988).

'The Fool and the Tiger' ('*Lyubov' tigra*') was first published in the journal *Strelets*, no. 4, 1991.

SERGEI DOVLATOV was born in 1941 in Ufa. From 1945 he lived in Leningrad (St Petersburg), where he studied at the Philological Faculty. After his military service he resumed his studies at the Faculty of Journalism. He worked as a journalist, and for three years he was correspondent for the paper *Soviet Estonia*. All his attempts to publish his prose in Soviet journals met with failure, and the proofs of his first book were destroyed on the orders of the KGB. In 1976 several of his short stories were published in the West in the journals *Kontinent* and *Vremya i my*, for which he was expelled from the Union of Journalists. He emigrated in 1978 and lived in New York, where he published the liberal *émigré* newspaper *Novy amerikanets*. He died in 1990 from heart failure.

During the twelve years he lived abroad he published in the USA and Europe twelve books. He was well known in Russia through *Samizdat* and regular broadcasts on Radio Liberty. Numerous collections of his stories have now been published in Russia. His works include: *The Invisible Book* (Ardis, Ann Arbor 1978; Engl. trans. by Diana Lewis Burgin and Katherine Tiernan O'Connor, Ardis, Ann Arbor 1979) and *The Zone*, (Ardis, Ann Arbor 1982; Engl. trans. by Anne Frydman, A. A. Knopf, New York 1985).

'The Fifth Compromise' ('*Kompromiss' pyaty*') was first published as 'Jubilee Boy' (*Kontinent*, Paris 1979; Engl. trans. in *New Yorker*, 9 June 1980); it forms part of *The Compromise*, (New York 1981; Engl. trans. by Anne Frydman, A. A. Knopf, New York 1983 and Hogarth Press, London 1983). The first publication in the Soviet Union of 'The Fifth Compromise' was in Sergei Dovlatov: *Zona, Kompromiss, Zapovednik*. PIK, Moscow 1991.

SASHA SOKOLOV was born in 1943 in Ottawa, Canada, where his father served as assistant military attaché in the Soviet embassy. In 1962 he enrolled in the Military Institute of Foreign Languages, but he gave it up and in 1967 started studying journalism at the Moscow State University. He first worked as a newspaper correspondent and then as a gamekeeper; he also worked as a boilerman and a lab assistant in a morgue. In 1975 he left the Soviet Union; he lived in Austria, Greece, France, Germany, the States and finally took Canadian citizenship.

His novels include *A School for Fools* (Ardis, Ann Arbor 1976; Engl. trans. by Carl R. Proffer, Ardis, Ann Arbor 1977; new edition Four Walls Eight Windows Publishers, New York 1988), which Nabokov called 'a charming, tragic and infinitely touching book', *Palisandria* (Ardis, Ann Arbor 1985, Engl. trans. *Astrophobia* by Michael H. Heim, Grove Weidenfeld, New York 1989) and *Between Dog and Wolf* (Ardis, Ann Arbor 1980).

'The Anxious Chrysalis' ('*Trevozhnaya kukolka*') was first published in the journal *Kontinent*, no. 49, Paris 1986. It was first published in Russia in the *Literaturnaya gazeta*, 2 May 1990.

p. 199   The Epigram comes from Irina Ratushinskaya's poem '*Po khlebam brodil dovoenny veter*'. The complete Russian text and Engl. trans. by Pamela White Hadas and Ilya Nikin may be found in *Stikhi – Poems*, Irina Ratushinskaya, Hermitage, Tenafly, NJ 1984 (poem no. 30).

p. 202   Я   Я is pronounced 'ya' and means 'I' in Russian, and is the last letter of the alphabet.

p. 203   *Much-respected wardrobe*   The Russian word for wardrobe here also implies bookcase, and the phrase echoes Gaev's apostrophe to the bookcase in Chekhov's *The Cherry Orchard*.

p. 204   *Sluggish megalomania*   Dissidents were often 'diagnosed' as suffering from 'sluggish schizophrenia'.

p. 205   *Walt Whitman*   A reference to 'Song of Myself', *Leaves of Grass*.

p. 206   *Ivan Turgenev*   Compare Turgenev's prose poem 'The Russian Language':

In these days of doubt, in these days of painful brooding over the fate of my country, you alone are my rod and staff, O great, mighty, true and free Russian language! If it were not for you, how could one keep from despairing at the sight of what is going on at home? It is inconceivable that such a language should not belong to a great people.

(Translated by George Gibian, *The Portable Nineteenth Century Russian Reader*, Penguin Books, Harmondsworth 1993).

EVGENY KHARITONOV was born in 1941 in Novosibirsk. He graduated from the school of acting of the All-Union State Institute of Cinematography in Moscow. He briefly worked as an actor, and then completed his postgraduate studies in 1966. He staged several of his own plays in various theatres in Russia; the most famous production was the *Enchanted Island*, a play for the deaf and dumb. He was actively persecuted by the authorities for his *Samizdat* publications and because he was homosexual. In 1981 he died suddenly of a heart attack.

None of his work was published during his lifetime. Some of his short stories appeared in the almanac *Katalog*, and later in Russian journals published in the West: *A-Ya* and *Strelets*. He achieved posthumous fame through publication in the journals *Vestnik novoi literatury*, *Stolitsa* and *Ural*.

'The Oven' ('*Dukhovka*') has not been published previously.
Dukhovka The word *dukhovka* (oven) also implies, not without irony, spiritual life or breathing space (in an oppressive culture) and is also an underground term meaning 'arsehole'. An alternative translation of the title could be 'The Airhole'.

VYACHESLAV PIETSUKH was born in 1946 in Moscow, the son of an army officer. In 1970 he graduated from the Historical Faculty of the Moscow Pedagogical Institute. He taught history in a secondary school, but was forced to give up his job when his work appeared in the almanac *Istoki* in 1978 – his bosses didn't approve. He has been the Chief Editor of the journal *Druzhba narodov* since 1993. He lives in Moscow with his wife and son.

His first book, *Alphabet*, appeared in 1983 and his work is now widely published in leading papers and journals. His published works include: *Happy Times* (1985), *The New Moscow Philosophy* (1987) and *Rommat* (1990).

'The Central–Ermolaevo War' ('*Tsentral'no-ermolaevskaya voina*') was first published in *Ogonyok*, no. 3, Moscow 1988.

p. 239   *Veche*   Popular assembly in medieval Russian towns.

EDWARD LIMONOV (real surname Savenko) was born in 1943 in Dzherzhinsk, the son of an NKVD officer. He was brought up in Saltovka, on the outskirts of Kharkov. He started working at the age of seventeen, as a steelworker, a fitter and on high-rise buildings. In 1965 he became involved in the Kharkov literary and artistic bohemian life. In 1967 he moved to Moscow, where collections of his poems were published in *Samizdat*. He became a member of the unofficial literary-artistic group 'Konkret' in 1971. He emigrated in 1974 and now lives in Paris and Moscow. He is politically active in Russia and publishes in anti-government publications.

Limonov's works have been translated into many languages. His best known works are *It's Me Eddie* (Ardis, Ann Arbor 1979; Engl. trans. by S. L. Campbell, Grove Press, New York 1983), *His Butler's Story* (first published in French in 1984; Engl. trans. by Judson Rosengrant, Grove Press, New York 1987 and Abacus, London 1989), *Diary of a Failure* (Index Publishers, New York 1982), *The Youth Savenko* (Sintaksis, Paris 1983), *The Torturer* (Chameleon, Jerusalem 1984), *The Young Rascal* (Sintaksis, Paris 1986).

'The Night *Souper*' has not previously been published.

EVGENY POPOV was born in 1946 in the Krasnoyarsk Region, Siberia. He graduated from the Moscow Geological Institute in 1968 and then worked as a geologist in Siberia for several years. In 1976 the publication of two short stories in *Novy mir* brought him recognition. Popov was an editor and author of the *Samizdat* almanac *Metropol* (see under Gorenshtein), which led to his being expelled from the Union of Writers. He had to wait until the time of perestroika to be published again in the Soviet Union.

His works include *Merry-making in Old Russia* (Ardis, Ann Arbor 1981), *I Await a Love that's True* (1989) and *The Splendour of Life* (1990). His novel *The Soul of a Patriot*, which was published in the journal *Volga* in 1989, has been translated into five European languages (Engl. trans. by Robert Porter, Collins Harvill, London 1994).

'How They Ate the Cock' (*'Kak s"eli petukha'*) was first published in *Merrymaking in Old Russia* (Ardis, Ann Arbor 1981).

TATYANA TOLSTAYA was born in 1951 in Leningrad (St Petersburg), the daughter of a professor of physics. After graduating from the Philological Faculty, she worked as an editor in the Oriental Literature department of the Nauka publishing house. She is married and has two sons.

She began writing in 1983, and her first short story was published in the journal *Aurora*. She writes regularly for the *New York Review of Books*, the *New Yorker*, *The Times Literary Supplement* and lectures in American universities. Her published works include: *On the Golden Porch* (1987, Engl. trans. by Antonina W. Bouis, A. A. Knopf, New York 1989 and Virago Press, London 1990) and *Sleepwalker in a Fog* (Engl. trans. by Jamey Gambrell, A. A. Knopf, New York 1992 and Virago Press, London 1992).

'The Poet and the Muse' (*'Poet i Muza'*) was first published in *Novy mir*, no. 12, 1986.
p. 289 *His ashes he would outlast, and the worms elude* A line from Pushkin's poem *'Pamyatnik'* ('Monument'), his version of Horace's *'Exegi monumentum aere perennius'*.

DMITRY PRIGOV was born in 1940 in Moscow. He studied sculpture at the Stroganov Art Institute in Moscow. He worked in the Architectural Directorate of Moscow, inspecting the paintwork on buildings. He is one of the founders of Moscow Conceptualism, and has tried his hand at poetry, prose writing, art, sculpture and design. He became a member of the Union of Artists, but has never had an exhibition in the Soviet Union. He lives in Moscow with his wife and son.

Poemograms, his book of visual texts came out in *A-Ya*, Paris 1985. He is now widely published in periodicals in Russia, and his first book, *Tears of the Heraldic Soul*, appeared in 1990. His poetry has been translated into English and has appeared in *Third Wave: The New Russian Poetry* (edited by Kent Johnson and Stephen Ashby, University of Michigan Press, Ann Arbor 1992), *The Poetry of Perestroika* (edited by Peter Mortimer and S. J. Litherland, trans. Carol Rumens and Richard McKane, Iron Press, Cullercoat 1991) and *Contemporary Russian Poetry: A Bilingual Anthology* (translated by Gerald S. Smith, Indiana University Press, Bloomington 1993).

'Description of Objects' ('*Opisanie predmetov*') appeared in 1979.

LEV RUBINSHTEIN was born in Moscow in 1947. After graduating from the Philological Faculty of the Moscow Pedagogical Institute, he worked in the institute's library for many years. A leading figure in the Moscow Conceptualist movement, he is the author of a new poetic movement: 'Poems on Library Index Cards'. His first publication appeared in the Parisian journal *A-Ya* in 1979. His work was first published in the USSR in 1989. He has frequently participated in international poetry festivals. English translations of his work may be found in *Third Wave: The New Russian Poetry* (University of Michigan Press, Ann Arbor 1992) and *The Poetry of Perestroika* (see Prigov). He lives in Moscow with his wife and son.

'The Six-winged Seraph' ('*Shestikryly serafim*') was published in 1991.

p. 300 *Six-winged seraph* The title, as well as sections 12 and 94, are taken from one of Pushkin's most famous poems, 'The Prophet' (1826), a poem which has come to symbolize the sacred role of prophet and sacrificial victim, which the Russian poet is destined to fulfil in that society.

p. 301 *17 Farewell, free element* The first line of Pushkin's poem 'To the Sea' (1824).

p. 305 *82 You're getting ideas above your station, Rozvalnev* These words (apart from the name Rozvalnev) are a quote from Nikolai Gogol's play *The Government Inspector*, act I, scene 2. 'Your rank doesn't entitle you to such big bribes.' The phrase is now used in the sense 'you're getting too big for your boots'.

p. 305 *89 She's not quite Missie . . .* 'Missie' is the heroine of Chekhov's short story 'House with a Mezzanine'.

ANATOLY GAVRILOV was born in 1946 in Mariupol (Zhdanov). After serving in the army he worked in the metallurgical factory. In 1978 he graduated from the Literary Institute in Moscow. He lives in Vladimir, where he is a postal worker. He was not published in the USSR until 1989. He is the author of two collections of short stories, some of which have been published abroad. He is married and has two children.

'The Story of Major Siminkov' ('*Istoriya Maiora Simin'kova*') was first published in Gavrilov's *On the Threshold of a New Life* in Moscow in 1990.

VLADIMIR SOROKIN was born in 1955 in Bykovo on the outskirts of Moscow. He graduated from the Institute of Oil and Gas, but has never worked in this field. He earns his living as a designer of technical books, but he is also a writer, playwright, dramatist, artist. His novel *The Queue* was published in Paris in 1985. His work is particularly well known in Germany, and he is a Laureate of the Prize of the West German Ministry of Culture. His work is extremely controversial in Russia. In 1992 the Moscow publisher Russkaya literatura issued a collection of his short stories. His works are published by the underground press for the most part. His other works include the novels *Marina's Thirtieth Love*, *Four Stout Hearts* (1994), the novella *A Month in Dachau*, the novel *Novel* (1994), and numerous short stories and plays. Translations of his work include 'Start of the Season' (translated by Sally Laird, in *Index on Censorship*, vol. 15, no. 9, London 1985), *The Queue* (translated by Sally Laird, Readers International, New York and London 1988), the story 'A Business Proposition', and an extract from 'Four Stout Hearts' (both transl. by Jamey Gambrell, in *Glas: New Russian Writing*, no. 2, 'Soviet Grotesque', Moscow 1991).

'Next Item on the Agenda' (original title '*Zasedanie zavkoma*' – 'Session of the Factory Trade Union Committee') was first published in *Strelets*, no. 3, 1991. p. 321 *All prepared then?* The watchword of the Pioneers, the Soviet organization for children was 'Be prepared!' to which the response is 'Always prepared!'

IGOR YARKEVICH was born in 1962 in Moscow. In 1985 he graduated from the Institute of Historical Archives. His works were first published in 1991. His works are mainly published by the press of the Russian underground. He is the author of the trilogy: *Childhood* (*How I Shit My Pants*), *Boyhood* (*How I was almost Raped*) and *Youth* (*How I Masturbated*). The first two parts form what is so far his only book, *Like I and Like Me* (1992, Engl. trans. by Andrew Bromfield in *Glas: New Russian Writing*, no. 2, 'Soviet Grotesque', Moscow 1991). He lives in Moscow.

'Solzhenitsyn, or a Voice from the Underground' ('*Solzhenitsyn, ili Golos iz podpol'ya*') was first published in the Moscow journal *Muleta* in 1991. The story has been slightly edited.

p. 346 *One word of truth can outpull a team of horses* A parodic echo of the key phrase in Solzhenitsyn's Nobel Prize speech, '*Odno slovo pravdy ves' mir peretyanet*', sometimes translated as 'One word of truth is of more weight than all the rest of the world.'

p. 347 *Fat greasy fingers* An allusion to Mandelstam's 'Stalin epigram' (1933).

VICTOR EROFEYEV was born in 1947 in Moscow in the family of a high-ranking diplomat. He spent part of his childhood in Paris. He graduated from the Philological Faculty of Moscow State University in 1970, and in 1973 completed post-graduate work at the Institute of World Literature. In 1975 he received his candidate's degree for his thesis on 'Dostoevsky and French Existentialism'. For organizing and publishing in the *Samizdat* almanac *Metropol* (see under Gorenshtein) he was expelled from the Soviet Union of Writers. His prose wasn't published until 1988. At the end of the eighties his first novel, *Russian Beauty*, became an international bestseller, and appeared in Russian as well as in twenty-six other languages (Engl. trans. by Andrew Reynolds, Hamish Hamilton, London 1992 and Viking, New York 1993). Author of the 1989 article 'A Wake for Soviet Literature', (Engl. trans. in *Glas: New Russian Writing*, No. 1, 'Soviet Literature: A Requiem'), which announced the *de facto* death of Soviet literature, and which became the subject of heated and prolonged argument. Alfred Schnittke wrote the opera *Life with an Idiot* based on Erofeyev's story of the same name.

He often lectures in various American universities. His collection of short stories, *Life with an Idiot* (1991) and the literary and philosophical essays, *In the Labyrinth of Accursed Questions* (1990) have been translated into various languages. He writes regularly for *The Times Literary Supplement*, publishes articles and reviews in *The New York Review of Books* and elsewhere. Recent articles include his introduction to Fyodor Sologub's *The Little Demon* (Penguin Books, Harmondsworth 1994).

He lives predominantly in Moscow, and is married with a son.

'Zhenka's *A to Z*' (original title '*Zhenkin tezaurus*' – 'Zhenka's Thesaurus') was first published in *Selections, or A Pocket Apocalypse* (Moscow 1993).

p. 349 *Bracie* Brother (Polish).

p. 355 *Nowy Świat* New World (Polish), one of the main streets in Warsaw.

p. 359   *Tato*   Daddy (Polish).

p. 360   *Rozumiem*   I understand (Polish).

p. 360   *Tak-tak*   Yes, yes (Polish).

p. 360   *Matka Boska*   Mother of God (Polish).

READ MORE IN PENGUIN

In every corner of the world, on every subject under the sun, Penguin represents quality and variety – the very best in publishing today.

For complete information about books available from Penguin – including Puffins, Penguin Classics and Arkana – and how to order them, write to us at the appropriate address below. Please note that for copyright reasons the selection of books varies from country to country.

In the United Kingdom: Please write to *Dept. JC, Penguin Books Ltd, FREEPOST, West Drayton, Middlesex UB7 OBR.*

If you have any difficulty in obtaining a title, please send your order with the correct money, plus ten per cent for postage and packaging, to *PO Box No. 11, West Drayton, Middlesex UB7 OBR*

In the United States: Please write to *Consumer Sales, Penguin USA, P.O. Box 999, Dept. 17109, Bergenfield, New Jersey 07621-0120.* VISA and MasterCard holders call 1-800-253-6476 to order all Penguin titles

In Canada: Please write to *Penguin Books Canada Ltd, 10 Alcorn Avenue, Suite 300, Toronto, Ontario M4V 3B2*

In Australia: Please write to *Penguin Books Australia Ltd, P.O. Box 257, Ringwood, Victoria 3134*

In New Zealand: Please write to *Penguin Books (NZ) Ltd, Private Bag 102902, North Shore Mail Centre, Auckland 10*

In India: Please write to *Penguin Books India Pvt Ltd, 706 Eros Apartments, 56 Nehru Place, New Delhi 110 019*

In the Netherlands: Please write to *Penguin Books Netherlands bv, Postbus 3507, NL-1001 AH Amsterdam*

In Germany: Please write to *Penguin Books Deutschland GmbH, Metzlerstrasse 26, 60594 Frankfurt am Main*

In Spain: Please write to *Penguin Books S. A., Bravo Murillo 19, 1° B, 28015 Madrid*

In Italy: Please write to *Penguin Italia s.r.l., Via Felice Casati 20, I 20124 Milano*

In France: Please write to *Penguin France S. A., 17 rue Lejeune, F–31000 Toulouse*

In Japan: Please write to *Penguin Books Japan, Ishikiribashi Building, 2–5–4, Suido, Bunkyo-ku, Tokyo 112*

In Greece: Please write to *Penguin Hellas Ltd, Dimocritou 3, GR–106 71 Athens*

In South Africa: Please write to *Longman Penguin Southern Africa (Pty) Ltd, Private Bag X08, Bertsham 2013*

READ MORE IN PENGUIN

INTERNATIONAL WRITERS – A SELECTION

The Stories of Eva Luna   Isabel Allende

'One could happily read more of these fantastic, sexy and sometimes macabre tales that treat the reader to Isabel Allende's extraordinary imagination' – *Guardian*

Marbles: A Play in Three Acts   Joseph Brodsky

Imprisoned in a mighty steel tower, where yesterday is the same as today and tomorrow, Publius and Tullius consider freedom, the nature of reality and illusion and the permanence of literature versus the transience of politics. In a Platonic dialogue set 'two centuries after our era' in ancient Rome, Nobel prizewinner Joseph Brodsky takes us beyond the farthest reaches of the theatre of the absurd.

Scandal   Shusaku Endo

'Spine-chilling, erotic, cruel . . . it's very powerful' – *Sunday Telegraph*. '*Scandal* addresses the great questions of our age. How can we straddle the gulf between faith and modernity? How can humankind be so tender, and yet so cruel? Endo's superb novel offers only an unforgettable bafflement for an answer' – *Observer*

Love and Garbage   Ivan Klíma

The narrator of Ivan Klíma's novel has temporarily abandoned his work-in-progress – an essay on Kafka – and exchanged his writer's pen for the orange vest of a Prague road-sweeper. As he works, he meditates on Czechoslovakia, on Kafka, on life, on art and, obsessively, on his passionate and adulterous love affair with the sculptress Daria.

A Scrap of Time   Ida Fink

'A powerful, terrifying story, an almost unbearable witness to unspeakable anguish,' wrote the *New Yorker* of the title story in Ida Fink's award-winning collection. Herself a survivor, she portrays Poland during the Holocaust, the lives of ordinary people in hiding as they resist, submit, hope, betray, remember.